MW01155626

TILL THE STARS BURN OUT ABOVE YOU

Volume 1 in the Series: "We May Never Pass This Way Again"

DANIEL HUDSON

authorHOUSE®

AuthorHouse™
1663 Liberty Drive
Bloomington, IN 47403
www.authorhouse.com
Phone: 833-262-8899

Published by AuthorHouse 07/20/2022

ISBN: 978-1-6655-6462-5 (sc)
ISBN: 978-1-6655-6460-1 (hc)
ISBN: 978-1-6655-6461-8 (e)

Library of Congress Control Number: 2022912675

TO CLEO HUDSON

Mother, Teacher, Editor, Constant Friend. You never ceased to encourage me in my writing, but never held back your positive criticism. You, more than any other person, molded my thought process and imagination.

You may be gone, but you live on in the hearts of those you taught and influenced, especially me.

Love, always....

LOVE bears all things,

LOVE believes all things,

LOVE hopes all things,

LOVE endures all things.

St. Paul's First Letter to the Corinthians

Marie Catherine LaVeau, the preeminent 19th century Voodoo Priestess of New Orleans, famously said, "My Granddaughter's Granddaughter will be born of a garden, and will carry my name and my reputation.

Her Granddaughter will be born of an Orangery, and her name will announce a dire warning to La Nouvelle L'Orleans, but it might not be recognized until it is too late...."

CONTENTS

ACKNOWLEDGEMENTS

Writing this book has been a true labor of love. It involved an incredible amount of research to get the locations, attitudes, personae, and culture correct over a period stretching from the 1950's in New Orleans to the 1970's in both New Orleans and New York City.

It is with great appreciation that I acknowledge the help of some truly outstanding people.

To my dear late wife: You always cheered me on, encouraged me, and was my first line editor. Thank you for your honesty. You were always truly been on this adventure with me!

To Sallie Ann Glassman, Mambo Asogwe, The New Orleans Healing Center: Thank you for taking the time to correspond with me and understanding my desire to include real Voodoo into this story. Thank you also for your videos that explain voodoo's connection to water, earth, herbs, and spirituality.

To Madame Cinnamon Black, The New Orleans Historic Voodoo Museum: Thank you for your specific advice about ceremonies and practices. You gave your time to answer what might have seemed to be odd questions. Thank you so much!

To the late Jane Randolph, First Lady of College Park: Having you as a maven of all things "Garden District" allowed me to get the finer details correct. Thank you for being a sounding board and having me over for "Captains Hour" to enjoy my readings. You were truly a gem, and are greatly missed!

CHAPTER ONE

AN UNEXPECTED VISIT FROM A HANDSOME STRANGER

Having finished her dinner, Mary Day dabbed her lips, and placed her napkin neatly on the table, to the left of her plate, and asked her mother to be excused from the dinner table. Hattie, the family's cook and maid, had already cleared her father's place, as he'd eaten quickly, and left the table rudely to return to his office. It was nearly 8:00. The Day family ate dinner somewhat later than most of the other Garden District families. Millicent Day, Mary's mother nodded in agreement to Mary's request.

Mary walked slowly up the stairs, and retired to her bedroom. She snuggled up in a comfortable **bergère à oreilles**, one of a matching pair of luxurious arm chairs, upholstered in polychrome silk damask, to read. She was seventeen years old, and a Senior, about to graduate from Miss. McGraw's School for Girls in New Orleans. Mary picked up her latest book, *Le Grand Meaulnes*, and opened it to the bookmark where she had left off. **Chapter Three**. It took her a few minutes to get back into the swing of the story. After about thirty minutes she was, once again, lost in the arching realm of the story, but suddenly there was an unexpected knock on her door. Startled, somewhat, she placed a book mark and said, "**Oui**, come in."

The door opened and Marie Cosette, another one of her father's domestics stepped in. In a strong Creole dialect, Marie Cosette said, "Dat boy's back down dere on de streed, Miss Mary." Mary looked at Marie Cosette. "Really?" After placing her book on a walnut **guéridon**, she switched the floor lamp off, so as to not draw attention. Slowly, she pulled the shears back, just enough to see the Streetcar stop in the middle of the Neutral Ground on Saint Charles Avenue below.

The young man was tall, muscular, tan, and exceedingly well dressed. He wore an ascot tied neatly in the "V" of his shirt collars. His thick brunette hair was parted on the right side of his head and brushed up and over, like a great brown waterfall. It was the kind of hair that women naturally wanted to run their fingers through. He was leaning against a lamp post that had been painted dark green countless years ago, but was now faded, and peeling. It was Saturday, March 15th., 1952, and a cool evening. The humidity and mosquitos hadn't yet returned to the Crescent City. He appeared to be staring at the funeral home that Mary's father owned, and that the Day family lived in. Mary found herself captivated by the handsome stranger. He had been there several times before, looking intently at the funeral home, but then leaving, somewhat unexpectedly, by the Streetcar. Tonight, however, he stood up and started walking toward the funeral home. Mary dropped the shear and stood up, completely surprised. "**Mon Dieu**, he's coming over!"

Mary's curiosity got the best of her, and she rushed into the hallway and down the stairs. Once down the stairs, she almost floated to the window in the parlor facing the corner of St. Charles Avenue and Louisiana Avenue without noticing her mother, Millicent Day, who was sitting in the darkness and sipping an exceptionally tall Gin and Tonic, the Garden District's "most civilized drink." The handsome stranger walked down Louisiana Avenue past the window from which Mary was watching. She rushed into the dining room and watched him continue past. He turned into the darkness of the back driveway of the funeral home. Mary rushed through the Butlers pantry and into the kitchen. She jumped onto the upholstered banquette in the oversized bay window behind the kitchen table. She observed him peering intently into the darkened window of one of the basement storerooms. She hadn't noticed that her mother was standing in the darkened kitchen door observing her actions.

Mary had never known anyone her age having any curiosity about the funeral home in which she lived. In fact, although she was hugely popular at school, she had no close friends. When she was very young, Mary's parents had invited her classmates to her birthday parties, but their parents generally found her home a tad too creepy, and always found excuses, not only to avoid her parties, but also to avoid inviting Mary to their children's parties. Sadly, they misjudged Mary, and thought she must surely be just as creepy as her home. She certainly wasn't. She was, in fact, the complete opposite of creepy. Mary Charmaine Day was well educated, quite poised, well-mannered, and strikingly beautiful.

The same wasn't exactly true of the young people Mary knew from her Church. Mary was extremely beautiful, with long blond hair and violet eyes, and there were always a few confident young men in her Sunday School Class at the Episcopal Cathedral of Christ Church who didn't know that she lived in a funeral home, or that her father was a textbook psychopath. They would occasionally ask her out on dates. Her father, Andrew Jackson Day, never allowed it. "He's not good enough for you," was all he ever said.

Mary's one true friend was Marie Cosette Jardin, who was more like a sister to her than one of her father's household domestics. Marie Cosette was only six weeks older than Mary. She came to live with the Day family when she was barely ten years old. Jackson Day convinced Marie Cosette's mother, Marie Catherine Jardin, that the addictions and melancholia with which "Cat" suffered would prevent her daughter's ability to achieve anything in life, and that she would be far better off living with, and working for the Day family. Andrew Jackson Day, who was sleeping with Marie Catherine, and had her believing that she was his **Placée**, made sure that the majority of Marie Cosette's earnings were sent to Cat. Like her mother, Marie Cosette was extraordinarily beautiful, and could have easily passed for white except for her Creole accent. She had luxuriant, long Chestnut brown hair, dramatically

3

arched eyebrows, full lips, and a dainty, upturned nose. Her waist and hips were smaller than normal, but her bust was larger than average. For a few months, Millicent Day had been worrying that her husband, Jackson, had been noticing that Marie Cosette's changing figure was making her resemble her mother more and more each day.

Millicent Charmaine Blanchard Day, unlike her husband, was not Creole, or Cajun, but of French descent. Her Blanchard and Ducatel ancestors were among the earliest French families to arrive in New Orleans. Millicent was tall and thin, with classic facial features, perfectly coifed blond hair, and beautiful "Blue Star" eyes. She treated Marie Cosette more like a daughter than a domestic, and home schooled her using Mary's school books and materials, after hours, and when Blackjack wasn't around. Marie Cosette was sharp as a tack with Mathematics, and Science. She had trouble, however, with English and French. While Mary grew up in a household that spoke standard English and French, Marie Cosette grew up, for her first ten years, in a home that spoke broken English and Creole French. To make matters worse, Marie Cosette's mother's addictions resulted in her rarely speaking to her daughter. Marie Cosette's main point of verbal contact, in her early years, was with her Great Grandmother, Marie Rosette Doliolle - de Jardin, the granddaughter of Marie Catherine Laveau - de Glapion, a name well known both in New Orleans, and around the world. Her English was far worse than Cat's, and her French was truly more Creole.

Millicent struggled to teach Marie Cosette proper French, and a standard English dialect. She never became frustrated, but worked tirelessly to eradicate the "D" from Marie Cosette's vernacular. She detested the "Dat," the "Dere," the "Dhey," and the "Dhem," among numerous other problematic pronunciations. Marie Cosette would never completely master an English accent while living in New Orleans, but her French greatly improved over the years. By the time Marie Cosette was sixteen years old, she could truly pass for white. While she was only 1/64th. Black, her accent condemned her in New Orleans. In addition to that, Jack Day required her to wear a **tignon**, a head wrap, that communicated, most vehemently, her status among his friends and clients in the Garden District. Millicent was convinced that Jackson took great delight in degrading Marie Cosette.

Mary Day stood at the kitchen door of the funeral home, unsure of what to do. Her gut instinct told her to go out and meet the mysterious handsome stranger. Her upbringing told her, unequivocally, to avoid him. After a moment's tender agony, she decided to to be brave and confront the Peeping Tom. Quietly, and stealthily, she opened the kitchen door and tip-toed down the stairs and out onto the driveway behind the funeral home. She came up behind the handsome stranger, leaned over him, and quietly whispered, "Can you see anything?"

Inman Emile Carnes, the Fourth was completely startled. He jumped, gazelle like, away from Mary. They both stared at each other, wide-eyed and breathless, for what seemed to both like an eternity. At last, they both convulsed in laughter. After a few moments they both regained their composure. Inman, always the gentleman, extended his hand. "So sorry, ...Inman Carnes, the Fourth, it's truly my pleasure to make your acquaintance!" Mary was impressed. "**Mon nom est Mary Day, Je suis enchante**." Inman was completely enchanted by Mary's voice and perfect French. After a moment he replied, "**Francaise, nous parley Francais. Merveilleux**!" Mary was suitably impressed with Inman's French as well. Inman extended his hand for a second time. Mary, still amazed, put her hand in Inman's. Inman pulled Mary's hand to his lips and kissed it tenderly. "**C'est vraiment mon honneur**." (It is truly my honor.)

It could be accurately said that it was truly a case of love at first sight. Neither Mary nor Inman had ever been in love before, nor had either been in a romantic relationship of any kind previously. Perhaps that was a good thing. Both were in a strange kind of state of shock. At last Inman had the presence of mind to suggest that they sit on one of the cast iron benches in the funeral home's Memorial Garden and get to know each another.

Mary took Inman's hand and led him to one to the white cast iron benches that were placed around an antique cast iron fountain in the funeral home's Memorial Garden. They sat. Each was captured in the other's eyes. Finally, Inman said, "Ask me anything, or ask me nothing, as long as I can stay here and adore your beautiful violet eyes!" Mary closed her eyes for a moment and a tear formed. It was the first compliment she had ever received from a boy, or even from a grown man, even her father. By the time the tear had transversed her cheek, she had recovered enough to ask, "Why are you here?"

Inman closed his eyes and bowed his head. He breathed deeply, opened his eyes, and looked Mary directly in her eyes. "My uncle Danton told me that my papa's funeral was held here. I was far too young to have any memories of it. My only understanding of what loss is comes only from what my mama and my aunt and uncle tell me. To this day, I don't really understand what happened to my papa. I don't even know what a funeral is. I was too young to remember my papa's funeral." He paused, then said, " How completely odd that must sound to you."

Mary closed her eyes as even more tears formed and cascaded over her cheeks. She opened her eyes and said, "No, there's nothing at all odd about that. Odd is being as completely comfortable with death as I am. There have been so many dead bodies, in and out of here in my lifetime, that I can't remember, or even count, and none of them ever meant anything to me, really. Sadly, they became more like temporary **objects d'art**. They might as well have been wax figures in a museum. I remember the faces that our morticians painted on them, but I was never able to develop any understanding of their importance to their loved ones."

Inman's face contorted into a grimace. "That's horrible! Where's the compassion?" Mary responded, "Compassion? Oh, sure, there's plenty of that here." She thought for a moment. "It has to be here. My mother would insist. I can tell you that no loved one has ever felt disrespected here. All of my father's employees exemplify professionalism." Inman was not completely convinced, but he let the point rest.

He thought for a moment and asked, "So, ...do you work here?" Mary covered her mouth and laughed. "Heavens no. I'm still in High School!" Inman blushed. "High School? What's that like?" Mary was flummoxed. "How could you not know what High School is like?" Inman, for the first time in his life began to realize how vastly different his upbringing had been. "Uh, ...I was schooled at home. My mama didn't want me to leave the property while I was growing up. She became terribly afraid of the outside world when my papa was murdered. My uncle Danton gave me a key to the gate outside of the **garçonnière** a couple of months ago, and lately I've been exploring New Orleans after my mama and aunt go up to bed."

Mary was intrigued with Inman's story. "Oh, I see. How interesting! **Excusez-moi, sil vous plait**, what is a **garçonnière**? " Inman chuckled. "Oh, you see, my home was once a huge plantation just up-river from the **Vieux Carré**. My mother's family, the Soleils gradually sold most of the land as the city of New Orleans expanded north and west of the **Vieux Carré**. At this point, we're left with about ten acres, the **manoir**, called **Maison Soleil**, the **garçonnière**, the stables, and my papa's **atelier**. The **garçonnière** is a dwelling space for boys after they reach adolescence. It was practical back in the day to keep them away from the daughters of visiting families. Visiting potential suitors of the Owner's daughters would also stay there on visits, which sometimes lasted for weeks.

Mary was a tad embarrassed that she didn't know that cultural tidbit and turned her glance downward. She noticed that her leg was touching Inman's leg. She thought briefly about shifting on the bench, but found that she was enjoying the sensation of human contact greatly. Moreover, she felt completely comfortable in Inman's company. Mary looked up at Inman and smiled broadly. Inman smiled back at her and reminded Mary that she was going to tell him what High School was like. "Oh, that's right! High School. Well, let's see. I am a Senior at Miss. McGraw's School for Girls on Prytania Street." Inman held up a finger and interjected, "Senior? What's a Senior?"

Mary froze in disbelief with her mouth agape. She grabbed Inman's hand and said, "You HAVE been sheltered!" Inman looked away. Mary continued, "A Senior is a student in the last year of High School. Before that, I was a Junior, before that a Sophomore, and before that a Freshman." Mary squeezed Inman's hand to reassure him. She gave his hand a pull, and he turned back to look her in the eyes. She smiled intently. "When I think about it now, it seems somewhat arbitrary. I think that I could have completed all of the work in far less time!"

Inman squeezed Mary's hand. "Yes, that was the best part about my education! I got to go at my own pace and master each subject. I'll tell you that I have always been my harshest critic! I surpassed my mama's abilities a couple of years ago. Uncle Danton has been supplying me with textbooks from Tulane ever since." Mary was amazed, "Really? What are you studying now?" Inman beamed with pride, "I'm studying Mechanical Engineering and Industrial Design!"

Mary looked off into the distance and said, forlornly, "I have no idea what I want to do after I graduate in May." Without thought, Inman put his arm around Mary and pulled her in close. "**Mon Cher**, why is that a problem?" Mary relaxed in Inman's embrace. She could feel his breath on the top of her head and her torso rose and fell with his respiration. "I'm supposed to make my debut at next season's Rex Ball. That's the last thing my father has on his list of expectations for me. I suppose he wants me to marry the "right" young man, whoever that is, but my father is so completely distant. I just don't know. No-one is ever good enough!"

They sat in silence with Mary's head on Inman's chest for a while. Both were more blissfully relaxed than either had been for many many years. Inman took advantage of the lull in the conversation to process the conundrum. Finally, he asked, "Why does it matter what you do? Who do you have to please? ...your father? Why don't you just wait until you know what it is that YOU want to do?" Mary breathed a cleansing breath and closed her eyes. "Ummmmm," was all she uttered.

They held their embrace silently for several minutes until Mary was startled by the light being switched on in her parent's bathroom directly above. She jumped up, nervously, and started to the kitchen door. "Sorry, I've got to in." Inman rushed over to her and caught her in his strong arms. Mary didn't resist. She turned to face Inman. Inman smiled broadly and asked, "May I see you again, **Mon Cher**?" Mary's eyes glinted in the moonlight. "**Certainement je te chercherai samedi soir prochain sous le lampadaire**. (Certainly, I will look for you next Saturday evening under the streetlight.) Mary kissed Inman on the cheek, spun out of his embrace, and disappeared into the kitchen. Inman, by now, was completely lightheaded. He closed his eyes for a moment to regain his composure, then retraced his steps to the Streetcar stop. He leaned against the lamp post, lost in unfamiliar and new feelings, until the Streetcar arrived. He spent the journey back to Howard Avenue reliving the evening. He was transfixed, and suddenly falling in love. Inman was so preoccupied with his thoughts that he didn't see a large black woman wearing a heavy coat and sunglasses sitting in the colored section of the Streetcar staring at him with great interest.

Mary rushed quietly up to her room so that she could watch Inman walk past the funeral home to the Streetcar stop. She was somewhat relieved that Marie Cosette was not there waiting for her. She watched Inman, adoringly, from her perch in the polychrome **bergère**, with the lights switched off, until the Streetcar arrived and took Inman away. Her body was pulsing with feelings that she had never experienced. She undressed and got into her night gown. She slid into her bed, but could not sleep. Her every thought was completely dominated by Inman.

Likewise, Inman got off of the Streetcar at Howard Avenue and walked back to the **garçonnière** at **Maison Soleil**. As tired as he was, Inman couldn't sleep either. His body was humming with hormones, and new, wonderful, and unexpected feelings. After trying to fall asleep in his bed, he went down to the lower level of the **garçonnière** and out onto the dance terrace beyond. He spent the evening on a **chaise longue** staring at the stars and dreaming of Mary.

CHAPTER TWO

A FIRST DATE AND A FIRST DANCE

The next week went by quickly for both Mary and Inman. They both derived a quiet peace from the afterglow of their first meeting. By the time Friday evening arrived, Mary's heart was racing with anticipation. She tried to read, but couldn't concentrate on the story. She changed into her nightgown and went to bed. She tossed and turned most of the night, and ultimately got out of bed early on Saturday morning. She went down to the kitchen and asked Hattie and Marie Cosette if there was anything she could do to help them get ready for breakfast. Hattie looked at Mary as if she had lost her mind. "We'z'uns got dis covered." Mary went into the dining room and sat at the table, She closed her eyes and imagined that she was dining with Inman.

Marie Cosette came in to set the table. She saw Mary with her eyes closed, and giggled. "Dat boy, he's gonna be here donight, ain't dat de druth?" Mary was startled for a moment, but quickly started laughing along with Marie Cosette. "Yes, Marie Cosette, he promised to call on me tonight." Marie Cosette started placing the plates around the table. "He's a looka!" Mary closed her eyes and smiled broadly. " Oh **Oui! Il est beau dans son ame**

aussi!" (He is beautiful in his soul too!) Marie Cosette paused and thought. "Oh, a beautiful soul!" Mary shook her head in agreement. "**Oui!**"

Marie Cosette finished with the plates, and started placing the napkins and silver. "When did he say he'd be callin'?" Mary said, "He told me that he can't leave his mother's property until she and his aunt go to bed. I suppose that it will be around 8:00, but I really don't have a clue." Marie Cosette finished with the silver and napkins. She crossed her arms and shook her head. "Dis is goin' a be a long day fo' ju!" Mary shook her head, "That's true! The bad thing is that I can't focus on anything to make the day go by faster." Marie Cosette paused before returning to the Butler's pantry for stemware. "Is a shame we can't call on my mama for some of her Gris Gris! Dat would help you get dru da day!"

Mary laughed heartily. "No doubt, but unfortunately, not today!" Marie Cosette laughed, and disappeared into the Butler's pantry. Mary closed her eyes and resumed her fantasy. Mary's mother, Millicent, was next to enter the dining room. She had an elegant quietness about her, and was able to enter the room without disturbing Mary's fantasy. Millicent paused and observed her daughter. After a few moments, she asked, "Mary, are you awake, or sleepwalking?" Mary quickly snapped out of her fantasy. "I'm awake, I was just resting my eyes."

Millicent Day loved her daughter more than life itself, but, was extremely unhappy in her marriage. She knew that it was foolish even to entertain thoughts of divorcing. Her husband, Andrew Jackson Day, was, if anything, a good provider, albeit extremely distant and completely preoccupied with making money. Millicent had everything that she needed, except love and affection from her husband.

Andrew Jackson Day had not been born into the aristocracy like his wife. Jackson was born into a working class family. His father was a Streetcar Motorman and Conductor. At an early age, Jackson felt bullied by passengers on his father's streetcar line who called him "Little Motorman." It wasn't bullying, the passengers absolutely adored young Jackson, but he thought that they were pigeon-holing into a career, and saying that he would never achieve anything better. He became a social climber at an early age. From the time he was eighteen, Jackson was determined to force his way into the most elite of social circles in New Orleans. …using whatever means it would take. Jackson was of average height, neither overweight nor muscular. He had a long oval face, smallish lips, and a somewhat over-sized nose. His eyes were grey, and his hair was jet black, parted on the right, and formed a "V" over his forehead, thanks to his liberal use of Vitalis.

Millicent and Mary exchanged the usual morning pleasantries as Hattie and Marie Cosette brought in the breakfast chafers and placed them on a walnut **buffet de chasse**. Millicent and Mary rose from the table and walked together to a towering **buffet deux corps**. Millicent poured coffee and warmed milk into a tea cup and added a brown sugar cube. Mary poured a glass of orange juice into an Imperial Cape Cod juice glass. Millicent and Mary returned to the table and sat stoically, waiting for Jackson as the expertly-prepared breakfast simmered in the sterling chafers. Eventually, Blackjack stormed out of his office, and entered the dining room. He said nothing to his wife or daughter. Blackjack thrust his stained diner coffee mug at Marie Cosette and grabbed his plate and started heaping food onto it. He sat down, ungraciously, and started eating. Blackjack didn't say a word when Marie Cosette brought his **café noir.** Millicent was appalled by Jackson's rudeness, but her exquisite rearing prevented her from indicating any displeasure. She gestured to Mary that it was now appropriate for her to go and fill her plate. Millicent waited patiently for Mary to return to the table before walking to the **buffet de chasse** to fill her own plate.

Millicent sat down and moved her napkin from the table to her lap. "Jackson, dear, would you like to have lunch at Antoine's today?" Jack grumbled, and shook his head as he stood up. He threw his napkin into the chair. "Can't, busy." He stormed back to his office with his coffee and slammed the door. Millicent sighed, "I'm so sorry, Mary." Mary looked off into the distance and said nothing, although she wanted to tell her mother that there was nothing to apologize for. Her father had been a boor all of her life, and would probably never change. Unexpectedly, Blackjack reemerged and yelled for Marie Cosette. "Marie Cosette, bring me some more coffee!"

Mary and Millicent looked at each other, heartbroken. Neither could bear to look at poor Marie Cosette when she passed through the dining room.

Millicent turned her gaze to Mary. "Why don't we go and get our hair styled and have lunch at Antoine's today. Mary had no trouble accepting that offer. At last there were things to do to pass the day, and the hairstyle was a huge bonus! Millicent dabbed her mouth and placed her napkin on the table. I'll just go and phone **Maison de Bringier** and set our appointments.

Mary was too excited to finish her breakfast. Marie Cosette came in to start clearing the dishes. "I'm going to get my hair styled today! How perfect is that?" Marie Cosette smiled. "You don' know what dat gonna do'da dat boy!" Mary beamed. "I hope so! There is something so different about him. He makes me feel like the most important person in the world!" Marie Cosette didn't want to puff up Mary's expectations, but also didn't want to shoot them down either. She picked up the plates and said, "You'n gonna get a new dose of him donight." Mary said, "Yep," and bolted out of the dining room, up the stairs, and to her bedroom.

Millicent and Mary enjoyed their Saturday afternoon in the **Vieux Carré.** The sun was setting as they returned to the funeral home, perfectly coiffed, just in time for dinner. As usual, they had to wait for Jackson. As usual, he bolted in, scarfed his food down, and bolted back to his office. When Marie Cosette came in to clear the dishes, Mary asked her mother for permission to be excused. She then went up to her room to watch for Inman, from her perch in the polychrome **bergère**. Once again, she tried reading, but her concentration was lacking. She jumped up every time she heard the Streetcar rattling past.

After what seemed an eternity, Mary saw Inman as the Streetcar rumbled away from the intersection. Her heart was racing. She rushed, in stealth mode, through the hallway, down the stairs and to the front door. Mary failed to notice that her mother was standing in the parlor with a tall Gin and Tonic in her hand, looking out of one of the parlor windows overlooking St. Charles Avenue. Mary was cautious to open the front door quietly, and close it even more silently. She walked swiftly across the **véranda**, down the steps and to the sidewalk gate.

Neither Inman nor Mary could contain their exuberance. Mary grasped the iron gate tightly and smiled the most genuine and unabashed smile in her lifetime. Inman returned Mary's smile with an equivalent exuberance. Their gazes locked upon each other. Neither said a word. Neither really had to, their eyes spoke volumes. Finally, Inman produced a bouquet of flowers from behind his back. They were, in fact, the first flowers that anyone had ever given Mary, and were so beautiful that Mary gasped. Mary accepted the flowers and slipped through the iron gate. She grasped Inman's arm, leaned up and kissed his cheek, sweetly. "**Merci beaucoup, mon cher**, they're awfully beautiful!"

Inman beamed. "**Ils pâlissent en comparaison de votre beauté!**" (They pale in comparison of your beauty!) Mary blushed. It was the most wonderful and heartfelt compliment she had ever received from anyone outside of her closest family. She reached up and kissed Inman on the cheek once again. "**Tu es trop gentil!** (You are so kind!) Would you like to go for a walk with me?" "**Certainment, mon cher!**" Mary put her arm in the crook of Inman's arm and they started walking down Saint Charles Avenue toward Lee Circle. Neither had noticed that Millicent had been watching them from the parlor window. Aside from a tear or two when Inman gave Mary the flowers, Millicent stood in the window, stoically, sipping her tall, Blanchard strength, Gin and Tonic.

As they walked down St. Charles Avenue, Inman, over time, slowly began to feel more comfortable. He had been tirelessly remembering, and following the rules of chivalry, passed on to him by his mother, Caroline Soleil Carnes, and had insisted on walking on on Mary's left, so that "his right hand could easily access his 'sword' positioned on his left hip and protect her from the rogue automobiles motoring past on their left. As he slowly calmed down, Inman began to better appreciate the sensory stimulations they were experiencing in the Garden District.

As they passed Harmony Street, they were overcome with the fragrance of Purple Lantana, and paused to attempt to understand the olfactory experience. The smell was only partially sweet. It also contained bitter and sour notes reminiscent of Marigolds. Mary was overcome with emotion and bowed her head and cried effusively. Inman was perplexed and grabbed Mary's arm. **"Mon cher, qu'est-ce qui te trouble?** (My dear, what troubles you?) Inman handed Mary his reserve handkerchief and Mary dabbed her eyes and did her best to regain her composure.

Mary persevered, and summoned her nerve. "I can't tell you how much that I don't want you to hear this the wrong way; but, in my whole life, the smell of flowers has meant only death to me. My father never sent flowers to my mother. There were never flowers on my birthdays, my mother's birthdays, or any important family occasions. These beautiful flowers, that you brought me tonight, are the first time in my experience, that flowers have been given for the living. They are precious to me, but the smell of flowers is regrettably, a great difficulty for me."

Inman cast his gaze to the sidewalk. "That's so horribly sad. In an odd and unique way, it makes me appreciate my mother's keeping me isolated for so long. One of my dearest pleasures, growing up, was spending the warming nights of spring and summer smelling the parade of different perfumes throughout the progression of the warm seasons." Mary looked up at Inman, dried her tears, and said, "I'd really like to appreciate that the way that you do. I'd like to loose my association with the smell of flowers with death." Inman smiled. He said nothing, but had already formulated a plan to change Mary's mind about flowers. Halfway down the block, Mary pointed across the street to Christ Church Cathedral. "That's where we go to church. I suppose that you didn't grow up going to church." Inman smiled. "No we didn't go to church. My mother didn't want to risk anything happening to me, so she arranged, from as far back as I can remember, for a priest from St. Patrick's to bring Mass to us every Sunday and on Feast Days. He even taught me the Catechism. My uncle Danton snuck me out of **Maison Soleil** to be confirmed. Luckily, St. Patrick's is only a couple of blocks from our home. The only other time I went to church was for my papa's funeral. I have no memory of it, and my mother has always found it pointless to tell me where he was laid to rest." Mary looked truly impressed with Caroline's ingenuity. "She must be a big donor!" Inman smiled, "No doubt."

Mary and Inman walked a while longer, and Mary suggested that they turn right on Phillip Street. Inman was curious. "Why are we turning here?" Mary looked up at Inman with a coy look, "I have my reasons...." After a block, Mary lunged to the right onto Prytania Street. Inman was confused by the circuitous route, but didn't object. In the middle of the block, Mary pulled Inman's arm to force him to stop. Inman quietly looked at Mary. She grabbed Inman around the midsection, gave him a smug look, and pointed to her right. "That's Miss. McGraw's. That's where I go to school!

Inman had a sudden realization. "Really, I hadn't thought so much about it before, but now that I do, that's where my mother said she went to school! Well, how about that!" Mary beamed, "That's wonderful, my mother went there as well!" They paused for a few moments admiring the antebellum building with extravagant two story **vérandas** adorning its three principal sides, before continuing on their walk.

They turned left on First Street. Along their walk they passed homes with windows open and radios playing. As they passed Coliseum Street, they heard the strains of Louis Armstrong's ***A Kiss to Build a Dream On*** floating in the air. For a moment, Inman froze in his tracks, then reached around, pulled Mary in close, and started dancing with her. She was, at first, taken aback, but quickly found that she was enjoying the dance immensely. They danced all the way to Chestnut Street before the song was lost in the air. They then turned to the right onto Chestnut Street.

They crossed Sixth Street and were half way to Seventh. They had stopped to admire a narrow Greek Revival house with an ornate two tier portico. The upstairs windows were open, and the golden silk sheers floated in and out of the windows on the breeze. The occupants had their radio on. While Mary and Inman admired the home, a commercial for Earl Kemper's Cadillac Dealership ended and ***Because of You*** started playing. It was the version sung by Tony Bennett. Mary and Inman were immediately starstruck, and were left with only the ability to stare into each other's eyes. They both felt the sudden impact of physical and emotional paralysis. They found themselves leaning against a brick pillar engaged in an tender embrace, slowly becoming transfixed in each other's visage. Neither could manage to move.

They simply stared deeply into each other's eyes for the duration of the song. It was a magical, romantic moment, and both found strong sensual feelings evanescing in their beings.

As the song faded away, Inman closed his eyes. A lone tear streaked down his cheek. Mary wiped Inman's tear away, put her hand behind Inman's head, and pulled it in close to hers. She kissed him tenderly and passionately on his full, beautiful lips. Inman placed his arms around Mary and held her close, careful not to crush her bouquet. He closed his eyes and wanted only to never let Mary out of his grasp.

After a few tender moments, Mary and Inman continued their walk, only now in a close side-to-side embrace. As they continued down Chestnut Street, neither could get the song ***Because of You*** out of their minds. Both were experiencing a tingling in their bodies that neither had ever experienced before. Nothing either could say at this point seemed relevant. They turned onto Louisiana Avenue, in blissful silence, on their final run to the funeral home. Neither wanted the walk to end, but both knew that it had to.

Mary and Inman turned onto Saint Charles Avenue and walked slowly to the funeral home gate. They paused and stared, star-crossed, into each other's eyes. Inman peered deeply in to Mary's magical eyes. "I don't want this evening to end." Mary closed her eyes and her head dropped. "I don't want this evening to end either." Inman reached his arm around into the small of Mary's back and once again pulled her in close to him. "Because of you, my life is now worthwhile, and I can smile …because of you." Mary closed her eyes. Tears welled up. They embraced tightly, without realizing that Millicent was watching them from the parlor window.

Mary opened her eyes and smiled at Inman. "Can we do this again next Saturday?" Inman beamed and said, "**Je souhaite que nous pourrions faire cela tous les soirs!**" (I wish we could do this every night!) Mary slipped through the gate and turned back to Inman. "**Je vous remercie encore une fois, ma chere, pour les fleurs!**" (Thank you again, my dear, for the flowers!) She turned and walked a couple of steps before spinning around to wave to Inman. This was repeated several more times before she reached the front door. Mary turned the knob quietly and cracked the heavy wooden door. She lingered for a few moments, blew Inman a kiss, and disappeared into the foyer. She closed the door quietly, turned and allowed her back to rest against the door and smelled her bouquet hoping not to have an association with death. She was lost in the memories of her incredible first date with Inman when she heard the clink of Millicent's ice cubes from the parlor. She froze for what seemed an eternity.

With great anxiety, Mary slowly walked into the parlor. She couldn't see her mama in the darkness. Millicent spent quite a lot of her time contemplating life in darkened rooms. Rather nonchalantly Millicent asked, "Who was that boy?" Mary hesitated. She was wracked with fear and trembling. "His name is Inman…. Inman…." Mary's eyes hadn't adjusted to the darkness enough to see that Millicent's mouth had dropped open, just a little, in surprise. Millicent interjected, "Inman Carnes?" Mary shook her head in agreement. "Yes ma'am. Do you know him?" Millicent sighed deeply. "It's so very complicated, my dear. …so very complicated." After a pregnant pause, Millicent asked Mary, "Are you in love with him?"

Mary let out a brief chortle. "Mama! I've only seen him twice. Tonight was the first time we had what some would call a date. I do really, really like him. He's not like the boys I know from Church. He's truly nice and kind. He is truly interested in me, and what goes on in my life. …but love? I don't even know what that is. It's way too early to even think about that."

Millicent had seen the two interact on both occasions, and knew from experience that her daughter was lying to her. She completely understood why Mary couldn't tell her that she was in love with Inman, and wasn't concerned about it in the least. Millicent took a deep cleansing breath, "Okay, first of all, your father can know nothing about this. You know how he is. No one is ever good enough for you. Inman Carnes, the Fourth is from one of the absolute finest families in New Orleans, but there is history between your father and the Carnes and the Soleil families. He can't know, at least until I figure out how to change his mind for him. You also need to be wary about who sees you two spending time together. Your father has his employees hidden everywhere." Millicent walked over to Mary. "My, what a lovely bouquet! We should get these into some water so you can take them up to your room."

Although she said nothing, Mary was completely shocked by her mother's reaction to the situation. They walked together into the kitchen. Millicent handed Mary a vase, and started to refresh her drink. Mary trimmed the stems of the flowers and placed them in the vase. Millicent reached into the pantry and grabbed a bottle of aspirin. She handed a tablet to Mary. "I've heard that this will help them last longer." Mary smiled and dropped the aspirin tablet into the vase. "Thanks, mama!" She added water and adjusted the blooms. "Mama, I think I'm going to go to bed now. I love you!" Millicent put her arms around Mary. "I love you too, sweetheart! Rest well."

Mary carried the vase of Inman's flowers up to her bedroom and placed them on the **guéridon** between the polychrome **bergères**. She had just climbed into the chair when there was a knock on her door. "**Oui**, come in." Marie Cosette opened and closed the door quietly and rushed over to Mary's side. She could hardly contain herself. Mary played it cool, and just looked at Marie Cosette, without the slightest look of emotion. Holding it in was killing her, but she was toying with Marie Cosette. Mary could see that Marie Cosette was about to burst. Finally, Marie Cosette could take no more. "Where'd ju go wid dat boy?" Still trying to keep her excitement under wraps, Mary sighed and looked out the window. "We went for a walk and got to know each other."

Suddenly, Marie Cosette noticed the flowers on the **guéridon**. "I know dat ju fader didn't give dose flowers do ju. Did dat boy give 'em do ju?" Mary smiled, "Of course he gave them to me. He's such a gentleman." Marie Cosette sighed. "Dat's so romandic!" Finally, Mary couldn't contain her emotions. "He is! He's the most romantic man ever! He surpasses all of the romantic heroes in any book I've ever read. Can you believe that he danced with me on the sidewalk to music that was coming from a complete stranger's radio. Marie Cosette's eyes opened wide. "No he didn'!" Mary grinned broadly. "Oh yes he did. It was magical!"

Marie Cosette looked back at the door to make sure it was closed and whispered, "Did ju kiss him?" Mary pursed her lips and looked up for a moment, "**Oui**." Marie Cosette gasped. "Oh no, yu're delling me an undruth." Mary shook her head. "No, I'm not. It started when I kissed him on the cheek

19

when he gave me the bouquet. …but, as we walked, I grew more and more fond of him. Then, out of the blue, he pulled me close and we danced on the sidewalk. Oh, I was lost! I was completely lost! By the time we were back home all I wanted was the night to never end. …but it did." Mary and Marie Cosette talked for an hour before retiring for the night.

Millicent had returned to the darkness of the parlor. She too was lost in thought. She thought about how wonderfully happy her daughter had seemed when she returned from her date with Inman. Millicent remembered a time in her own life when she too had been that happy. That happiness, however, ended long before Mary was born, and even before she married Andrew Jackson Day. She thought about how her husband had sucked the life and joy completely out of her, and that she had no choice but to endure her own personal hell. She sadly realized that her dreaded husband was on a trajectory to do quite the same to her precious daughter, Mary. Millicent thought about how Jackson's businesses had prevented Mary from having any close friends.

Millicent started to become angry. She realized, however, that to protect Mary, she would have to maintain her **sang froid**. Millicent crushed an ice cube with her teeth and finished her drink. She was fully composed when she elegantly ascended the stairs to her bedroom. Millicent was thankful that Blackjack rarely slept in the master suite.

The next morning, after Jackson left the table, Mary told her mother why Inman had come to the funeral home in the first place. "Inman told me that his papa's funeral was held here. Is that right?" Millicent put her **café au lait** down on the saucer. "Well, that's partially true. His wake was held here. His funeral was solemnized at St. Patrick's. Why do you ask?" Mary leaned in closer to her mother. She said quietly, "He told me that his mother had never told him where his father is entombed. I guess because she never had any plans for him to leave their property."

Millicent sighed. "Caroline was devastated when Big Inman died. She was so upset, she lost the baby girl she was carrying. … and about six months later, she and Little Inman were coming home from a shopping trip. A thug demanded her purse. When she at first refused, the thug pulled a gun and threatened to shoot little Inman. For whatever reason, the gun didn't go off.

That's when Caroline became a recluse. Prior to the assault, she had always been an extraordinarily genteel and social person. Her parties, especially her Tea Dances, were legendary." Millicent stood and walked to the window. She looked out at the driveway. Jackson was fussing with Eddie Smith, one of the funeral home's Porters. Millicent turned around and said, "I'll tell you what, when your father is out, we'll look through the books to see where Big Inman is entombed." Mary smiled and thanked her mother. Millicent turned back to the window and stared, with contempt, at her husband.

CHAPTER THREE

EXAM WEEK AT MISS. MCGRAW'S SCHOOL FOR GIRLS

Mary was thankful that she had exams to prepare for. The wait for Saturday night seemed excruciatingly long. She was surprised to see her mother sitting at the table reading *The Times-Picayune* when she crossed from the parlor to the dining room. Millicent let the top half of the paper flop over her hands. "**Bonjour chérie Mary!**" Mary smiled. "**Bonjour chère mama!**" She took a Cape Cod juice glass and filled it with chilled, freshly squeezed, Orange Juice from a cut glass pitcher on her mother's walnut provincial **buffet deux corps**. Mary sat down to wait for Hattie and Marie Cosette to bring in the breakfast chafers.

Blackjack had evidently developed a food radar. As soon as Hattie placed the first sterling chaser on the marble top of the **buffet de chasse**, Jackson's office door burst open and he charged the room and pushed ahead of Millicent and Mary. "Marie Cosette, go fetch my mug from the office and fill it up." Yassir, Mistuh Day." He piled his plate high with no consideration for anyone else, and quickly retraced his steps to the office. He slammed the door, practically in Marie Cosette's face. After delivering Blackjack's **café noir**, Marie Cosette returned to the dining room. She looked at Mary and started to grin. Mary gave her the "stop it, mama is here" look, but it only made it worse. Marie Cosette found herself struggling to keep from giggling. Millicent looked up and saw Marie Cosette grinning and had to purse her lips to keep from grinning herself. "Marie Cosette, dear, would you mind topping off my **café au lait**?" Of course, Millicent knew why Marie was grinning. She too was secretly grinning that Mary was seeing a young man of such quality and breeding. She was also secretly worried about "fixing" the situation where Blackjack would give his blessing. Her Blanchard confidence convinced her that she could prevail. The Blanchard family was known for their fierce determination in all things.

After Marie Cosette brought Millicent's **café au lait** and returned to the kitchen, Millicent asked from behind her newspaper, "Evidently, Marie Cosette is excited that you are seeing Inman tonight." As Millicent turned the page, Mary was convinced that her mama was smiling. "**Oui mama.** We are going out tonight." Millicent folded her newspaper and put it down next to her plate. She leaned in and put her hand gently over Mary's. After a deep breath, she said, "I hope that you both have a wonderful evening, but remember what I said last week. You have to be especially careful not to be seen by any of your fathers cohorts." She wanted to say "goons," but Mary didn't have a complete knowledge of her father's financial activities. Mary sighed. She knew, but not the true extent of the danger. "**Oui mama, je comprends.**" Millicent stood up and looked at Mary, "**Ma douce,** I was just about to call **Maison de Bringier**, shall I make an appointment for you also? Mary's entire face bloomed with joy, "**Oh oui, mama, ce serait merveilleux. Merci beaucoup!**" (Oh yes, mama, that would be wonderful. Thank you so much!) Millicent turned to walk to the telephone nook in the foyer. Over her shoulder, she added, "Antoine's or Broussard's?" Mary contorted her face as if ashamed to ask, "Might we go to The Court of the Two Sisters?" Millicent paused, and looked off in the distance. "What an excellent suggestion. Yes, we'll eat there."

Marie Cosette had been listening at the swinging door. As soon as she thought that Millicent was out of earshot, she slipped back into the dining room. "Juz goin' all outn fo dat boy, ain' ju?" Mary folded her napkin and placed it to the left of her plate. She stood up to retire to her bedroom. "I suspect that he'd still want to spend time with me even if I hadn't brushed my hair, or taken a shower." Marie Cosette blushed. "Oh, now dat's a real gen'ul'mun." Mary grabbed Marie Cosette's hands, "That's what he's shown me, and my mother knows his family, and says there isn't a finer family in Louisiana!" Hattie called Marie Cosette from the kitchen. "I'z gots do go. Maybe wez'll dalk lader." Mary smiled, "**Oui**, of course," and made her way through the home and upstairs to dress for the day. She was happy to have pleasant distractions to help her pass the hours until Inman arrived.

Mary showered, and toweled off with a turkish towel so large, and so thick it was almost decadent. Blackjack had gotten a "deal" on them. Every bathroom was outfitted with enough towels, hand towels, and wash cloths to supply a small European Principality, each in a different color. Mary's bathroom was outfitted with bright pink towels, hand towels, and wash cloths. When Mary turned sixteen, Millicent persuaded Jackson to renovate Mary's bathroom. He agreed, begrudgingly. Millicent pointed out, strategically, that it was one of those things he could do that just might impress the Garden District Old Guard with whom he was so determined to curry favor with. By the time Blackjack was done, Mary's bathroom was a pretentious Pepto Bismol pink palace. The room was anchored by a pink corner tub. It was a huge square behemoth of pink ceramic over cast iron. The actual tub opening was a diagonal chasm, requiring an extra long shower curtain that had to travel around two sides of the tub. The toilet and sink were pink, and the counters and floors were pink and white geometric designs. The lower walls were tiled in pink, with a white and black border. The upper walls, thankfully, were painted a light ivory, but the trim was, as you'd imagine, bright pink.

Mary put on her undergarments, including a slip. For the day, or more specifically, for the date, she had chosen a floral circle dress with a wide belt, white gloves, kitten heeled pumps, and a **Beaucoiff** adorned with silk flowers. Millicent approved of her wardrobe, and suggested that Mary take the **Beaucoiff** to **Maison de Bringier** to make sure her hairstyle would compliment it. Millicent and Mary stepped out onto Saint Charles Avenue just before 9:00 to take the Streetcar to Canal Street. Neither noticed the large black woman in sunglasses with a heavy coat and carpet bag sitting on the back bench.

Once downtown, they walked a short distance, and went through the door into the studio of **Maison de Bringier**. All of the ladies took notice of Mary's ensemble. The "oooohs" were audible. Mary's stylist was René, who was new to New Orleans, but not to coiffure, especially elaborate coiffure. He suggested a classic chignon. "Darling, you have the perfect hair. It's thick, and long, and strong. It'll easily hold together, especially with a little help from Revlon!" Mary was excited about having an elaborate coiffeur. It was her first, but not her last, by far. When René was satisfied, he pinned Mary's **Beaucoiff** on, expertly. Mary's face announced her complete joy when she saw the results in a hand mirror. Millicent too, was taken aback. "René, you are truly a genius!" René was a tad too full of himself to thank Millicent for her heart-felt compliment. All he uttered was, " but of course!" Genius was one of the few excuses for bad manners among the Old Guard of New Orleans. René would go on to have a star-studded and storied career in New Orleans.

Millicent and Mary stepped out on the sidewalk and hailed a cab. "Court of the Two Sisters, please." The cabbie negotiated the narrow one-way streets of the **Vieux Carré** and let the two elegant ladies out at 613 Royal Street. They went in and were escorted to a shaded table in the courtyard. A waiter came over to take their drink orders. Mary ordered a soft drink, but Millicent interjected, "This is a special day, my dear. I'll order drinks." Mary was confused, but went along. "We'll share a bottle of **Chateau Fuisse Pouilly-Fuisse Tete de Cru.** Do you have a '48? The waiter said, "**Oui, madame, tres bien.**" Mary looked at her mother with a look of utter confusion. Millicent smiled, "It's not like you haven't had a "sweetened" drink before. Besides, you are a Senior at Miss. McGraw's. It's high time you learned how to drink like a lady." Mary laughed. "I feel like I'm in school!" Millicent looked down her elegant, boney Blanchard nose at her beloved daughter. "Yes, you are. Miss. McGraw's would teach this if the State would allow it. ...but the school can't, so responsible parents have to take up the slack." Mary innocently asked, "So, responsible parents teach their children to drink?" Millicent appreciated Mary's irony. "…not TO drink, but rather, HOW TO drink. There is a huge difference." Millicent had Mary's attention. "Okay……" Millicent continued, "Right now, just one block over, on Bourbon Street, there are countless people in countless dive bars, drinking with wild abandon, just to get drunk. Some of them enjoy that behavior; Some just can't help it, and they suffer it until they get help, or until they die from it."

Millicent now had Mary's full attention. Mary watched intently as the Sommelier brought the chilled bottle of wine to the table with an ice bucket and two stems. He cut the foil over the cork, and twisted his cork screw deep into the cork before wrenching it out. Mary was intrigued by the petit "pop" the cork made as it exited the green bottle. The Sommelier then poured Millicent a taste. She placed her fingers on the base of the stem and swirled the glass around on the heavily starched table cloth before lifting the wine glass, by the stem, to her nose. She breathed in deeply before taking a small taste. While the wine was still in her mouth, Millicent drew in a deep breath through her slightly open lips. Millicent closed her eyes for a few moments and enjoyed the sensations she was experiencing. She opened her eyes and nodded to the Sommelier, who poured a glass for her and a glass for Mary.

After the Sommelier left the table, Millicent looked at Mary. "What questions do you have so far?' Mary had many, but she started with, "Why did you go through that elaborate routine to taste the wine?" Millicent said, "My dear, it's an old custom. Some people really think that they can ward off a bad vintage, but no one ever does!" Mary laughed. Millicent added, "Just wait until you have to listen to 'wine connoisseurs' describing the subtle flavors in their wine. I think 'stone' was the most absurd one I've ever heard!" Mary had to put her hand over her mouth to keep from belly laughing. When she regained composure, she said, "Please tell me you are making that up!" Millicent smiled a shy smile. "My dear, you have no idea what is out there in the world." Mary then asked, "Why is the glass only partially filled?" Millicent perked up. "That is an excellent question. The prevailing response is, 'so the wine can breath,' but I personally find that bogus. If I'm honest, the wine never tastes even remotely different, regardless of how it is poured." Mary added, "…but there's still the ceremony." Millicent looked off into the distance, "Yes my dear, with wine, and so many things, there is always the ceremony."

Mary looked at her glass of what otherwise would have been called "Chardonnay" and wondered if she dared pick it up. Millicent grasped her stem and lifted her glass. She gave Mary her look of permission to raise her glass by the stem also. Mary raised her glass and Millicent said, "Here's to our unwritten rules for drinking in New Orleans Society!" When Mary didn't know the correct response, Millicent explained, The correct response is, 'Santé" Mary sat up straight and repeated, "**Santé!**" Millicent was happy with Mary's desire to learn the rules for social drinking. "Now you need to learn how to pace yourself. To begin with, you must sip, and not gulp. In time, you'll learn to appreciate the sip. …just enough to put flavor in your mouth, not enough to cause embarrassment. A glass of wine can last a long time, but a lady's reputation can be ruined in an instant!" Mary said, "Yes, I see, but what if I'm really thirsty?" Millicent welcomed that question. "My dear, in New Orleans, drinks are consumed 24 hours a day, but there are always alternative beverages to minimize your chances of intoxication. Say you're at brunch, there's coffee, or in polite society, **café au lait**. For the rest of the day there is water or iced tea. The bottom line is… Drink socially, or be shunned socially." Millicent raised her glass, and said, "To Social Drinking," Mary raised her glass as said, "**Santé!**" She took a micro-sip and smiled at her mother. Millicent smiled back at her. With the lesson learned, mother and daughter enjoyed a fabulous luncheon before enjoying a tour of the antique stores along Royal Street. They spent as much time as possible enjoying themselves in the **Vieux Carré** before it was time to make their way back to Canal Street and the Streetcar back to their home on Saint Charles Avenue.

When they got back home, Mary retired to her room and continued reading her novel, ***Le Grand Meaulnes***. While she was slightly less anxious than she had been the previous week, the Streetcar caught her attention with every pass, even the passes before the sun went down. In truth, she didn't have to worry. She had a true ally. Marie Cosette manned a window and kept a vigilant lookout. When Inman finally showed up, all Marie Cosette had to say was, "Um…." Mary bolted up and extinguished the light by her **bergère**. She looked through the crack in the shears. It was Inman. Mary slipped quietly through the house, not to evade her mother, but to evade her father's notice. She needn't have worried. Jackson was comfortably ensconced in his lair, going over the books from his gambling racket Bank Houses.

Mary slipped out of the front door and met Inman at the gate. He stood with his left hand hidden behind is back. Mary slipped out of the gate, determined to discover what Inman had hidden behind his back. Inman dodged Mary's advances until she faked right, then went left. She grabbed his arm, only to find nothing. She was immediately hurt. Mary had been sure that Inman had brought her flowers. If she had waited just a moment more at the window, she'd have noticed that Inman had placed them at the base of the fence. Inman recognized immediately Mary's hurt, and felt horrible that he was jesting her. "No, look over there. I just put them down for a minute." He bent down and picked up the bouquet that he had personally picked at **Maison Soleil**, and arranged himself. Mary took them and forgave him immediately.

Inman was relieved. He asked, "What should we do tonight?" Mary thought for a moment. "Did you tell me that you hadn't been to a movie?" Inman blushed. "Yes, I did. Would you like to go to a movie?" Mary said, "Yes, and no. Yes, because it will be with you. No, because we'll be watching and not talking." Inman said, "Wouldn't we be talking about the story afterwards?" Mary said, "Perfect. We can discuss the film afterwards." Inman made a joke, "So you want to go to a movie so no one can see us!" Mary was mortified. "No, I want everyone to see us, and know that we have strong feelings for each other. …but it's my father. He'd tear us apart if he knew." Inman asked, "You know this because…." Mary replied, "Because my mother told me so." Inman asked, "Your mother knows about us, then?" Mary said, "Yes, she does. In fact, she knows your family, and is happy that we are seeing each another." Inman was confused, "So what's the problem?" Mary said, "The problem is my father. He hates everyone, and everything." Inman was incredulous, "Not you?" Mary sighed, "Maybe. Sometimes I think that I'm only useful for his social advancement." Inman asked, "If it's only him, what are you worried about?" Mary answered, "Mama said to be wary of being seen where his cronies hang out. Inman found a grasp on the problem and said, "...so let's go see a movie." Mary took his arm and said, "Yes, lets!"

Mary and Inman rode the Streetcar to, and up Canal Street. The Loew's State was showing **The Belle of New York**. Mary said, "It's full of dance, but the reviews aren't great." Inman said, "I love dance. Let's give it a go." Mary said, "At least we'll be together!" Inman stepped to the Box Office and said, "Two, please." Inman paid for the tickets, and they entered the movie palace, the first theatre Inman had ever seen. He was quite impressed, "This building is beautiful!" Mary agreed. Inman bought soft drinks and popcorn, and they made their way to their seats in the balcony. They cozied up and shared their fresh-popped popcorn, Coca-Colas, and intimate snuggles.

When the movie ended and the lights came back up, Mary asked if they could stay a while and snuggle. Inman had no objections. When Mary was sure that anyone who could rat them out had left the theatre, she stood up. "Why don't we go back to the Garden District. We can sit in the garden until I have to go in." Inman agreed. They rode the Streetcar back to the front of Mary's home, and avoided Blackjacks "operatives." Mary and Inman walked with arms around each other's waists, unaware of Millicent's gaze from the various windows, around the funeral home, to the Memorial Garden, and the cast iron bench upon which they sat the first day they met. They both sat, entwined within each other, and just enjoyed the company of each other. Inman said, "I hope you don't find this too strange, but I feel complete when I spend time with you." Mary pondered Inman's thought for a moment, "Yes, I get that, and I feel the same way. In fact, I feel more and more comfortable with you each time we see each other."

Inman said, "It would be so much better if I could call you, but there is no phone at the **garçonnière**." Mary said, "Even if there was a phone at the **garçonnière**, my father wouldn't allow me to talk to you." Inman was confused. "I thought you said your mother knew my family, and my family's worthiness." Mary said, "She does, but my father rules this roost, unfortunately, and no one is good enough to please him. ...and my mama said that there was some unpleasantness between your papa and my father." Inman was intrigued, and wanted to know more about the "unpleasantness." He decided that the only avenue available to him was to ask his uncle Danton. He certainly couldn't ask his mother. That would raise unanswerable questions. He pushed that to the back of his mind and concentrated on being in the moment with Mary. He leaned over and kissed her. She sighed and put her arms around Inman's neck. They kissed until they heard the chimes ring out 11:00. Mary turned away. "I have to go in now." Inman pulled her back. "...**juste cinq minutes de plus**." (...just five more minutes.) Mary couldn't help herself and embraced Inman tightly, kissing him passionately. When the light went on in her parent's bathroom she pulled away. "We can't be caught out here! I have to go in." As Mary started through the kitchen door, she paused and said, "**... même heure la semaine prochaine?**" (...same time next week?) Inman smiled from the shadows and said, "**Oh, Oui!**" His heart was pounding and it felt like electricity was coursing through his body as he walked around the funeral home and to the Neutral Ground dividing Saint Charles Avenue to wait for the Streetcar.

While Mary and Inman thought calling upon each other would be a wonderful option, another option would soon rear its beautiful head.

CHAPTER FOUR

MOVIES, MAY DAY, AND THE CITY OF THE DEAD

April was Mary and Inman's Month of Movies. They saw **Phone Call From a Stranger** at the Tutor Theatre, **Here Come The Nelsons** at the Globe, then **Singin' in The Rain** at the Saenger Theatre. On Saturday the 26th, their final Movie Month selection was **Anything Can Happen** at the Orpheum. They had extremely strict criteria when choosing their movies. They had to be shown in extremely dark theatres; the theatres had to have comfortable seats, and a decent concession stand. …and the theatres had to have exits that led to alleys so they could avoid people after the show let out. Going to movies was working well for Mary and Inman's budding relationship. They waited to buy their tickets and enter the auditorium until after the house lights had dimmed and the Previews were playing, so, hopefully, no one would notice them. They always used the fire exits when the credits were almost to the end.

The following Saturday, the third of May, was May Day at Miss. McGraw's School. It is a delightful tradition dating back to the Teens. Millicent and both Inman's mother and her twin, his aunt Virginia, had graduated the same year and participated in May Day festivities. The idea of her daughter's participation in the tradition warmed Millicent's heart. After the skit, Mary introduced her Little Sister, Hélène Boudreaux, to her parents. Millicent was terribly excited to meet her. "You were so delightful on stage!" Hélène blushed, but curtseyed and thanked Millicent for the compliment. Jackson was uncharacteristically pleasant the entire morning. When the third graders started dancing around the May Pole, Millicent clasped her hands and held them over her heart. She wept with pure joy. Finally, it was time to announce the May Day Court, which consisted of the May Day Queen, and her fair maids. Millicent had been a maid, which was a high honor, based upon kindness and School Spirit. When it was announced that Mary Day was the Queen of May Day, Millicent was so excited that she almost told Mary that Inman's mother Caroline had been the May Day Queen, and that she and Virginia were her maids. Thankfully she caught herself in time. It was difficult to tell who was prouder of Mary, Millicent, or Blackjack. Blackjack; however, had a selfish motive to be proud of Mary. Her achievement would invariably help his social aspirations.

From across the iron fence and the street, Inman watched as best as he could. He had asked Uncle Danton to lie for him and get him out of his confinement for the morning. He could tell that there was a major celebration, but couldn't see that it revolved around Mary. After the program ended, the Day family walked back to Jackson's limousine. Johnny Hardwick opened the door for them. This was the first time Inman had caught a glimpse of Mary's parents. Blackjack was oblivious to his surroundings, but both Mary and Millicent spotted Inman. Millicent wanted to tell Mary that Inman was the spitting image of his father who had been considered the handsomest man in New Orleans in his day, but for the second time that morning, she held herself, and said nothing. Mary, obscured from her father's view by her mother's getting into the Fleetwood, smiled at Inman, patted her heart, and waved her fingers from close to her chest. Inman quietly enjoyed Mary's daring greeting.

That evening Mary and Inman saw ***Young Man With Ideas*** at the Joy Theatre, which was diagonally across Canal Street from the Saenger Theatre and directly across Basin Street from the Loews State Theatre. The film had just been released, and the Joy Theatre was crowded. Inman held Mary's hand and they made their way up to the balcony. They emerged from the house left vomitory onto a mid-balcony cross over. From there they climbed the stairs to the uppermost row of seats. They were happy that there weren't many patrons up that high, but there were a few. Several of them ogled Mary. Mary and Inman settled in and enjoyed each other's company. Something told Inman to hold back for a minute as the credits were rolling. When the last of the balcony patrons had exited through the vomitories to the lobby below, Inman took Mary's hand and they walked down to the crossover. Inman pushed open the fire exit door. He and Mary found themselves on a covered iron platform with steps leading down to Basin Street. They decided to sit on the steps and wait, just in case there were theatre patrons on the sidewalk below waiting for a bus. After the next bus passed, Mary and Inman walked cautiously down the stairs to the sidewalk, ever vigilant. They were relieved that the sidewalk was empty. Inman dropped their empty popcorn bucket and drink cups in a rubbish bin, and they walked along Basin Street and turned left onto Common Street, avoiding the people on Canal Street. They got on the Streetcar at Common and St. Charles for the ride back to the Garden District. On the ride back, Mary was worried that she had recognized one of her father's employees at the theatre. They decided that Mary would get off the Streetcar at Louisiana Avenue and get up to her bedroom as quickly as possible, and Inman would continue on a few stops, get out and transfer to a Streetcar headed back toward the Central Business District. As the Streetcar approached Louisiana Avenue, Mary and Inman kissed as passionately as they dared on public transportation. The door opened, and Mary snagged one last kiss then hurried across Saint Charles Avenue and into the funeral home. Her mother was at the foot of the stairs. She said only, "Hurry, the phone just rang." Mary began unbuttoning her dress as she raced up the stairs. After closing the bedroom door behind her, Mary laid the dress across one of the matching polychrome silk **bergères,** dropped her slip and laid it across the **bergère** and slid quickly into bed.

Millicent stood in the cased opening that led from the foyer into the parlor looking at the antique French parlor furniture. Jackson came into the foyer from the rear of the house, fuming and red faced. "Where is Mary?" Milled continued to stare at the furniture. "She's been in bed for a while now, why?" Jackson replied," I just got a call from Jack Bates telling me he just saw Mary at the movies with a boy!" Millicent shook her head. "...and from where did he call you?" Jackson thought for a moment. Millicent jumped back in. "You don't have to tell me. He's at The Little Gem, that dive bar that used to be a pawn shop. ...and he's probably already drunk." Jackson insisted, "He said that he saw Mary at the Joy Theatre, with a boy." Millicent shook her head, "Go up and check. I've been here thinking about new furniture for an hour and a half. I'd have seen her go out." Jackson Day huffed and trudged up the stairs. He knocked on Mary's door. When she didn't answer, he cracked the door and called her name. In a quiet voice, Mary answered, "**Oui**, father?" Jackson was stunned. "Were you asleep?" "Yes, father, I was. Is there anything wrong?" Jackson grumbled, "No," and pulled the door closed. Mary waited for a few minutes before slipping out of bed and changing into her nightgown. She got back in bed. Her heart was racing, and she worried about being seen in public. Canal Street was too close to her father's other enterprises. She and Inman would have to stay in the Garden District. None of the funeral home employees lived there, and she couldn't think of anyone Blackjack was friends with. No one, that is, who would call her father and rat her out.

Jackson brushed past Millicent. "You were right, she was asleep. ...and Jack IS probably drunk." Millicent said, "Jackson, I saw some high quality furniture at Hurwitz Mintz earlier today. What do you think about redecorating this parlor with modern furniture?" Blackjack frowned. "There's nothing wrong with the furniture I already own. ...and even if there was anything wrong with it, I'd never trade with those Hurwitz Minz hebes. You can just forget about that store and do your day dreaming at Doerr's." Even after all of the years Millicent had been married to Jackson Day, this level of racist contempt stabbed her in the heart. Her Blanchard upbringing had left no room for racism of any type. Jackson tromped through the back of the house and slammed his office door. Millicent turned, and elegantly climbed the stairs to visit Mary. Millicent knocked, then stuck her head through the door. She whispered, "Are you still awake?" Mary sat up in bed, "**Oui**, mama, come in." Millicent slipped through the door and closed it behind her. She switched on the floor light next to Mary's favorite **bergère** and dragged a **fauteuil** close to Mary's **lit à la polonaise**, an elaborate canopy bed that Millicent had given Mary for her 13th birthday. It was an exact replica of one owned by Marie Antoinette. As Millicent sat down, she chuckled and asked, "Do you still love this bed, Mary?" Mary, with a look of confusion, said, "**Oui, mama! Mais pourquoi?**" (But why?) Millicent shook her head, "Your father just said the most racist thing before I came up, and seeing this bed made me think that it's a good thing he doesn't speak French, or he'd never have allowed me to buy it for you." Mary stared at her mother blankly. Millicent said, "In English it's a 'Polish' bed." Mary started to giggle and it wasn't long before Millicent joined in.

Millicent got ahold of her giggles and said, "You almost got caught tonight." Mary said, "Yes, I know. I've been thinking about that quite a bit. We can't go to Canal Street anymore." Millicent said, "Yes, there are too many eyes over there." Mary asked, "I was thinking that we'd be safe here in the Garden District. None of his employees live here or hang out here. What do you think?" Millicent thought about it and said, "Yes, I suppose you're right. I can't think of anyone here who would betray you like his hired muscle." Millicent smiled at Mary, "You put a lot of thought into this. **Je suis très fier de toi mon coeur**!" (I'm very proud of you my sweetheart!) Mary smiled and said, "Thank you so much, mama!" Millicent stood up, leaned over and kissed Mary on the forehead. "**Bonne nuit ma fille chérie**." As Millicent returned the **fauteuil** to its place, Mary replied, "**Bonne nuit, mama!**"

After church the next morning, and lunch at the Camellia Grill, Mary went up to her room to hit the books. The next day was the first day of Exam Week, and she wanted to finish strong. She wasn't worried about her Literature class, or her French class. She simply had to finish the last couple of chapters in *Le Grand Meaulnes*, and be ready to answer questions, **en Français, naturellement**! As Exam Week progressed, the only time Mary had to think about Inman was in her bed before falling asleep. Those loving thoughts caused her to dream beautiful dreams and wake up happy and refreshed. By Friday afternoon Mary was exhausted. She put her school satchel up in her room and came down stairs and collapsed onto a richly upholstered **méridienne**. She kicked off her saddle oxfords and lay back, propped up by one of the bolsters against the higher arm of the sofa. Millicent walked through the dining room and asked, "How was your last exam?" Mary said, "It was fine. I'm glad it was today and not earlier in the week. Chemistry has been my most challenging class." Millicent smiled, "I'm sure you did just fine! Now, rest, your father is taking us to Brennan's for dinner." Millicent walked on through the parlor to the foyer, and up the stairs to change for dinner.

Being in public with Jackson was always stressful for Mary and Millicent. This dinner was no exception. Jackson was critical of Millicent's drinking. "It's one thing at home, but must you drink so much out in public?" Millicent crunched an ice cube, and said, "We're in New Orleans, in the **Vieux Carré**. This is drinking central. ...I dare you to recall any occasion when I was even remotely spiffed!" Mary was astonished that her mother would even consider standing up to her father. In truth, Millicent knew that she was right, and that Jackson wouldn't argue with her. That might be bad for business. For the rest of the meal, there was a frosty silence at the table. The only conversation was with the waiter. After Jackson settled the tab, they got into the Fleetwood. Jackson asked Johnny Hardwick to drive him by his Bank House on Esplanade Avenue. Mary let out a heavy sigh and turned to look out the window. Her father grumbled, "Young lady, I've worked years of long hours to afford to send you to that fancy school and pay for your wardrobe, hairdos, and the like. The very least you could do is be a little appreciative." Mary started to say that she was appreciative, just exhausted, and wanted to go home and go to bed, but Jackson cut her off as they approached the corner of Esplanade Avenue and Marais Street. Johnny turned right onto Marais Street then into the yard behind the two story clapboard house. Johnny and Jackson got out and went into the back door.

Mary asked her mother, "Whose house is this?" Millicent replied, "This was your grandfather's house. Your father grew up here." Mary seemed shocked, "Father grew up in **Tremé**?" Millicent explained, "Technically, it's

Esplanade Ridge, but it might just as well be **Tremé** which, by the way, was called 'Back of Town' at that time." Mary still wasn't sure why they were there. "So… do these people rent the house from father?" Millicent laughed. "Oh, heavens no. These people work for your father's other business." Mary scrunched her face. "…other business?" Millicent leaned in close and kept a lookout for Jackson. She whispered, "This is a Bank House. It was your father's first Bank House. He has other business interests, but you can't tell anyone, or let him know that you know. Is that clear?" Mary was shocked, a little confused, and speechless. She nodded her head. Jackson and Johnny Hardwick were in the Bank House for just under twenty minutes. They strode out of the Bank House. Jackson climbed into the Cadillac. Millicent asked him if everything was okay. Jackson replied, "Everything's fine. I just wanted to set Jack Bates right. He could't have seen Mary at the movies. She was home in bed." Mary's eyes got really wide, and she turned to look out the window. Millicent asked, "Did you mention his drinking?" Jackson huffed, "Yes I did. He knows better than to drunk call me anymore." Johnny drove them back to the funeral home. They got out of the car in the motor court and went into the kitchen. Hattie and Marie Cosette were getting things ready for Saturday breakfast. Mary shot through and up to bed. Millicent stopped to check on Hattie's and Marie Cosette's preparations. Jackson went back to his office and slammed the door. Within five minutes he opened the office door, and bellowed for Marie Cosette to bring him coffee.

Mary slept in on Saturday morning. When she didn't come down for breakfast, Millicent sent Marie Cosette up to check on her. "Ask her if she would like to have her breakfast sent up on a tray." "Yassum." Marie Cosette went upstairs, knocked on Mary's bedroom door, and stuck her head in. "Is ju up?" Mary yawned, and stretched her arms, "Yes I am, please come in." Marie Cosette walked over to the bed. "Yo mama wansa no if'n you wan yo breffas brod up hea." Mary thanked her. "That won't be necessary. I'd appreciate it if you would make me a plate and leave it in the oven." Marie Cosette agreed and left Mary to get ready for the day. When Mary came downstairs, and started through the parlor, her mother was coming from the dining room. "Well, good morning, sleepyhead!" Mary replied, " You know how Exam Week has always wrecked me." Millicent added, "No doubt, all 'A's'" Mary seemed buoyed. "Perhaps, except maybe Chemistry." She thought for a moment and added, "I can't possibly understand why I needed to take Chemistry in the first place." Millicent said, "Perhaps it has something to do with cooking." They both laughed. Millicent suddenly remembered, "Oh, I almost forgot! I was going to give it to you yesterday, but 'circumstances' got in the way." Mary asked, "Give me what?" Millicent went to her **dos d'ane,** a fancy french drop front desk and retrieved a paper. She handed it to Mary. Mary looked at it and asked, "What is this. It's like a cipher." Millicent said, "It's where Inman Carnes, the Third is entombed. Mary was buoyed. "Really, and which cemetery?" Millicent said, "Lafayette Cemetery, Number One." Mary was relieved. "Good, at least it isn't Saint Louis, Number One." Millicent agreed. "Yes, that would be too close to your father's 'associates.'" Mary had Millicent explain the logistics, then thanked her and made her way to the kitchen to eat, what would now be more appropriately called her "brunch."

Mary spent the rest of Saturday studying the map of Lafayette Cemetery, Number One, to ensure that she could accurately tell Inman how to get to his papa's tomb. After dinner, Mary went up to her room to relax. She thought about reading, but hadn't chosen a new book. Between her close call in the Central Business District, Exam Week, and everything else, it was no wonder. She sat in her **bergère** and looked out the window. Time passed quickly, and soon she saw Inman as the Streetcar cleared the intersection. Mary raced down the stairs, through the front door, and to the iron fence. She had just enough time to slip through the gate before Inman got there. Mary threw her arms around Inman's neck and kissed him passionately. "We almost got caught last week." Inman was shocked. "What?" Mary continued, "I was right, one of my father's employees saw us. Thankfully, he went to a bar, and got drunk before calling my father. That's the only way I made it home and into bed in time to deny that we'd been out." Inman was having trouble understanding the fact that they weren't doing anything wrong, and were, in fact doing what teenagers had been doing across the globe, every night of every week, of every month, of every year since time began. Mary sensed that Inman was steaming, so she changed the subject to a less negative subject. "I have a present for you." Inman was taken back. "A present? What's the occasion?" Mary teased, "Didn't you tell me that you wanted to know where your papa is entombed?" Inman had to admit that he had indeed told Mary that, and that he did still want to know where his father was entombed.

Mary said, "Drum roll, please." Inman looked at her blankly. Mary laughed and said, "Oh, I forgot, sheltered life!" She leaned in close to Inman and said, "Your papa is entombed in Lafayette Cemetery, Number One." Inman thought for a moment. "That's such good news! Where exactly is Lafayette Cemetery, Number One?" Mary kept herself from pondering how someone so obviously brilliant could have next to no cultural understanding of his home. "It's just a few blocks from here." Inman said, "That's great! Let's go." Mary protested. "It's dark." Inman was confused. "You told me about all of those dead people who 'lived' in your home. What's different about the ones sealed in marble tombs?" Mary repeated, "It's dark, and people say that the spirits wander the cemetery at night."

Inman asked, "Do they wander your home at night?" Mary had to admit that she never experienced it. Inman said, "Well in that case, let's go." Inman's rational, and Mary's desire to be with him conspired against her irrational fears. "Okay, I'll get some flashlights." Inman was ecstatic. Mary went back to the funeral home. Surprisingly, there were flashlights laid out on an elaborate mahogany **enfilade** in the foyer. She took them, without any reservations, and rejoined Inman on the sidewalk in front of the funeral home. Together, they walked hand-in-hand down Saint Charles Avenue, toward town, until they came to Washington Avenue and turned right. They only had to walk a block and a half until they were at the gate to Lafayette Cemetery, Number One. As they crossed over into the land of the dead, Mary's grasp on Inman's hand became a death grasp. She was truly afraid. Inman paused and put his arm around Mary. "**Pas de peurs, je vais te protéger mon amour.**" (No fears, I'll protect you, my love.) Mary sighed and got as close to Inman as humanly possible. She led him to the Carnes Family Tomb. Inman was suddenly humbled. He shown his light all over the tomb, reading the names and dates. He was immediately confused. "How can so many people be entombed in this amount of space?"

Mary had to explain, "The recently deceased are placed in the upper vaults. Over time the heat and humidity cause rapid decomposition. Usually, by the time of the next funeral, all that is left are bones and dust. They are placed in the lower vault, allowing another entombment above." Inman looked at the lower vault that contained many generations of his ancestors." Mary was worried about Inman's reaction to the news. Inman squatted down and placed his hands on the marble slab sealing the lower vault. He said a prayer, then stood up. "This is remarkably efficient. I suppose, one day, I'll be here." Mary said, "Maybe, but not for a long time." There was an unusual chill in the air. Mary shuttered. Instinctively, Inman removed his blazer and draped it around Mary's shoulders. Inman put his arm around Mary's waist as they started to walk out of the cemetery. As they reached the gate of the cemetery, Inman was overcome by incredible culinary scents. Inman asked, "Where are those amazing food smells coming from?" Mary chuckled. "Why, they're coming from Commander's Palace. Inman stared at Mary with a look of utter puzzlement. "Commanders Palace? What's that?" Mary, by this time should have been prepared, but Inman's question took her off guard. "You seriously don't know about Commander's Palace?" She added, "It's one of New Orleans' best restaurants. You haven't ever eaten there?" Inman's face flushed a bit. "No, actually I've never eaten in any restaurant. My mother never allowed it. We've always had cooks and a full household staff." Mary was once again dumbfounded. On the walk back to the Memorial Garden behind the Jackson Day funeral home, Inman reminded Mary that after his father's murder, and the run in with the thief who threatened to kill him, his mother had secured her family in her home on Howard Avenue. She had the walls built higher and the gates made stronger.

Once they were all sequestered, Inman's mother home schooled him to the limit of her abilities. There were servants to do the shopping, and keep the family afloat. His uncle Danton kept his mother supplied with books and managed the family businesses. Inman sighed and said, "It's easy to be eccentric when you have money." They sat on their accustomed iron bench, locked in a passionate embrace. Inman sensed that his time that evening was waning, so he went bold. "Mary, would you make me the happiest man in New Orleans by having dinner with me at Commander's Palace. Mary was overjoyed at the thought of a dinner out that she could actually enjoy. Her emotions got the better of her and she quickly said, "Yes!" She thought for a moment and added, "We'll have to wait until after graduation on the 24th. ...but YES!" They relished in their delight for the upcoming BIG date and necked until the light went on in Mary's parent's bathroom. Reluctantly, Mary pulled away. "Next Saturday, my love." Inman replied, "Yes, my love, next Saturday." Mary went in to he kitchen, and Inman sat back down on the iron bench to decompress. Parting with Mary was becoming more and more difficult each time. In truth, Inman didn't want to part with her, but he had no choice. Inman reluctantly understood that things could get much worse, unless he could think of a way to impress Mary's father enough to approve of their relationship.

He was tired, and realized that the solution to that problem wouldn't come that night, so he moped back to the Neutral Ground between the lanes of Saint Charles Avenue and rode the Streetcar back to Howard Avenue.

CHAPTER FIVE

GRADUATION AND A CRUEL BETRAYAL

After what had seemed an eternity for Mary, her graduation from Miss. McGraw's was upon her. Johnny Hardwick drove the family to the school. It was a blue-clear, cloudless day, perfect for an outdoor graduation in the Garden District. Mary was resplendent in her pink gown. It had originally been her mothers, but Millicent insisted on having it altered to better reflect more modern tastes. Mary had done even better on her exams than she'd expected. She graduated Summa Cum Laude, and the school's Valedictorian by only one tenth of a point. Mary made her family extremely proud. As on May Day, Inman watched, as best as he could, from across the street. When Inman saw Mary crossing the dais to thunderous applause, Inman's heart started to race. He was genuinely happy for her. Her father was genuinely happy that Mary's success would bode well for his social aspirations. This time, as the family left the school grounds, Jackson saw Inman. In fact, Jackson locked eyes with Inman. Inman nodded politely. Jackson smirked, and got into the Cadillac. Millicent, who had witnessed the exchange, was aghast that Jackson hadn't realized that the handsome young man was a Carnes. After all, Inman did look just like his father.

As much as Mary wanted to see Inman that night, she couldn't. Her parents had invited what was left of their family in New Orleans, and what few friends they had, to a graduation party for Mary. She was trapped. Everyone was trapped. …trapped at a party, that was, who would guess, more like a funeral. It wouldn't have been like that if Jackson had simply allowed Millicent to plan it. Jackson insisted, however, that Roger Whacker, one of his Funeral Directors, plan the **fête**. Roger was, after all, being paid a generous salary! During the party, Millicent made her rounds, apologizing for the party. No one blamed Millicent. They all were supportive and understood her consternation. Mary, more than anyone else, was on a desert island. There were no young people there. Mary had been taught to be polite and be "the hostess with the mostess." She was surely put to the test that night. The worst was when she happened into the company of Dr. Scrope. Mary didn't know it, but the good doctor was on her father's "retainer." That is, he had a gambling problem, and perpetually owed Jackson Day money. Dr. Scrope told Mary, "I was supposed to deliver you, dear child, but an emergency prevented it. The midwife came here to the funeral home to deliver you. I think I remember being told that you were born in the Embalming Room. Mary was truly shocked, and was having trouble maintaining her composure. Finally, Mary said, "Please excuse me, Dr. Scrope, my mother is waving to me." Dr. Scrope bowed, and said, "By all means my dear, don't keep Millicent waiting."

Mary bounded across the room looking for a safe spot from all of her fathers morbid "friends." Millicent found Mary hiding in a corner, hoping not to be seen. She pulled Mary aside. "I know how awful this is. It hurts my soul that you had to give up an evening with Inman for this." Mary smiled because of her mama's kind understanding. Millicent added, "Go on up to bed, I'll make your excuses." Mary didn't have to say a word, her face said it all. She hugged her mama and walked briskly through the house and up the stairs to her bedroom. The day had exhausted her. Mary undressed and put on her nightgown. She slid into her magnificent bed and concentrated on her dreams of a life spent with Inman. She looked forward to her date with Inman the following Friday evening. Mary couldn't figure out if she was happier for the expectation of her own culinary experience, or for that of Inman. At least they would be together, and away from the prying eyes of her father's "employees" in the Central Business District and beyond.

The next week was abysmal for Mary. Without school, she was stuck at home with nothing to do. She realized that this must be very much like Inman's forced confinement. She didn't like it at all. As much as possible, Mary tried to get her mother to tell her stories about Inman's mother and aunt, and their mysterious brother Danton. While Millicent was adamant in her lies that she knew little of Danton, she did tell Mary about the Tea Dances and **fêtes** at **Maison Soleil** back in the day. Mary asked, "Did they really have a Dance Terrace?" Millicent said, "Of course they did! It was between the **garçonnière** and the pool. Oh, it was so elegant! Caroline's mother Francine had supervised the construction personally, especially the plantings."

"There were fragrant blooms surrounding the Dance Terrace all year long!" Millicent welled up with emotion. "I'm so sorry." Mary waited patiently for her mother to regain her composure. After a few moments, Millicent continued, "Social life in New Orleans was dealt a hard cruel blow when Inman Carnes, the Third was murdered at Lee Circle. The finest home, the best parties, and the finest family were walled off from the rest of us who loved them. We all cried, and yearned for them." Mary was fighting back tears. Millicent continued. "I would never have thought that you'd be dating Inman Carnes' son. ...and I'd never have thought he'd be everything you say he is. ...but I'm not surprised, not with his family, even with the horrible duress he grew up with." Mary wiped her tears away and hugged her mother. "**Merci mama, il est vraiment merveilleux!**" (Thank's mama, he is truly wonderful!) Millicent hugged her daughter. "It will all be okay. I just need to make your father think it's his idea. ...just don't go where his associates are!" Mary agreed.

At last, Friday night, the 30th. of May arrived. It was Mary and Inman's date night at Commander's Palace. Even Millicent thought that Commander's Palace was mostly a safe venue. She took Millicent to Maison Blanche for a new outfit, then Adler's for earrings, a necklace, and bracelet. They then went to **Maison de Bringier** and had their hair expertly coifed. By the time Millicent and Renè had finished, Mary looked positively regal. For a change, that evening, Mary stood in the parlor window with Millicent waiting for Inman to arrive. While they waited, Millicent reminded Mary, "Please remember that your father had 'business' with Inman's family and I haven't figured a way to convince him that Inman is the right beau for you." Mary was breathless. "Yes, mama, I know, but there couldn't be any of father's associates at Commander's Palace, now could there?" Millicent couldn't conceive it. " just be on the look out, that's all." Mary agreed, just as the Streetcar began to pass. After it passed, there was a single person standing in the neutral ground dividing Saint Charles Avenue. It was Inman, bedecked in a new suit, and carrying an amazing bouquet of flowers.

Inman started walking toward the funeral home. Mary wanted to break for the front door, but Millicent grasped her wrist. "Patience, my dear. He'll soon be at the gate. Ladies sometimes keep their gentleman friends waiting, just for a little while. Millicent noticed that Mary was hyperventilating like a greyhound at the slip. Finally, Millicent couldn't take it any longer. "Go on then, just be careful!" Mary ran to the front door, paused, then opened it somewhat slowly. She slipped around the door and paused on the **véranda** ever so briefly. Mary then glided down to the iron gate. Inman presented Mary with his huge bouquet of flowers. Mary asked, "Do we have time for me to take these in?" Inman said, "If that's what you think is best, then yes, of course." Mary ran to the door and slipped inside. Millicent interceded, "Sweet one, let me take those. I'll put them in a vase and water them, so you can get back to your beau." Mary thanked her mother, then slipped back through the front door.

When she got back to the sidewalk, Mary slid her hand into the crook of Inman's muscular arm. As they walked down Saint Charles Avenue toward Washington Avenue, Mary told Inman all about their close call the previous Saturday. "I just had time to take off my belt and dress and slid into bed. It's a good thing that my father didn't switch the light on." Inman seemed perplexed. "Why?" Mary guffawed, "Because I hadn't taken my hat off, silly!" Inman started laughing too. By the time that Inman regained control over his facilities, he became curious. "Do you know who called him." Mary said, "Yes I do, and fortunately, he is a notorious alcoholic, and called father from a bar, almost two hours after he saw us walking up the balcony stairs. Thank God he didn't call from the theatre lobby." Inman agreed. Mary continued, "…so, I'm afraid that movies on Canal Street are not going to be an option anymore." Inman agreed. "I just wish that I could prove my worth to your father." Mary assured him, "My mama is working full time on that problem."

As Mary and Inman approached the intersection of Washington Avenue and Coliseum Street, the smells emanating from the kitchen at Commander's Palace perfumed the air. They were intoxicating. At the intersection, Inman looked across the street. The restaurant was a two story Victorian structure, surrounded on the two street fronts by a patinated copper porch roof to protect waiting patrons from sudden summer storms. The corner of the building was topped with an octagonal church-like spire. The building's clapboards were painted sparkling white, but, unlike buildings in the **Vieux Carré**, there were no shutters, just oversized windows and venetian blinds. Inman chuckled. Mary asked, "What's so funny?" Inman pointed to the support columns for the porch roof. "I was wondering if they had to paint them green half way up to keep people from running in to them." Mary stopped to study the columns, then began to laugh too.

Inman put his arm around Mary's waist, and they crossed Washington Avenue, passed under the yellow neon sign, and went into the restaurant. The **Maître d'hôtel** greeted them and asked if they had a reservation. Inman said, "Yes, we do, the name is Carnes." The **Maître d' hôtel** seemed surprised when he heard the Carnes name. He studied Inman carefully. "**Mon Dieu!** Can it be? You look just like Inman Carnes!" Inman smiled. "That's good, because I am Inman Carnes." The **Maître d' hôtel** almost passed out. "Please tell me that you are the son of Inman and Caroline Carnes." Inman puffed up like a peacock. "I am! I'm Inman Carnes, the Fourth, to be precise. The **Maître d' hôtel** was delighted, "I knew your parents. I was a very young waiter back then. They were so nice, and so generous. I was devastated when your father died, and I haven't seen your mother for so many years!" Inman shook the **Maître d' hôtel's** hand and thanked him for his tribute to his parents. **The Maître d' hôtel** made some changes in his book of reservations, and guided Mary and Inman to the best table in the main dining room. Mary thought that she heard the **Maître d' hôtel** mutter, "Mayor Morrison will have to sit elsewhere!" under his breath. Both Mary and Inman noticed the approving looks of the diners as they were escorted to their table.

The main dining room was papered in a multi-colored flocked wallpaper above the Ionian white chair rails and wainscoting. The square tables were draped in heavily starched linen tablecloths, and set with silverware, water goblets, and napkins folded into triangular pyramids. The chairs were relatively modern. They were all arm chairs with curved backs and comfortable seats, upholstered in sky blue rayon. The **Maître d' hôtel** called a waiter over and had him clear away the twenty-or-so other silverware pieces, the napkins, plates, and goblets from the other two places at the table. The **Maître d' hôtel** sat Mary and Inman with their backs to the kitchen doors. Mary had a view of the comings and goings of patrons. Inman had a view across the room to the garden. The **Maître d' hôtel** handed them menus, and excused himself. "Gaston will be waiting on you tonight, Mr. Carnes. He'll be right over." Mary and Inman looked over the menu. Mary suggested that they order off the ***Table D'Hôte Dinner*** side of the menu. Gaston arrived and took their drink orders. When he returned with their drinks, Gaston took Mary and Inman's orders. For starters, Mary ordered the Crabmeat Cocktail. Inman opted for the Turtle Soup au Sherry. For their main courses, Mary selected Breast of Chicken Marchand de Vin, Fried Hominy. Inman ordered the Trout Almandine, Brabant Potatoes. They both ordered the Combination Salad. For dessert, Mary suggested the Doberge (Dough-Bash) Cake. "It's not on the menu, but they get them custom baked by Beylah Ledner, herself. Inman hadn't understood any of Mary's story, but took her at her word, and ordered it for two.

As the food started coming out, Mary and Inman found themselves in culinary Nirvana. Between the delicacies on the table, and their loving attention to one another, there was no room to observe the other diners as they came and went. Mary completely missed that Dr. Scrope came in, sat down, ordered, then suddenly noticed her. She also didn't see him get up and walk to the **Maître d'hôtel's** station and ask to use the phone. While Mary and Inman were lost in a paradise of their own making, the phone rang in Jackson Day's office. Millicent's heart sank when she heard the phone ring from her seat on the **méridienne** in the parlor. Then, there was the screaming. Jackson went out to the motor court, and even through closed doors and many rooms, Millicent heard her husband yelling for Johnny Hardwick to pull one of the Fleetwoods out. She breathed in deeply as she heard the kitchen door open violently. "Millie! Come on, Mary's out with some boy!"

Mary and Inman had just started enjoying their Doberge Cake, when Mary saw the last thing she wanted to see. Her father was stalking through the restaurant looking for her. Millicent had refused to get out of the Cadillac. It was then that she saw Dr. Scrope. He pointed Jackson to the table that Mary had been enjoying with Inman. She froze. Her red-faced, maniacal father demanded to know who the boy was. Mary was still frozen in panic. Inman very calmly wiped his mouth and laid his napkin next to his plate. He stood and extended his hand. Blackjack was still focused on Mary. Inman said, "It's a pleasure to meet you, Mr. Day. I'm Inman Carnes, the Fourth." Blackjack, still staring through Mary said, in a voice far too loud for polite society, "Carnes?" He turned to stare at Inman. "Carnes, you said?" Inman, still extending his hand, said, "Yes sir! Inman Carnes. …the Fourth. My family has been in New Orleans since day one, I'm told."

Blackjack, now completely exasperated, said, "Yes, I know all about your family. Your aunt is as crazy as a bat, and your mother hasn't left the house in twenty years. But, more importantly, YOU! …you don't have an education, a job, or any prospects. You aren't good enough for my daughter!" Inman tried to point out that he had been home schooled, was planning on joining his uncle Danton to learn the Factorage business at the family Wharf, and had income from his family's up-river plantation, **Beau Cadeau.** Blackjack wasn't interested in listening. Blackjack turned his glare back to Mary. The diners, who had been truly delighted by the young couple with impeccable manners, were now shocked and dismayed by Blackjack's horribly boorish display. Blackjack said, "We're leaving." Mary hesitated. "We're leaving, now, Mary Charmaine Day!" Mary looked at Inman. The full extent of her disappointment, sorrow, and horror was evident in her face. Inman tried to interject into the situation, but Blackjack wrenched around and shouted, "Sit down, boy!" Inman defiantly stood his ground. Mary held her beautifully

48

coifed head down in shame and followed her father out. The other diners, with the possible exception of Dr. Scrope, felt great pity for the elegantly dressed, and well-mannered young man who had so obviously been done wrong. One of the diners sent Inman a double Bourbon/rocks. Not knowing who exactly had sent it, Inman stood and raised his glass and slowly spun around to salute the entire restaurant. When all that was left were a few skeletons of ice cubes, Inman motioned for Gaston. "Check, please." Gaston leaned down and whispered into Inman's ear. "Sir, your tab has been paid." Inman asked who, but Gaston said that the benefactor didn't want to be named. "...but sir, there was a competition. Several other diners asked to pay your tab after it had been arranged. Inman hung his head and thanked Gaston. He then stood up. For once, the restaurant grew really quiet. Inman started to leave, but stopped. He breathed in deeply, and puffed out his chest. Inman surveyed the room and said, "Regardless of what her father said, I WILL marry her! ...and I thank you all for your gracious hospitality." As Inman walked toward the door, the entire restaurant erupted in applause. Inman smiled through his tears all the way to Saint Charles Avenue and the Streetcar ride back to Howard Avenue.

Jackson Day said nothing to Mary during the ride back to the funeral home. When they got out of the car behind the funeral home and went into the kitchen, Millicent fixed herself a Blanchard strength Gin and Tonic and went into the parlor. Mary stayed close to her mama. Jackson, still beet red yelled, "She was on a date!" He paused, "She was on a date with Inman Carnes, of ALL people." Millicent stared at her husband with utter contempt, that he, of course, missed. She took a sip of her drink and crunched a fragment of an ice cube. Jackson continued his verbal assault on Mary. "Do you have any idea how much money I've spent to prepare you for the right kind of husband?" Mary began to cry. Millicent felt her blood pressure rising. Jackson continued, "Well, do you???" Millicent handed Mary a tissue. She wiped her eyes and got control of her sobbing. "Father, he's the nicest, and kindest boy I've ever met."

Jackson huffed with contempt. "Mary, while it may be true that his family is old New Orleans, older, by far than most, they like to say, they are no longer socially relevant in New Orleans." Jackson looked at Millicent. "There's no way he's good enough for her." Millicent crushed a second ice cube fragment.

"You mean that he's not good enough for YOU!" Jackson completely ignored Millicent's keen observation, and pondered how Inman had evaded Caroline's lock down policy. Millicent was aghast when Mary said, innocently, "He sneaks out after his mother and aunt go to bed." "Is that so" Jackson started. "Well then, until further notice, you, young missy, aren't allowed to leave the house after dark. Is that understood?" Mary felt defeated and began to weep. Hesitantly, she said, "Yes, sir."

Jackson said, "Good, now that this is sorted, I've got a lot of work to do. It didn't help having to drop everything to go rescue you from that... that mongrel." Jackson stormed back to his office and slammed the door. It wasn't a minute before he was yelling for Marie Cosette to bring him coffee. Mary looked at Millicent with tears in her eyes, "Mama!" Millicent took a sip of her drink. "I had a feeling something like this might happen. I just didn't think it would happen in the District. I'm sorry, but we're just going to have to let this die down." Mary said, "...but mama." Millicent put her arm around her daughter and said, "You heard him, you can't go out at night without one of us. ...and I promise you, he'll have spies watching both you and me."

Mary gave her mother a pitiful look, "...but mama, I want to date Inman. He makes me feel so special!" Millicent sipped her drink. "You don't have to convince me. I know that family. That's how they are. ...the absolute best! You'll just have to have faith. In time this will work itself out. Your father's grand scheme will be complete when you debut at the Rex Ball. He's dead set on keeping that from derailing." Mary said, "Mama, that's almost a year away! I could loose Inman!" Millicent said, "**Mon cher Chéri, laisse-moi m'inquiéter à ce sujet.**" (My dear darling, let me worry about this.) Mary said, "**Merci mama, Je suit fatiguée. Ja vais aller me coucher maintenant.**" (Thank you mama, I'm tired. I'll go up to bed now.) Millicent wished Mary a good night's sleep. Mary left the parlor and went up to bed. Millicent walked over to the window overlooking Saint Charles Avenue, peered out the window, and sipped her drink, lost in her thoughts, and in her schemes. In her mind, it was bad enough that Jackson Day had destroyed all of her hopes and dreams.

Millicent silently swore that she'd be damned if she'd allow that bastard to do the same to her beloved Mary.

CHAPTER SIX

MILLICENT BLANCHARD DAY HATCHES AN AWESOME SCHEME

After a night of tossing and turning, sheet wrenching, and tears, Mary forced herself to get out of bed. On her way to the bathroom, she paused and stood at the window overlooking the Neutral Ground, desperately wanting to see Inman. She sighed and found her way to her Pepto Bismal bathroom. After a luxurious soaking bath, she dressed, and walked slowly and sadly down the stairs and to the dining room. She was surprised to see her father sitting at the table, reading the *Times-Picayune*. He had finished his breakfast. Millicent, who had been reminded the previous evening of her husband's nickname, looked up at Mary and said, "**Bonjour mon amour**!" Mary put her arms around Millicent's shoulders and kissed her cheek. "**Bonjour, mama.**" "Blackjack" refused to acknowledge Mary's presence. Mary took her plate to the **buffet de chasse**, and served herself. She wasn't particularly hungry, and took small portions. As Mary sat down to eat, Millicent couldn't help noticing Mary's malaise. She put the toast point she had been enjoying down on her plate and leaned closer to Mary. "I thought that you might like to go shopping with me today." Mary perked up a bit. From an early age, shopping with her mother had been one of her favorite pastimes. Purchasing wasn't obligatory, it more about the experience. She adored exploring new fashions, and feeling the materials against her skin. Mary loved the way new shoes smelled. …not necessarily the way they felt being broken in, though. Had she been queried, Mary would have said that between shopping and spending time with Inman, she'd choose spending time with Inman. …but that just wasn't an option at the moment.

Mary's face bloomed into a smile. "**Oh merci, mama!**" Millicent sat back straight in her chair and looked over at Blackjack. "Jackson, dear, would you like to meet us for lunch in the Quarter?" Blackjack made a disgusting noise in his throat and grumbled from behind his newspaper barrier, "I have two funerals Monday. It's damn impossible!" Millicent's face drew itself into a Gioconda smile. She turned to Mary, arched her eyebrow, and winked. Mary had to put her hand over her mouth to keep from giggling. When she calmed down, Mary said, "I'm not dressed to go to town. I won't be long, mama." As Mary was leaving the dining room to change, she heard her mother ask, "Jackson, is there a car and a driver free?" Blackjack compressed the newspaper in his fists. "Seriously! Did you not hear me when I said that there are TWO funerals Monday?" Of course Millicent had heard Blackjack, but she needed to get a jab in that would contribute to her strategy. She forced a sly smile, "That's okay, Jackson, we'll take the Streetcar. Blackjack looked down at his ruined newspaper. He started to smooth it out but descended into frustration, that led to outright anger. "Marie Cosette, why don't you get in here and clean away these damn dishes!" Marie Cosette was startled by Blackjack's outburst and came right in and started to clear away the dishes. Blackjack looked at Millicent and grumbled deeply. "I'm not exactly sure how you persuaded me to eat out here Millie, but I'm going back to my office. Marie Cosette, take a break and fetch me some coffee."

Blackjack grabbed his suit jacket from the back of the chair and stormed back to his office and slammed the door. Marie Cosette had frozen, conflicted by the two overlapping directives. Millicent said, "…better take him his coffee. These dishes can wait." Marie Cosette nodded her head, grabbed Blackjack's horribly tannic-stained diner mug and took it to the **buffet deux corps**, and filled it with **café noir**, then rushed it back to Blackjack's office.

Millicent gently dabbed her lips and the corners of her mouth. She folded the napkin over and placed it beside her plate before standing and walking to the parlor.

Millicent was sitting on an elaborately carved and gilt **bergère à oreilles** next to the fireplace when she saw Mary descending the stairs. She stood and walked toward the foyer to meet her daughter. Mary said, "I hope that I didn't keep you too long, mama!" Millicent shook her head, "Nonsense, I'm just so glad we can get out of this house and have a wonderful day together shopping, and planning." Mary beamed. Together, they walked to the Washington Street intersection and crossed to the Neutral Ground where they waited for the Streetcar. When it arrived and the doors opened, Millicent and Mary boarded, and Millicent dropped a token in the fare box for her, and pointed to Mary, "She's a student." They took seats on the right side of the Streetcar, and settled in for the ride to Canal Street. As the Streetcar neared the traffic circle around the Lee memorial, Millicent pointed out the window, "If you look down Howard Avenue, toward the river, about a block, you'll see the main gate to **Maison Soleil**, Inman's home. The walls are high and very secure. You probably won't be able to see the **manoir**, or any of the other structures, but they're there. Caroline Soleil Carnes, and her twin sister Virginia, receive virtually no callers, but they're there. They even have a full household staff!" As Millicent was talking, Mary kept craning her neck and changing positions to catch a glimpse of the gate. Millicent smiled. "Don't worry, when we start home, you'll have another chance to catch a glimpse."

Millicent and Mary's shopping day out started on Canal Street. Their first stop was Adler's. Millicent took Mary to the jewelry counter to look at necklaces, bracelets and rings. They both tried on countless pieces of costume and fine jewelry. The salesperson had a hunch and brought over a velvet lined mahogany tray of heart-shaped necklaces. Mary was stunned. One piece in particular spoke to her. She picked it up and placed it over her **décolletage**. Her heart started to race. Millicent said, "We'll take it." The salesperson located the jewelry box, and placed it in an embossed paper bag. Millicent opened her purse and handed the salesperson her charger plate. As Millicent was handed the receipt, she was asked, "Is there anything else we might do for Madam?" Millicent thanked the salesperson, "Thank you, no. We're going to the Stationary Department, and I know the way." Mary was confused as to why they needed to go to the Stationary Department, but followed her mother through the throng of New Orlean's finest, well-dressed citizens. When they reached the main counter in the Stationary Department, Millicent asked the salesperson if they had any leather bound journals. The salesperson reached into the display case and produced a stylish and beautiful kid leather bound journal. The cover was embossed with leaves of gold. Millicent was impressed. She told Mary, "You can write about the things you and Inman have done, and the things you two will do." Mary found herself intrigued. "Yes, that sounds appropriate." After Millicent agreed to the purchase, the Salesperson commented about Mary's necklace. She told the salesperson that it was a constant reminder of someone she loved. After that day, Mary rarely ever took it off.

Millicent looked down at her Diamond encrusted Cartier watch. She had received it as a graduation present from her parents when she graduated from Miss. McGraw's. It was white gold, rectangular, and set with three emerald cut diamonds at the top, and three more at the bottom. The bracelet was a yellow gold rope design, cinched by white gold collars studded with rose cut diamonds. "I thought it was close to time for luncheon. Today, I'd like very much to know where you would like to eat. If your father were here, we'd be forced to go to Brennan's." Mary said, "We're out of the house and away from the smell of dead flowers. Anywhere is fine. How about Antoine's?" Millicent was ecstatic with Mary's choice. They took a cab to the **Vieux Carré**. The cabbie stopped and let them out in front of Antoine's. As Millicent and Mary walked through the front door, Millicent's waiter, Henri, spotted her. He ran over, **"Bonjour, madam Day! Table pour deux?"** Millicent smiled serenely, **"Oui, Henri!"** Henri sat them at the best table in his domaine, and presented them with menus. **"Que puis-je vous faire boire?"** (What may I get you to drink?) Millicent said, we'll have a bottle of a good White Bordeaux, and water, please." Henri replied, **"Très bien madame!"** After Henri left, Millicent and Mary perused their menus. Henri brought the bottle of wine in a two bottle silver-plate wine bucket with an ice compartment. He poured Millicent a taste. She sampled it and was delighted. "If it gets too low, bring us a second bottle, Henri." "**Oui, madame.**" Henri then asked them for their orders.

Henri knew instinctively that Millicent would order **Pompano Montgolfier** and that Mary would order **Filet of Beef Périgueux.** As expected, Henri was correct. Henri rolled Millicent and Mary's main courses out on a **guéridon.** Using a clean starched white linen towel, Henri presented Mary's **Filet of Beef Périgueux** first. The heavenly scents of fine Madeira and black truffles teased Mary. Henri then presented Millicent's **Pompano Montgolfier.** It was truly an Antoine's experience. The chef had started with a heart shaped piece of parchment paper, then added a layer of crab meat and shrimp. On top of this he perched a well buttered Pompano fillet, and topped it with sautéed onions, celery, dill and tarragon. He then poured a sauce consisting of white wine, lemon juice and just a splash of tangy Tabasco Sauce. Then the parchment paper was folded over and sealed around the edges. It was cooked in a medium oven, allowing the steam to balloon the parchment paper sheath. Henri placed the plate in front of Millicent and picked up a knife and fork. He slit the parchment paper with the knife, releasing the heavenly fragrances from their captivity. He used the fork to roll the Parchment paper back, revealing the decadent entrée within. For dessert, Mary asked for **Meringue Glacée au Chocolat,** and Millicent ordered **Pêche Melba,** and **Café Brulot Diabolique pour deux.** The **Brulot** was expertly flamed at the table by Henri. As lagniappe, Henri brought Millicent a snifter of VSOP Cognac to augment her **Café Brulot.**

After a leisurely luncheon, Millicent and Mary made their way to Maison Blanche. After several hours of shopping for everything from hats to shoes and all of the fabric in between, and multiple purchases, Millicent had a brainstorm. She looked at Mary. "You should have your own charger plate. I know that you won't abuse it. It'll just make things easier." Mary had no clue what Millicent was alluding to, but went along. Millicent, however, had thought her chess game out for multiple plays. Mary accompanied Millicent to the Business Office. Millicent stated to a clerk that she wanted her dear daughter to have a charger plate connected to her account. The arrangements were made, and the clerk assured Millicent that the charger plate would be delivered within a few days. As they walked out onto the wide concrete sidewalk outside of Maison Blanche, Millicent caught sight of the Roosevelt Hotel across Canal Street. She sighed. "My dear, I'm parched. Why don't we go across the street and get something cold to drink before we go home?" Mary agreed. She would do anything to keep from having to go home during a funeral.

Millicent and Mary crossed Canal Street along Baronne Street and stepped into the Sazarac Bar. Millie strode to the bar and ordered a Sazarac. "When in Rome…." The bartender looked at Mary. **Un Sazarac pour vous aussi mademoiselle?**" Mary blushed, "No, a soft drink, with ice, please." Millicent looked at the bartender, "She'll have a Coke, but sweeten it." That was the publicly accepted genteel colloquialism for, "give her a "weak" drink. After their refreshments, Millicent and Mary boarded the Canal Street Streetcar, and transferred onto the Saint Charles Line. Mary stared intently out the windows, hoping for a glimpse of **Maison Soleil.** As the Streetcar started it's loop around Lee Circle, Millicent told Mary, " The Soleil family used to own all of this land. They made a fortune developing it. Their home is the oldest building above Canal Street. …1795, I think. Their surveyors made a huge mistake which put Howard Avenue right up next to the **manoir.**" Mary was intrigued by her mother's story. She turned to listen. Millicent continued, "I'll tell you something else; I don't care what your father said last night, Caroline Carnes and Virginia Soleil aren't crazy. It's true, Caroline rarely receives visitors, and that she has rarely ever left the property. She doesn't have to, everyone comes to her. …but the big thing is, she manages her household. She has domestic help, a yard crew, and her brother, Danton manages both the Day and Soleil businesses."

Millicent continued, "Caroline Carnes personally educated Inman. According to several of my dear friends, Danton Carnes told them that Inman is fluent in both French and Spanish. It suddenly hit Mary, and she interjected, "**Excusez-moi**, please tell me more about about Inman's uncle." Sudden thoughts of Danton caused Millicent to look way off in the distance and become emotional. "Danton Soleil manages his family's Factorage on the Wharf as well as the Day Plantation, **Beau Cadeau**, up river, near Baton

Rouge in Morrisonville. Caroline and Virginia have access to everything they could ever need or desire through their brother Danton. I hear that Danton has been spending a lot of time mentoring Inman since he became a teenager. He probably arranged for Inman to 'go exploring.'" Mary smiled, "He sounds like an extremely nice man." Millicent sighed heavily, "He truly is…. If only." Mary gazed intently at her mother. Millicent replied, "…but that's a story for another day. Oh, look, we're home."

Millicent and Mary arrived home just before dinner had been scheduled. Marie Cosette had been vacuuming the large Persian rug in the parlor, and saw them struggling across Saint Charles Avenue with their bags, bundles, and packages tied up in string. She threw open the front door of the funeral home and rushed to the gate to ease them of their burdens. The three made it to the foyer, and started laying their burdens down. Blackjack heard the commotion, and rushed from his office. He was aghast at the number of parcels. "I was about to call the Police Chief!" Millicent rolled her eyes and brushed past Blackjack on her way to the stairs. "Nonsense, we weren't gone that long." Blackjack surveyed the bags and packages and asked, "How many stores did you buy out?" Millicent was nonplussed, "It's just a few odds and ends." Blackjack started back to his office, "Thank God business is good!" Something caught him, and he turned and retraced his steps to the banister. Blackjack grasped Mary's wrist tightly as she started to ascend the steps. "Young lady, you know that you're forbidden from leaving this house after dark, without one of us, don't you." Mary almost got upset, but happened to be looking upstairs at her mother. Millicent stood, statuesque, displaying that **la Gioconda** smile she was so famous for. "Yes, father, I understand."

Marie Cosette helped Mary take the bags and bundles upstairs to Mary's bedroom. She had to rush back down to help Hattie serve dinner. After dinner, Marie Cosette accompanied Mary upstairs to her bedroom to help her unpack and store her new treasure. For each outfit that Mary unpacked, she offered Marie Cosette one of her gently used older outfits. Completely by accident, Marie Cosette happened to have a glance out the window. She was shocked. "Dat boy be down dere ride now." Mary said, "No, really?" Marie Cosette shook her head, "Ju'se come and see fo ju self." Mary stiffened and crept to the window. Sure enough, Inman was leaning against one of the Streetcar wire support poles. Mary looked at Marie Cosette and started running for the door. Marie Cosette, of course, followed. They ran down stairs, and to the parlor window. Mary and Marie Cosette piled into the window with Millicent, who had been there for a while. Millicent put her index finger over her lips, and moved to a beautiful petit desk called a **bonheur du jour**. It had been her mother's, her grandmother's, and her great-grandmother's before she had inherited it. Millicent pulled out a formal note card from one of the drawers and thought before she wrote. Firstly, she struck through her formal monogram at the top. She then wrote:

Dearest Inman,

My husband has made it clear that Mary is forbidden to leave this house after dark without his permission and without his or my company.

Would it be possible for Mary to call on you and your dear mother, Caroline, at **Maison Soleil** on days when there are funerals here? Our girl, Marie Cosette, would be available to bring you word in advance of Mary's visits.

Most Sincerely,

Millicent Charmaine Blanchard Day

When she finished writing the note and screwed the top back on her Mont Blanc pen, Millicent allowed Mary to read the note. Mary beamed, and hugged her mother, trusting in her mother's emerging scheme. With Mary's approval, Millicent placed the Crane note card into a matching envelope and handed it to Marie Cosette. "Marie Cosette, please go out the back door and take this note to Inman. …and wait for an answer." Marie Cosette agreed, and sprinted around the funeral home to the Neutral Ground. From the parlor window, Millicent and Mary watched as Marie Cosette handed Inman the note and waited for his response. They both were on tender hooks as Inman carefully read the note. His face lighted up like a summer fair midway. Millicent and Mary couldn't hear him, of course, but saw him nod his head enthusiastically. Millicent and Mary witnessed a lot of words evanescing from Inman's mouth, but had to wait for a synopsis from Marie Cosette when she returned from her mission.

Inman said, "Don't call at the main gate. Walk on down Howard Avenue to the gate at the **garçonnière**." Marie Cosette scrunched her brow and looked quite puzzled. Inman saw the problem. "Oh, I'm sorry, a **garçonnière** is a lodging where the family's teenage boys lived to keep them away from teenage girls who were on extended visits with their parents, and staying in the **manoir**." Marie Cosette said, "Iz can see how dat was a necessidy." Inman agreed and added, "Please don't tell Mrs. Day that I have 'my own place.'" Marie Cosette chuckled and agreed to keep all of Inman's and Mary's secrets. Inman thanked Marie Cosette, and as she turned to walk back to the funeral home, Inman had a sudden realization. "Oh, one more thing." Marie Cosette stopped and turned back to face Inman. He said, "I almost forgot… There is a cast iron handle on a chain just inside the gate. It's connected to a bell. Give it a couple of pulls to let me know that you've arrived." Marie Cosette nodded, then turned and crossed back over to the sidewalk on Louisiana Avenue.

Millicent watched Marie Cosette walk down the block. Mary continued to watch Inman intently until the Streetcar arrived, and he was gone. Marie Cosette walked through the dining room and stepped into the parlor. Millicent asked, "Well?" Marie Cosette said, "De boy said jes, he'd love to hab Mary visid him." Mary could hardly contain her excitement. She put her arms around Millicent and whispered, "**Merci, mama**!" Mary went up to her room and read for almost an hour before going to bed. Millicent freshened her drink and returned to the front window. She continued to stare out into the night and consider the next steps in her grand scheme.

The next morning was Sunday the first of June. The Day ladies assembled in the dining room for breakfast. As usual, Blackjack heard the chafers being set on the **buffet de chasse**, and bolted out of his office, snatched his plate and filled it. As he sat down, Millicent motioned for Mary to serve herself, then looked at Blackjack and said, "Jackson, I laid out a red tie for you today."

59

Blackjack replied, "Red's not really my color. I can't figure out why you bought it in the first place!" Millicent sighed, "Andrew Jackson Day, you know perfectly well that today is Pentecost Sunday. All of those Garden District gentlemen you are always trying to impress will be wearing red neckties." Blackjack grumbled. He wolfed the rest of his breakfast down and went up to change his necktie before the family was driven to Christ Church Cathedral for the celebration of Pentecost. The necktie was only the first thing in a string of habits and behaviors that Millicent would have to contend with, as Blackjack had informed her, the previous evening, that he had decided to run for Orleans Parish Coroner. As usual, Blackjack was overconfident about the run. Millicent, on the other hand, knew that for Blackjack to win, she'd have to use her Blanchard family connections, and charms to compensate for Blackjack's shortcomings. It would be an uphill battle, but it would play well in her scheme to give Mary and Inman plenty of time to enjoy their summer and get to know one another. After the service, Millicent pointed out various couples that Blackjack should socialize with. "Don't say anything about the race, just yet. ...just be interested in their work and families. Pretend that you care!" She spent the next forty-five minutes or so, giving Blackjack family histories and interesting tidbits about the men and their families so he could feign interest in them. As difficult as it was for Blackjack at first, and as much as he resented having to do it, Millicent was a rock, and kept her candidate on track.

During the drive to Brennan's, Millicent laid out several strategies for Blackjack to implement. "You're going to have to join the Rotary Club, and become involved with the Chamber of Commerce. You should have done that years ago to help the funeral home!" Blackjack grumbled, but, deep down, in his tint heart, he knew that Millicent was right." After they were seated and had ordered, Millicent accompanied Mary to the Ladies. While they were adjusting their makeup, Millicent said, "We need to enthusiastically support your father in his campaign." Mary asked why. Millicent smiled devilish, "I'm going to keep him so busy, between funerals, and campaigning, that you and Inman can have a completely enjoyable summer."

The ladies finished their makeup and returned to enjoy their Sunday Breakfast at Brennan's in spite of the fact that Blackjack was there.

CHAPTER SEVEN

THE "SUMMER OF LOVE" BEGINS

Inman woke up early on Pentecost Sunday. The thought of Mary's first visit had lit a fire deep within him. He started cleaning and arranging the furniture in the **garçonnière**, the dance pavilion, and out on the dance terrace. As he worked, Inman began to ask himself just what did he have in the way of entertainment to offer Mary. He rummaged through his father's **atelier**, one of the outbuildings that had served as his father's design studio and workshop, when he wasn't at the Wharf. After his father's death, Caroline insisted upon preserving all of the projects that Big Inman had been working on. They were all still in place, but the space had become more of a storage room. Inman's uncle Danton called it the "Plunder Room." If he had commented to Inman once, he'd commented a hundred times, "You have to do the 'Hinsley step' in there, and at your own risk, too." Inman had heard him use that description to his mother many times growing up, and never thought anything of it. When it had become apparent that Inman was going through puberty, Caroline decided that Inman needed more privacy and had Danton set him up in the **garçonnière**. He suggested that Inman take his old room upstairs in the back, overlooking the pool and dance terrace. They had used old leather suitcases to transport Inman's clothes and sundries. Not wanting to lug them back to the **manoir**, Danton sighed. "I guess we'll just put them in the Plunder Room. I'll have to teach you the 'Hinsley step.'" Inman was finally curious enough to ask. "What is this 'Hinsley step?'"

Danton put his suitcases down and told Inman a story. "When your father and I were at Tulane, there was an old janitor named Mr. Hinsley. He must have been eighty years old. It was said that he had been retired for years, but still came to work every day. The other janitors did all of the regular chores, but allowed Mr. Hinsley to run errands and such. Well, he had some gait issues and a few eccentricities thrown in for good measure." Inman said, "So, I'm guessing that he had a peculiar walk." Danton said, "Here, I'll show you." Danton took two steps forward, then took a step to the left. He took three steps forward then two steps to the right. Inman started to snicker. "Please tell me he did't raise his knees that high!" Danton said, "Oh yes he did! ...but no one ever mocked him. The students had great affection for him. He would greet everyone he met, and raise his old pork pie fedora." When they went into the **atelier**, and started having to shuffle around through the stacks and piles, Inman began to chuckle. Danton said, "See, now you get it!"

After some effort, Inman found what he had been searching for, an ancient croquet set. He did the 'Hinsley step' and maneuvered himself and the Croquet Set out of the **atelier**. Inman placed the elegant wooden caddy with room for four mallets, four color banded wooden balls and a brass handle on the dance terrace with the flags and heavy cast iron hoops. He reasoned that he'd have time to figure the game out later. Inman then decided to explore the **manoir** for interesting items. The first thing that he discovered was in the **bibliothèque**. It was a stereopticon and several wooden boxes of slides from around the world. Inman stepped into the salon where his mother Caroline was reading. His aunt Virginia was elsewhere, no doubt "entertaining" one of her gentleman friends. Inman had learned years ago not to inquire about his aunt. His inquiries had been the straw that broke the camel's back and landed him in the **garçonnière** in the first place. "Mama, may I take these to the **garçonnière** to study.

Caroline looked up from her book. "Yes, of course you can. I don't believe that anyone has looked at them for many years." Inman thanked her and took the Stereopticon and boxes of slides to the dance pavilion. When Inman returned to the **manoir**, he truly hit pay dirt. He happened to open the doors to a cabinet in the library. It was jammed with 78 rpm recordings. He pulled out an album that was marked 1928. Inside there were recordings of ***Because My Baby Don't Mean Maybe Now*** by Ruth Etting, ***That's My Weakness Now*** by Paul Whitman, ***Diga Diga Doo*** and ***Mississippi Mud*** and ***Let's Misbehave*** and ***I Wanna Be Loved By You*** by Helen Kane, among many others. Inman took the album and stepped back into the salon. "Mama, I didn't know that you had records." Caroline looked up and placed her book, pages down, in her lap. "Let me see that album, please." Inman took the album to his mother who proceeded to peruse the song titles. A warm and radiant look overtook her countenance, as if she were taking a delightful trip down memory lane. "Where did you find this?" Inman said, "It was in a cabinet behind stacks of magazines." Caroline said, "Your papa and I loved music, and we dearly loved to dance. After he was gone, they caused more pain than happiness. I had forgotten about them." Inman asked, "Would it be okay if I took them to the **garçonnière**?" A broad smile illuminated Caroline's face, "Of course, but you'll need to find the Edison phonograph to play them." Inman asked if she knew where it was. Caroline thought for a moment, "I believe it was placed in the **grenier**. It was thought that it would be too hot for the records up there, though." Inman said, "I'll go take a look." He sprinted up the stairs. Fortunately for him, they extended up into the **grenier** (attic). After a search, Inman found the phonograph, covered by a sheet in a corner. He went back downstairs and out into the gardens where he persuaded Moses, the head groundskeeper to help him cary the phonograph down out of the **grenier**, and to the **garçonnière**. After that, they carried the matching cabinet of records to the **garçonnière**. When Inman went back to the **manoir**, his mama told them that there were probably many more cabinets or boxes of recordings. "All of the records that were shipped to Louisiana arrived at the Soleil Factorage. Uncle Danton and your papa always got to pick first. It was quite wonderful."

Ultimately, Inman found two more cabinets and numerous wooden fruit crates of records. By the time he had carried the last crate to the **garçonnière**, it was nearly dinner time, and his uncle Danton showed up as was his custom. Danton walked down to the **garçonnière** and found Inman trying to figure out how to set up the Croquet Set. "You know that Croquet isn't a solo game. You have to have an opponent." Inman replied, "Playing Croquet by yourself wouldn't be much fun, but I'll be having a friend over to visit occasionally." Danton became slightly pensive. Inman continued. "Would you have the tennis court rehabilitated?" Danton thought for a moment and said, "Well, yes. I suppose so." It was then that Uncle Danton noticed the phonograph and the collection of records. "Would you like me to get you a nice radio and record player combination?" Inman was excited. "Yes, that would be wonderful!" As Danton was about to return to the **manoir**, he asked, "What's this fellow's name, and how did you meet him?" Inman stopped dead in his tracks and looked at his uncle Danton. "Well, to begin with, he is a she. Her name is Mary, and I met her at her home, which is a funeral home on Saint Charles Avenue over in the Garden District."

Uncle Danton suddenly had a look of utter astonishment on his face. "You don't mean Mary Day, do you?" Inman said, "Yes, that's her. I found the funeral home you and mama said handled my papa's funeral. Mary saw me get off the Streetcar and walk around the back of the funeral home. I was looking in a window, and she snuck up behind me and scared me half to death. After that, we sat in the garden and got to know each other. The next week we started going on long walks through the Garden District to look at homes and gardens, and to talk. A few weeks ago, she told me that she had looked through the books and found the spot where papa is entombed."

Danton interrupted, "Do her parents know that you are spending time with her?" Inman hung his head. "Her mother knew about it, but her father didn't until one of his associates called him while we were enjoying an amazing dinner at Commander's Palace." Danton asked, "I can't imagine he was happy about that, was he?" Inman said, "No, he charged into the restaurant and yanked her out. It was awful." Danton probed just a little deeper, "What about her mother?" Inman said, "I think she knew about us from the very beginning. ...and I believe she supports us. Here, look at this note." Inman reached down to the note that he had placed on a **guéridon** next to a wicker **canapé**. Mary's mother asked if Mary could visit when her father is occupied. Danton looked at the note. He held his thoughts, but the penmanship was immediately recognizable, and he almost smiled when he saw that she had crossed out her formal monogram. "Are you two in love?" Inman was caught completely off guard. He guffawed. "Uncle Danton! We've only known each other for about two months. We're great friends. She's super nice, and you're really going to like her!"

A sudden realization suddenly hit Danton. His face became deadly serious. "You know that we're going to have to find a way to make your mother think that your having company, especially female company, is a good idea. We'll have to make this her idea." Inman too had a sudden realization, and agreed. Danton thought for a few moments, "Okay, it's time for **dîner**, let's do this. I have a plan. While Danton and Inman made their way from the **garçonnière** to the **manoir**, Danton said, "When we get there, don't say anything. Let me do the talking." As Danton and Inman arrived at the **manoir**, which faced southwest, the sinking sun was sending broad red rays straight toward the **manoir**. All of the exterior shutters were closed to help keep the home cool. As a courtesy, Danton knocked twice on the salon shutters, then opened them and stepped in, followed by Inman. Caroline was seated in her accustomed place, an ancient, but beautiful and comfortable **bergère confessionale** next to the fireplace, reading, as usual. Before Caroline could look up from her novel, Danton pointed to a spot and told Inman, "You stand right there." Caroline was startled and closed her book. "**Danton, quel que soit le problème**?" (Danton, what ever is the problem?) Danton walked over to his sister feigning extreme anger. "When I got here, Inman was talking to people through the **géarçonnière** gate! He knows full well that you despise contact with the outside world. This behavior is unacceptable. He has to be punished. Just how do you want to handle this egregious behavior?" Caroline laid her book on the **étagère** next to her **bergère** and asked, "Punished for talking to people, Danton?" Danton dug in deeper. "They were common people. People who have no couth and don't see the world the way we do."

Caroline looked across the room to her son. After a few moments of thought she asked, "Inman, is this true?" Inman kept quiet and nodded his head in agreement. Caroline grasped her left shoulder with her right hand and grasped her chin wth her left hand. She sank back into the damask luxury of her **bergère** and stared off into space considering the situation. After a few tense moments, Caroline said, "Danton, we've given Inman everything he could possibly need except company. While I'm not wild about his mingling with common folk, I would be open to his having friends from our echelon of society. In fact, I think that would be a fine idea!" Danton bowed up. "...but you swore that you'd protect him from the world!" Caroline leaned forward in her **bergère**. "That's true, but that was many years ago, when he was but a child. He's grown up now. Frankly, I'm embarrassed that I didn't think about this sooner. Would you arrange for some suitable young people, his age, to call on him?"

Danton looked over at Inman. He started tapping his left foot and acted as if he was coming to terms with his sister's request. "Well, I suppose that I could do that. If you're going to open this door, I could use some help at the Factorage. ...and he needs to learn the business, I can't work forever." Caroline asked, "What do you have in mind?" Danton said, "I think that he should enjoy his summer, and start work in September." Caroline smiled, "Yes, I was just thinking the same thing. He's going to have to take the helm some day." Inman was having difficulty both keeping from grinning and playing his part. Danton then said, "Caroline, please excuse us. In what light we have left, we need to go survey the tennis court. I think that it would be a grand idea to have it renovated for Inman's new friends. Caroline had already put her reading glasses back on and opened her novel. "What a wonderful idea. ...but don't be too long. ....**dîner**."

Danton and Inman didn't actually go to the tennis court. They needed to get out of earshot, so they walked back to the **garçonnière**. Once there, Inman gushed. "That was brilliant! How did you ever think of that?" Danton breathed in deeply and let out a breath of relief. "Inman, my wonderful nephew, I've known your mother longer than anyone living on this Earth. She may live in her own made-up world, derived from her books, but she is still a very human being. She's obstinate. She always has to have her way, even when what she wants makes no sense. However, she is super intelligent, and she thrives in reason. You have no way to know this, but I've tried to get her to let me bring young people, your age, here for years. The problem was aways that it was <u>my</u> idea, not <u>her</u> idea. Today, at least, I was able to turn her mind against her practices. I forced her to make the decision to change her paradigm." Inman thanked his dear uncle profusely.

As they stood on the dance terrace, the cast iron farm bell rang. Both Inman and Danton were surprised. They walked to the **garçonnière** gate together. When they got to the gate, they found Marie Cosette waiting. She hadn't expected to see anyone other than Inman, and showed her fright. Inman picked up on her fear immediately. "Marie Cosette, this is my uncle Danton Soleil. He knows that Mary is going to be visiting, and is completely on our side." Danton, who, in a way, knew all about Marie Cosette, smiled and nodded through Inman's explanation, and his actions had put Marie Cosette at ease. "Deys gonna be a funeral on domorro. Miss Marry wona no if'n she'n come by aroun doo fo a wile?" While Inman was telling Marie Cosette that 2:00 would be wonderful, his uncle Danton had pulled a notepad and fountain pen from his jacket pocket. In haste, he scribbled down his name and telephone number on the page. He yanked it out, and handed it to Marie Cosette. "Sweet girl, I want you to to take this note to Mrs. Day. Mrs. Day only! No one else can know about this. …understand?" Marie Cosette looked like she was about to cry, but held it together. "Yas'ir, I'z can do dat." Danton was overjoyed and gave her a quarter as a tip. Danton said, "Please ask her to call me when it's convenient." Marie Cosette nodded, then turned and walked up Howard Avenue toward Lee Circle.

After Marie Cosette was out of earshot, Danton asked Inman, "How did she know to come to this gate?" Inman responded, "I asked her to." Danton sighed, "I get that, but when Mary comes, have her go back up to the main gate and ring the bell. You'll have to present her to your mama. It'll be okay. Once you make the introduction, your mama will go back to her reading. It has become an obsession since she had to give up teaching you. It's becoming difficult to keep her in books!" Inman threw his muscular arms around

Danton and pulled him close. Danton was worried that his nephew was going to injure him. Inman thanked Danton effusively, and then the two walked back to the **manoir** for **dîner**.

After **dîner**, Danton fabricated a story and told Caroline that he had arranged for Inman to have a visitor the next afternoon. Caroline seemed pleased. "What's his name? Who's his family?" Uncle Danton smiled, "Actually he's a she, from a good family." Caroline was just a little shocked. "A girl?" Danton shifted in his chair just a little. "Caroline, I just found out that they've been talking through the gate, I suppose, for some time now. She's from a good family in the Garden District, not like those people I found him talking to earlier. …but I won't say anything else, you'll just need to be prepared to be pleasantly surprised."

As Danton got up to leave, he spied the huge stack of books next to the door leading to the loggia. "It looks like it's time for me to visit the library. Any requests?" Caroline looked at her brother across her readers and smiled. "No, Danton, you always bring me a great selection. …and I appreciate it." Danton pressed Inman into service to help him carry the stack of books to his Packard. "Hopefully, you'll be available to held me carry the next load in." Inman grinned.

Earlier, Marie Cosette had walked up Howard Avenue and gotten on the Saint Charles Streetcar line. She got off at Louisiana Avenue and walked to the back door of the funeral home. She waited until after dinner, when Millicent was alone in the darkened parlor. Marie Cosette stepped into the parlor, almost terrified. She extended her hand with the note to Millicent with her head bowed. Millicent took the note from Marie Cosette, read it, and then looked at Marie Cosette with a puzzled look. With newly-found bravery, Marie Cosette leaned in close to Millicent and whispered, "Dat mistu Solay be da boy's unkle. He don wan no'n to no 'bout dis." Millicent nodded in agreement, but said nothing. She folded the note and put it in a hidden pocket in her purse. "Thank you, Marie Cosette, for everything you have done for us today!"

68

CHAPTER EIGHT

THE FIRST DATE AT MAISON SOLEIL

The next morning, Blackjack ate at the table with his family. Millicent had insisted. "This will be our time to discuss strategy for your campaign." As much as the thought aggravated him, Blackjack sucked it up and agreed to eat his breakfast and remain in the dining room for thirty minutes each morning for the duration of the campaign. This morning, Millicent reminded Blackjack that he'd had been invited to the weekly luncheon meeting of the Rotary Club. "Their meeting will start at 12:12 on Wednesday, but I'd suggest that you get there at least thirty minutes early to hob-nob." Blackjack begrudgingly said the he'd make time. Millicent then said, "Jackson, I hope that you can spare me today because I'm going to **Maison de Bringier** for a style." She turned to Mary. "**Aimerais-tu te joindre à moi?**" (Would you like to join me?) Mary looked up from her plate, swallowed, and dabbed her lips with her napkin. "**Oui, mama, j'aimerais beaucoup ça. Merci beaucoup!**" (Yes, mama, I'd like that very much. thank you very much!) Blackjack grumbled. "There's a funeral today. You two would just be in the way." He looked at his watch and stood up. "Marie Cosette, get my mug and bring me some coffee." Blackjack grabbed his jacket and walked back to his office. Millicent looked over at Mary and smiled. Mary smiled back.

By 1:30, family members of the deceased were strolling into the funeral home. Blackjack and his minions were in full show mode. Millicent and Mary quietly slipped out of the front door and and walked across their side of Saint Charles Avenue to the Street car stop in the Neutral Ground. After a short interval, the Streetcar arrived, and they boarded. As the Streetcar neared Howard Avenue, Mary hugged her mother and exited the streetcar. Millicent took the Streetcar to Canal Street and exited. She walked a short distance, and entered the salon of **Maison de Bringier**. After her style, Millicent continued along Canal Street and stopped at a public telephone booth. She dropped a nickel in the slot and dialed the number on the note from Danton. The line only rang twice before an operator picked up and said, "Soleil and Carnes, Factors, how may I assist you?" Millicent said, "Danton Soleil, please." The switchboard operator replied flatly, "One moment, Madam."

After a moment, Danton's secretary, Lucy Butler, answered the call. "Mr. Soleil's office. How may I assist you?" Millicent said, "I'd like to speak to Danton. …he requested that I call." "Whom may I say is calling?" "You may tell him that Millicent Day is calling." Without saying a word, Lucy Butler placed Millicent on hold. It wasn't but a few moments before Danton picked up the call. "Millie, is it really you?" Millicent almost melted upon hearing Danton's voice. "Yes, Danton, it is." Danton told Millicent how wonderful it was to hear her voice. Millicent felt the same way but said nothing. After a few moments of catching up on each other's lives, Millicent said, "You know, my daughter Mary is calling on Caroline and Inman, even as we speak." Danton told Millicent how he had manipulated his sister into thinking the meeting was her idea. Millicent laughed wholeheartedly, for the first time in decades. "Danton, you haven't changed one bit!" Danton laughed too, "No, I suppose not, but I was surprised that you allowed this. Blackjack surely doesn't know." Millicent looked around her perimeter and leaned into the phone. "Oh, heavens no! He's still trying to figure out the best candidate for her to marry. It's all about social climbing with him." Danton said, "Yes, I remember that, all too well. There was a short silence. Danton summoned his courage and came straight to the point. "Millie, I'd love to buy you a drink."

Danton's request knocked the wind right out of Millicent. After she regained her composure, Millicent responded, "I'd like that, very much Danton, but how?" Danton considered the options. "Before the next funeral, send your girl to let Inman and me know. After you drop Mary off, you can meet me at the Sazarac Bar." Suddenly Millicent was experiencing feelings that had been hidden away for years. Her eyes darted around, looking at all of the people milling about on Canal Street. "What if someone sees us?" Danton didn't miss a beat. "It's a free country. Two old friends happen to walk into the same bar and have a drink and a conversation together. They finish and leave separately. What's wrong with that?" Millicent was breathless, "Not a thing, but I won't be dropping Mary off. I don't have a car. We'll be taking the Streetcar." Danton was shocked. "Milly, it's 1952! All of the wives of successful businessmen have a car of their own to drive. If you were my wife, you'd have whatever car you wanted." Millicent smiled. "Well, Danton, I better be going. Mary and I can't be out too long on the first day." Danton said, "Until we meet at the Sazarac Bar...." Millicent sighed as she returned the handset to the public phone. The nickel dropped into the coin box as she opened the phone booth door.

Millicent had watched Mary walking down Howard Avenue from the Streetcar earlier. Mary got to the gate at the the **garçonnière**, reached through the gate and pulled the wrought iron handle. The bell rang. Inman had been lounging on a **chaises longue** on the dance terrace. He sprang up, greyhound-like. His heart was racing. Inman found a mirror and checked his hair. To be on the safe side, he ran a comb through it, up and over. Mary could't keep from smiling broadly when Inman turned the corner and came into view. Inman's face erupted into the most appealing smile, the moment he laid eyes on Mary. Mary was the picture of loveliness, wearing an ecru linen and silk tunic dress, gloves, and a matching beret. A small beige purse was hanging elegantly from the crook of her left arm.

Inman, short of breath, walked to the gate and grasped two of the wrought iron uprights. He pressed his face between the two central uprights and said,

"**Je suis vraiment heureux de te voir ma chérie!**" (I am truly happy to see you my darling!) Inman stared deeply into Mary's beautiful violet eyes. Mary looked up and down Howard Avenue. "**Je ne peux pas vous dire à quel point je suis heureux de vous voir aussi, mais allez-vous me laisser entrer?**" (I can't tell you how happy I am to see you too, but are you going to let me in?) Inman snapped back into reality and jerked back from the gate. "Oh, there's been a change. My uncle worked it out so my mama knows you are coming. She's expecting you. I'm so sorry, but would you walk back to the main gate, and ring that bell. I can't wait to introduce you to my mother."

Mary seemed a tad perplexed, but agreed. Inman said, "Please hurry, I don't want to waste a single minute of the time we have together today." Mary said, "No, I don't either!" Mary and Inman walked swiftly on either side of the wall to the main gate. Inman got there first. When Mary arrived, she asked, "Aren't you going to open the gate?" Inman laughed, "Yes, of course I am, but you have to ring the bell first. Mama has to hear the bell!" Mary put her gloved hand over her heart and said, "Oh yes, of course. Mary rang the bell, and Inman opened the gate. He offered Mary his arm and she slid her hand into the crook of Inman's elbow. Inman escorted Mary around the drive and up onto the **véranda**. They stepped into the **salon principal**, and walked over to Caroline's nest. Caroline had taken her reading glasses off, and had looked Mary over. Inman started, "**Mama, puis-je présenter...**" Caroline cut him off. "**Mon Dieu**! Can it be... My dear, you are the spitting image of Millicent Blanchard! Is it possible that you're Millie's daughter?" Mary's smile warmed the room. She walked over to Caroline and extended her graceful arms and hands. "Why, yes ma'am, I'm her daughter, Mary Day." As Caroline clasped Mary's hands, her smile faded just a touch. "That's right, your father is Jackson Day." "Yes ma'am."

Caroline released Mary's hand. "Did you know that your mother and I were in the same class at Miss. McGraw's?" Mary was enthusiastic. "Yes ma'am, she told me that recently, and your sister too, I seem to remember. 1922?" Caroline said, "Yes, 1922." Mary added, "She also told me that the three of you were in the May Court." Caroline was over the moon. "We were! It was magical!" Mary said, "Yes, I know, it still is. Mama told me that you and I share something extremely special." Caroline asked what the special something was. Mary said, "…that we are both May Day Queens." Caroline was completely dumbfounded. "Oh that says an awful lot about you, my dear!" Caroline turned her gaze to her son. "Inman, is this fine young lady one of the people your uncle tells me you have been talking to through the gate?" Inman looked at Mary and said, "Yes, mama, Mary and I have had conversations 'through the gate.'"

Caroline seemed happy and relieved. "Well it certainly is a small world." Both Mary and Inman agreed with her. "Inman, what fun activities have you planned for Miss. Day?" Inman's face lit up, "Uncle Danton helped me set up the Croquet Set. We're going to learn how to play Croquet!" Caroline had by now settled back into the luxury of her **bergère confessionale**. "What a marvelous game, and such good weather for it!" Inman smiled, "Yes ma'am, it truly is!" As Inman turned to escort Mary to the Croquet lawn, Caroline added, "I'll send Monique down to get you when we've had time to prepare some **rafraîchissements**." Inman smiled at his mother, and Mary said, "**Merci beaucoup, madam Carnes!**"

After the nervous excitement of the start of their date, both Inman and Mary could exhale and enjoy their time together. It wasn't until they got out into the light that Mary noticed what Inman was wearing. He was dressed in a white linen jacket and trousers. The trousers were lined to the knees with silk. His white oxford cloth shirt was long sleeved, but Mary would see later that he had rolled the sleeves up almost to his elbows. His shoes were white bucks and his socks were silk. His shirt was open and he was sporting a paisley ascot. His outfit was crowned with a rakish straw boater with a crimson grosgrain hatband that matched the soles of his white bucks. In the sunlight, Inman was positively radiant. Mary thought that he was the most beautiful person she'd ever laid eyes on. Mary snuggled her hand into the crook of Inman's arm and allowed him to stroll her to the Croquet lawn.

Mary had played Croquet for most of her life, but feigned ignorance. Inman explained the rules for Nine Hoop Croquet. Mary looked deep into Inman's eyes. "I'm not sure that I know how to hit the ball." Inman asked, "Would you like for me to guide you?" Mary nodded her head coyly. Inman got behind Mary, put his arms around her and placed his hands over hers on the mallet. They might just as well have been spooning. They were both completely in paradise. Inman guided Mary to use the broad side of the mallet for distance, and the narrow end for accuracy. Eventually, the cuddling had to stop and the game begin. It wasn't long before they both abandoned the formal rules of Croquet. They talked, told jokes, laughed heartily, embraced, and completely enjoyed each other's company. Around 4:00, Monique walked down to the Croquet lawn from the **manoir**. "Mistuh Inman, yo mama's reddy fo yo'sn's to come fo refressmens." Inman smiled, "Thank you Monique! We'll be right along."

Mary and Inman joined Inman's mother and aunt Virginia in the **salle à manger** for **rafraîchissements**. Mary looked at the offerings and thought that it must have taken a huge staff to produce that many high quality delicacies. Caroline asked everyone to take a plate and help themselves. The dessert plates were Rosalinde by Havilland, of course. Monique had placed starched embroidered linen cocktail napkins next to the plates. Everyone placed a few **hors d'oeuvres** on their plates and returned to the **Salon principal**. As they enjoyed their **hors d'oeuvres** and pleasant conversation, the bell from the main gate rang. It was Millicent Day. Caroline asked Monique to go to the gate. When she got there, Millicent told her who she was, and that she was there to collect Mary.

Monique opened the gate. "Miz Carnes say she'd lik-do say hallo." Millicent stepped through the gate at **Maison Soleil** for the first time in decades. As Monique escorted Millicent across the threshold of the **Salon principal**, Caroline stood and shouted, "Millie!" Millicent rushed over to her oldest friend. "Caroline!" They embraced, tearfully oblivious to their children. Millicent sniffled, cleared her throat, and said, "It's been far too long, dear Caroline. I can't begin to tell you how much I've missed you!" A tear coursed down Caroline's cheek, "Millie, I can honestly say that you're the one person I've missed the most over the years!" The old friends released their embrace, but continued to hold hands. They looked deeply into each other's eyes, and just knew. Tears of joy for their meeting flowed. Mary and Inman looked at one another. They hadn't anticipated that their mothers would meet. ...and they certainly hadn't anticipated the depth of affection that had been buried so deeply for so many years.

The meeting gave Mary and Inman hope that their relationship would eventually be approved. Caroline said, "Millicent, where are my manners. Please go into the **salle à manger** and get a plate. We're all having such a fine time." Millicent looked at her Cartier watch and sighed, "Caroline, I know your treats have always been the best, but I'll have to take a rain check. I need to get Mary home before Jackson starts 'supposing.'" Caroline breathed in deeply. "Yes, I completely understand. Well then, another time!" Millicent thanked Caroline for her hospitality and promised that they would find a time to catch up and talk about the old days. Inman escorted Millicent and Mary to the gate. After they left, Inman climbed a ladder he'd placed against the wall and watched Millicent and Mary make their way up Howard Avenue to Saint Charles. As Millicent and Mary got just a little past the gate, and supposedly out of earshot, Millicent said, "He's even more handsome than his father!" Mary said, "He is handsome, and it goes all the ways to his bones!" Inman smiled, and climbed down the ladder.

At dinner, Millicent armed with a stiff drink, and buoyed by Danton's comments, said, "Jackson Day, it's positively disgraceful, in this day and age that I have to ride the Streetcar like common women." Mary's eyes became as large as saucers, but she said nothing. In truth, Millicent had never minded taking the Streetcar, but she suddenly wanted more freedom. Blackjack looked up, stunned. "What? What has happened. Where did this come from?" Millicent didn't miss a beat, "I saw several of my classmates from Miss. McGraw's today at **Maison de Bringier**. They were all talking about the cars their successful husbands had bought them. I was mortified to have to admit that I still ride the Streetcar. It'll be a wonder if we are invited to any of their parties. …and that won't help your election chances."

Blackjack became highly agitated and turned red in the face. He blurted out, "Okay, there are no funerals tomorrow. Would you be able to free up your dance card to go and look at cars? Millicent, who had already been dreamily looking at cars advertisements said, "Yes, I should be able to work that in." Mary's eyes had been darting back and forth between her parents. She was both taking in, and enjoying immensely, her mother's skillful manipulation of her father.

Saturday morning, at breakfast, Blackjack asked Millicent, "Are you ready to go look at cars?" Millicent said, "Yes, Jackson I am. ...but I don't want to waste the whole day. I've been looking at car ads in my magazines and I think that I know exactly what I want." Blackjack looked Millicent in the eyes and said, with just a touch of derision, "Really, are you sure?" Millicent stood her ground. "Yes, Jackson. I've talked to all of my friends, and I feel that the Buick Riviera would be the perfect car for me. It's midrange, and has all of the perks of a Cadillac." You, gentle reader, should know that Millicent really wanted a Cadillac, but knew instinctively that she needed to play Blackjack's weaknesses against him. After a few moments of thought, all Blackjack said was, "We'll see."

After breakfast, Millicent and Blackjack went out the kitchen door to the motor court behind the funeral home. Johnny Hardwick was standing by the open door of one of the Fleetwoods. Millicent got in. Blackjack whispered some instructions in Johnny's ear, before getting in. It was a short drive, but tense. Blackjack stared out the window, and Millicent rummaged through her purse. Johnny pulled the Cadillac into the dealership lot. Blackjack was immediately greeted by the owner of the dealership with furious handshaking. Millicent stepped out of the limousine and realized that they were not at the Buick dealership. "Jackson, I thought that we were looking at Buick Rivieras today." Blackjack huffed. "Why buy a Buick, when I can get a Cadillac for the same price, right Earl?" The dealership owner turned on all of his charm. "Why yes! Mr. Day has bought so many Cadillacs from me, I give him the 'family price.'"

Earl Kemper was a somewhat short and stout man. He wore a relatively conservative wool three piece suit, but his tie and shoes were very much over-the-top. He ushered Millicent and Blackjack into his brand new dealership. It was a garish example of Googie architecture. The roofline plunged down from both corners, forming a huge shallow V, similar to the V emblem under the Cadillac crest. Earl escorted Jack and Millicent directly back to his office and pulled over a chair for Millicent. Once they were all seated, Earl offered

Blackjack a cigar. Blackjack put his hand up. "Thanks, no, I don't smoke. Earl closed the lid of his humidor, and leaned back in his chair. He studied the two of them. "You've brought Mrs. Day today. Can I guess that you're not interested in a hearse, limousine, or flower car today?" Blackjack scrunched back in his chair. "My wife has been taking the Streetcar and busses to shop and to visit friends. Business is good, her friends all have cars, and I think that she needs a car befitting her status.

Earl essentially ignored Millicent. "She said something about Rivieras when you got here. What is she looking for?" Blackjack leaned forward. "She wants a convertible. The last time I had an open top was before I bought the funeral home. It was a 1920 Essex touring Phaeton. ...practical, but no frills. I traded that car for a flower car." Earl leaned forwarded rested his elbows on his desk. "Mr. Day..." Blackjack cut him off. "Earl, please, we've done enough business for so many years now, that you should call me Jack." Earl smiled. "Jack, the Buick Riviera isn't even the top end Buick. That'd be the Buick Roadmaster." Earl paused for a moment then said, "So, just how nice of a convertible do you want her to have?" Blackjack thought about it for a few moments. ...not about what Millicent wanted, but about how good the car purchase would make him look. "I want her to have the absolute best." Millicent, who had been made redundant in the conversation, had been staring at the paneling. When she heard that, she rolled her eyes.

Earl thumbed through a stack of flyers and brochures that filled one of many baskets on his desk. "Cadillac is celebrating it's Golden anniversary in 1953. There'll be a once-in-a-lifetime opportunity to own the absolutely most wonderful convertible ever produced by any car company on October First." Blackjack stopped Earl. "Earl, we want a car today." Earl was noticeably excited, "Yes, I know, and we're going to make that happen, but you need to know about the Eldorado! GM is only going to build five to six hundred of them! You could be the only owner in New Orleans, hell even in Louisiana! Pardon my French, ma'am. Earl's use of "hell" was the least insulting **faux pas** he had imposed on Millicent that afternoon. "Pardon my French" was high on her list, but treating her like cheap wallpaper was the worst. Even still she smiled and said nothing.

Blackjack's gears started rolling. "Well, Earl, I'm intrigued. This car doesn't sound cheap, even with the 'family price.' What's it going to cost, and how will Millie have a car in the meantime?" Earl took out a sheet of paper and started figuring. $7,750.00 invoice, $250.00 +++ equals $8,000.00. $2,000.00 down now, $1,500.00 in July, August, September, and on delivery October 1st. ...at the new model party." Earl slid the paper across the desk to Blackjack. "Of course, she'll have our best demonstrator to drive until the First. ...with full service, at no cost." Blackjack looked at the paper and nearly passed out. " Ahhh, are you sure that this is the family price!?" Earl shook his head affirmatively. "I can sell you a cheaper car, but they'll be all over New Orleans. I've got plenty of those. But, if you want the Eldorado, I'll have to order it and pay for it while they are still available. I could do that and give it a real mark up, or I could give you a good deal, Jack. People are interested in this car. Danton Soleil has expressed his interest in purchasing it. Millicent perked up. The mention of Danton's name sent a shiver through her person. A little smile was impossible to suppress. She made sure not to let either Blackjack or Earl see it.

Blackjack, on the other hand assumed a look of fierce determination. "Earl, you said the demonstrator would would be at no cost, with service included, right?" Earl Kemper, the King of Cadillac in New Orleans knew absolutely at that point that he'd sold the most unique and the most expensive automobile ever in his career. "At no cost, and our porters will wash it as often as your wife wishes. You'll always be first in line for service, and we'll even carry the insurance on the vehicle." Blackjack was slain. He pursed his lips, and tried to resist, but folded and slowly nodded in agreement.

Earl picked up his phone, "Send in the salesman who has the next 'up.'" He returned the phone handset to the base. It wasn't long before a salesman knocked on his open door. Earl looked over to the door. "Great, it's Phillip. Come in Phillip, and meet Mr. and Mrs. Day. Phillip walked over and shook both of their hands. "Pleased to meet you both." Earl stood up. "Phillip, I want you to show Mrs. Day some convertibles. Mr. Day and I are about to order a new Cadillac Eldorado. Phillip looked confused. He mistakenly thought that he had been recruited to babysit a wife, when, in fact, he was about to be the official salesman on the most unique car to date. He and Millicent left the office to test drive convertibles.

After they left, Blackjack scooted his chair closer to Earl's desk. "How are you going to tell Soleil he isn't getting the car?" Earl laughed. "I'm not. I've told everyone that I'm taking bids, and the winner will be revealed at the New Model Party on the first of October." Blackjack burst out in laughter. "Oh, hell no, you didn't!" Earl joined Blackjack in celebratory laughter. "Oh, hell yes, I did!" When they laughed themselves out, Earl got down to the paperwork. His only question was about the color, Blackjack asked for the darkest blue possible, so it could be used for funerals if absolutely necessary. When he had finished, and the deal was done, Earl opened his bottom desk drawer and pulled out a bottle of Old Grandad Bourbon, and two old fashioned glasses. Earl and Blackjack enjoyed numerous rounds of fine Bourbon before Millicent decided on a demonstrator.

After Millicent had made her choice, Phillip sent the car to the detail lot and returned Millicent to Earl's office. Earl and Blackjack calmed their party down and waited for Phillip to bring the key to the freshly pampered demonstrator. When the time came, Earl tried to pass the keys to Blackjack. It was probably the Bourbon talking, but Blackjack said, No, Earl, I think that Milly should have the keys. It's 'her' car, after all, and she should drive us home." Earl tried, unsuccessfully, to to resist laughing, and handed Millicent the keys. As Millicent and Blackjack got into the Cadillac, Earl reminded them, "Don't forget about the washes." Both Millicent and Jackson smiled. As Millicent started to maneuver the huge land yacht out of the lot, Blackjack yelled, "Hey Earl, don't forget to vote for Day for Coroner. Earl waved back. His vote had been bought and paid for for years. For the entire journey back to the funeral home, Blackjack had an expression on his face as if he were looking so forward to October first. Millicent, however, invariably saw someone she knew at each intersection and at every corner. Being in full campaign mode, she waved, and insisted that Blackjack wave too.

When Millicent pulled the new Cadillac into the motor court behind the funeral home, Blackjack's employees were offloading a body from one of his hearses. Blackjack got out and started asking questions. The family would be in at 4:00 to make the arrangements. Millicent turned to look over to the kitchen Window. As it happened, Mary was there observing the goings on. Both Millicent and Mary, knowing the ramifications of the situation, smiled slightly to each other. Millicent turned to Blackjack. "Please have the porters make room in the garage for 'my' car,'" She handed the keys to Blackjack and walked into the funeral home through the kitchen door.

Mary was waiting for her mother in the kitchen. Millicent smiled broadly. "It looks like we'll be going 'shopping' in a couple of days." Mary clapped her hands together as Millicent made herself a tall Blanchard strength Gin and Tonic. "I can't wait."

CHAPTER NINE

MARY AND MILLICENT BOTH HAVE DATES

The next morning at breakfast, Blackjack flipped his *Times-Picayune* down and announced to Mary, "Your mother is going to drive us to church today in "her" new car. You both are going to have to look your best, it's the start of campaign season." Both Millicent and Mary went up stairs and put on tailored suits, silk blouses, elegant heels, gloves, and fascinators. Blackjack avoided his usual dreary black suit and wore the blue worsted gaberdine, double breasted suit that Millicent had forced him to buy earlier in the week. Against Millicent's fashion advice, Blackjack insisted upon wearing spectator shoes. Millicent speculated that it would be impossible to ever completely separate Blackjack from his gangster side. She was pleased, however, with his sharp new Panama Hat.

Christ Church Cathedral was only a short walk from the funeral home, but, as in the past, Blackjack insisted upon arriving in a Cadillac. The only change for this day was the fact that Johnny Hardwick got the morning off, and Millicent was driving. Blackjack presumed that his "gift" to his wife would really impress the Cathedral's communicants as he pressed hands. After all, it was campaign season. The Cadillac and the good deal that Earl Kemper had given him would be a good "topic of conversation." After the service, Blackjack insisted on staying in the parish house until the last of the Coffee Hour holdouts decided to leave. Mary's stomach was growling. As they walked to the Cadillac, Blackjack said, "I can't speak for you two, but I'm hungry. Let's go to Brennan's." Millicent looked at Mary, and said to Blackjack, "Couldn't we go to Galatoire's instead?" Blackjack shook his head, "No, you don't understand. I want Owen to help with my campaign. His restaurant is the hottest place in New Orleans." Blackjack looked over at Mary. "...and you love the Bananas Foster, don't you? Mary nodded, more in resignation than in agreement. She didn't smile, however.

Once Millicent found a parking space, the family walked to Brennan's. Blackjack had fully embraced campaigning, and glad-handed everyone they met on the street. ...even the tourists. Once they entered Brennan's, and were seated, Blackjack asked Millicent to order for him. He left the table to work the room. Millicent ordered a stiff drink, and looked at Mary. "I'm so looking forward to the endless meetings he's going to have to attend between now and November!" Mary grinned, "That will leave more time for our 'shopping trips.'" Millicent perked up in her seat, "Yes, absolutely! You are exactly right!" Their "Breakfast at Brennan's" turned out much better than usual, mostly because Blackjack spent most of the time away from their table.

As Millicent piloted the huge Cadillac back to the funeral home, she asked, "How many this week, Jackson?" Blackjack was caught up in his thoughts and didn't hear the question. "JACKSON!" Millicent said loudly. Blackjack was startled and snapped his head around to see what the problem was. "What???" Millicent shook her head. "I just asked you how many funerals are on the books for this week." Blackjack thought for a moment. "Two, unless something else has come in today. Tuesday and Thursday. As Millicent pulled the Cadillac into the motor court, she said, "Well, you're going to have a busy week!" Blackjack puffed up like a peacock. "You bet! They're both big high-end affairs." He smiled and positively strutted off to his office. Millicent handed the keys to a porter and went in the kitchen door with Mary.

Marie Cosette was sitting at the kitchen table frenching green beans. Mary sat at the table and offered to help. Marie Cosette let Mary cut the ends off of the beans while she ran them through the wire to bisect them. Millicent went to her **Bonheur du Jour** and wrote out two notes, one for Inman and the other for Danton. While the note for Inman was short and to the point, Danton's note was longer and more convoluted because it contained directions to the location where Millicent wanted Danton to meet her after their "chance encounter." Millicent sealed the notes in envelopes and waited until Marie Cosette had completed the chores that Hattie had assigned. She then dispatched Marie Cosette to Howard Avenue.

Marie Cosette rang the cast iron bell at the main gate. Inman stepped out onto the **véranda** to see who it was. Danton followed him out, and stood on the **véranda** as Inman walked over to the gate to greet Marie Cosette. They talked for a couple of moments before Marie Cosette passed the notes through the gate to Inman. After Inman had the notes, Marie Cosette excused herself and made her way back to Saint Charles Avenue and the Streetcar. Inman, puffed up with expectation, took the notes back to the **véranda**, and passed Danton his note. They both opened their notes, but Inman was the first to speak, "Tuesday and Thursday. How wonderful!" Uncle Danton continued to read his note with Inman looking on. Finally Danton looked up. "Milly wants to meet me at the Sazarac Bar, like we planned, then at Maison Blanche." Inman was puzzled. "Maison Blanche? Won't there be a lot of people there?" Danton shook his head. "No, the store doesn't use all of their space. The upper floors in the rear building are let out. Evidently, Millie's brother, a well-known antiques dealer in New York City, rents a huge space on the top floor as a warehouse."

Inman scrunched up his face. "She has a brother? I remember hearing about her sister who killed her husband in bed with a stoned prostitute." Danton smiled. "Irene! Oh my God! She got away with it! The jury wouldn't convict." Danton lost himself with fond memories of the Blanchard family. Inman asked, "...her brother?" Danton shook his head and came back to reality. "Oh, yes, Millicent's brother. His name is Phillippe de Marigny Blanchard. He was one of my great friends growing up. He really wanted to be an actor. Fortunately, the Blanchard's could afford to let him follow his dreams. Your father and I went to work. Phillippe went to New York to act, but that didn't work out. He did, however, have a torrid affair with one of the most successful antiques dealers in the north-east. Inman asked, "What was her name?" Danton almost busted a gut. "Her? …she was a he." Inman's eyes exploded open. "No!" Danton said, "Yes, Phillippe told the old queen that New Orleans was a honey hole for antique furniture, especially antique French furniture, so Colin asked Phillippe to rent space and hire buyers to accumulate stock that would ultimately be sold in their New York City store. Caroline stepped to the French door, then out onto the **véranda**, and said, You boys have gossiped enough. Virginia and I are famished. Come on in so we can enjoy **dîner**, Danton and Inman slid their notes into their jacket pockets and accompanied Caroline to the **salle à manger** for their Sunday **dîner**.

Millicent and Mary ate an early lunch on Tuesday so that they could sneak out before the mourners started to arrive. Millicent drove the small segment around Lee Circle before exiting onto Howard Avenue. Just outside the main gate at **Maison Soleil,** she pulled to the curb and waited. Mary pulled the iron bell pull. Monique stepped out of the kitchen door and walked over to the gate. As she unlocked the gate, Monique said, "Miz Carnes is happy dat youz hea. but Iz speck Mr. Inmanz a bit mo happy." Mary smiled and walked with Monique up the stairs to the **véranda** and into Caroline's **salon principal**.

As Mary entered Caroline's realm, Caroline smiled and placed a leather bookmark in her latest novel. She placed it on the **étagère** next to her **bergère confessionale**. "How nice to see you, **ma douce fille!**" (my sweet girl!) Mary walked over and extended both hands. "**Je suis ravi de vous voir, madame Carnes!**" (I am delighted to see you Mrs. Carnes!) Caroline beamed with joy, "My dear, **ton Français est vraiment magnifique!**" (your French is truly magnificent!) Inman has been speaking French since birth. I've tried for years to teach Monique, but she learned to speak up river on a non-French speaking plantation. Mary smiled. "My mother and I are trying to teach Marie Cosette both standard English and standard French. I completely understand." Caroline sighed. Mary waited for a minute or two before asking,

"Is Inman home, I thought he was expecting me." Caroline grinned, "Oh yes, he is. I sent him to the **grenier** (attic) to retrieve a few items I wanted to sort. He'll be down in a moment. Please, have a seat." Mary took a seat in the matching **bergère confessionale**. Mary actually enjoyed her short chat with Caroline. After a moment, they both heard Inman coming down the stairs. He popped through the loggia French doors carrying a big pile of clothes. The pile was so immense, that Inman failed to notice that Mary was in the room. Inman dumped the pile of clothes onto a **canapé** and only noticed Mary when he stood up.

Caroline said, "Look Inman, **vous avez un visiteur.**" (you have a visitor.) Inman said, "Mary, you're early, how wonderful!" As Inman walked over to Mary, she extended her gloved hand. Inman took Mary's hand gently in his, bowed, and kissed her hand. "**Bienvenue chez moi, mon cher.**" (Welcome to my home, dear one.) Mary didn't miss a beat. "**Je suis ravi d'être ici mon cher ami!**" (I am delighted to be here my dear friend!) Caroline was happier than she'd been since before Inman's father's murder. She radiated pure delight. "**Mon fils,** (My son) your father would be so proud of what a gentleman you've become!" Inman blushed. Caroline asked, " What are you two up to today?" Inman looked at Mary. "I thought that we'd dance, if that's alright with you." Mary liked the idea. "Oh yes, that sounds wonderful." Inman continued, "Good, Uncle Danton brought me even more old records and a book of dance steps. Foxtrot, Waltz, Charleston, Baltimore, the Black Bottom Stomp, and others." Marry grinned. "We used to have oldies dances at Miss. McGraw's. ...no boys, but great songs and great dance steps. We'll have a ton of fun! Caroling smiled broadly. "An early Tea Dance! Oh, the memories! Mama and papa gave the best Tea Dances. They always gave one for your father when he came down to visit. He'd stay in the **garçonnière** with Danton. The day would start with a garden party and a light luncheon, while the Palm Court Orchestra set up. ...but I go on. Monique and I will put together some **rafraîchissements**. They won't hold a candle to mama's, but she always had a full staff and days to prepare."

Caroline gave Mary and Inman leave to walk to the dance terrace to spend their time together. Inman picked up the huge pile of clothes and walked through the French doors out onto the **véranda**. Mary followed him, and once down the stairs, and on the path to the **garçonnière**, slipped her hand into the crowded crook of Inman's elbow. Neither Mary nor Inman had even guessed that Caroline had any suspicions. ...but she did. She sent Monique over to one of the French doors to spy on Mary and Inman through the shutters. After a few moments Monique giggled. "Yas'um, youse right, dey's ina crush." Caroline picked up her novel. With a look somewhere between satisfaction and excitement, she said, "Good, just as it should be."

On the walk to the **garçonnière**, Mary asked Inman about the clothes. Inman told her that they were his parent's clothes from before he'd been born. "Mama is going to have Uncle Danton take them to the Church Shoppe." Mary was curious. "Do you think that she'd mind if we looked through them first?" Inman stopped dead in his tracks. "I was thinking the exact same thing!" Mary and Inman finished the walk to the **garçonnière** and Inman put the pile on a large table. It was the very table that the Soleil's famous **hors d'oeuvres** had been served from at their legendary Tea Dances.

Back at the **Manoir**, Monique crossed the loggia on her way to the kitchen. She asked Caroline, "Mr. Danton ain't coming fo dose clos, now ain't he? It took Caroline a minute to deconstruct and reconstruct Monique's grammar successfully. She smiled. "Well, actually, no. He told me about Inman's plan to give Mary a Tea Dance. Those clothes are the clothes that Inman's father and I wore to dances around the time we married. I put them away when he died. I never thought they'd ever see the light of day, but Inman is a carbon copy of his father, and Mary is almost the exact same size I was at her age. Monique laughed, "You sure iz somthin' else, Miz Caroline!"

Mary and Inman sorted the clothes, men's on one side of the massive table, and woman's on the other. Mary could hardly believe her eyes. "They're beautiful. ...and hardly worn." Inman was nodding his head in agreement. Mary picked one of the gowns up. "Would your mother mind if I tried this on?" Inman said, " I can't see why, she's planning on getting rid of them all." Mary asked, "Where can I change?" Inman pointed to the stairs that led up to the bedrooms and bathrooms. There's an empty room on the right when you get upstairs. Mary picked one of the gowns up with enthusiasm and kissed

Inman on the cheek. Inman watched her gracefully climb the stairs. As Mary disappeared into the the upper floor, Inman closed his eyes and laid his hand carefully over the spot where Mary had kissed him. While it hadn't been their most passionate kiss, it was a kiss of promise. It was a kiss that, somehow, said that they were a couple, and that everything would resolve itself. Their mothers were making it possible for them to date. Somehow, some way, Mary's father would be convinced, and life would be grand.

The thought of it all paralyzed Inman for a few moments. When he regained his facilities, Inman returned to the tasks at hand. He walked over to the Edison phonograph and wound it. He pulled the first record out of one of Danton's fruit boxes and placed it on the green felt topped turntable. It was **Charmaine**, recorded in 1927 by the B.F. Goodrich Silvertown Cord Orchestra. Inman busied himself moving chairs during the song intro, then looked at the phonograph. He went over to the elegant mahogany machine and opened the lid, and slid the lever controlling the volume to full volume. He then started practicing his waltz steps with his back to the stairs. During the instrumental interval, Mary appeared at the base of the stairs and was astounded at Inman's moves and his dedication to make her time with him enjoyable. It was't until Inman waltzed around, that he discovered Mary watching him. He froze, then noticed her gown. Inman was overcome with adoration. He and Mary locked their glances and slowly moved toward one another. They instinctively began to dance. Mary asked, What is this song?" Inman thought about it. He had looked at the label. "I think it's called **Charmaine**." Just before the singer started his bit, Mary said, "**Charmaine**, really! My middle name is 'Charmaine!" Inman was flabbergasted. He laughed. "You don't say! That's amazing, simply amazing! I had no idea, it was just the first record in the box." As the song ended, and Inman went to change it for a new selection, Mary asked, "Play it again, Inman. I want that song to be our first dance." Inman was smiling almost to the point of tears and said, "It will be my pleasure!"

Inman rewound the phonograph and moved the tone arm back to the beginning of the record. Inman extended his left hand and Mary draped her right hand across his palm. She put her left hand on Inman's shoulder, and

Inman rested his right hand in the small of Mary's back. They waltzed. The song lasted for almost five minutes, but they both thought it was over way too soon. When the song ended, Inman led Mary to the boxes of records and said, "You pick out the next song." Mary looked through uncle Danton's boxes of unfamiliar tunes, and picked out *Them There Eyes*. It was a 1930 Foxtrot from Hal Kemp and his Orchestra. After they danced to it, Inman started to put it at the front of the record box. Mary placed her hand on Inman's. "Could we keep *Charmaine* in the front position?" Inman smiled, and put *Them There Eyes* behind *Charmaine*. Inman picked next. It was *Any Time's The Time To Fall In Love*, a jaunty Foxtrot from Philip Spitalny and his Orchestra. Mary followed with *I Was Made to Love You*, from Freddie Rich and his Orchestra.

As the song ended, Monique arrived carrying a giant tray. She brought Mary and Inman cold freshly squeezed lemonade, and assorted freshly baked cookies. Monique set the tray down on the massive table, between the stacks of party clothes. As Monique left to return to the **Manoir**, she paused and remarked, "Youse'uns relly havin' a dime down do hee a!" Mary and Inman both nodded their heads in agreement. Inman said, "Monique, I really appreciate your bringing these **rafraîchissements**. Please thank mama too!"

After **rafraîchissements**, Mary and Inman danced to a few more songs before Mary said, "Inman, let's stop, just for a few minutes. I need to change back into my clothes before my mama comes to get me." Inman agreed, albeit regrettably. Mary went up and changed back into her clothes. She draped the dance gown over her arm and started back to the stairs. As she started to go down, something caught her eye and she was drawn into another of the bedrooms. It was Inman's. She looked at his collections, and projects. They were wonderful, and interesting, but she was drawn to his bed. She turned down the covers and smelled his pillow. The scent nearly drove her wild. She spread the covers back and went downstairs where she laid the elegant gown atop the pile of women's clothes on the massive table. Inman was ready with the next record. They hadn't been dancing long when Mary and Inman heard the bell at the main gate ring. They looked at one another for a moment, smiled, and continued dancing. They were mid-dance when Monique and Millicent came around the corner.

For the first time, Millicent saw absolute joy in her precious daughter's face. The song ended, and Inman shut the phonograph down. Millicent grinned at Mary and said, "You two are quite good at the Foxtrot!" Mary beamed. "We have that one and the Waltz down. Our Charleston is getting better, but the Baltimore is giving us fits! Millicent looked at the boxes of records. She pulled the front record out. ***Charmaine***. She was just a little taken aback. "I remember this song. I always liked it. It's my middle name." Inman let out a "Haw!" "Your's too? Mary said that it was her middle name." Millicent smiled. "It's wonderful song." Both Mary and Inman agreed, not knowing that Millicent was feeling extreme loss at the thought of that song.

Millicent turned away from the records and noticed the piles of evening clothes on the table. "What have we here?" Inman moved closer to the table. "My mama had me bring these down, so that my uncle Danton can take them to the Church Shoppe. Millicent was more interested in the dresses. She picked the top one up to get a better look. It was the gown that Mary had been wearing. Millicent could immediately tell that it had been worn recently. It was moist with perspiration, warm to the touch, and she could smell Mary's perfume, **L'Heure Bleue** by Guerlain. "What a shame. These are lovely!" She carefully laid the gown back across the pile of dresses on the table. "Inman, you'll have to excuse us. Mary's father will be looking for us. Thank you, for your, and your mama's kind hospitality. I'm sure that Mary is looking forward to the next time you can get together."

Inman looked over at Mary. They were both dreamy-eyed. Millicent said, " I'll just go and say '**Au revoir**' to Caroline. Mary, be a dear, and meet me at the car in five minutes." She turned as Monique picked up the tray, and the two women walked, deliberately slowly, back to the **manoir**. Inman walked over and put his arms around Mary. He looked deeply into her eyes and said, "Oh how I wish that you did't have to go, **chere**." Mary closed her eyes and wrapped her arms tightly around Inman. "I wish I never had to be away from you!" Inman closed his eyes too, and they held each other snuggly in complete contentment. After a few moments, Mary and Inman slowly released their embrace and began to kiss. They kissed each other deeply and passionately. It was the most passionate kiss either had ever experienced. By the time they had to part, they were both shaking. Inman put his arm around Mary's waist and escorted her to the main gate. Millicent was already in the Cadillac, just out of their view. Inman kissed Mary again, forgetting that Millicent was ready to leave, and baking in the June sun. Finally, Millicent honked the horn. Mary and Inman were immediately snapped back into reality.

Inman opened the gate for Mary. "I can't wait until you can come back, **chere**." Mary smiled, "Me, either. I'll send Marie Cosette to let you know." Mary turned around to look at Inman so many times walking to the car, that she might just as well have been walking backwards. Millicent had every reason to be annoyed, but she wasn't. Perhaps she saw a younger version of herself, before her youthful fancies were crushed by the crueler realities of life.

Earlier, after Millicent had dropped Mary off at **Maison Soleil**, she had pulled away from the curb and motored into the Central Business District, and onto Canal Street. She parked the Cadillac, and started walking toward the Roosevelt Hotel. She may not have known it, but she was walking more confidently than she had in years. Millicent had no apprehensions until the last minute before she had to open the door to the Sazarac Bar. She looked all around to make sure she didn't see anyone she knew. She also was besieged with irrational questions. "Will he be here?" "What is he going to say?" "What am I going to say?" "Will he tell me why he broke off our engagement in 1930?" Millicent knew, in her heart, that she still loved Danton. She had always loved him. ...but she was married, and to a passive-aggressive narcissist. She couldn't figure out what she feared the most. Was Danton still in love with her, or did he hate her? She became a little lightheaded and hesitated at the door. It was short-lived, and her primal desires for Danton propelled her through the door into the Sazarac Bar.

Danton Soleil was sitting at the bar enjoying a Sazarac cocktail with his rain coat draped over the bar stool next to him. Every other seat at the bar was taken. Millicent nonchalantly walked over and asked, "Is this seat taken?" Danton set his drink down, turned, and gasped at the complete vision of loveliness standing before him. He stood up, removed his coat from the bar stool, and said, "No, it isn't. ...and it would be a great pleasure to sit next so such a refined lady!" Danton pulled the bar stool out for Millicent, and helped her get the chair situated. Millicent ordered a Sazarac, and Danton subtly motioned for the Bartender to put it on his tab. Millicent, pretending not to know Danton, asked, "Do you come here often?" Danton looked up and to the right off in the distance. He closed his eyes and said, "I used to come here frequently with someone I loved dearly, but that was a long time ago." Millicent bowed her head. A warm purring "Ummmm'" was all she said.

Danton ordered two more Sazaracs. Millicent and Danton made small talk. Millicent asked, "What do you do for a living?" Danton replied, "I'm a Factor. I'm in shipping, warehousing, wholesaling, and transportation." He paused. "What about you? Millicent forced a smile. "I'm a kept woman. My husband is a Funeral Director. . . .at least that's what his business card advertises. He has other, . . .other, less honorable incomes, and is richer than Roosevelt. He couldn't care any less about my happiness, or my daughter's happiness." Danton, staring straight ahead, said, "That's tragic." Millicent finished her Sazarac and put her glass down. "Thank you for your kind company, and the drinks, but I've got to go across the street to Maison Blanche to buy a dress for one of my husband's campaign events." Danton stood and offered Millicent his hand. He helped her down from the bar stool. "It has truly been a pleasure, Madame. I wish you only the very best life has to offer!" Millicent and Danton held on to the one thing they could, a look. Millicent started to walk toward the door, but stopped and turned. "Do you like antiques?" Danton knew immediately what Millicent was communicating, "They're in my blood!" Millicent arched her left eyebrow, smiled, and strolled elegantly out of the Sazarac Bar. Danton ordered one more Sazarac, just to be careful. He sipped it slowly, remembering with fondness, the wonderful times he and Millicent had passed in this bar. After Danton settled his bar tab, he walked out onto O'Keefe Street. He crossed Canal Street and walked to Dauphine Street. Mid way up the block, there was an entrance into the Maison Blanche building that revealed a bank of elevators that weren't associated with the famous department store.

Danton pressed the "UP" button and waited for one of the elevator cars to arrive. When it did, he boarded and pressed "14," the top floor. As Danton was carried aloft by the automatic elevator, he fondly remembered the days of

Elevator Operators. He was conflicted, both missing them, and happy they weren't around to know everyone's business. At last, floor 14 was achieved. Danton stepped out into the elevator lobby with his raincoat and attaché. He looked down the long hallway to his left. There were endless wood and glass doors with gold letters advertising Doctors, Attorneys, Dentists, and Accountants. He looked to the right and the hallway ended abruptly at one gold-lettered door. It said, "Phillippe de Marigny Blanchard, Fine Antiques —- To The Trade, Only" Danton hesitated. He stared at the brass door knob and pondered what was going to happen on the other side of the door.

Danton gathered his strength and turned the knob. The door was unlocked, and he entered the massive space crowded with fine antiques. It took Danton a minute to fully grasp the vastness of the space. He was frozen in his tracks, barely able to turn and look around. "Millicent?" There was a faint echo. Millicent stepped from behind a large screen. "**Oui**, Danton?" Danton walked over to Millicent. "It's time." Millicent looked quite perplexed. "It's time? Time for what?" Danton looked around. "Is there somewhere we can sit down and talk?" Millicent, still taken aback, paused for a moment. "Yes, just over here." She led Danton to an enormous dining room table and chairs. They sat down next to one another.

Again, Millicent asked, "Time for what?" Danton pulled his leather attaché case into his lap and opened it. He pulled out a manilla folder and placed it on the table in front of Millicent. She looked perplexed, so Danton tapped his index finger on the folder several times. Millicent opened the folder and started to peruse the documents and photographs within. After she started to connect the dots, Millicent experienced a sudden realization. Tears manifested themselves in her eyes. "Oh, Danton, is all of this true?" Danton closed his eyes and breathed in and out several times deeply. "Of course not! At the time there wasn't anything Tom, or Inman, or I could do, but pay Blackjack his demand money. and I had to give you up, or he'd have made sure that the three of us would have gone to Angola, and had dates with Gruesome Gertie. Millicent closed her eyes, hung her head, and began to cry. "Trapped!" Danton, who was becoming emotional, rolled his eyes up in an attempt to keep from crying. "Yes, both of us were trapped. I had to give up the only woman I have ever loved, and you were trapped into marrying that beast."

Millicent was still weeping. In a painfully quiet whimper she asked, "Is there any chance you still have any feelings for me?" Danton stood up, offered his hands to Millicent, helped her up, and wrapped his arms around her tightly. He looked deeply into her piercing blue eyes and said, **Mon chere**, I've NEVER stopped loving you. No one could ever take your place! You may be married, but you are the only woman I've ever loved, or ever will love." Millicent buried her face in Danton's neck and cried. After a few minutes she was able to talk. "Every thought, since I married Jackson, has been of you. I had to close my eyes and and convince myself that it was you, when he forced sex on me. Fortunately that wasn't often, especially after Mary was born. Danton sighed, "At least Mary seems to be all you." Millicent chuckled, "She is! Especially since Jackson yanked her out of Commander's Palace on her 'date' with Inman. She's figured him out, but doesn't yet have a clear idea just how dangerous he is."

Danton pondered that last statement. "Just how dangerous is he?" Millicent stood up and walked over to her purse. She moved items away from a hidden compartment, and removed a glassine envelope. She handed it to Danton. Danton took the glassine envelope, opened it and removed a blood-stained and bullet-riddled note. He read the note and all of the color drained from his face. "I forgot all about this! When we heard the shots, I jumped into the hearse with Jack. We found Inman at the base of the Lee Memorial. I helped Jack get Inman on the gurney and into the hearse. He drove off after telling me he was taking Inman to Touro Infirmary. I went to **Maison Soleil** to sit with Caroline and wait for news."

Millicent looked deeply into Danton's eyes. "There should have been news, and quickly, but Jackson made sure that there would be no good news. He had all of the lights on when he turned the corner and pulled into the motor court. It was so completely unusual. It caught my attention. Jackson didn't take Inman to Touro Infirmary. He had the interior lights of the ambulance on, and I watched my husband search all of Inman's pockets. After he found the I.O.U., Jackson sat in the jump chair and waited until he couldn't detect a pulse, before he drove Inman to Touro Infirmary. It was almost an hour. Danton's jaw slacked. "He let Inman die?" Millicent nodded her head. Danton protested, "Inman would have worked it out the next morning. He wouldn't have taken the funeral home. He wouldn't have taken Jack's means of supporting his family!" Millicent put her hand on Danton's. "I believe you Danton! Jackson has always been ruthless and impulsive." She paused to think for a moment, then continued, "Do you know another attorney besides Emile LaRoque?" Danton replied, "Oh sure, yes, many, why?"

Millicent stared plaintively into Danton's eyes with a steady stream of tears escaping her own eyes. "Danton, **mon chéri**, I want MY life back. I'm so afraid of what Jackson would do if he figured out what Mary and I have been up to. I need a dossier like that one he put together on you." Danton thought, "Couldn't Emile squash all of that in court?" Millicent cut Danton off. "The idea isn't to turn Jackson in, it's to have overwhelming dirt to hold over him that could crash his high society dreams, and allow us to be together." Danton said, "Oh, yes, I see. We'll need pictures of the I. O. U. to go with the affidavit, and everything will need to be notarized, of course." Millicent took Danton's hand into her's. "Could we, together, get several safe deposit boxes at different banks to keep copies of the evidence?" Danton said, "Yes, of course, and our new attorney will keep the originals in his safe. Millicent breathed in and out heavily for a couple of breaths and asked, "Do you think you can get us an appointment for Thursday? It's a funeral afternoon." Danton agreed. "I'll put Lucy Butler on it. Call me tomorrow afternoon." Millicent agreed.

Millicent and Danton, both exhausted by the sheer drama they had both relived, sat and stared at each other. Each could see that the other was completely spent. After a few moments of quiet, Danton stood up and offered Millicent his hand. He asked, "Is there somewhere that we can go and just hold each other? I have missed your warm embrace every day for the last twenty something years." Millicent stood up and grasped Danton's hand. She led him around a massive support pillar to a deeply padded and tucked brown leather Chesterfield. They both collapsed into each other's arms, and held each other quietly for almost an hour. There were no words. There was no need for anymore words. There was only love. It was a love that had been held prisoner for twenty plus years.

Eventually, Danton thought about the time that had passed, albeit, so enjoyably. He asked Millicent, "When do you need to pick Mary up at **Maison Soleil**?" Millicent told Danton. He consulted his Patek Philippe pocket watch, and was relieved that they had a few precious moments left before Millicent would have to leave. The business manager in Danton took over from the grand romantic, for a few brief moments. "Millicent, **mon cher**, our meeting on Thursday will have to be 'All Business,' as unfortunate as that is, so that we can protect ourselves. I'll do whatever is necessary so that we can love each other without conditions. Millicent raised herself up. "I allowed myself to become convinced early on that I could never deserve a love like the one that we had. The Beast took his toll on me in so many ways over the years." Danton tightened his grasp on Millicent. "**Mon chere**, there is so much that you don't deserve, but for so many years I've been '**waiting, my Charmaine, for you.**'" Millicent sighed at the song reference, and went limp in Danton's arms. The once and future lovers held each other tightly. Millicent asked, "**Mon amour**, what time is it?" Danton opened the lid of his pocket watch and sighed. "It's time for you to start back to **Maison Soleil**. Millicent sighed. "I'll send Marie Cosette to your office tomorrow to get the particulars." She slowly wrapped her arms around Danton and pulled him in tightly. They embraced passionately for a few more minutes before Danton reluctantly broke Millicent's hold. "Oh, that this never need end, but we can't let Blackjack get suspicious of you, or of Mary."

Millicent agreed, also reluctantly. Danton left first and made his way back to the Factorage on the Wharf. Millicent rode the elevator down, but didn't exit out onto the street. She went into Maison Blanche. She had to have at least a few bags when she got home. Millicent, remembering **Maison Soleil's** decadent, by 1920's standards, pool, bought a bathing suit, cap, and robe for Mary. The bathing suit was for …just in case. She decided to leave it in the custody of Caroline. Millicent made her way back down Canal street to the parking lot. She motored through the Central Business District and turned down Howard Avenue. Millicent parked outside of the main gate, got out of the car, and rang the great iron bell. Monique stepped out of the side door from the kitchen and walked to the gate with a huge grin on her face. As Monique unlocked the gate, she said, "**Bonne après-midi, madame Day.**" (Good afternoon…)

Millicent was completely charmed. "Caroline's been working on your French, no?" Monique blushed as she swung the gate open. "**Oui, madame!**" The two ladies walked together to the French doors leading to Caroline's **salon principal**. As Millicent stepped across the threshold, Caroline put her book in her lap, and removed her readers. "**Mon Dieu, Millicent, regarde toi! Vous êtes radieux!!** (My God, Millicent, look at you! You are positively radiant!) Millicent beamed, "Oh, Caroline, for the first time in many years, I feel like I'm alive again. "**Il y aura tellement d'amour dans l'air cet été!** (There will be so much love in the air this summer!) Millicent walked over to Caroline's nest and clasped both of her hands. They kissed each other on both cheeks. Millicent remembered the Maison Blanche bag that was hanging with her purse in the crook of her left elbow. "Caroline, I hope that you don't mind, but I bought Mary a bathing suit. I thought I'd leave it with you in event that Mary and Inman get a chance to swim in the pool." Caroline grinned. She took the bag and peeked in. "Extraordinary, nothing like the wool bathing costumes we wore in the '20s and 30's! It's beautiful! I'll have Monique put it upstairs for when Mary needs to change." Millicent was relieved and smiled at Caroline. "Good!"

Millicent paused for a moment then asked Caroline, "Are they having fun?" Caroline looked at Millicent with a twinkle in her eyes. "Oh, yes, I expect so. The music has gone on non-stop all afternoon. …and Monique tells me that they are both quite accomplished dancers." Millicent smiled, "I'd love to see that!" Monique spoke up, uncharacteristically. "If we wait fo de nex song do staat, I'zl wok you down dere." Millicent said, "Oh, thank you Monique! That'll be just fine. The song ended, and there was a pause. …a longer than expected pause. Millicent chuckled, "Well, I guess I don't have to wonder about that pause!" All three had a chuckle. Caroline chimed in, "They aren't any different from us when we were that age!" Millicent's memories came flooding back. "I suppose that you're right. I hope that this is real, and that nothing gets in the way of their happiness…" She paused to let that comment sink in. "Okay, Monique, let's go check on the 'dancers.'"

As Millicent and Monique arrived at the dance terrace, Mary and Inman were dancing to Paul Whitman's ***When My Dreams Come True*** featuring Bix Beiderbecke and Frankie Trumbauer. Millicent was absolutely delighted at seeing Mary having such a good time. She and Monique enjoyed the spectacle greatly. After the song, Mary and Inman knew that it was time for this date to come to an end. Millicent left Mary to say goodbye to Inman and waited in the car, baking in the hot June New Orleans sun. Mary eventually made it to the car, and Millicent pulled away from the curb. Mary watched Inman's face at the gate fade from view as they motored away from **Maison Soleil**. Mary turned and smiled at her mother. "Was your 'date' as magnificent as mine?" Millicent beamed. "Oh, yes! It was wonderful!" Mary was exceedingly happy to see her mother happy, for the first time in her memory. They swapped highlights of their dates all the way back to the funeral home.

As Millicent turned the Cadillac onto Louisiana Avenue, she remembered, "Oh, I almost forgot. On Thursday, if you and Inman get too hot from dancing, I bought you a bathing suit, and left it with Caroline." Mary's face lit up with excitement. "Oh mama, **c'est merveilleux**! We were getting awfully hot today. Thank you so much!" Millicent pulled the Cadillac into the motor court behind the funeral home. None of Blackjacks minions were anywhere in sight so she left the key in the ignition. Mary helped her cary the Maison Blanche bags into the funeral home. Hattie and Marie Cosette were sitting at the kitchen table prepping for dinner. Marie Cosette noticed the shopping bags and looked over to Mary. Mary smiled, shook her head, pointed to her mother, and mouthed, "All hers."

When Danton stopped by **Maison Soleil**, Inman dragged him out to the tennis court. Danton's crew had finished resurfacing the clay surface earlier in the week and installed the new net. After Mary had left earlier, Inman rummaged around in the Plunder Room and found his parents's collection of tennis rackets. While the wooden rackets from the earliest years of the twentieth century were in pristine form because of the tightly fastened braces, Inman presented one and proceeded to press his thumb through the mummified cat gut strings. Danton frowned. "Well, that's a problem." Inman asked, "Can they be ready for us to play on Thursday?" Danton sighed, "I'll send Sam Godwin with them to the Lawn Tennis Club in the morning. I'll pull some strings, pardon the pun, if I need to. I'll have him get you fresh tennis balls too." Inman thanked his dear uncle profusely.

CHAPTER TEN

FOUNDATIONS

The city of New Orleans has routinely been described as "Paris in a swamp." The fact that homes, streets, apartments, and commercial buildings have survived aquatic calamities of biblical proportions for three hundred or so years, must begin with their strong foundations. When describing homes, Real Estate Agents talk about the light flooded rooms, the fine appointments, manicured gardens, and attention to detail. No mention is ever made of the foundation. Foundations remain hidden, and completely, for the most part, out of sight. No building, however humble, or grand, could stand without a secure foundation. The same must be said of relationships. Like New Orleans, relationships experience fowl weather from time to time. There has never been a truly life-long fair weather relationship. All are tested. The next couple of weeks saw Mary and Inman, as well as Millicent and Danton, settling into new relationships, and building strong foundations for their future happiness. Sometimes, after plans are made, foundation excavations reveal problems that have to be overcome, before continuing with construction.

Over the remaining weeks in June, both couples would experience trials, some minor, and others major. On Wednesday the Eleventh, Millicent sent

Marie Cosette to the wharf to call on Danton. The **tignon** wrapping her hair raised suspicion when she said she was there to speak to Danton Soleil. Dominic Delevingne, Chief of Security, couldn't believe that she knew who Monsieur Soleil was, much less had any business requesting to see him. He picked up the house phone and rang Lucy Butler. He explained what was going on and asked her to phone the police. Lucy too, was troubled with the scenario, but opted to ask Danton before calling the police. "Chief, Dominic has a black teenaged girl asking to see you. Should I call the police?" Danton was puzzled for a moment until he remembered that Blackjack forced Marie Cosette, who was as fair as any of them, to wear the badge of oppression. "Ask him what her name is." Lucy put the receiver back up to her ear. Monsieur Soleil asked for her name." Dominic, quite aghast, asked Marie Cosette for her name. "Marie Cosette Jardin," was her reply. Dominic relayed it to Lucy, and she told Danton. Danton laughed. "Oh, yes, I know that young lady. She works for a friend. Please have Dominic send her on back." Lucy suggested that Dominic have one of the stevedores escort Marie Cosette back to the offices. He was initially shocked, but got over it and called out for Ken Cracker who was the closest security detail member. "Ken, Monsieur Soleil is expecting this girl. Could you take her to Mrs. Butler's office?" Ken looked shocked. Dominic shot him a look that snapped him back into reality. "Okay, Dom, I'll take her. If'n that's what the boss-man wants."

By the time that Ken got Marie Cosette to Lucy Butler's office, Danton was out of his inner sanctum and waiting for her. Marie Cosette said "**Bonjour, monsieur Soleil.**" Danton said, "**Merci d'être venue, Marie Cosette.**" (Thank you for coming, Marie Cosette.) Danton handed Marie Cosette a sealed envelope. "**S'il vous plaît, donnez ceci à Millicent uniquement. Assurez-vous que personne ne le sait. Oui**?" (Please give this to Millicent only. Make sure no one knows. Yes?) Marie Cosette was calmed by the kind look in Danton's eyes. "**Monsieur, vous pouvez compter sur moi!**" (Sir, you can count on me!) Danton was suitably impressed with Marie Cosette's improving French. Millicent had been far more successful in correcting Marie Cosette's French than fixing her tell-tale Creole-English accent. Danton smiled and handed Marie Cosette a Half Dollar. "**...pour vos efforts.**" (...

for your efforts.) Marie Cosette curtseyed and thanked Danton. She allowed Ken to escort her back to the main security station. As she left, Ken shook his head and looked at Dominic, "The boss-man gave that girl fifty cents to deliver a letter!" Dominic seemed shocked and said, "My God, what is the world coming to?"

Marie Cosette rode the Streetcar back to the funeral home. She walked around back and slipped into the kitchen. Hattie wasn't terribly happy about how long she had been gone. Marie Cosette apologized and told Hattie that she had gotten back as quickly as she could. Hattie pulled a face and gave Marie Cosette her chores for the evening. Around 4:00, Millicent came into the kitchen for a glass and ice cubes. Marie Cosette looked at Millicent and smiled. She shook her head in a way that indicated to Millicent that she had a message. Millicent said, "Marie Cosette, after dinner, could you help me upstairs for a minute. I want to flip the mattress on my bed. Marie Cosette looked worried and cast her gaze at Hattie. "Oh, don't worry about Hattie, you'll only be gone about five or ten minutes." Millicent turned to Hattie, "That won't be too long, now will it?" Hattie pursed her lips and said, No'm, I speck not."

As was his custom, Blackjack wolfed his dinner down with manners that would embarrass a pig. He ran off to his office, demanding coffee from Marie Cosette. After Blackjack left, Millicent asked Mary if she and Inman would be swimming tomorrow. Mary said, "Mama, I want to, but I'm not sure that I'm ready to be that open." Millicent said nothing, but was proud of what a young lady her daughter had become. When Marie Cosette returned from her coffee run, she said, Miz Day, can we go do dat ding naw? I don' wanna make Hattie mad at'un mes." Millicent pressed her napkin to her lips and stood up. "Yes, let's go up, and flip that mattress." Mary thought nothing of the exchange, and went up to her room to read. When Millicent and Marie Cosette were safely behind Millicent's bedroom door, Marie Cosette reached into her blouse and produced Danton's envelope. Millicent thanked her. "Don't keep Hattie waiting. You did a fine job flipping this tired old mattress." Oblivious to any hidden meaning, Marie Cosette smiled and went back down to help Hattie finish the dishes and do some prep for the following morning's breakfast.

The following day, as Blackjack was greeting mourners, Millicent and Mary slipped out to the motor court. Marie Cosette had been previously dispatched to have Johnny Hardwick pull Millicent's magnificent, albeit temporary, Model 62 Cadillac convertible out into the motor court behind the funeral home. They got in the automobile and breezed past the mourners entering the funeral home, then motored on to their happiness. Millicent let Mary out at the main gate of **Maison Soleil**. She waited until Monique stepped out to let Mary in, then motored over to the Hibernia Bank building on Gravier Street. After parking the Cadillac, Millicent walked into the elevator lobby, just off the main banking room and pressed the call button centered on the wall of brass elevators. As she waited for a car, Millicent worried that her regular attorney, Emile LaRoque, or one of her friends would see her, and wonder why she was there. The elevator car whisked her to the twenty first floor quickly. Millicent exited the car and made her way to the office of Olivier deVezin, Attorney at Law. Danton was waiting in the ante-room when Millicent entered the office. She walked over and sat next to him. After a moment judging her surroundings, Millicent asked, "His name is old, as old as ours are, but how do we not know him?" Danton replied, "He's a half generation off. His father was younger than our parents, and he is a few years younger than us." Millicent added, "…but you vetted him, didn't you?" Danton leaned in close, "Yes, I put Lucy on the task. She had to call in a few favors to get the information back so quickly. When she told me that he had sued one of Emile's clients and beat the pants off of Monsieur LaRoque, I ceased worrying." Millicent said, "That's good news! Will it be possible to wind this up, and have some together time?" Danton said, "I do hope so, but I can't see how it'll be possible today. Attorneys!" As unpleasant as it would be, Millicent resigned herself to the necessity of building an unbreakable foundation for her and Danton's rekindled relationship.

Back at **Maison Soleil**, Inman had heard the bell ring, and went to the **manoir** to greet his date. She was having a grand time talking to both Caroline and Virginia about Miss. McGraw's School for Girls. Inman's aunt Virginia was saying "Some things never change," as Inman set foot across the threshold from the **véranda** to Caroline's **salon principal**. Caroline greeted her son, "**Cher fils, notre chère Marie est ici, quelles danses allez-vous apprendre aujourd'hui?**" (Dear son, dear Mary is here, what dances will you two learn today?) Inman dropped his head and grinned. I had thought that we'd play tennis today. Uncle Danton had the court rehabilitated, but the rackets aren't back just yet. We'll have to move that to another date. Aunt Virginia pressed, "So, the dances???" Inman shook his head, "Don't laugh, but the Black Bottom Stomp, and the Varsity Drag." Aunt Virginia cheered, "Oh those were two of my favorites!" Caroline agreed. "You two go on and have fun dancing. We'll help Monique put together some **rafraîchissements**, and send them down to the **garçonnière**."

Millicent and Danton, meanwhile, were enduring mind-numbing questions about every aspect of the various scenarios from their past. **Monsieur** deVezin had to have a clear understanding of every element of their shared history before he could set up a plan for a comprehensive interrogation upon which to build solid depositions that would completely stymy Blackjack into unequivocal submission. As she sat through the ordeal, Millicent envied Mary, whom she presumed to be innocently enjoying the company of her beau. She had no way to know that Mary and Inman had decided to "work" that day. They had to "work" to understand the steps of two new, unfamiliar dances. The dances weren't easy, but Mary and Inman were grateful to discover that they both worked well together. Neither became frustrated with the other. They found positive ways to show each other both errors as well as new possibilities. The copious mistakes they both made when they first started both dances could have ruined other couple's relationships, but Mary and Inman focused on the outcome, the fun they would both have when they mastered the steps. By the time Millicent arrived to retrieve her daughter, Mary and Inman had achieved a sound fundamental understanding of the two new dances. All stress had disappeared, and they had regained their happiness. They were both extremely exhausted.

As they rode together, Millicent admitted, "There were times today when I just wanted to change places with you, and enjoy a stress-free afternoon." Mary had to run back through the exchange to make sure that she hadn't heard it wrong the first time. She hadn't. She snipped, "We worked on two new dances this afternoon. It was 'work.' I had to think about the time we could dance these dances effortlessly, just to cope." Millicent let out a warm, "hummmmmmm." Mary looked at her mama questioningly. Millicent said, "**Ma chère fille, tu ne te rappelleras pas de ce jour où tu étourdis les gens avec tes pas de danse!**" (My dear daughter, you will not remember this day when you are stunning people with your dance moves!) Mary responded, "**Je l'espère vraiment! Mama, comment s'est passé ton après-midi avec monsieur Soleil?**" (I truly hope so!) Mama, how was your afternoon with Monsieur Soleil?) Millicent said, "Darling, the start of the afternoon was abysmal. ...but it was in no way, Danton's fault. ...those damn attorneys. ...damn shame we can't live without them. Mary hit the nail on the head when she observed, "So we both were builders today?" Millicent was completely confused, "Builders?" Mary said, "Yes, builders of our loves, our relationships." Millicent closed her eyes and thought about her daughter's keen, yet, in her opinion, partially flawed, observation. "Yes, we both are building our relationships. I just wish you had the evidence that I have to shut your father down. You have the opportunity to build a strong relationship with Inman, but your father has the resources to destroy anything you and Inman build. He won't be able to do that to Danton and me." Mary responded, "My greatest desire is that it never come to that for either of us." Millicent agreed wholeheartedly, but wasn't optimistic. She knew that they both had the time to be with their beaux from the funerals, the business meetings, and the campaigning. She also knew what Blackjack was capable of, if cornered.

The next date opportunity was on Monday the 16th. As they motored away from the funeral home, Millicent asked Mary, "What do you two have planned for today?" Mary told her, "I think it's tennis. Inman said that his Uncle Danton had the court surface rehabilitated, put up a new net, and had all of the racquets restrung. Millicent was just a little jealous. "Danton and I played many sets of tennis on that old court!" As much as she may have wanted to, Mary stopped short of inviting Millicent and Danton to join her and Inman. Millicent turned down Howard Avenue, and waited at the main gate at **Maison Soleil** until Monique stepped out of the kitchen, and opened the gate. As she escorted Mary to the **manoir**, Inman stepped out onto the **véranda** to greet his one true love. They were both too afraid to kiss in front of anyone, but he took her hand and said, "**Quel plaisir de vous revoir, ma chérie!**" (How wonderful to see you again, my darling!) Inman then said, "Let's stop in and say 'Hello' to mama." Mary agreed.

Millicent drove across the Central Business District and found a parking space near Maison Blanche. She rode the brass elevator up to her brother's warehouse, took her bags of **rafraîchissements** over to a **buffet á glissant** and began to set them out. She had brought cheese and crackers, grapes, figs, olives and pickles, and apples that were soaked in orange juice. From the other bag, she produced bottles of Bourbon, Gin, and Tonic Water. As she finished arranging her goodies, there was a knock on the door. She strolled over and opened the door, revealing her one true love, Danton. He presented her with a bouquet of flowers. Unlike Mary, this wasn't a new experience for Millicent. "**Oh, Danton, ils sont si beaux!**" (Oh, Danton, they are so beautiful!) Danton replied, "**Je me suis rappelé à quel point vous adoriez les fleurs de la Maison Soleil.**" (I remembered how much you used to adore the blooms at **Maison Soleil**.) As tears welled up in Millicent's eyes and they began to flutter, she accepted Danton's personally harvested bouquet, and threw her arms around his neck. "**Combien plus cette horrible bête peut-elle nous infliger?** (How much more can that horrid beast inflict upon us?) Danton sighed, "Nothing more on us, but it's not us that I believe that we need to worry about." Millicent released her bear hug and looked up into Danton's piercing hazel eyes. "Yes, you are so right. Mary and Inman." As the annunciator for the elevator dinged, Danton cringed, "Perhaps we should go in my dear?" Millicent pulled Danton into the **entrepôt antique**, and closed the door before the brass doors of the elevator opened. She started walking deeper into the space, and Danton followed. When they got to the **rafraîchissements**, Millicent apologized that she hadn't any ice for the drinks. Danton asked, "Where is the phone?" Millicent took him to the office, and Danton called the Wharf. He asked for the Commissary, and specifically Sammy Furno. When the line was connected to Sammy, Danton said, "Sammy, this is Danton Soleil. I wonder if you could do me a favor?"

Sammy said, "Sure boss, anyding." Danton said, "I'm in a meeting with a client and we need a block of ice and an ice pick. Could you bring them to me?" Sammy said, "Sure, dat's nuddin' Wad's de address?" Inman told him and hung the phone up. "Problem solved! Sammy will be faster than you can imagine." Millicent smiled, "Danton Soleil, is there any problem that you can't handle?" Danton said, "Thank God that I've never been challenged with anything too overwhelming!"

While Millicent and Danton were waiting for Sammy Furno to bring them ice for their cocktails, Monique was squeezing lemons to make Lemonade, and smoothing peanut butter between Ritz Crackers to make **rafraîchissements** for Mary and Inman. Inman proudly escorted his beautiful girlfriend into Caroline's **salon principal**, to speak to his mother. Caroline looked up from her book, removed her readers, and smiled broadly. "**Oh, ma chère fille, c'est vraiment un plaisir de te voir!**" (Oh, my dear girl, it's truly grand to see you!) Mary rushed over to Caroline's nest and took her outstretched hands. "**C'est tout à fait mon honneur et ma mère lui adresse ses meilleures voeux.**" (It is completely my honor, and my mother sends her love and best wishes.) Caroline, still grasping Mary's hands, turned to her right and cried out, "Virginia, our dear Mary is here. Do come in and say hello to her!" Inman's aunt Virginia excused herself from the company of her "friend" and bounded into Caroline's **salon principal**. They exchanged warm pleasantries, and Virginia asked, "What are you two doing today?" Mary looked back at Inman, "Tennis?" Inman stepped just a step closer to his mother and aunt and said, "Yes, tennis. Uncle Danton went to a lot of trouble to rehabilitate the court and equipment. We're going to give it a go!" Caroline clapped her hands together, "That's so wonderful, Inman and I played tennis every chance we got! Mary looked over at Inman, a little confused. He smiled, "My father." Inman could see that Mary's minor **faux pas** was causing her embarrassment. "Mama, aunt Virginia, we'll take our leave now. There is a chance it might rain." Caroline said, "Of course you should go. Monique will be down with **rafraîchissements** shortly. Both Mary and Inman thanked the sisters, especially Caroline, for their hospitality.

Millicent and Danton, meanwhile were enjoying their **hors d'oeuvres**, but hoping that Sammy Furno would hurry up and arrive with the ice. He actually arrived quite quickly. There was a knock on the door, and Millicent stepped into the office and allowed Danton to see who was calling. It was Sammy. "He's yo ice, boss, and de ice pik, do." Danton said, "Sammy, I knew that I could count on you! Thank you so much." Sammy smiled, "Dat's okay, boss, I'd do 'bout anythin' fo yu!" Danton smiled back at Sammy. "You can expect a little extra in your pay packet this week." Sammy said, "Boss, you don' need do dat...." Danton appreciated the feigned protestation. "None the less...." Sammy left, and Millicent found a large metal container for the ice. Sammy had wrapped the ice in kraft paper and tied it up with sisal twine. He had also crafted a carry loop. Danton untied the twine and freed the twelve inch cube from the kraft paper. He put it in the basin and grabbed the ice pick. As he picked at the cube, Millicent said, "Pretend it's Jackson." Danton's complexion reddened, and the veins in his neck throbbed. His blows became more savage and intense. Within a few moments, the block was reduced to interestingly shaped shards. They were perfect for drinks because their surface volume was large enough to ensure that they melted slowly in the New Orleans summer heat. Danton looked at Millicent, "I suppose you still drink the most civilized drink in New Orleans?" Millicent nodded and Danton made her a Blanchard strength Gin and Tonic. He poured himself a tall glass of iced Bourbon. Millicent and Danton took their wildly perspiring glasses and linen napkins to a **canapé a confidante** so they could enjoy their drinks and remembrances of their legendary courtship.

As much work as Danton had invested into rehabilitating the ancient tennis court and equipment, the suddenness of the tennis date had created a crossed wire situation with Mary and Inman. Both hadn't thought through the idea of a tennis date. Neither was wearing the appropriate clothing, for starters. Inman was wearing heavy gaberdine trousers and a dress shirt. Mary was wearing a knee length skirt and pleated blouse. At least she had chosen flats. Inman was wearing Bass Weejuns, hardly appropriate footwear for tennis. They stopped at the dance pavilion to choose rackets and to collect the new tennis balls. Mary locked her arm into Inman's and they promenaded to the court. Inman asked Mary to choose which side she preferred. He took the other. When they were in place, Inman shouted over to Mary's side, "Should we just lob the ball back and forth to get used to the whole thing?" Mary shouted back, "What???" Inman ran to the net and motioned to Mary. When Mary got to the net, Inman repeated his question. Mary agreed. "We're not in any competition, we're just here to have fun." Inman agreed, "Yes, no score, just fun." With both partners in complete agreement, they returned to their opposing spots. Inman served to Mary. She approached the ball, but her racquet got caught in her skirt. The tennis ball rolled out into the grass. Mary looked embarrassed, but Inman waved his racquet and showed her another tennis ball. Mary curtseyed to telegraph Inman a signal to serve on. Inman served, and this time Mary was able to catch the tennis ball with her racquet. The only problem was that the angle of her antiquated racquet sent the ball hurtling high over the net, past Inman, and ultimately into in the pool.

After an unimpressive start, they considered giving tennis up, but they persevered. After all, Danton had put so much into the whole tennis scheme. For two more hours, Mary and Inman braved hurting feet, blisters on their hands and their feet, and overwhelming fatigue. When they finally knew it was time to throw in the towel, Mary and Inman were drenched in more perspiration than Millicent and Danton's cocktail glasses. They found themselves tired and frustrated, and retreated to the dance pavilion to cool down, enjoy Monique's **rafraîchissements**, and discuss their afternoon. As they nestled in each other's embrace, all of their stress, aggravation, and pain faded from their consciousness.

They talked through the activity, and instantly realized that the first strike against them was their inappropriate clothing. That was; however, a convenient scape goat, upon which to blame for an afternoon that neither had particularly enjoyed. During the process of blaming their clothing, footwear, and even the lack of a fence to keep the balls from escaping, it became apparent, almost concurrently to both Mary and Inman that none of their complaints were the real problem. Mary was the first to name it. "All I wanted to do was spend the day with you, but you were way over there, and we couldn't talk." Inman said, "You're absolutely right. I felt the same way.

This is so much better!" Mary said, "I feel so bad. Your uncle put so much into arranging this for us." Inman thought through the problem. "Yes, he did. ...but, if you think about it, our problem isn't about the game, necessarily. It's about our proximity." Mary gave Inman a look of inquisitiveness. Inman continued, "Perhaps we can agree that singles tennis doesn't work for us, not even with appropriate clothing." Mary agreed. Inman continued, "So what if, in the future, we could play mixed doubles. You and I could be together on the same side." Mary looked intrigued. "Ohhh, but who would play with us?" Inman had to admit, "Right now, I have no idea. Maybe we should move it to the back burner, and just enjoy each other's company now." Mary agreed.

As the time to go approached, Millicent arrived at the main gate. Before Mary and Inman could walk up from the **garçonnière**, Caroline had come out onto the **véranda** and waved to Millicent. Millicent waved back. Monique opened the gate and Millicent walked quickly over to her oldest and dearest friend. Caroline told her, "They played tennis today." Millicent said, "That's so wonderful!" Caroline added, "I'm not sure who wore that old court down more, you and Danton, or Inman and me?" Millicent said, "Well, it certainly got a lot of wear back in those days! Maybe it got the most when we played mixed doubles." Caroline placed her left hand over her **décolletage** and said, "Yes, wasn't that the absolute best!" Millicent had to agree. As they talked, Mary and Inman staggered up from the **garçonnière**, looking completely beaten down. Caroline and Millicent looked at them with great concern.

Inman took their challenge. "We weren't dressed appropriately for the occasion." Both Caroline and Millicent could tell that Inman's explanation was 100% accurate, but just the tip of the iceberg. While it hadn't taken either of them a moment more to comprehend the real problem, neither of them said anytime, at least to them. They would save that for a future conversation. Millicent sighed, and told Caroline that Jack would soon be wondering where they were. Caroline, of course, understood completely. "**Ma maison est toujours honorée lors de la visite de mesdames dames Blanchard!**" (My home is always graced when dear Blanchard ladies visit!) Millicent was almost weeping as she embraced her dear friend Caroline on the **véranda**. Inman and Mary looked at each other stoically, each knowing the pain of the other not being able to admit their love, and embrace as they wanted. While neither of them "enjoyed" their mother's involvement, both Mary and Inman understood, and accepted the necessity of it.

While they were driving back to the funeral home, as much as Mary wanted to tell her mother that she couldn't be comfortable around Inman when "the mothers" were "prowling" around them, she couldn't. Neither could Inman, back at **Maison Soleil**. Millicent wanted only to tell Mary how much she supported her relationship with Inman, but her fears of Blackjack's potential reaction caused her to hold her tongue.

CHAPTER ELEVEN

LOVE IS IN THE AIR

As had become their routine, Millicent and Mary arrived back at the funeral home just as Hattie and Marie Cosette were putting the final touches on dinner. As much as Marie Cosette wanted to go with Mary up to her bedroom, and hear all about Mary's date with Inman, Hattie had her incredibly busy, and she couldn't break away. Mary went up, shucked out of her clothes and took a long hot shower. The heat of the water and steam pulled the aches and pains out of her body and feet. It also relaxed her so much that once she put on fresh clothes, and sat in her accustomed **bergère,** she drifted off to sleep. When Mary wasn't at the table when dinner was served, Millicent went up to check on her. She stepped into Mary's room and lovingly laid her hand on Mary's shoulder. "**Ma chère fille, c'est l'heure du dîner.**" (My dear daughter, it's time for dinner.) Mary struggled to open her eyes. She sighed, and said, "Mama…." Mary found the strength to stand and walk with her mother down to dinner. Blackjack, not surprisingly, had not waited for his family, wolfed down his dinner, and returned to his office lair. Millicent was actually relieved that her husband wasn't at the **table à manger** when she and Mary arrived for dinner.

Even without Jackson at the table, neither Mary nor Millicent dared talk about their activities. After dinner, Millicent went up to Mary's bedroom, and they sat in the **deux bergères à oreilles.** Millicent started the conversation, "Did you enjoy the tennis?" Mary sighed exceedingly deeply. "We both thought that we would. ...but we really didn't. We weren't so good at it, especially at first. We got a little better, but our clothes and especially our shoes made it a drudgery. ...but the worst part was being so far apart!" Millicent asked, "Why didn't you two go swimming? I bought you a bathing ensemble weeks ago." Mary blushed. "I have never been swimming with a boy. I guess I've been really self conscious." Millicent almost fumed. In her mind, it was Blackjack's fault. His "professions" had caused Mary's lack of experience with people of her age. **"Mon cher chéri, tu n'as rien à craindre, Inman Carnes est un bon gentilhomme."** (My dear darling, you have nothing to fear, Inman Carnes is a fine gentleman.) Mary teared up. **"Pourquoi mon père ne voit-il pas cela?"** (Why can't father see that?) Millicent looked down into her lap. "Mary, Your father has always wanted to fit in with the gentry in New Orleans, That's why he did everything necessary to marry me. That's why he put you at Miss. McGraw's, and why we go to Christ Church, even though I'm Catholic. He hasn't let you date because he's too dense to figure out the best match for you that would benefit him, socially, the most. Inman is the ideal, and logical choice to help with your father's ambitions, but... With Inman, he can't see past the "business" with Inman's father and uncle. I can't tell you about that now, but I will one day, when the time is right."

Mary thanked her mama for her support. "I feel confident enough to go swimming on Friday afternoon!" Millicent hugged and kissed her daughter. "Inman's a keeper! We just have a struggle to convince your father." Millicent left Mary, and went through the Butler's pantry to the kitchen, and poured herself a Blanchard strength Gin and Tonic. She wandered through the dining room and to the large window overlooking Saint Charles Avenue in the parlor. "Parlor? **C'est un fichu salon!**" (It's a damn salon!)," she thought to herself. **"Tu es un bâtard de classe basse!"** (You damn low class bastard!)

When Friday the 20th. arrived, passions were running on overdrive. Millicent had stewed over Blackjack's boorish deficiencies all week, and was longing for the genteel company of the only man she had ever loved. Mary had steeled herself in her mother's encouragement, and was ready to present herself to Inman in a bathing suit. Millicent dropped Mary off at the main gate of **Maison Soleil**, then continued on to her rendezvous with Danton atop Maison Blanche. This time, Danton arrived with a well wrapped cube of ice in tow. Danton made drinks, and Millicent put out a buffet spread. It wasn't long, however, before Millicent's rage against Blackjack overcame her, and she took her new-found relationship with Danton to a new level. They made wild passionate love on countless pieces of fine provincial French antique furniture. Outside, the wind blew raindrops against the over-sized warehouse windows. Claps of thunder accentuated their animalistic groans and moans, and shrieks of exhilaration.

Mary and Inman heard the approaching thunder as they met at the main gate and walked to the **véranda** to enter the **manoir** to spend a few minutes with Caroline. Caroline asked, "Was that thunder I just heard?" Inman said, "Yes, I think it was." Caroline said, "Well, that's just too bad. I know you were both looking forward to swimming today." Mary said, "Yes ma'am, we were." Caroline added, "Well, maybe next time. It won't be safe if there's going to be a storm. What will you do?" "Inman said, "We can dance, or we could listen to the radio. ...oh, and there are board games. We'll have a fine time!" Caroline smiled and returned her readers to the bridge of her nose. "**Bon, vous deux passez une bonne après-midi**" (Well, you two have a great afternoon.) Inman grabbed Mary's hand and pulled her out onto the **véranda**. He could barely wait a few steps down the walkway before he grabbed Mary's waist and pulled her in to him and kissed her passionately. Mary melted into his arms and lost herself in the passion of the moment. As difficult as it was, they paused, and made their way to the greater privacy of the **garçonnière** before submitting a second time to their growing passions. Inman walked over to the phonograph, but had second thoughts. He switched the radio on and retired to one of the comfortable chintz covered settees with Mary. They resumed their passionate make-out session. Their only interruption was when they heard Monique walking down the walkway with a tray of **rafraîchissements**. By the time Monique arrived, they were sitting on the settee with an appropriate gap talking about the programming on the radio.

Monique had been young once, and in love. She wasn't fooled one bit, but said nothing. In truth, Caroline, who had been this age in the Roaring Twenties also knew the passions of teen-aged love, but said nothing and smiled, both on her face and in her heart. Monique put the tray down and said, "I'z got'a lot'a do fo' dinna. If'n y'all needs anythin' Iz'l be in da kidchin." Both Mary and Inman thanked her for the treats. After waiting a few moments for Monique to get out of earshot, Mary leaned over Inman, pressing him deep into the upholstery and started French kissing him with wild abandon. Electricity began to arc through both of their beings. Mary could feel her nipples engorging and pressing against her tight brassiere. She also felt Inman's penis grow erect in his trousers. It was a new, unexpected experience for Mary, but her shyness suddenly evaporated. She liked the new feelings she was experiencing, and was confident that this was true love. Inman knew that he was completely in love with Mary. He ran his hand up Mary's leg. She bit his lip and stopped his hand before it managed to cross the boundary of her panties. After a while, Inman ran his hand across Mary's breast. She grasped it tenderly and moved it up to the nape of her neck. Without realizing it, Mary began to grind on Inman's groin. It felt spectacular, like nothing she had ever experienced. Inman was beyond bliss. He was on the verge of orgasm when the main gate bell rang.

Mary started to cry. "I don't want to leave you, my darling." Inman said, "I want this to go on for the rest of our lives. I wish that we could be together forever." Mary asked, "Are we in love?" Inman said, "I know that I love you completely, and I hope that you love me too." Mary said, "**Je t'aime de tout mon cœur et je le ferai toujours!**" (I love you with all of my heart, and will always!) Inman, with a tear flowing over his left cheek, kissed Mary on her forehead, then her cheeks, and finely on her eyelids. "**Avec le temps, j'embrasserai chaque partie de toi mon amour**." (In time, I'll kiss every part of you my love.) Mary closed her fluttering eyes and dreamed of that day. Mary and Inman allowed themselves time to deescalate their passion before starting the walk to the **manoir**. They did allow themselves the confidence to hold hands. It was rewarded when they walked in to Caroline's **salon principal**, and both Caroline and Millicent melted into beautiful heart-warming smiles. Both mothers apologized for the weather not cooperating with the notion of swimming. Mary and Inman both said, "We'll swim next time," Millicent pointed to her watch, and said, "Dear, we can't keep your father waiting." Caroline stood up and walked over to Millicent. She whispered into Millicent's ear, "**Vous savez que nous devrions être des soeurs.**" (You know that we should be sisters.) Millicent pulled away and looked square into Caroline's face. "**Oui!**" was all she said, but it was enough. The entire exchange was lost on Mary and Inman, as it needed to be, for a while longer.

Millicent and Mary walked through the main gate and got into the Cadillac. There was silence for an extended time. Millicent could tell that there was something on Mary's mind, but waited, and let it be Mary's conversation. As they motored down Saint Charles Avenue, Mary asked, "Mama, am I too young to be in love?" Millicent uttered a "Hummmmm." and was silent for a few moments. "No." She hesitated, then added, "…not if it's the right person. I was in love, with the right person, when I was your age. Age has nothing to do with it. Eighteen, twenty-eight, forty-eight, eighty-eight, it doesn't matter. What matters is how you treat each other." Mary fretted for a few moments, then asked, "Mama, would you be upset if I told you that I thought that I was in love with Inman?" Millicent breathed in and out slowly and deeply. "Mary, would you be shocked to know that I saw the chemistry between you and Inman on your first date? Would you be shocked to know that I watched you two on the first day that you met in the motor court? Knowing that he is the son of Inman and Caroline Carnes only reinforces my confidence in him. I will do everything in my power to support your courtship. …but I can't vouch for your father." Mary thanked her mother. "Hopefully, we'll have a lot of time to convince him." Being on the same page was comfortable for both Mary and Millicent. Their next opportunity to escape Blackjack and the oppressive funeral home, and experience the love of their beaux would be on the 24th.

Over the course of the four days before their next date, Mary replayed her previous date with Inman over and over. The passion she had experienced, almost overwhelmed her. She was confused. Should she give in to it, or should she risk loosing Inman by rebuffing his advances. There wasn't a right or a wrong answer. It was clear that her sexual feelings were growing, and could, if not repressed, overwhelm her. The only thing she was sure of was that she was completely in love with Inman. She humored herself, and believed that Inman was having the same feelings for her. While she couldn't know for sure, Inman was, in fact, truly, madly, and completely in love with Mary.

When Millicent pulled to the curb at **Maison Soleil**, she said, "Have a fun time today. Wear your bathing suit. Based on what I've seen, Inman completely respects you. As long as everything is good, enjoy the ride. Hopefully it'll go on from now on." Mary thanked her mother and got out at the main gate. She rang the bell. That day, Inman came out to the gate and greeted his beloved. He escorted Mary to Caroline's **salon principal**. After warm greetings, Caroline said, "Well, it looks like the pool is an option today? No?" Inman said, "It seems so." He turned to Mary, "Would that be good for you?" Mary smiled. "**Oui, mon amour**." Caroline beamed. "**Tres bien**! Monique, will you take Mary upstairs to the suite where her bathing ensemble is, so that she can change?" Monique stepped out of the shadows and said, "**Oui, madam**!" Monique motioned for Mary to follow her upstairs. Caroline said to Mary, "Inman will meet you at the dance pavilion." Inman thanked his mother and went back to the **garçonnière** to change into his bathing suit. If truth be told, he was as nervous about showing himself so uncovered, as was Mary. When Mary and Monique made it down to the dance pavilion, both she and Inman were sporting robes over their bathing suits. Monique placed the **rafraîchissements** on the table and excused herself.

Mary and Inman looked at each other with looks containing both desire and fear. Inman decided to be fearless, and whipped his robe off and threw it across a chaise. Mary gasped when she saw Inman's muscular and evenly tanned body and tight reveling bathing trunks. She thought to herself that she'd never seen anything as beautiful as Inman's body in her entire life. Without thinking, Mary released her tight grasp on her robe. It opened, slid over her shoulders, and dropped to the floor. Inman gasped immediately, and had to cover his mouth with his hand to avoid embarrassment. Mary had put on a stunning white one-piece suit that had a black appliqué running from decorative triangles atop her thighs on both sides, up and over her breasts to matching triangles that that terminated at the strapless top edge of the suit. Inman thought that they looked like elongated hour glasses. He found that thought quite appropriate for the hours he desired to spend with his beloved Mary. After a few moments of frozen gazes, Inman walked over to Mary and reached out to her. Her trepidation melted instantly, and she embraced Inman. Touching warm subtle skin was a new sensation, but they both enjoyed it completely. Inman put his arm around Mary's waist and together they walked to the pool. Mary walked elegantly down the stairs. Inman was more playful, and dove off of the diving board. His Jack Knife dive impressed Mary to no end. He surfaced, and swept his thick dark hair out of his eyes and over his forehead. He breast-stroked over to Mary who was sitting on the steps. She grinned, "**Très bien, mon amour**!" Inman said, "I've had a lot time growing up, by myself, to practice." Mary feigned a frown. "**Oh, pauvre bébé**! Are you going to miss that alone time now that I'm in your life?" Inman swept in and threw his arms around Mary. He kissed her passionately and said, "**Non, pas du tout**!" (No, not one bit!) Inman and Mary traded places. Inman sat on the step, and Mary climbed into his lap and put her right arm around Inman's broad shoulder and back. They started making out. Their bodies were wet and hot. Mary could easily feel Inman's erection under her, and was conflicted. She wanted all that it promised, but her upbringing told her that she had to resist all temptation.

As before, Inman started probing. He started running his hand up Mary's thigh. With each pass, he drew closer and closer to the boundary of her bathing suit. Unlike before, Mary put up no resistance. Inman took another pass and ran his fingers under Mary's bating suit edge. When she said nothing, and didn't resist, he made another pass, yet deeper. Mary let out a mild moan, but made not protestations. With the next pass, Inman encountered Mary's pubic hair and vagina. The shock almost caused Inman to remove his hand, but Mary grabbed his forearm and steadied him. Without knowing what he was doing, Inman began to explore and fondle Mary's privates. He took his queues from Mary, who began to moan and sigh. She bent her neck around and kissed Inman passionately. Inman continued to stimulate Mary until she started to make animalistic noises, and climaxed. Inman didn't truly realize what he'd just done. Mary lovingly removed Inman's hand and rotated around and straddled him. As she kissed him passionately, Mary dropped one side of her bathing suit exposing a full beautiful breast. She guided Inman's head to it. He kissed her perfect nipple and began to stimulate it. Mary's eyes once again began to fluter. As Inman stimulated Mary's perfect nipple, he ran his fingers under her swimsuit and found her still well stimulated vagina. Inman inserted his fingers, and took Mary to the moon and back for a second time.

Fearing that they'd be caught, Mary and Inman decided that it would be prudent to dance for a while. As they climbed the stairs out of the pool, Mary couldn't help herself, and marveled at the massive bulge in Inman's tight swim trunks. She may not have understood the attraction, but she felt it, and enjoyed it completely. Inman put on a waltz. They danced, practically naked. Inman's massive engorged penis rubbed against Mary's groin. Both were in paradise. After a few dances, Inman was more in pain than in paradise. He asked Mary if they could stop and talk for a minute. She agreed, of course. They went over to one of the chintz covered settees and fell into each other's arms. Inman explained that, like what Mary had experienced earlier, men needed something similar.

Mary thought for a moment. "That seems fair. Is it at all similar to what we women experience?" Inman said, "Yes, I believe that it is." Mary said, "Tell me what to do." Inman, somewhat embarrassed, took Mary's hand and guided it into his swim trunks. He helped her grasp his erect penis. "All you need to do is stroke it." As Mary stroked Inman's penis, he kissed her passionately. Before long, he knew the time was fast approaching. He started to moan and praise God. Before he orgasmed, Inman forced his trunks down and grabbed an oversized beach towel. When he ejaculated, Mary was completely startled. Nothing like that had ever happened when she had experienced an orgasm. Inman picked up on Mary's shock and said, "I guess they didn't tell you about that at Miss. McGraw's, now did they?"

Mary started laughing hysterically. "No they didn't!" Both Mary and Inman were able to stop thinking about their erogenous zones for a few minutes and concentrate on how much they loved each other. They cleaned each other up. Inman went upstairs in the **garçonnière**, and Mary went to the **manoir**. They both got dressed. For the rest of the afternoon, they danced to the records in Inman's father's and his uncle Danton's collections.

There was only one more date in June, and two dates in July before the big Bastille Day party on Saturday, the 12th. of July. Bastille Day parties always occurred on the Saturday closest to Bastille Day, July 14th. While Mary knew that her parents would be out of the house until at least 10:00, Inman knew nothing of the significance of the date. His mother knew. His aunt and his uncle knew. They were reared in the Bastille Day traditions. Inman wasn't. It was just another day to someone who had been confined in his home. Before that date, Mary and Inman had three more dates at **Maison Soleil**. The last was on the 10th. of July. Mary and Inman started out in the pool. They couldn't help themselves and started making out and pleasuring one another. At long last, they realized that they really wanted to dance with each other. They lovingly danced to many recordings. The last record that Inman placed on the green felt turntable, before Millicent rang the main gate bell, was Paul Whiteman's 1927 version of ***Mary (What are you waiting for?)*** featuring Bix Beiderbecke, and vocals by Bing Crosby. As they danced, ignoring the fact that Mary's mother was at the **manoir** gossiping with Inman's mother, Mary contemplated the title of the song. …but midway through the song, the lyrics began. They got into her head and began to speak to her. Mary found it impossible to escape from that song and the quandary it imposed upon her.

The dilemma interfered with the conversation Millicent tried to have with Mary on the way back to the funeral home. It preoccupied her during dinner. Mary ate very little, and asked to be excused before dessert so she could go up to bed. Millicent looked at Mary, "Are you coming down with something?" "No mama, I'm just completely exhausted." Blackjack who rarely ever engaged in family conversation asked, "Exhausted, how could you possibly be exhausted?" Mary's face contorted, and she blushed. Millicent said, "Jackson, I told you weeks ago that Mary has been taking tennis lessons." Blackjack huffed, "Tennis lessons, what a complete waste of time. …and money!" He stood up and threw his sullied linen napkin into his chair and yelled into the kitchen for Marie Cosette to bring him **café noir**. He shook his head in a condescending manner and stormed out of the dining room, and made his way back to his office.

Millicent sighed, "From what I've been told, your grandfather could never afford for your father to participate in school activities, or take any lessons. It's a shame that he never took the time to teach your father to be polite, charming, and social." Mary went over to Millicent and wrapped her in a warm loving embrace. "**Merci mère pour m'avoir appris ces grâces!**" (Thank you mama, for teaching me these graces!) Millicent smiled, "**Vous êtes les bienvenus, vous les honorez bien!** (You're welcome, you honor them well!) Now, you go up and get some rest. Mary smiled at her mother and walked slowly from the dining room, through the parlor, and up the stairs to her room.

Mary walked to her window and looked down to the Neutral Ground, irrationally hoping to see Inman leaning on the support pole at the Streetcar stop. When he wasn't there, she sighed and pulled the drapes to block out most of the early evening summer sunshine. Mary changed into a pale pink silk nightgown trimmed in ecru Chantilly lace. She slipped under the covers and stared up at the **Baldaquin** that crowned her bed, draped in pink and white **Toile de Jouy** and lavish **passementerie**. She muttered under her breath, "What are you waiting for Mary?" In the solitude of her closed-off bedroom, free from distractions, Mary pondered her carnal desires, and what the future might hold for her if she succumbed to them.

Just who was she considering becoming intimate with, anyway? Was Inman kind? Yes, he was, kinder than anyone she knew, other than her mother. Was Inman puffed-up? No, he displayed more desire to please her in every possible way than to please himself. Was Inman honest or deceitful? Other than participating in a secret relationship, that only their mothers, and Inman's uncle were aware of, no, she couldn't think of a single time he had ever told her an untruth. …and he had, most certainly, answered all of her questions, even the most intimate questions, without evasion. As Mary started to nod off, she came to the realization that she was completely, madly, and utterly in love with Inman, and couldn't conceive of her life lived with anyone else. She smiled, closed her eyes and rolled over on her side. Mary was blessed with a peaceful night's rest and beautiful dreams of her love.

The next morning at breakfast, Millicent noticed a paradigm shift in her daughter. While Mary had gone up to bed a fatigued and introverted, insecure young girl, at breakfast, she was almost regal. She displayed confidence, and intrepidity. Millicent commented, "Well, one of us got an exceptional night's sleep." Mary breathed deeply, closed her eyes, and nodded in agreement. After breakfast, Mary retired to her bedroom to read. When she came down for luncheon, Mary asked Marie Cosette to come see her after the food was put up and the dishes were washed. Mary was back into her novel when Marie Cosette knocked on her door. Mary invited her in and asked her to go on a mission for her. "Marie Cosette, would you go to **Maison Soleil** and tell Inman that my parents will be away tomorrow night from 6:00 to 10:00 at a Bastille Day party. I'd like for him to come here to visit me for a change." Marie Cosette's eyes grew as large as coasters. "OH no, iz you dat crazy? He can't come here. You'll gid caugd!" Mary laughed. "Don't be silly. Hattie will be off, and you'll be standing guard. If anything goes wrong there are several staircases, and multiple hiding places and exits." Marie Cosette asked, "Iz any boy wordh all dat?" Mary looked out her window to the Streetcar tracks below. "I've asked myself that question, and hundreds more like it. The bottom line is, I would go through hell and back for him, and I truly believe he would do the same for me." Marie Cosette started to tear up. "...an you'll defy dat fader o your'n fo dat boy?" Mary sat up straight and arched her back. "Yes, if that's what it takes. My mama is on my side!"

Marie Cosette received her instructions for the message and left the funeral home through the kitchen door and headed for the Streetcar stop. She boarded the Streetcar and rode to Lee Circle, where she got off and walked down Howard Avenue to **Maison Soleil**. Marie Cosette breathed in deeply and rang the heavy main gate bell. Monique stepped out of the kitchen. "Iz gots a message for Mr. Inman." Monique recognized Marie Cosette, and opened the gate to allow her to enter the property. "Please wait here, I'll go and get Mr. Carnes." Monique disappeared back into the kitchen, and a few moments later, Inman stepped out onto the **véranda**. When he saw that it was Marie Cosette, Inman made his way down the stairs, and across the driveway to greet Marie Cosette. In an unusual move, Caroline, who was restless, and just a bit curious put her book and readers down and walked to the French doors. She hesitated for just a moment, then stepped out onto the **véranda**.

Inman had his back to his mother and had no idea she was watching him. Marie Cosette could see Caroline studying her. She relayed Mary's message and made her exit as quickly as possible. Inman paused to smile about the invitation for the next evening. When he turned around, Caroline had retreated to her reading nest. After Inman stepped back into the room, Caroline asked, "Inman, who was that girl that just visited?" Inman said, "That was Marie Cosette. She works for the Day family. She was out on errands, and Mary asked her to stop by and thank me for our date yesterday." Caroline nodded, and continued reading. Inman couldn't resist, "She also said that Mary's mother went on and on about how much fun she has when she visits you." Caroline smiled, "That Marie Cosette seems like a nice girl. …and she seems so familiar.

I just can't seem to put my finger on it just now."

CHAPTER TWELVE

BASTILLE DAY

Millicent Day arose early on Saturday morning, the 12th of July. When she entered the kitchen, Hattie and Marie Cosette had just started breakfast. Coffee, Community Coffee, was in the percolator on the stove, but it would be ten or twelve minutes before it was ready. She looked around the kitchen, wanting something to do. Hattie continued stirring the grits and said, "We's got dis, Missus Day." Millicent saw that she wasn't needed. "I just know everything is going to be wonderful. " After an awkward pause, Millicent turned, and went into the dining room. As Millicent was pushing the swinging door open, Hattie added, "Cosett'll be bringin' ju jo coffee soon'uns it's done."

Millicent went to her usual chair and sat down at the table. Marie Cosette had already set the table. Instinctively, Millicent picked up her spoon and looked at her reflection on the bottom. She smiled. She had taught Hattie the "Blanchard" way to polish silver, and Hattie always achieved perfection. Her linen napkins were also perfect. …perfectly laundered, perfectly starched and pressed, and perfectly folded. Marie Cosette backed through the swinging door with a sterling tray containing a matching sugar bowl and warm milk pitcher. She placed the tray on the **buffet a deux corps**, keeping the **buffet de chasse** free for the breakfast chafers.

Marie Cosette returned to the kitchen to pour the coffee into the sterling coffee pot that had been sitting in the sink full of scalding water. No sooner did the door swing shut behind her, Blackjack stormed into the dining room and rudely began shouting. "Where the hell is the god-dammed coffee, Hattie." Hattie shook her head and simply ignored him. Marie Cosette dumped the scalding water, dried off the coffee pot and poured the coffee into it. Her hands were trembling as she pushed the kitchen door open. "Here 'dis Misduh Day, nice an' fresh." Blackjack grabbed the pot out of Marie Cosette's hand and poured himself a cup, not in Millicent's Limoges tea cups, but in his accustomed old stained diner coffee cup that he'd brought from his office. Had he not been ignoring Millicent, Blackjack would have seen her close her eyes and sigh in exasperation.

When Blackjack put the coffee pot down on the Buffet, Marie Cosette picked it up and took the coffee over to Millicent and poured her tea cup half full. She returned the coffee pot to the Buffet and brought the tray holding the sugar and warm milk over to Millicent. Millicent looked up at Marie Cosette, smiled, and mouthed "Thank you." Marie Cosette nodded and returned to the kitchen to help Hattie fill the chafers. Millicent added sugar to her cup and filled it the rest of the way with the warm milk. Mary strolled into the dining room and took her seat as Hattie and Marie Cosette brought the first chafers into the Dining Room and placed them on the **buffet de chasse**. She looked at her mother and said, "**Bonjour, mama.**" Millicent smiled at her daughter, "**Bonjour, Mary.**"

Blackjack folded his paper over and noticed the food had been put out. "It's about damn time. I've got a lot of work to get done before that damn party tonight." He grabbed his plate and rushed to fill it, ahead of Millicent and Mary. Millicent simply stared down at the table. She wanted to weep, but was determined not to give Blackjack the satisfaction. Blackjack returned to the table and began to shovel the food into his mouth. Millicent and Mary accompanied each other to the **buffet de chasse**. They made their selections and returned to the table.

Millicent took a few bites of her breakfast. "Jackson, will you be ready to leave by 5:45 this afternoon? The party starts at 6:00." Blackjack, still with food in his mouth, said, "We'll be leaving just before 5:15. I want to be early, there's only so much time before the election and a lot of votes to secure. Millicent started to remind him that the Long's invitation had said that the **fête** would be between the hours of six and ten, but she didn't want to reinforce the notion that Jackson hadn't been brought up in the same social circles as had she.

Millicent sipped her coffee. "I'll be ready, but you should know that I'm going to get my hair fixed this afternoon, and I'm taking Mary with me." Blackjack grumbled and gulped down the rest of his breakfast. He walked over to the buffet and slammed down his coffee cup before returning to his office. "Marie Cosette, get off your ass, and bring me my coffee!" Although Blackjack said nothing to either of them as he left the dining room, both Mary and Millicent breathed a sigh of relief when he was gone; although, both tried to conceal their feelings from each other.

After breakfast, Millicent went out back and found Eddie Smith washing one of the hearses in the Motor Court. "Eddie, I'll need my Cadillac by 11:00 this morning, top down, please." Eddie didn't miss a beat, "Yes, ma'am. I'll have it ready for you." Millicent thanked him and returned to the kitchen. She told Hattie that she and Mary would be out for luncheon and that she should ask Mr. Day what he wanted for his lunch. Hattie was hunched over the sink washing the breakfast dishes. She frowned to herself, but said, Yes'um."

Millicent and Mary walked out of the kitchen door to the motor court behind the funeral Home at 11:00. The loaner Cadillac was there waiting for them. It was white with chrome everywhere, and supple white leather upholstery. Eddie had washed and waxed it and it was glinting in the harsh July sunshine. He had left the keys in the ignition for Millicent. She and Mary slid in over the supple leather. Millicent fired the beast up, put it into gear, and she and Mary motored down Saint Charles Avenue toward the Central Business District. Millicent parked in a lot and she and Mary walked to **Maison de Bringier**. While they were having their hair styled, Millicent said, "Mary, my dear, I fancy a manicure. …how about you?" Mary waited a moment and said, "**Oui, mama**. Thank you so much! That would be lovely."

After their makeovers, Millicent and Mary made there way over to **Galatoire's** on Bourbon Street for lunch. After being seated, Millicent ordered a Fruit Salad, and Mary requested her usual soft-drink with ice chips. Millicent added, "She'll have her soft drink sweetened, please." The waiter was well aware that "sweetened" was a euphemism for "Add a little Bourbon, please." When the waiter returned with their drinks, Mary ordered the Chicken Clemenceau with Brabant Potatoes and Green Peas. Millicent ordered the Veal Chop Bonne-Femme with Lyonnaise Potatoes and Green Beans Almandine. She also requested an order of Canapé Lorenzo to share with Mary. Neither could finish their meal, and neither had room for dessert. Since neither was especially eager to return home, Millicent ordered a coffee, and asked the waiter to bring Mary another soft-drink. The waiter brought Millicent a demitasse cup of strong coffee and a small tray of cream and brown sugar cubes. He served Mary another sweetened soft-drink over ice chips. Together, Millicent and Mary sipped their drinks, and enjoyed each other's company.

By 2:30, Millicent realized that it was time to make their way back to the funeral home. Reluctantly, she and Mary made their way back to the Cadillac and began the drive back out Saint Charles Avenue, slowly. They were relieved that Blackjack was still in his office when they got home. Millicent excused herself to go up to her room. "I'm going to need to rest before going to this party with your father. I know that he's going to embarrass me." Mary hugged her mother tightly. "**Merci Mama, pour nos friandises aujourd'hui**." (Thank you Mama, for our treats today.) Millicent went up to her room while Mary went into the kitchen looking for Marie Cosette. She found her in the pantry, grabbed her hand, and said, "Come on, we need to talk." They ran up the stairs to Mary's bedroom and sat in the matching polychrome silk damask **bergères à oreilles**.

Marie Cosette took Mary's hands and looked at her manicure. She looked at Mary with an inquisitive expression. "You gonna make dat boy suffa when he git here donight wit dose nails and dat hair!" Mary smiled and pulled her legs up into the chair. "I hope so!" was all she said. They talked and giggled until they heard Mary's parents walking down the stairs. Quietly, they followed them down to the foyer. In the foyer, Millicent picked up a **boutonnière** from a Sevres bowl on the marble top **enfilade**. It was for Blackjack, not her. It was a red Carnation with blue and white ribbons. Mary and Marie Cosette held back a few steps, in the shadows, and listened. Millicent started to pin it on Blackjack's dinner jacket lapel. He bristled, "What is this?" Millicent leaned in and she pinned it to Blackjack's lapel said, "It's a Bastille Day **boutonnière,** of course. It's a social requirement for this party!" After she finished pinning the **boutonnière** on Blackjack's lapel, Millicent took her ivory crocheted silk gloves from a rectangular Limoges platter on the same **enfilade** and pulled them onto her graceful Blanchard hands.

Blackjack looked at Marie Cosette in the shadows. "I suppose you can serve Mary her dinner tonight? Hattie is off, and Mrs. Day and I will be at a party." Marie Cosette nodded her head. Blackjack looked at his watch. "Okay, it's almost 5:15, we need to be going." He looked at Mary. "We'll be home shortly after 10:00." Millicent added quietly, "Maybe later, there may be an after party." Out of the corner of her eye, Mary saw her mother shaking her head as if to say, "Hell no. That won't be happening." Mary said, "I hope you both have a great time tonight!"

Millicent sighed, and Blackjack ignored Mary's warm sentiment. "We're wasting time. We need to leave. He and Millicent walked through the dining room and kitchen to the rear vestibule. Millicent had left the Cadillac in the Motor Court after returning from her afternoon out with Mary. Blackjack brushed past Millicent and walked to the Driver's side of the car and got in. Millicent, knew better than to think that Blackjack would ever be a gentleman, She opened her own door and slid onto the seat. Blackjack fired the Cadillac up. They motored the short distance to **General Long's Villa** on the the corner of Prytania and Fourth Streets.

As they turned the corner and pulled up next to the corn stalk fence, Blackjack was surprised that there were no other cars or people there. He asked, "Where is everyone?" Millicent shook her head slightly. "The party starts at 6:00. It's only 5:20." Millicent suggested pulling past the gate and waiting in the car. Although fuming, Blackjack said nothing and pulled past the gate. He switched off the ignition, and they sat there in silence in the blistering midsummer afternoon sun. Millicent was mortified that the Longs might see them there so early. The heat made the minutes waiting seem like hours to Millicent. Her only saving grace was that the Cadillac was white and had white leather upholstery. She stared at the clock on the dashboard of the Cadillac until other cars started pulling around the corner. At 5:55 she told Blackjack that it would be okay to walk to the **véranda** and wait for the door to open.

Earlier, neither Millicent nor Blackjack had noticed Mary watching from the front window, as they turned right onto Saint Charles Avenue in front of the funeral home. Mary watched her parents leave, and watched for the Streetcar. Marie Cosette scampered into the parlor, "Dey's gone, now." Mary continued to stare out the window. "Is he ever going to come?" Marie Cosette joined Mary in the large window to get a view. "Hes'un be here. I no dat!" They both heard the Streetcar bell as it approached the stop at Louisiana Avenue. Mary could scarcely breath. The Streetcar rumbled to a stop, and stayed for what seemed an eternity to Mary. When the Streetcar continued on down Saint Charles Avenue, Mary and Marie Cosette finally saw Inman leaning against the center support pole in the Neutral Ground, waiting for the car to pass.

Mary asked Marie Cosette to go down and ask Inman to come to the funeral home front door. Marie Cosette gasped, "Yose wants him in hea? What if'n you'se gets caught!?" Mary's newly found confidence shown through. "It'll be okay, I have you looking after me. Go on, I don't have all night! Marie Cosette opened the front door quietly and walked quickly, albeit apprehensively to the Neutral Ground between the Streetcar tracks where Inman was perched against the support pole. Inman stood and smiled when he saw Marie Cosette. She was a tad stressed, and came right to the point. "Miz Mary be ready do se you'sn now!" Inman was just a little confused about the change of how their dates worked, but he allowed Marie Cosette to lead him across the street, through the iron gate and up onto the **véranda**. Inman looked around, still puzzled. "Where's Mary?"

Blackjack got out of the car, and made a show of opening Millicent's door. They walked side-by-side through the front gate and up to the **véranda**. Millicent was happy to see people with whom she had grown up. She enjoyed catching up with them, but was embarrassed by Blackjack's attempt to turn every social conversation into a political campaign. To her relief, General Long's Butler opened the front door precisely at 6:00.

General and Mrs. Alexander Long were standing in the cavernous hallway, framed by a floor-to-ceiling window across from the open pocket doors leading to the Front Parlor. They greeted every guest warmly as they entered their elaborate Italianate Renaissance home. Blackjack shook the General's hand. General Long's icy stare unnerved Blackjack. "We're delighted that you could make it to our little **soirée** today." Blackjack forced a smile. "Thank you, General." At that moment, Blackjack knew that he was out of his league, but suppressed his all too real fears. General Long took Millicent's hand and kissed it. "Millicent, my dear, it's been far too long since Alice and I have had the pleasure of your company." Millicent smiled broadly. "Indeed it has! I am truly happy to be here today." Millicent embraced Alice Long. Alice whispered into Millicent's ear, "I do miss playing Bridge with you." Millicent whispered back, "I miss that too, but you know...." Alice nodded, knowingly.

Marie Cosette did her best to hold back a chuckle. "Lordy! She's be ride in dere! Marie Cosette grabbed the door handle, opened the door, and swung around to hold the door for Inman. Inman immediately saw Mary standing in the center of the foyer under its Bohemian crystal chandelier. Mary smiled and stretched out her hands. Without thinking, Inman was lured across the threshold. He took Mary's hands, kissed them and said, "**Bonne soirèe mon amour!**" Marie Cosette closed and locked the door, and melted into the background. Mary could immediately sense Inman's discomfort. She kissed him elegantly and passionately on the lips, and said, "We are alone, and safe, for a few hours." Mary led Inman into the parlor, and together, they sat on her mama's elegant **méridienne**. "My love, please calm down. Marie Cosette is the only one here in the residence, and she's agreed to stand watch for us. We have time, but there are plans if my parents happen to come home early." Inman breathed several cleansing breaths and sank back onto the bolster.

Mary thrust one arm behind Inman's neck and used the other to pull the two together into a passionate embrace. She leaned in close to Inman's ear. The feel of Mary's breath and her words intoxicated Inman with love. "**Ma chérie, je n'attends plus…**" (My darling, I'm not waiting anymore…) Upon hearing those words, Inman's breathing was practically paralyzed. His short breaths caused him to become light headed. All he could do was to gaze into Mary's beautiful violet eyes with a look of complete love and desire.

Inman managed to find the strength to pull Mary in close, and he kissed her passionately. Mary swung her legs over and straddled Inman. They began to make out with wild abandon. Inman's hand found its way up Mary's thigh and under her panties to the sweet wetness of her clitoris. Remembering the details of their last encounter, Inman instinctively began to massage Mary's clitoris and run his finger tips shallowly into her vagina. Before Mary could climax, she grasped Inman's wrist. "**S'il te plait, un moment mon amour.** (Please, a moment my love.) Mary stood up and took Inman by the hand, "Please come with me." Inman stood and followed Mary to the stairs. While ordinarily Inman was thoughtful and rational, with these circumstances, he was in a complete love trance. Mary led him to the stairs. Inman put up no resistance. His eyes were closed and Mary was completely in charge. By the time Inman opened his eyes, he found himself in Mary's pink palace of a bedroom.

Millicent stepped over to Blackjack. "Well Jackson, which group should we join?" Blackjack had no idea which group to join. "Let's work all of the rooms." They went first into the music room. Millicent was overjoyed to see that the Long's had engaged 'Fess' to play the piano for the evening. 'Fess' was short for Professor Longhair, whose real name was Henry Byrd. 'Fess' was tall, lanky, and black. He wore a white dinner jacket over black pants. Blackjack was at a loss to understand why 'Fess' kept his white silk gloves on while he played. He couldn't take his eyes off of 'Fess's' hands, and was startled when one of the three circulating bartenders asked Millicent and him what they'd like to drink. Before Millicent could answer, Blackjack blurted out. "Scotch, rocks, not too much soda." The bartender gave Millicent a sympathetic look.

She sighed and said, "I'll have White Wine, please." The bartender replied, "Very good, ma'am."

When the circulating bartender was safely out of earshot, Millicent pulled Blackjack aside. "Jackson, you should have ordered Bourbon." Blackjack pulled a face. "Millie, it's the 1950's. Scotch is the drink these days." Millicent shook her head. "Not here, not with these people." She looked across a row of dining chairs that spanned the opening to the stair hall, which had been turned into a working bar. She saw their bartender starting to mix the drinks. He was talking to the two main bartenders. They looked over toward the Music Room and shook their heads. Millicent was completely embarrassed. She knew that word would get around that Blackjack was "**Gauche**."

From her spot in the music room, Millicent could see past the grand stair hall and into the dining room. The elegant mahogany dining table, that could easily seat eighteen, had been turned into a sea of sterling serving trays, holding **canapés** of all descriptions, strategically placed to keep the waiters constantly supplied, and the guests always within reach of delectable finger foods. Many were served on toothpicks. The catering staff had placed cut glass bowls strategically around each room for guests to deposit their spent toothpicks. The waiters changed them out periodically.

Among the **hors d'oeuvres**, there were smoked oysters baked in puff pastry, stuffed olives baked in biscuit dough, shrimp, marinaded for days, on toast points, and, of course, cheese straws. Around the room there were bowls of toasted pecans and monogramed linen party napkins. The most coveted **hors d'oeuvre**, by far, were the Rhum Babas, crushed vanilla wafers, chopped nuts, confectioner's sugar, cocoa, and rum, rolled into balls and sealed in tin containers for a week prior to the party. Each batch was rolled in confectioner's sugar before being placed on a serving platter.

While Blackjack was working the Music Room, he asked Millicent, "Where's that waiter with our drinks?" Millicent sighed, "Jackson, he's not a waiter, in this home he's 'the gentleman serving this room.' He'll be along soon." Blackjack was asking for votes when the gentleman brought a tray with drinks for several of the couples in the group. Bourbon for the men, except Blackjack, of course, and White Wine in stemmed glasses for the ladies. Blackjack was the last to receive his drink. The other couples noticed the Scotch immediately, but decorum prevented them from expressing their utter disdain. Millicent's ordering the correct drink helped Blackjack. He'd have had a difficult time getting any votes had Millicent not been brought up in a proper home, and had ordered a less gentile drink.

Inman looked around. Mary's bedroom was truly feminine and completely French. All of the upholstered furniture, other than the **bergère à oreilles** that formed an intimate seating area in the bay window overlooking the front garden were upholstered in pink and white Toile de Jouy matching Mary's bed curtains. Her other principle pieces of furniture included a **poudreuse**, or make-up table, a **bonheur du jour,** a feminine desk, a tall **semanier**, and of course a pair of **chevets**, night stands. Near Mary's bed there was a radio that sat upon a beautiful walnut three tier **Étagère**. It was playing quietly in the background. Over the course of the next several hours, the playlist included, *Would I Love You* by Patti Page, *I Apologize* by Billy Eckstine, *You Belong to Me* from Jo Stafford, *Because of You*, sung by Tony Bennett, *You're Just in Love* from Perry Come and the Fountain Sisters, *My Heart Cries For You* by Guy Mitchel, *If* again by the sultry Jo Stafford, *Too Young* from Nat "King" Cole, *I'm Yours* sung by Eddie Fisher, and *The Little White Cloud that Cried* crooned by Johnny Ray.

Mary placed her palms gently on Inman's cheeks and gently entwined her fingers just under his ears. Inman looked deeply and longingly into Mary's eyes as she pulled him closer and closer. Mary held Inman's cheeks and kissed him passionately, then released her grasp on his face. As they stood there in the long rays of the setting sun, looking longingly at each other, Mary began to unbutton her blouse. She allowed it to drop off of her shoulders and fall to the Persian rug below. After it fell, Mary's eyes glanced down at Inman's buttoned shirt, then back up at his eyes. Inman kept his gaze into Mary's eyes, and unbuttoned his shirt. He untucked it, shucked it off, and let it fall to the rug. Mary reached to her side, unbuttoned and unzipped her skirt. It slid effortless across her silk slip and landed on the rug. Mary then slid her slip down to join her skirt. Inman slowly unbuckled his belt, unbuttoned his trousers and slid the zipper down. He allowed his trousers to slide over his boxers and land in a pile around his ankles.

Inman stepped out of his trousers and looked lovingly at Mary. Mary reached over and stroked Inman's chest with the back of her fingers. She guided them downward to Inman's midriff where she grasped his singlet with both hands and pulled it up confidently over Inman's head. Mary let the singlet sail across the room before taking Inman's hands and placed them behind her back where her bra straps converged. Inman struggled initially with the hooks. He said, "**Je t'aime tellement complètement, es-tu sûr?**" (I love you so completely, are you sure?) Suddenly, Inman deciphered the code to the hooks on Mary's bra. The back straps snapped around and the entire apparatus slid over Mary's arms and fell to the rug revealing the most perfect and beautiful breasts Inman could have ever imagined, even with his earlier sneak peak. Mary, said, "**Je n'ai jamais été aussi sûr de rein dans ma vie!**" (I've never been so sure of anything in my life!) Mary slowly pulled Inman closer for a kiss, but paused to caress his chest with her breasts. Inman was instantly overcome with raw passion. Both of their bodies were crackling with pleasurable sensations.

Inman reached around Mary and ran his fingers down her back, slipped his hands under her panties and grasped her butt cheeks tightly. He kissed her passionately and confidently. As they kissed, Mary began to work Inman's boxers down below his waist. His erection gave her trouble at first, but she figured it out, and slid down with them to her knees. As she slid down, Mary grazed Inman's engorged penis with her cheek. Her eyes fluttered and she sighed. As Mary stood back up, Inman slid his hands into her panties and began to slide them down. As he descended, Inman kissed Mary's beautiful body each step of the way. He kissed her lips, then her neck, the canyon between her breasts, her stomach, then her navel, and finally her mons venus. He then kissed Mary's quivering body all the way back up to her mouth.

Mary and Inman, both quivering in anticipation, were now standing naked before each other in the last rays of orange sunlight that were flooding into Mary's bedroom over the Café curtains. They wrapped their bodies around each other and kissed, with intense passion. They explored each other's bodies uninhibitedly. After a few minutes, Mary took Inman's hand and led him confidently to her magnificent bed. Mary turned back the spread and the sheets and said, "**Si vous voulez de moi, je veux être complètement à vous.**" (If you'll have me, I want to be completely yours.) Inman kissed Mary tenderly on her eyelids. He reached around and grasped her by her buttocks and pulled her body in as close to him as possible. He whispered, "**Je suis à toi pour toujours et un jour.**" (I'm yours, forever and a day.)

While Millicent was happy to stay with the group in the Music room, Blackjack insisted that they move on to another room. They worked their way slowly through the hallway and into the Front Parlor. Blackjack's Scotch was like a beacon lighting their way. Millicent made sure that her wine was visible and held, properly, by the stem of the glass. She hoped to be the antidote to Blackjack's **faux pas**. The circulating bartender made his way to the group with a tray of drinks. The ladies exchanged their near empty glasses for fresh stems of wine. The gentlemen exchanged their glasses for fresh Bourbons. The bartender asked, "A fresh Scotch for you, Mr. Day?" Blackjack shoved his glass at the bartender and waited for him to hand him a fresh drink. Several of the ladies were Millicent's friends, although she saw them only rarely, usually at church. One of them asked Millicent, "How does it feel to be a politician's wife?" Millicent leaned in close to the ladies and out of Blackjack's earshot. "Well, to be honest, it isn't any worse than being married to a Funeral Director. It can't really do me anymore damage socially!" The ladies had a nice chuckle over that.

Mary sat on her ostentatious bed and pulled Inman in on top of her. They both reveled in the sensuality of warm skin contacting warm skin. Inman, although inexperienced, proved to be a gentle and compassionate lover. He took his time and made sure that Mary was comfortable, and that she was completely enjoying each moment of their love making. Mary's new-found confidence in her love and her mate, left her completely unafraid of anyone's hearing their love making. She wouldn't try to stop Inman when she got close to climaxing. Mary's nostrils began to flare, and she started panting deeply. She closed her eyes and tossed her head back into her pillow. After letting out an unashamed "Oh God!" Mary grasped the sheets in the tight grasps of her clenched fists and started hyperventilating. "Oh, yes! Yes! YES! Mary let go of the sheets and relaxed just a bit. She suddenly dug her nails into Inman's butt and said, "I want you in me. I want you deep in me. I want us to be one."

Inman was in nirvana, and completely incapable of speaking. He started massaging Mary's clitoris with the head of his penis. He also started rubbing it between her labia. It was enough to bring Mary to orgasm for a second time. As she climaxed, Mary grabbed Inman's penis and guided it to her vagina. She grabbed his butt and forced him into her. The moment that Inman's penis reached the depth of Mary's vagina, they both felt the world move. They were one. They were one, forever. Their love was locked. Their lives were locked. Their destinies were locked.

Inman worried about Mary's comfort. He knew that his athletic frame would be a great weight for Mary to support, so he relied on his engineering studies and balanced on his knees and elbows to keep the bulk of his weight off of Mary to enhance her pleasure. Instinct kicked in, and Inman began to thrust in, and withdraw from Mary. They both were in a state of pure bliss. Both were oblivious to the fact that Inman was about to climax, until the last minute. Not knowing exactly what he was doing, Inman pulled out at the last minute and came on Mary's belly. Inman dropped and rolled next to Mary. He lay flat on his back staring at the baldaquin crowning Mary's bed. Mary rolled on her side facing Inman. She slid one arm under Inman's neck, and laid the other across Inman's chest. She bent her knee and laid it across Inman as if he was her favorite pillow.

While Mary and Inman were both completely physically spent, the pleasurable sensation from their love making would last, in waves, and echo throughout their bodies until almost noon the next day. No words were spoken for what seemed like an eternity. No words were needed. Mary lay contented in Inman's arms and caressed his massive chest. After a pleasurable while, Mary started to kiss Inman. He sat up in Mary's bed and pulled Mary into his lap and began to kiss her. When his erection returned, he manipulated his penis into Mary's vagina and began to use his muscular legs to lift her up, and lower her down over his penis. Mary's spectacular breasts caressed

Inman's chest as she rode up and down, and they were able to kiss passionately for the entire love-making session.

Millicent spent the remainder of the evening engaging the wives. It was her mission of damage control. After the party, they would all tell their husbands how wonderful it was to see Millicent that night, and that they hoped that Blackjack would win the election. Sadly, Blackjack never understood that Millicent was the only reason he won his race. When they worked their way into the Grand Parlor, which was separated from the Front Parlor by only a double archway, Millicent saw Danton Soleil standing between the fireplace and a floor-to-ceiling window that had been opened to allow guests out onto the rear **véranda** and expansive slate terrace. Blackjack hadn't noticed his old nemesis and continued to work the room. Danton and Millicent caught each other's eyes from across the room. They both tried not to show the longing they felt for each other. The circulating bartender walked up to the group. Once again, this one called Blackjack out by name. Most of them exchanged their drinks and continued listening to Blackjack groan on. Ladies limited themselves to two stems of wine, and white was preferred as it didn't stain. After a short while, they were happy for Blackjack to move on through the room, yet sorry to see Millicent go.

As they got closer to the fireplace, Blackjack spotted Danton. Blackjack gave Danton a cold stare, and pushed through the open window onto the **véranda**, and then onto the terrace. Millicent noticed that she didn't recognize most of the guests on the terrace. It was then that she noticed many of the men were drinking Scotch and the women were either drinking mixed drinks or holding their wine glasses by the bowls. She thought to herself that she'd been sent to "**Gauche**" hell. Blackjack, however, fit right in and received enthusiastic support for his campaign. Millicent was able to take a well needed break from damage control.

At 9:30, Marie Cosette knocked hesitantly on Mary's bedroom door. "Miz Mary, it be haf pas nine! Dat pardie's gon be over'n real soon! Mary was still locked in Inman's embrace with his engorged penis buried satisfyingly deeply in her body. They had been exploring each other's bodies lovingly as if they were one being. Inman showed no emotion, and no embarrassment.

Mary took her paramour's lead. "Thank you, Marie Cosette, we'll be down shortly. Inman kissed Mary's ear and whispered, "I don't like this one bit. I don't want what we're experiencing to ever end." Mary put her index finger across Inman's lips and said, "**Amoureux, sis patient, nous avons le reste dos vies**." (Lover, be patient, we have the rest of our lives.) Inman knew in the depths of his being that his one true love spoke the truth, and said only "**Oui**." as he wilted inside of Mary.

Mary and Inman made out for a while longer, but reluctantly got out of bed. They spent a few more minutes caressing and admiring each other's bodies, before Inman dressed in the clothes in which he arrived, and Mary put on her silk night gown and robe. Inman almost cried as he hugged and made out with Mary in her silk cocoon. Mary put her arm around Inman's waist and Inman reciprocated. Together, they walked down to the foyer of the funeral home and began to make out. They weren't worried about being caught, Marie Cosette was standing guard at the window. As the chimes from the cathedral rang out 10:00, Mary stroked Inman's cheek and said, "**Bonne nuit mon amour, dort bien**." (Good night my love, sleep well.) As Marie Cosette opened the front door for Inman to leave, he paused and said, "**Je ne vais pas dormir ce soir. Je vais me coucher sous les étoiles et me concentrer sur mon amour pour vous**." (I won't sleep tonight. I'll lie under the stars and concentrate on my love for you.) Inman wrapped his arms around Mary, started kissing her passionately, and lifted her off the ground. Once again in paradise, Mary didn't want the encounter to end.

They both knew that it had to end, however. Inman put his lover down and took her hand. He had her follow him down the front steps and to the iron gate. They made out at the place of their first kiss. Mary and Inman could both tell that Marie Cosette was getting extremely worried on the **véranda**, so they reluctantly parted company. Inman started across Saint Charles Avenue. He stopped, in the emptiness of traffic, turned and blew Mary a kiss. From inside the iron gate, Mary placed her palm to her cheek and smiled as broadly as she could. Inman made it to the Neutral Ground just as the Streetcar arrived. Mary watched until the Streetcar was completely out of sight and told Marie Cosette that she was going to bed. Mary went up to her bedroom, got into her bed, and relished in the residual scents of her love-making session with Inman.

Just before 10:00, General Long motioned to 'Fess, and the piano fell silent for a few moments to get everyone's attention. Without any introduction, 'Fess started playing "**La Marseillaise**," and the entire assemblage began singing it **en Français**. As the final strains faded away, everyone lifted their glasses and yelled, "**Vive la France!**" Millicent looked at Blackjack. "You need to go in and tip 'Fess." Blackjack frowned. "Why, didn't the good General pay him?" Millicent sighed. "Of course he'll pay him! …and give him an expensive bottle of Bourbon to boot. That's not the point. If you ever want to hire him for a party, you better go in there, thank him, and give him a nice tip. …and don't be chintzy. …and be sure to tell him that if he'll play for us, you'll have him picked up and driven home in a Cadillac limousine." Blackjack shook his head. He and Millicent walked back through the open window into the grand parlor, and then into the hallway.

Millicent waited for Blackjack in the hallway. Blackjack joined the queue of gentlemen in the music room waiting to thank Professor Longhair for his performance. Blackjack noticed that when 'Fess' took a gentleman's hand, he'd rotate the grasp, leaving his gloved hand on the bottom. When the handshake finished and the gentleman removed his hand, there was a tip in Fess' hand which he acknowledged and slipped into the pocket of his dinner jacket. Blackjack reached into his pocket and pulled out a Quarter and Half Dollar. He debated how much to tip, and settled on fifty cents. When it was his turn, Blackjack took 'Fess' hand, thanked him, and left the silver Half Dollar. 'Fess, said, "Thank you, Mr. Day, and good luck to you." Blackjack smiled and said, "Thank you. I hope one day you will play for one of my wife's parties. I will have you picked up and taken home in my best Cadillac limousine, and agree to the arrangement you have with General Long." Roy nodded his head, "Let me know as early as you can. If I do says so myself, I'm pretty popular." Blackjack agreed, then turned and joined Millicent in the hallway. General and Mrs. Long were working their way through the crowd. Every so often, one of them would lean in to a guest and say, "You know we'd love to see you later." Millicent wasn't surprised when the Long's didn't say that to them. They thanked their hosts for a marvelous Bastille Day party and made their way to Millicent's Cadillac.

Blackjack started the Cadillac and asked Millicent, "Why were they telling people they'd love to see them later?" Millicent turned to look out of the window, "That was the Long's way of telling the 'in crowd' that they would see them later at the **Carousel Bar**, for the after party. I'm afraid we didn't make the cut, dear."

General and Mrs. Long waited for the guests to leave. General Long opened a cabinet and produced an expensive bottle of Bourbon and gave it to "Fess" along with a sealed envelope of cash. "**Caldonia Club** tonight, Roy?" 'Fess smiled. "Yas'sir, if'n you don't mind." The General and Mrs. Long walked through the stair hall, dining room and kitchen to the back door with "Fess." They all got into the car. As he slid into the back seat, the coins in "Fess's" dinner jacket pocket sang out the song that only silver coins sing. General Long said, "...sounds like you had a really good night Roy!" 'Fess said only, "I do think so, sir." They dropped "Fess" at the **Caldonia Club** and made their way to the **Monteleone Hotel**, home of the **Carousel Bar**.

Millicent and Blackjack got into the loaner Cadillac and immediately began to argue about crashing the after party. Blackjack wanted to go, in spite of not being invited. "It's a free country! Why can't we go out for a drink, that just happens to be at the bar the Long's chose for their after-party? Millicent reminded her husband, "You want to be Coroner. To win that election, you've got to do things that you don't want to do, like adhering to social etiquette norms. ...and one of those is, you don't crash a party you weren't invited to." They drove home in silence. Blackjack pulled the Cadillac into the motor court behind the funeral home. He honked the horn and Eddie stepped out of the office. Millicent and Blackjack walked to the kitchen door. Eddie drove the Cadillac into the garage.

Marie Cosette was sitting at the kitchen table when Millicent and Blackjack came in. She stood up respectfully. Blackjack said nothing and rushed past her to his office. Marie Cosette looked warmly at Millicent and said, "**Bonsoir, madame**." Millicent smiled at Marie Cosette. "Good evening, dear one. How has your evening been?" Marie Cosette blushed because, secretly, she knew that she was about to lie, something she wasn't at all comfortable with. "I's been quiet donight. Mary went do bed early, so I'se been on my own, mos'ly." Millicent was concerned. "Is she ill?" Marie Cosette said, "No'me. She'us jus' dired." Millicent said, "Okay." She took a tall glass out of the cabinet, added ice cubes, and poured herself a tall, Blanchard strength, Gin and Tonic. She strolled into the dark Parlor and stared out of the front window across Saint Charles Avenue to the Streetcar Stop, lost in thought.

As she stared out the window, Millicent sensed a familiar odor, that wasn't common in the funeral home. She associated it with Danton, but didn't over think it. When her ice cubes were dry, Millicent walked to the kitchen and placed her glass on the counter by the sink, then walked up stairs. She paused at her bedroom door, and decided to look in on Mary. She knocked on Mary's bedroom door, then opened it and stepped in. Almost immediately, the same smell hit her again, only much stronger. Millicent paused for a moment and looked across the room to Mary's bed. Mary was so still, and Millicent didn't want to disturb her. Mary was, however, wide awake, and frozen by fears of being found out. Millicent closed the door and walked to her bedroom. She convinced herself that the olfactory sensation was a response to her fantasies of Danton. She changed into an azure satin night gown and slipped into bed alone. Millicent engaged her fantasies until she fell asleep. Her fantasies transitioned into to sweet dreams. Across the hallway, Mary lay awake in the moonlight, hopelessly lost in passionate thoughts of Inman. Her body convulsed with the echoes of their evening of passion.

Inman had a difficult time tearing himself away from Mary. He too was experiencing the echoes of their passion. As the Streetcar approached, Inman looked up at Mary's darkened bedroom window. He blew her a kiss, that he hoped she would see, then climbed onto the Streetcar. Inman strode down the aisle with his chest puffed out and found an empty row just ahead of the colored section. He plopped down, sprawling across the entire row. From the colored section, Inman heard, "Um um, um, You done bin up do sum ser'us lovin' donight!" Inman looked across the aisle and a couple of rows back, There was an enormous black woman wearing a heavy wool coat and sunglasses, in spite of the fact it was dark and July in New Orleans. She had an old carpet bag at her feet, and was staring at Inman and laughing quietly. Her hair, unattended for decades, was matted and gnarled, had curled around itself to produce silver-grey locks that looked like fierce snakes. For years people had called her "Medusa," but her name was actually Delphine Voyante. She was a Seer, and based her initial predictions on the scents emanating from people. Delphine could smell love, sex, hatred, remorse, fear, and even anger. She filled in the blanks by how a person reacted to what she was saying. Inman stared inquisitively at her. She shifted in her seat just a bit, "Oh, boy, ju no ju love dat girl, an' ju prob'ly no dat girl be lovin' ju. ...bud, whad ju don' no iz dat iz gonna cosd a lod fo ju do keep'er." Inman was perplexed. "Cost? ...cost what? ...a lot of money?" Delphine looked straight through Inman and leaned forward. "Chil'! Deys lots mo dan money dat coss' peop'l." She started laughing creepily, "Hee, hee, hee, hee, hee."

Inman's eyes grew wider and wider to their physical limitations, and his mouth gaped ever so slightly. He was wondering what the lady would say next. "Boy, ju got somth'n most'n us neva gon' hab. Ju hol' on do dat girl, ju hea' Tain'd gon'a be a eze rid, but id'l end jus fin fo ju boy! Hee, hee, hee, hee, hee, hee, hee." When the Streetcar stopped at Lee Circle, Inman stood up, "Ma'am." He tipped his hat and stepped off the Streetcar. As it rattled on around Lee Circle, and Inman started walking down Howard Avenue, he could still hear the mysterious lady's laughter from the open Streetcar window. "Hee, hee, hee, hee, hee, hee, hee. Hee, hee, hee, hee, hee, hee, hee..... When Inman got back to the **garçonnière**, his mind was racing, mostly with passionate feelings for Mary and memories of their incredible evening of love-making, but also, to an extent, with what, as he described her, the Prescient Mulatto, had foretold to him on the Streetcar. Inman rolled a **chaise longue** out onto the dance terrace and lay awake all night under a canopy of twinkling stars and the arc of a beautiful waning gibbous moon. His body continued to hum with the echoes of multiple orgasms. As he relived the passion, Inman imagined what it would be like if Mary were there atop him, **faire l'amour sous les étoiles**. (Making love under the stars)

CHAPTER THIRTEEN

CAROLINE LEARNS THE TRUTH

The second half of July was a slow time at the funeral home. On the Wednesday after Bastille Day, Blackjack went to the Rotary Club's luncheon meeting in the Central Business District. Millicent and Mary were restless. They both wanted to spend time with their beaux, but knew that a Rotary Club meeting wouldn't afford them the time necessary for a proper date. While Blackjack was out, and at the last minute, a funeral was scheduled to take place on Friday afternoon. Millicent and Mary heard the phone ring in the office. They listened from the hallway and heard Robert "Rob" Reece taking down the pertinent information to prepare for the meeting with the family that afternoon. As soon as they learned that the funeral was to be Friday afternoon, Millicent and Mary went into the parlor to write notes to Danton and Inman.

When the notes were completed and sealed in envelopes, Millicent asked Marie Cosette to deliver them to **Maison Soleil** for them. Marie Cosette accepted her mission with pleasure. These trips were some of the only chances she had to get out of the house, and out from under Hattie's thumb. As Marie Cosette started to leave, Mary had a sudden thought. "What if father comes home and wants to know where Marie Cosette is?" Millicent agreed, and removed her coin purse from her handbag. She gave Marie Cosette two quarters and said, " Stop on the way home and get me some Tonic Water. ...and get yourself a treat too!" Marie Coset smiled and said, "**Oui, madam!**" She went out the kitchen door, down the back stairs, and up Louisiana Avenue to the Streetcar stop.

It had been almost a week, and Inman found that he was starting to worry that "things" had goon too far, too fast. He was sitting in his mother's salon when Marie Cosette rang the bell at the main gate of **Maison Soleil**. He almost jumped right out of his skin, and bolted for the doorway to the **véranda** to see who was at the gate. His whole body was aquiver as he made his way down to the gate. When he recognized Marie Cosette at the gate, his breathing became partially paralyzed, out of fear of bad news. He stood ram rod straight and could only muster one word, "Mary?" Marie Cosette giggled, "Yous'n be hap'y d'no dat Mizz Mary be missin' ju sump'um ter'bal!" Inman exhaled and his entire being relaxed. "Thank you so much Marie Cosette! You can't possibly know what that news means to me." Marie Cosette said, "Druth be dold, is been a slow week ad de fun'ril home. Da on'list fun'ril be on Frysdy. Here, Iz gots notes fo ju and Monsieur Soleil." As Marie Cosette started to offer Inman the notes through the gate, Inman suddenly realized that he was being self-centered and rude. He opened the gate and beckoned for Marie Cosette to come in.

Marie Cosette was completely taken aback by Inman's generosity and acceptance. She hesitated for a moment, but Inman insisted that she come in. "Marie Cosette, my uncle Danton is here visiting my mother and aunt Virginia. He'd want to receive the note directly from you. Please walk with me to the **véranda**, so that uncle Danton can step out and receive your message in person. Marie Cosette's eyes grew wide in astonishment. She paused for one more moment, then stepped through the gate and accompanied Inman up to the **manoir**. They climbed the steps to the **véranda**. Marie Cosette grew wide-eyed when she saw the two semicircular staircases that ascended to the upper floor of Inman's ancestral home. The French doors to Caroline's **salon principale** were open. Inman stepped across the threshold. Danton and Caroline were seated in his mother's matching **bergères**.

Although Caroline and Danton had been engaged in a lively discussion of current events, they both fell silent when they realized that Inman had entered the room. They could also just make out that there was another person on the **véranda**, obscured by the sunshine. Inman couldn't help picking up on his mother's and uncle's pregnant pause. He glanced at his mother, "Mama," then at his uncle, "Uncle Danton, there is someone here with a message for you. Would you like to come out onto the **véranda** to receive it?" Danton looked at the door, but the glare of the sunshine made it impossible to recognize anyone or anything. He then looked at Caroline. It was, after all, her home. Caroline looked at her brother, then at the indistinguishable shape in the doorway, and finally at Inman. "Inman, **cher fils**, (dear son) you've brought this messenger this far, have him come in, **s'il vous plaît**.

Inman found himself in completely unchartered territory. He froze, but for only a moment or two. He motioned for Marie Cosette to enter his mother's **salon principale**. "Mama, may I present Marie Cosette Jardin. She is employed by Mr. and Mrs. Jackson Day of Saint Charles Avenue." Marie Cosette crossed the threshold, but not by much. Caroline squinted to see Marie Cosette, but the glare was too intense. "Dear girl, please come closer, I'm having trouble seeing your face." Marie Cosette, full of apprehension, moved closer, slowly, and curtseyed before Caroline. When Marie Cosette got close enough, Caroline grasped. She caught herself and summoned her wits within a microsecond. Caroline turned her gaze upon her brother for a few seconds, that to him seemed like hours. "So, you work for the Day family? ...do you work in the funeral business?" Marie Cosette grinned, "No ma'am. Iz hep in da kitch'n and wid Miz Day, an Miz Marry."

Caroline stood up and offered her hand to Marie Cosette. "Welcome to **Maison Soleil**, Marie Cosette. Do I understand, correctly, that you have a message for my brother, Danton Soleil?" Marie Cosette shook Caroline's hand, "Yass'm, yass'm, I doos." As Caroline held Marie Cosette's hand, she studied her at close distance. Caroline released Marie Cosette's hand. "Dear child, you have nothing to be nervous about in this home, or anything to fear from anyone in this family. Please... you may give your message to my brother." While still in a state of shock, Marie Cosette turned to Danton,

"Dis be fo ju." She handed the note to Danton. He smiled at her. "Thank you!" Marie Cosette nodded and turned back to Caroline. "Ma'am, I'z be 'specked bak ad de Daze houze. May I'z be goin?" Caroline smiled, "Marie Cosette, thank you so much for taking the time to hand deliver this message to Danton. When you get to the Day's home, please remember me fondly to Mrs. Day." Marie Cosette let out a cleansing breath. "Yass'm. yass'm I'z'l do dat fo ju." She then bolted out of the door headed for the gate. Inman bolted after Marie Cosette so that he could open the gate for her.

When Caroline and Danton were suddenly alone in Caroline's **salon principale**, she stared intently at her brother. Danton squirmed for a few tortuous moments. "What horrible things are you thinking, Caroline?" Caroline sat down and sighed. "I'm not thinking 'horrible things Danton. I know that you are seeing Milly, secretly. While that poses some potential issues, I'm not opposed to it. She is the only person, other than your family that you've ever loved. ...Hmm. Mary and Inman? Dear brother, I've read almost every book ever written, and I can't find a pair in love anywhere in literature better suited for each other, or more in love." Caroline paused. Danton welcomed her pause because he suddenly knew that Caroline now knew the truth, the truth that he had only suspected until he saw his sister's reaction to Marie Cosette.

At last, Caroline summoned the where-with-all to broach the subject of a difficult truth. "Danton, ...that Marie Cosette. ...she's big Inman's daughter, isn't she?" Danton's head sank. "I've suspected it, but there isn't any concrete proof. Her features suggest so. ...but it is all so complicated." Caroline asked, "How is it complicated?" Danton sighed and propped his head in his hand. "Blackjack Day, that evil scoundrel, followed Inman to Marie Catherine's apartment and waited until Inman left to go home. When Inman was safely gone, Blackjack barged into Cat's apartment and forced himself on her, threatening to tell you about her relationship with Inman." Caroline pursed her lips. "So Jackson raped her?" Danton signed, "Yes, and he's been raping her regularly ever since. His abuse led to her drinking, the drugs, and the loss of her career." Caroline could only say, "**Mon Dieu!**" She took a few moments to process all of her thoughts and dry the tears welling op in her eyes. Caroline sat up ram rod straight. "Well, my dear brother, there is no doubt in my mind that this girl is Inman's daughter. There's thankfully not a bit of Andrew Jackson Day in the child." Danton tried to interject, but Caroline raised her right index finger to stop him. Waving her finger, Caroline said, "You don't know that I knew about Inman's betrayal, but I did. It cut me to the bone, but when I confronted Inman, he humbled himself, so very completely. He did everything possible to put things right with me. …but he never had the chance to make things right with Marie Catherine, like he had planned before he was murdered. Danton, we are going to make things right when the time is appropriate. Danton was in a state of complete shock. "Yes. …I agree. …in time."

Inman popped back into the **salon principale**. He looked at his mother and uncle and said, "**Mon Dieu**, it looks like both of you have seen a ghost!" Caroline chuckled, **Mon cher fils**, if that were the case, we'd look like this eternally. There are too many ghosts here in this home from the last 167 years to count!" Inman smiled and sighed. He had no idea that Marie Cosette was his half sister, or that his mother had put all of the puzzle pieces together. Inman excused himself and returned to the **garçonnière** to rest before **dîner.**

CHAPTER FOURTEEN

LAST DAYS OF THE SUMMER OF LOVE

The rest of July and all of August progressed as had June and the first half of July. Millicent kept Blackjack busy with funerals, and campaign appearances, while she and Mary spent much quality time with Danton and Inman. The Friday following the Bastille Day party, Inman told Mary about the mysterious woman on the Streetcar. "She was very large, with wild unkempt wiry hair that looked like snakes!" Mary didn't even have to think about it. "Oh, yes, I've seen her several times. Mama remembers seeing her for years." Inman was surprised. "Could she be that old?" Mary said, "Mama thinks that she is well over a hundred years old. She said that many generations of New Orleans families have called her 'Medusa.' What did she say?" Inman related the encounter with Delphine. "She said that you and I have something that not many people have. ...a strong, true love." Mary clapped her hands together. "Oh, I like that!" Inman continued, "She also said that we would have some hard times ahead." Mary frowned. "...not because of either one of us, though?" Inman smiled, "No, and she said that we would both get through the hard times and be just fine." Mary sighed, "All I know is that I want to spend every minute of every day with you, **mon amour**." Inman smiled and embraced Mary. "**Je ressens exactement la même chose, mon amour!**" (I feel exactly the same way, my love.)

As they walked back to the **garçonnière**, Mary remembered a ride on the Streetcar earlier in the summer before her mother got her Cadillac. "Now that I think about it, I saw Medusa on the Streetcar with my mama. It was June, maybe? I felt an odd feeling and turned around to see her behind us, staring at me. She was rocking back and forth and grinning. I punched mama to get her to turn around. Medusa started this weird laugh, and asked mama if she was still in her 'darkness.' Mama nodded. Then Medusa said that it had a ways to go before it would pass, and that it was going to pull me in too. Mama protested, but Medusa didn't back down. She said that mama was going to have to get strong, and fight the darkness with everything in her being." Inman was amazed at the two encounters with Delphine that, while so random, connected so completely. They made their way down to the dance pavilion and Inman put the first record on the phonograph, a 1932 Ray Noble Orchestra version of *I'll Do My Best to Make You Happy* featuring vocals by Al Bowley. As they foxtrotted, Inman slid his right hand down over Mary's bottom and pulled her in super close. She sighed, and lay her head on Inman's shoulder. He could feel the warmness of her breath on his neck and in his ear. He started breathing deeply and his passion increased.

As the song ended, Inman ignored the spinning record, switched the radio on and guided Mary to the same **chaise longue**, he had routinely wheeled out onto the dance terrace to spend nights dreaming of her under the stars. Inman laid back and pulled Mary on top of him. They started to make out. Inman said, "I'd give anything to not give a damn who knew what we were doing." Mary kissed him, "Un huh. Me too." Inman playfully nibbled at Mary's ear. She melted. "If that were only my breast." Inman smiled, "Yes, but that might be a bit dangerous." Mary said, I don't know how much longer I can take this." Inman nodded. After a few more torturous moments, Mary said, "**... juste un instant, ma douce.**" (...just a moment, my sweet.) She stood up, removed her shoes, then Inman's. She then ran her hands up her legs under her skirt and slid her panties down and tossed them into a chair. Mary unzipped Inman's fly and pulled his engorged penis out. Inman started to hyperventilate. "Are you sure?" Mary smiled coyly, and climbed atop Inman and guided his penis to her wet vagina. Mary was able to orgasm multiple times while keeping a lookout for Monique, in case she was dispatched to check on the teens. When it became apparent that Inman was about to climax, Mary stood up, grabbed a beach towel, and helped Inman to a pleasurable orgasm. After Inman was cleaned up, and his pants zipped back, Mary lay next to Inman on the **chaise longue**, and draped her arm over his chest. They spoke in hushed tones about love and the things they wanted to do together.

Eventually they both became quiet. Neither felt the need to engage in unless dialogue. They were laying there together caressing each other when Monique arrived with **rafraîchissements**. She placed them on a table close to the **chaise longue**. As Monique stood up, she noticed the panties in the chair and smiled. Their secret, however, was completely safe with her. Inman turned on his side so that he could gaze into Mary's extraordinarily beautiful violet eyes. They were connected both mentally and emotionally, and completely. Inman caressed Mary's cheek and said, "**Je t'aime Mary.**" (I love you, Mary.) Mary moved closer and kissed Inman lightly on his lips. "**C'est si bon, parce que je t'aime aussi, Inman.**" (That's so good, because I love you too, Inman.)

Mary and Inman spent the rest of their time that day locked in each other's embrace, adoring each other, and listening to the radio. When the bell rang at the main gate, they both sighed in unison. They stood up and Mary and Inman kissed passionately. "We can't do this up there, so I'll say it here. I love you completely, Mary!" Mary's eyes filled with tears. "I love you with every bit of my being, Inman." They locked themselves in an embrace for as long as they dared, then Inman pulled out his handkerchief and Mary dried her tears as they walked up to the **manoir**. It wasn't until Mary got home and went up to her room, that she realized that not only did she have Inman's handkerchief, infused with his musk, but she had also left her panties at the **garçonnière**. She giggled and thought to herself, "…it's a fair trade." She changed for dinner, and went down to eat with her mama. Her father had taken a heaping plate into his office lair. During dinner, mother and daughter could tell that both had had a wonderful afternoon with their beaux. After dinner, Mary went up to read, but the residual feelings coursing through her body prevented it. She changed into her night gown, and slid beneath the covers with Inman's handkerchief. She fell asleep with it next to her on her pillow. Inman did exactly the same thing with Mary's panties.

Between her scattered August dates with Inman at **Maison Soleil**, Mary thought about, and wondered about what Medusa had said to her mama and Inman. Millicent and Mary were eating luncheon together on Wednesday while Blackjack was at Rotary. "Mama, do you remember that old Mulatto woman whom we talked to on the Streetcar earlier in the summer?" Millicent thought for a moment, "Medusa! ...Yes I do. I'd almost forgotten." Mary asked, "Didn't you tell me that she has been riding the Streetcar for generations?" Millicent put her fork down, and smiled slyly. "Yes, I remember her from when I was a young girl riding the Streetcar to go shopping with **grand-mère**. ...In fact, Caroline Carnes would remember her too. She has always looked the same. ...same coat, same dark glasses, same scary hair, same carpet bag."

Mary asked, "Did she scare you when you were young?" Millicent let out a guffaw. "Scare us, heavens no. We were too busy enjoying her sessions with the other riders. She never said anything to me until... just before..." Mary perked up, "Just before what, exactly?" Millicent started to tear up. "...just before my life came crashing down, that's when." Mary thought, "...so that's the darkness she was speaking of???" Millicent looked away, through the parlor and to the Streetcar stop. "Yes." Mary was intrigued. "Mama, I want to see her. I want to see if she has anything to say to me."

Millicent sighed, "...be careful what you wish for. You may not like what you hear." Millicent added, "...and your father won't let you out alone." Mary said, "You could send me on errands. ...and insist that Marie Cosette go with me. ...short errands, day errands, when Inman can't leave **Maison Soleil**. We could go to the drug store, to the dry cleaners, to anywhere that wouldn't take too long. ...a ride out, and a ride back." Millicent said, "You never know when she'll be there. It's almost like she's only there when she has something to say to you." Mary smiled, "That's it! I can be useful, and if she has a message for me, she'll be there. If not, Marie Cosette and I will come home." Millicent agreed, reluctantly, mostly to get Mary to end her line of questions about Delphine's prophesy for her.

Several times a week, mostly when Blackjack was preoccupied, Millicent sent Mary and Marie Cosette on errands on the Streetcar. For weeks they came back without seeing Delphine. Towards the end of August, on the way back from the drug store, Mary and Marie Cosette boarded the Streetcar. They were preoccupied with their hysterics over the plight of a young Tulane student who was trying to buy condoms at the Drug Store. He was being given the third degree from a Mrs. Todd, one of the cashiers. She was about four feet tall, four feet wide, and four feet thick. She had on a tight dark navy wool dress over unforgiving foundations. The dress would have been more attractive if it had been made out of used burlap. Her rakish, cat style reading glasses hung on a beaded chain around her neck, and she displayed her pride and joy, a gaudy Sara Coventry broach over her massive left bosom. "What do you need these for, you Playboy?" Mary and Marie convulsed with laughter as they bounded out of the Drug Store headed for the Streetcar. For once, they weren't looking for Delphine. They sat on the slatted Streetcar bench and tried to gather their composure. It took a couple of tries to assuage their hysterical laughter.

Before long, they heard, "Well, well, well, I hurd ju wan'd do dalk do me." Mary and Marie Cosette jumped up and turned around. It was Madame Delphine Voyante. Mary started, "How…" Delphine cut her off. "Ho'd I no ju wan'd do dalk do me? A bedder quesdun be, 'Wy'd I make ju waid zo lon'?'" Mary found some courage. "Madame Medusa, I…" Mary was cut off for a second time. "My nam ain' 'Medusa!' …an' I'm only dellin' ju dis becas ju are only de secon' do say id do my face. …an ju, like de las' was 'speckful. 'Madam!'" Mary couldn't breath. "Chil' dey's a lod o' guud in ju. My name is **Delphine Voyante**." Mary breathed in and out deeply, "Madam Voyante, a while ago, you said that my mother's darkness was going to come after me. I wanted to ask you about that." Delphine grinned, "O kose ju do! …caus ju no dat boy be in love wid ju." Mary smiled, "Yes, that's true. Do you remember seeing him recently?" Delphine laughed, "Hee, hee, hee hee, ob kose I do. I dol im dat ju two gonna hab sum dark days, bud ju'll be fine 'vend'lly."

Mary thought for a moment, " so, I can trust him?" Delphine said, "Jes, ju wan' ne'er no no'un else. De darkness iz gon come don on yu bodth like nuttin' ju culd 'magin'. Ju jus gotta drus' dat he's'l fin a way outt'n dey darkness. Ju hea?" Mary nodded and said, "Yes ma'am, I hear you." Marie Cosette asked, "Madam Voyante, why do ju wea' dose dark glasses ad night?" Delphine bowed up. "Chil,' ju'd no betta, if'n de darkness han' ruin'd jo mama. Ju grand-mères are weepin' fo ju, caus' ju ain't ben daughd. I ware dese do prodec' ju. I'd be deaf fo' ju or anyon' else do look in my eyes. Ju shud be mo worr'd about dat damn darkn's dat's dryin' to dak ju." Marie Cosette looked surprised, "Dake me?" Delphine said, "Look, iss Louisiana Abenu, jo sdop. bud jes, ju nedda no dat de dark one is drying do dake ju. Ju bot' hab som' dougf dimes ahed' bu ju's got por'ful forces on ju side. an' ju go' love. hol' on'a dat. Now go, an be car'ful!" Mary and Marie Cosette stood up. Mary, said, "**Merci madame Voyante et bonne soirée.**" (Thank you Madam Voyante, and have a nice evening.) Delphine smiled at Mary and Marie Cosette as they left the Streetcar. As the Streetcar continued down Saint Charles Avenue, Mary and Marie Cosette could hear Delphine laughing. "Hee, hee, hee, hee, hee, hee, hee. Hee, hee, hee, hee, hee, hee, hee….." They liked arms and walked down Louisiana Avenue to the motor court behind the funeral home and climbed the stairs to the kitchen door. Hattie swung around. "Is about time, Missy. Dis here dinner ain't gonna cook itself!" She gave Marie Cosette her chores as Mary walked into the dining room intent upon going straight up to her bedroom to consider Delphine's frightening words.

As Mary walked through the parlor, she heard her mother's voice from the shadows of the far corner of the room. "Mary, you look as if you've seen a ghost!" Mary froze in the center of the room. …and said nothing. Millicent stepped out of the shadows and looked carefully at Mary's face. "You saw her. You saw Medusa." Mary nodded her head, slowly. "Come on, I want to hear all about this, but you look you've gone through the ringer. Let's go up to your room." Mary followed her mother up the stairs and into her room. She sank onto an ebony and guilt **récamier**, upholstered to match her pink palace.

Millicent disappeared into Mary's bathroom and returned with an enameled basin of warm water and wash cloths. Mary laid her head on the bolster and propped her ankles on the low side of the **récamier**. Her mother squeezed out a cloth and laid it over Mary's forehead and eyes. The warm and calming sensation caused Mary to breath in deeply, and sigh. Millicent changed Mary's warm compress. "I should have prepared you better for a meeting with Medusa. There were several times it knocked all of the air out of my sails too." Millicent walked over to the window and looked down at the Streetcar stop in the neutral ground between the lanes of Saint Charles Avenue for a few moments. She then returned to Mary and freshened her compress. "**Ma chérie, je suis ici pour te parler, seulement quand tu seras prêt.**" (My darling, I'm here to talk you through this, only when you're ready.) Mary smiled, and said only, "Hummmm." Millicent added, maybe it's time to start telling you some of our family stories. Did I ever tell you about the day you were born?" Mary shook her head. Millicent changed warm compresses and began her story.

"By early November of 1934, I was near term with my pregnancy. I was having difficulty walking and rarely left the funeral home. Your father's business had picked up exponentially. Not only was he receiving a great number of death calls, but also the quality "profitability" of the booked funerals was improving steadily as well. I had been helping families with the arrangements for their loved ones. It kept me quite busy, and prevented me from focusing on how much excruciating pain I was feeling both physically and emotionally."

"On Thursday, the 22nd. of November, the phone rang. Your father answered it and took down some notes. He went into the garage and gave Johnny Hardwick a slip of paper with an address and a contact person. He said, 'Take the Cunningham, it suits her.' Johnny and Harry Cawe got into our jet black 1929 Cunningham Hearse and went out to retrieve a body."

"They returned with the body of Lulu White, the legendary Grand Madam of Storyville. Some had said that Lulu died in 1931, and still others insisted that they had, in fact, witnessed her make a bank withdrawal in 1941. Her storied legend blossomed into mythology in New Orleans, and sightings continued for many years. But, there she was, one week, exactly, before Thanksgiving Day of 1934, on a gurney in the basement of our funeral home. Your father and I couldn't resist temptation, and pulled the shroud back to gawk at Lulu's face."

"Now, Lulu White was a large woman. She was of mixed race, although the degree was never proven. Her face was round and full. Her eyes were somewhat small and sunk deep beneath her brow. Her nose and lips were average in size. Her hair was cropped just above her shoulders. Her bosom was enormous, which wasn't unheard of for women of her era. She was barely five feet tall, but weighed at least 180 lb. Lulu was dressed in a nightgown, and had evidently died peacefully in her sleep. There was no evidence of her extravagant jewelry other than the patches of lighter hued skin where the jewelry had shaded her skin from the Sun's rays."

"After a few minutes of gawking, I noticed the folded towel that draped over Lulu's head and was tied beneath her jaw. I said, 'Jackson, do you suppose that she had a toothache?' Your father doubled over in laughter, and said, 'Oh, no. That was tied there after death to keep her mouth closed!' Jackson was still amused about the toothache and forgot to replace the shroud as we walked slowly back to the office to plan Lulu's funeral."

"We hadn't been in the office long when I shouted out in pain. I shot up out of my chair gasping for air. Jackson looked up as I leaned over and grabbed the edge of the desk. With a queer look on his face, Jackson asked, 'Are you okay? What's going on?' I was gasping and panting. I cried, 'Call Doctor Scrope. It's time.' Your father leaned back in his chair and quipped, 'How do you know that it's time, exactly?' I slowly lifted my head and looked your father dead in the eyes. I'd like to think that the look nearly burned holes through his skull. Angrily, I said, 'My - water - just - broke. Call - Doctor - Scrope!'"

"Your father picked up the phone and with trembling hands dialed the Touro Infirmary. As it happened, Dr. Scrope was tied up in an extremely difficult delivery. The Infirmary instructed Jackson to make me comfortable, in my bed, and they would send a Midwife. Jackson had never found it especially easy to accept instructions from anyone. He slammed down the phone and went to the door. He called for Johnny Hardwick and Harry Cawe. He intended to have them put me on a gurney, put me in the Cunningham Hearse, and drive me around the block to the Touro Infirmary."

"Johnny and Harry were able to get me on the Gurney, but you were coming real fast. The Midwife arrived in the midst of the chaos of my screams and the men trying to load me into the Hearse. She wasn't happy at all to see me on a gurney, and not in my bed, but, by then, it was too late. The Midwife asked if there was a room that was cleaner than the garage. Your father instructed Johnny and Harry to wheel me into the embalming room. I was too preoccupied with the pain to hear where I was headed."

"By that time, Rob Reece and Roger Whacker, your father's embalmers, had with great effort, moved Lulu White's body onto the great white porcelain embalming table. Her nightgown had been removed, and minimal drapes covered her bosom and privates. Johny and Harry wheeled me next to Lulu White so that they could reposition the overhead lights to aid the Midwife. They elevated my head and upper torso. My clothes were cut off, discretely under drapes, thankfully. My contractions were coming closer and closer. I decided that I needed something to focus on. For some inexplicable reason, it turned out to be Lulu White's towel wrapped head."

"As your head began to crown, Harry accidentally bumped into the embalming table. The shock caused Lulu's head to roll to the right. Her eyes were open, and as her head turned to face me, the towel holding her jaw loosened. Lulu's mouth dropped open and a guttural rush of air escaped her that sent cold shivers all throughout my being. I shut my eyes and held them closed with trembling hands."

"In my self-imposed darkness, I could see clearly the irony of the juxtaposition of Lulu White, who, in her life, exuded strength and independence, with myself, who was weak and dependent upon a husband she didn't love. In my depression, I thought my only worth to society was as a high class breeder. I thought about the only man I had ever truly loved, and cried."

"You were born with no complications. The Midwife cut the cord and cleaned you with great tenderness. She wrapped you in sheets that Hattie had brought from the linen closet upstairs. It was a fight to get me to open my eyes and meet you, **Ma fille chérie**. (My darling daughter.) The Midwife assured me that she had covered Lulu's face. Hesitantly, I removed my hands and opened my eyes. Upon my first glance at you, I began crying tears of overwhelming joy. I took you into a warm embrace, and completely forgot about Lulu White's lifeless body next to me on the embalming table. For the next several minutes, the Midwife delivered the placenta and placed it in a slop jar."

"Just as a precaution, your father had Johnny and Harry load you, me, and the Midwife into our 1929 Packard Ambulance. I was relieved not to be transported in the un-sanitized Cunningham Hearse but refused to allow anyone to take you as I was loaded into the Packard. The Midwife sat next to me in an Art Deco chrome and purple velvet jump seat. Johnny and Harry sat in the front seats. Johnny drove us slowly around the block to the Touro Infirmary, near the intersection of Louisiana Avenue and Prytania Street. Once unloaded at the Emergency Department, The Midwife took you to the Nursery, and I was moved into the Maternity Ward, consoled by promises that the Nursing Staff would bring you to me soon."

"Instead of visiting us, your father went back to his office. There were Funeral plans to be made, and gambling books to review. I was told later that it wasn't long before Jackson became extremely annoyed by the mess in his office. Your father went to his door and yelled for Eddie Smith, one of our Porters, to come in and clean up the birthing mess in his office. At the same time, Rob Reece was hard at work preparing Lulu White's corpse for her service and burial. Roger Whacker was pressing Lulu's burial gown and gloves. He had already called the Hair Stylist and Make-up Artist. They were due to arrive momentarily. Jackson stepped into the embalming room and reminded Rob and Roger how important this funeral was. They both later told me that they looked at each other, desperately wanting to say that your father should be at Touro Infirmary with you and me. The staff was perfectly capable of caring for the Madam's arrangements without the boss. ...but no-one was brave enough to say anything."

Millicent's story had yanked Mary back into present. She sat up. "I think that I'm starting to understand the "Darkness." Millicent sighed deeply and said, "Medusa said it would eventually pass." Mary said, "Her name isn't Medusa. She told me her name. It's Delphine Voyante." Millicent was astounded, "She told you her name?" Mary said, "Yes, I made the mistake of calling her Madam Medusa, and she corrected me. She said that I was only the second person brave enough to call her that, but since I had been polite, she told me her real name." Millicent said, "Really? That's good to know, I don't think that our business is over, and I'd like to be as respectful to her as possible." Mary said, "Mama…." Millicent replied, "Yes, dear?" Mary hesitated for a moment then asked, "Mama, in your story, you said something about 'gambling books, and we had to wait for father at his 'Bank House' recently. What does all of that mean?" Millicent stood up and smiled, "My dear, I've told you one deep dark secret today. Let's save that story for another day, okay?" Mary grinned, "Okay, mama, you're right, I've taken in quite a lot today. We'll save that story for another day."

Mary's and Inman's dates continued through August. When September arrived, they had but one more weekday date planned before Inman was slated to begin working at the family Factorage on Monday, September the 8th. It was on Friday, September 5th. Mary and Millicent eagerly wrote their notes to Inman and Danton on the 2nd, as soon as the funeral was booked and sent Marie Cosette to Howard Avenue to deliver the news to Inman and Danton. Marie Cosette was completely taken aback when Monique came out to open the gate. "Madam would like for you to join her for **rafraîchissements**." Marie Cosette had no idea how to respond. She tensed up and followed Monique to the **manoir**. Monique stepped into the **salon principale**, and announced, "Mademoiselle Marie Cosette Jardin…." Caroline stood and walked toward Marie Cosette. "**Bon après-midi, jeune femme!**" (Good afternoon, young lady!) Marie Cosette curtseyed, "**C'est un plaisir ma dame.**" (It's a pleasure, my lady.) Caroline was thrilled. While she didn't say a word, she knew that Millicent had been a good tutor of both French and manners. Caroline smiled broadly and said, "**Je sais que vous avez des messages, mais rejoignez-nous d'abord pour un rafraîchissement.**" (I know that you have messages, but please join us for refreshments first.) Marie Cosette smiled and accepted. She was completely out of her comfort zone, and had no idea why Inman's family was treating her so kindly. Caroline led her family into the **salle à manger** (dining room) and described the various and sundry treats to Marie Cosette. She overcame her trepidation and slowly started to sample the **hors d'oeuvres** and took a glass of Coca - Cola and ice chips. After Marie Cosette was served, Caroline asked her sister Virginia to join her at the buffet. Finally, Caroline beaconed for Danton and Inman to tuck in. The odd group snacked, drank, and exchanged small talk for just under thirty minutes. Danton and Inman were growing anxious to receive their notes, and Marie Cosette was growing anxious to be released from a situation that made no sense, and made her uncomfortable.

Danton and Inman escorted Marie Cosette out to the **véranda** where she gave them their messages. She waited for them to read the notes, just in case there would be an answer. Marie Cosette rather enjoyed seeing the smiles bloom on Danton and Inman's faces. Almost in unison, they both said, "**Oui!**" Marie Cosette was caught up in their enthusiasm and grinned. "I'z'll dell diem, dat ids a dade, den! Danton reached into his pocket and pulled out four quarters. "Marie Cosette, you have gone to a lot of trouble to keep us informed this summer. You may know that Inman starts work on this coming Monday, the eighth. Please take this small honorarium to know that Inman and I appreciate your efforts above and beyond your responsibilities for the Day household." Marie Cosette had been a courier simply out of love for Millicent and Mary, and didn't think a tip was warranted. She froze, and suddenly found herself with an ounce of coin silver in her palm. Slowly, she closed her fingers around the coins, and somewhat reluctantly accepted them. Inman walked her to the gate and stood out on Howard Avenue as Marie Cosette walked slowly up to Lee Circle to get on the Streetcar.

When Friday finally arrived, Millicent suggested at breakfast that she and Mary pay a visit to **Maison de Bringier**. Mary was overjoyed. "I suppose that we won't be swimming today!" Millicent chuckled, "I suppose not. ...nor will I!" Just after an early lunch, Millicent and Mary made their escape. Millicent drove them down to Canal Street and parked. They walked to **Maison de Bringer** for several hours of beauty. Hair, nails, pedicures, the works, even makeup. They both walked out of the Salon looking like fashion plates.

Wolf whistles came from every corner. Neither broke their straight ahead stares, but were smiling on the inside. They got back into the Cadillac, and Millicent drove to Howard Avenue. She let Mary off and continued back to Canal Street and found a parking space near Maison Blanche. Millicent rode the brass elevator up and opened her brother's warehouse. She worked on her **hors d'oeuvres** while she waited for Danton.

Mary rang the bell at the main gate at **Maison Soleil**. Caroline had persuaded Inman to allow Monique to answer the bell. It was, after all, the way upper class households functioned. It took all of his breeding, and all of his being, to resist running to the gate. Inman stood next to his mama's nest and waited for Monique to escort Mary to the **salon principale**. After Monique stepped across the threshold from the **véranda** and introduced "Miss. Mary Charmaine Day." Inman stepped lively across the floor and took Mary's hands. He kissed her on both cheeks, as was the custom, and walked with her, holding her hand, over for her to greet his mama. Mary leaned down and took Caroline's hands. "**Je suis si heureuse de vous voir madame Soleil, ma mama me fait de grands voeux.**" (I'm so happy to see you Madam Soleil, my mama sends warm wishes.) Caroline's face lit up. "**Je suis sûr que votre mère est extrêmement fière de vous. Vous êtes tout à fait la jeune femme!**" (I'm sure your mother is extremely proud of you. You are quite the young lady.) Mary blushed. "Thank you, I am a Blanchard, after all." Caroline let out an enthusiastic "Ha" and said, "Yes, my dear, you are, and you wear it well!"

To Inman's surprise, Mary asked Caroline, "Madam Day, my mother told me that when you were both young friends, you sometimes saw a Mulatto woman riding on the Streetcar and predicting the future. Is that true?" Caroline sighed, Yes, I suppose you're speaking of Delphine." Mary was dumbfounded. "You know her real name?" Caroline said, "Of course I do, I've spoken to her many times over the years. Why are you so surprised?" Mary paused for a moment, then said, "I saw her the other day. I called her Madam Medusa. Everyone I know calls her that. She told me that Medusa wasn't her name, but she'd tell me her real name because I was only the second person to call her that to her face, and was respectful." Caroline sank back confidently into the well-worn silk luxury of her **bergère à oreilles**. The truth hit Mary immediately. "It was you, wasn't it? You made a bond with her, didn't you?"

Caroline confessed. "Yes, I have known Delphine since I was a little girl. I admired her from afar for years. It was just before Inman was born that she spoke to me. She told me that he would be born during a dark moon, an eclipse. …and he was. She also told me that an evil 'Darkness' would descend on my family not long afterward. At the time, I didn't think much of it, but when big Inman was murdered, I rode the Streetcar many times desperately wanting for Delphine to clarify her predictions. When Delphine finally made an appearance, she hedged. She told me only that the 'Darkness' would hang over my family, and other families, for years, but that it would eventually be driven away. She said that there were many others who would suffer, but that there were many good souls who would endeavor to vanquish the 'Darkness.'" Out of desperation, I invited her to call on me here. She did so, on several occasions. I plied her with expensive Bourbon, but she held onto most of her visions. She always said it for my own good. The last thing that I managed to extract from her was about Inman. Delphine said that Inman would be the cause of all of the healing, both in my family, and in the other families that had been affected by the 'Darkness.'"

Inman guarded himself. He knew that it wouldn't be a good idea if he admitted to seeing the prescient Mulatto on the Streetcar. After all, he thought that his mama had no clue that he regularly left the property at night. Inman also had no idea that Delphine had told his mama that at a certain point he would venture out and find a solution to their problems. Delphine conveniently forgot to say that the solution to the problem might ultimately be more bitter, for a while, than the actual problem. Inman found himself stressed, and wanting to escape to the **garçonnière** to have some private time with Mary. Caroline could sense her son's agitation and said, "You two go on down to the **garçonnière** and dance, and have fun. I'll send Monique in a few minutes with **rafraîchissements**. Inman found himself amazingly relieved. He grabbed Mary's hand. "Thanks, mama." He almost yanked Mary off her feet in an effort to leave the conversation about Delphine.

When Mary and Inman got down to the **garçonnière**, they cleared their romantic air of the tense moments they'd experienced with Inman's mother. That tension was the least of their worries. They both worried about Delphine's predicted "Darkness." They both worried that their love wasn't strong enough to survive the "Darkness." At last Inman took a stand. "'Darkness,' or no 'Darkness,' I pledge to you that for as long as I am alive, I will love you. ...you only, and you unconditionally. Mary started to cry. She buried her face in Inman's shoulder for a few moments, then lifted her face and said, "I pledge to you, **mon amour**, that I will be, forevermore, true to you, and to you only." As much as they both wanted to dance and have a good time, the mood had been completely destroyed. Inman switched the radio on. Its tubes warmed up, and began playing the best of AM standards. The major revolt in popular music had just started in cities like New York and San Fransisco. New Orleans was still playing the classics. While the commercials were playing, Mary and Inman made their way to their accustomed **chaise longue**. As they reclined together, the commercials ended, and Mary and Inman found themselves serenaded by Frank Sinatra. He was singing his hit, ***All the Way***. Mary and Inman melted into each other deeper and deeper with each line of the song. By the dramatic musical bridge, they were both weeping. They kissed. While their kissing, this time, was more romantic than passionate, it seemed extraordinary, and they began to truly comprehend what a relationship truly encompassed. Maybe Madam Delphine was right. Mary and Inman decided to expel all doubt and embrace a connection that they knew to be complete and unbreakable.

When the inevitable bell at the main gate rang, Mary and Inman, who had been quite content simply to be in each other's arms for the last couple of hours, sighed. They untangled themselves and stood up. Mary put her arms around Inman and said, "I hate that our dates have to change." Inman reminded Mary that the funeral home could always schedule funerals on Saturdays and Sundays. Mary smiled. "That's true, but father charges more for Saturday, and even more for Sunday." Inman's face lit up and he said, "That would be a good reason to push those days!" Mary replied, "That's true. I'll mention that to mama on the way home."

They walked arm in arm up to the **manoir**. Caroline and Millicent were having an animated conversation when they crossed from the **véranda** into Caroline's **salon principale**. Both mothers looked up at the couple with big smiles on their faces, and endless love in their hearts. Millicent asked, "So Inman, are you excited about starting to work on Monday?" Inman beamed, "Yes ma'am, Madam Day. There's so much to learn. I'll be so busy that the days will pass too quickly. Millicent added, "Will you miss your lazy hazy days of summer?" Inman looked at Mary. "I'll only miss the time that Mary and I spent together. We'll just need to figure out when we can spend time together now."

Caroline offered a partial solution. "Milly, what if you and Mary had lunch with Danton and Inman on funeral days? Danton has fine chef in the commissary. I'm sure he might have an occasional afternoon meeting, but surly he could take time to eat with you and Mary." Caroline smiled, "I'll speak to him later at **dîner**." Mary and Inman immediately loved the idea. Millicent kept her composure. She didn't know how much Caroline knew, or if she'd approve of her extra-marital relationship with her brother. "That would be wonderful for Mary and Inman. Please, do speak to him about it." With it being time for Millicent and Mary to get back to the Garden District, Caroline stood and met Milly halfway across the room. They embraced and told each other how much their visits meant to them.

Inman walked with Millicent and Mary down to the gate to see them out. As he opened the gate, Millicent said, "Mary, I'm going to go and crank the car. Say '**Bonsoir**' to Inman, and for heaven's sake, forget that I'm here. I've seen you kiss him many times! **Bonsoir**, Inman!" Inman's mouth dropped open a little, and he responded out of muscle memory, "**Bonsoir, madam Day**!" Millicent had pulled the car past the gate, when she had arrived, not wanting to be in the young couples' line of sight. She had, however, positioned the rear view mirror so that she could revel in the sight of two such fine young people so deeply in love. Mary and Inman cuddled and kissed sensually for a short while, knowing that it would be better for Millicent and Mary get back at a respectable time so as to not arouse any suspicion in Blackjack. Finally, Inman took the plunge and walked Mary to the loaner Cadillac. He opened

Mary's door and offered his hand to assist her entry. He closed the door and leaned through the open window. "**J'ai hâte de déjeuner lundi**." (I'm looking forward to lunch on Monday.) Mary beamed and said, "**Je peux difficilement attendre**!" (I can hardly wait!) She then reached up and pulled Inman's face to hers and kissed Inman in such a beautiful way that Millicent had to turn her head away and sigh deeply. Inman patted the car door with his hands twice and said, "Monday." Millicent pulled away from the curb, and Mary leaned out of the window and yelled, "Yes, Monday." After several moments of silence, Mary said, "Mama, Inman asked why Father doesn't actively encourage funerals on Saturdays and Sundays, since they bring in more money." Millicent stopped at a traffic signal and pondered the notion. She pondered it through the light and got honked from behind. As she regained her composure, Millicent said, "Genius, that's pure genius!

I'll figure a way to make Jackson think that it's his idea, too."

CHAPTER FIFTEEN

WINDS OF CHANGE

On Monday, September 8th., Danton pulled to the curb at the **garçonnière** gate at 7:30. He was surprised that Inman was standing on the sidewalk outside of the gate, raring to go. Inman jumped into his uncle's Packard, and Danton started down Howard Avenue toward the Wharf. Inman was confused when Danton turned left onto Saint Peter Street. Danton sensed Inman's confusion. "First of all, we own the company. We don't punch time clocks. Second, Lucy Butler is a gift from God. You will grow to appreciate her as much as I do, but, the dear woman couldn't brew a drinkable cup of coffee if her life depended upon it. Ironically, for some unexplainable reason, our employees love her coffee. We're going to Café du Monde for **café au lait** and **beignets**. Inman found himself quite happy. He was away from **Maison Soleil**, about to enjoy a new experience, and then start to work, learning the family business. Danton found a parking space on Decatur Street, and he and Inman strolled into Café du Monde. They took seats at a small round table and a waiter came over and took their orders. They both ordered **beignets** and **café au lait**. While they waited for their order, Danton first told Inman about the Café du Monde lean. He explained, " If you don't lean way over the table, the confectioner's sugar will get all over your clothes." Inman appreciated the simple solution to a sugary problem. Danton then told Inman, "There is a 90% chance that the sugar that we'll eat here today, was grown at **Beau Cadeau.**" Inman said, "I've heard so many stories about my papa's plantation, but I've never seen it. Do you think now that I'm working, that we could go up there?" Danton was elated. "Yes, that part of the business belongs entirely to you and your mama. It's a huge undertaking, and you need to learn that part too."

The waiter brought Danton and Inman their **café au lait** and **beignets.** In the silence of enjoyment, Inman started to look around the **café**. He was amazed with the number of tables, and the number of orders being rushed out. "How do they ever keep up with demand?" Danton signaled to their waiter. "Would you take my nephew back to see how the kitchen produces so many **beignets**?" The waiter replied, "**Certainement! Si vous me suivez monsieur.**" (Certainly! If you'll follow me sir.) The waiter took Inman back to the kitchen. There were several stations, each providing their part to the recipe. There was a prep kitchen where the ingredients were weighed out and sent to the mixing room. In the mixing room, there were several massive Hobart mixers outfitted with dough hooks. When the ingredients had been combined in the the mixers and turned into dough, it was sent to a machine that pressed it flat, and stretched it. From there the dough was heavily flowered and run through a rotating cutter that produced uniform ingots of dough. The oddly shaped pieces were cleared away and thrown back into the waiting dough.

The perfectly uniform squares of dough were picked up by a portly employee, and tossed into the fat. In testimony to his prowess, and years on the job, the cook never looked back to where he was tossing the dough. They always landed squarely in the bathtub sized fryers. When the entire sheet of dough had been cut and tossed into the fat, the portly gentleman used what looked like a stainless steel basket at the end of a long pole to turn and manipulate the frying French doughnuts. For the last few minutes of the frying session, the cook lowered a mesh grid to keep the **beignets** submerged in the boiling fat. After a few minutes the grate was lifted, and the **beignets** were floating and dancing on the surface of the rolling molten fat. The cook then dipped them out with the stainless steel basket and transferred them to a large stainless steel box in the service area where they were plated and heavily dusted with confectioner's 10x sugar. Inman watched until he instinctively knew the process. In so doing, Inman determined several ways that the process could be made more efficient, but he held his thoughts. Not wanting to keep his uncle Danton waiting on his first day of work, Inman returned and suggested that they both go to work. Danton agreed, but not before ordering a to go order for Lucy Butler.

Millicent and Mary were enjoying their breakfast, at last. Blackjack had boorishly gobbled his breakfast and retreated to his office lair. After Blackjack left, Millicent turned to Mary and said. "I was successful." Mary looked at her mother with a look of complete confusion. Millicent added, "I got your father to come to the conclusion that he should actively advertise weekend funerals," Mary was suitably impressed. "How'd you pull that off?" Millicent looked up and to the left. "I told him last night how much I admired him for sticking to his guns about the boys working overtime. I told him that other funeral homes had given their employees salaried positions that were more than the full time hourly rate, but far less than what the overtime for even one weekend funeral would be, but I thought that it was wise to pay the employees a set weekly rate and forget weekend business." Mary's face erupted in a huge grin. "Oh no. You didn't!" Millicent breathed in deeply and sat up straight in her chair. "Oh, yes I did. You could see the numbers flying around in his head on his face. He told me first thing this morning that he had come up with a new business model. He was going to give the boys a raise, but make them salaried. He was so proud of himself. He took it a step further, and decided to make weekend funerals the same price as week day funerals. ...all of a sudden, he's determined to be the King of weekend funerals." Mary wanted to cheer, but knew that she oughtn't. Instead, she got up, ran to her mother and hugged her tightly, Mary whispered into Millicent's ear, "**Remercier vous tellement mama!**" (Thank you so much mama!) Millicent replied, "Well, it's as much for me as it is for you, but you're very welcome!"

Mary returned to her seat, but, uncharacteristically, picked up her plate and went back to the chaffers for seconds. Millicent had another of her moments when she found herself suspecting the impossible. She let it go. By 9:45, the entire funeral home staff was in a swivet. The "guest's" dress didn't fit, and was fighting with the staff against all of their tricks to make it "fit." In addition to that, the make-up lady and hairdresser hadn't arrived. Blackjack was completely beside himself. He was shouting at employees and pounding his fists. Millicent distracted Blackjack for just long enough to say, "We're leaving." Blackjack made a disagreeable noise with his mouth and brushed past his wife and daughter to make his staff's lives just a little more miserable, without offering any solutions for their problems.

Millicent and Mary went out the kitchen door, down the stairs to the motor court, and got into Millicent's loaner Cadillac. Millicent fired it up and they were off on their way to Canal Street and the Salon of **Maison de Bringier**. After just over two hours of beauty, Millicent piloted the Cadillac back to Lee Circle, and then down Howard Avenue to the Wharf. She drove into the warehouse and pulled to a stop outside the General Offices. As Millicent and Mary exited the car, they were greeted by Lucy Butler. Danton had told Lucy that Millicent was a potential client, but Lucy knew better. She escorted Millicent and Mary deep into the General Offices, and to the Board Room. As the door swung open, Danton arose from his papers and greeted the ladies. Mary was distracted and looking around for Inman. Danton saw her discomfort. "My dear, Inman is out on the Wharf watching a ship being unloaded. Would you like for me to have someone take you out there?" Mary said, "Yes, please. That would be lovely. Thank you!" Danton said, "Lucy, if you please, take Mary to the Security Office and have Clement escort Mary out to where Inman is." Lucy nodded to Danton, and motioned for Mary to follow her. Together, they walked to the Security Office. Lucy smiled at Clement. "This is Mademoiselle Mary Day. Monsieur Soleil would like for you to escort her to Monsieur Carnes, if you please." Clement looked first at Mary, then at Lucy and said, "**Certainment**." Mary thanked Lucy Butler for her troubles and then followed Clement through the warehouse. They passed a huge object covered in a massive canvas tarp. Mary asked Clement, "What is that?" Clement said, "Why, that there be **Terpsichore!**" Mary frowned and shook her head. "**Terpsichore?** What's that?" Clement said, "Well, you sees, the family has a farm up river. ...near Baton Rouge, I's thinks. Well, **Terpsichore**, you sees, is de boat theys goes up in. ...or at least theys used too. I can't remember de last time theys used dat boat." Mary smiled. Clement continued to a door that went out on the riverside Wharf. Inman was out there with an Engineer's Notebook watching a ship unloading bananas, and busily taking notes. Clement excused himself and Mary thanked him for his kindness. Clement doffed his hat and turned to walk back to the central warehouse.

Mary could see the same intensity of observation in Inman as she had observed on the very first night she met him, peering into the windows at the funeral home. Not wanting to startle him, Mary decided to promenade around Inman and let him discover her. As Mary passed Inman, he buried his face in the notebook and began to intently scribble notes. When he looked up, Inman was completely surprised to see Mary standing in front of himself. An enthusiastic "Haw!" escaped when Inman first laid eyes on Mary. She turned, and Inman dropped his engineering notebook and placed his pencil back in his pocket. "**Quelle merveilleuse surprise! Je suis ravi de vous voir!**" (What a wonderful surprise! I am so delighted to see you!) Mary smiled as broadly as she could as they walked toward each other and embraced. She kissed him passionately on the lips, in public, for God and everyone to see. As the stevedores whistled and hooted, Mary leaned in close. Inman could feel her warm breath on his neck, and became highly aroused. Mary whispered, "After lunch, is there some where we can go to be alone?" Inman whispered back, "I'll build a place if I have to!" Mary grinned, "Good!" Inman reached down, picked up his notebook, put his arm around Mary's waist, and promenaded her for almost a mile up river along the wharf, showing her the ships, the cargo that was being off-loaded and on-loaded, and the warehouses where commodities were stored until Danton and their other Factors could sell them. Inman guided Mary into one of the warehouses where green coffee was stored. Mary was surprised that there was no telltale "coffee" odor. Inman explained, "The beans haven't been roasted yet. The Buyers will come in, roast samples, and choose the lots they want to buy." He pointed to an office in the distance. "That's Mr. Henry Saurage from Baton Rouge. His father started buying our coffee before 1920. Mr. Henry's son is in there learning "the business" from his father, Cap, just like I'm learning "the business" from my uncle Danton. Inman started to tear up. Mary felt his pain, and pulled him in close so that he could rest his head on her shoulder and not be seen crying. Mary teared up too. While she had one, she knew what it like growing up without a father. Quietly, Mary envied the fact that Inman had an uncle like Danton.

While Mary and Inman were touring the Wharf and assorted warehouses, Danton got busy describing the menu he envisioned his chef, Jean Claude, preparing for their luncheon. As Danton finished reading the proposed menu, Millicent gushed, "**Il est parfait!**" (It's perfect!) Danton had earlier called for Sam Goodwin and dispatched him to Gambino's Bakery with a wad of cash. "Sam, there's enough money for you to order yourself a lunch too." Sam took the money, grinned, and said, "Thanks, Boss!" As Inman was touring Mary around the sprawling Wharf, she asked, "Are they waiting for us?" Inman laughed, "The first thing I learned this morning was that if my uncle wants anyone, someone is sent to fetch them." Mary laughed. Inman continued, "They're probably trying to settle on what's for lunch." Mary sighed, and Inman continued on his tour. They were in the raw sugar warehouse, admiring the literal mountains of partially processed sugar when Ken Cracker informed them that luncheon was ready. As they walked back to the central warehouse and the General Offices, Mary asked, "Did you say that a third of that sugar came from your farm. Inman said, "Yes, but technically it's my mama's plantation, **Beau Cadeau de Dieu**. (Beautiful Gift from God)" Mary was enthusiastic. "Clement showed me a covered boat that was used to go up to the plantation?" Inman pulled a face. "I suppose so. I've never been to **Beau Cadeau**, or seen the boat." In her discomfort, all Mary could muster was "Hummmmm."

When Mary and Inman reached the Board Room, Millicent and Danton had pulled chairs from the massive Board table over to a small side table. They were drinking Fruit Salads and telling stories from back when they were young. When Mary and Inman entered the room, they both immediately felt the warm love coming from both Millicent and Danton. It was an extraordinary feeling for both of them. Inman walked over and shook his uncle/partner's hand, "We thought that we were holding up lunch." Danton laughed, "Nonsense! When Millicent arrived, she immediately agreed to the menu I'd put together. Which was good, because I'd already sent Jean Claude out to Schwegmann's to buy the provisions that weren't in the commissary. I gave Sam money to order his lunch too, while he was picking up our dessert, so it may be a few more minutes." Mary was curious, "What's on the menu?" Millicent grinned, You'll find out." Danton added, "...and your father would hate it intensely!" Both Mary and Inman were intrigued. When Sam returned, the scents from Jean Claude's chafers were perfuming the air to an extent that all were paralyzed with desire. Sam placed the cake box on a buffet. As the chafers were opened, Inman began to notice a trend. "Crabmeat Cocktail, Turtle Soup au Sherry...." Mary exclaimed, "Those are menu items we ordered at Commander's Palace! **Comme c'est parfait!** (How perfect!)" Inman smiled and continued his inventory, " Breast of Chicken Marchand de Vin, Trout Almandine, Brabant Potatoes, **haricots verts**, Combination Salad...." Danton jumped in and said, "...and a whole Doberge Cake. I sent Sam to get it from Gambino's. Inman began to get a little choked up. "This is exactly what we ordered at Commander's Palace..." Mary grasped, "You're right!" She teared up and Inman gave her his handkerchief. Danton said, "It's your meal interrupted." Millicent added, "We thought that you'd both like to enjoy the meal in peace and surrounded by love." Mary ran to Millicent and threw her arms around her. "**Merci mama, je t'aime tellement!**" (Thank you mama, I love you so much!) Inman looked across the table at Danton, "Well you were absolutely right." Danton, lost in all of the emotion of the moment, was confused, "What, right about what?" Inman said, "You said that Mary's father would hate this meal." They all got a hearty laugh at the thought, and settled in for a long slow luncheon over glorious Creole culinary perfection. Danton looked down at his glass, "Well, my ice cubes are getting dry, your's are too, Millie. I'll just refresh these. ...how about you two?" Mary looked to her mother. Millicent had no objections. Inman asked, "...but we're at work?" Danton replied, "Yes, we are, but, like I said this morning, we own this business and can have a drink with friends if we want to." ...and that settled that.

For the rest of September, Millicent and Mary joined Danton and Inman for luncheon at the Wharf as often as they could. Each time, Danton had Jean Claude duplicate fabulous cuisine from New Orleans' finest restaurants, without duplications. Inman took great pride in showing Mary the progress he was making on the various projects he was working on. His first was inspired by his first day on the Wharf. On Monday the 22nd., Inman took Mary into a large warehouse room that he had commandeered as an **atelier**. On a massive oak work table, Inman showed Mary several compilations of corrugated cardboard. Try as she did, Mary couldn't figure out what they were. Inman patiently explained. "Do you remember the first time you and your mama visited? Mary remembered the visit fondly. "Well, if you'll remember, I was watching a ship of bananas being unloaded." Mary said, "Yes, I remember. I was amazed at how big the bunches were, and how heavy they must have been." Inman continued, "Yes, that's certainly true. They are extremely heavy. ...and labor intensive. It shocked me that we needed so many people to load the bunches onto the canvas slings in the ship, off-load them on the Wharf, then move them to conveyor belts, where even more men hoisted them on their shoulders to move them to delivery trucks and rail cars."

Inman could tell that Mary was understanding the problem, but not getting his solution. The only evidence of his solution that Mary could see on display was, after all, just a flat irregularly shaped collection of corrugated cardboard and kraft paper. Inman grinned, "**Excusez-moi une seconde, ma douce, j'ai quelque chose qui simplifiera cela** ...." (Pardon me for just a second, my sweet, I have something that will simplify this....) Inman stepped into another room and returned with a completed Banana Box prototype. He placed it on the work table and removed the lid. While in outward appearance, is seamed to be a basic cardboard box, Inman had studied all of the varieties of bananas that were being imported into the Port of New Orleans, and had designed a shipping container that would keep 12 - 18 bunches of five to seven bananas each safe for shipping. They would be arranged in two layers of two rows separated by perforated kraft paper, and topped, under the lid with perorated kraft paper. "Insulation from shock, but breathable," Inman explained. Mary was impressed. She looked at the mock up on the work table and asked, "So what's keeping you from starting to use these?" Inman sighed. "I am still working on the final measurements, and a final prototype. Our attorney is preparing the Patent request. Once that goes through, we'll start producing them.

Mary turned sullen. "What about the poor dock workers that won't be needed anymore?" Inman reacted immediately, "We're not looking to get rid of anyone, we'll find jobs for them, even if we need to expand the business. Mary hugged Inman, "**Je doute que vous puissiez être un homme plus parfait. Je t'aime**!" (I doubt that you could be a more perfect man. I love you!) Inman closed his eyes and said, "**Je suis désespérément amoureux de toi ma douce**!" (I'm hopelessly in love with you my sweet!) They kissed passionately until there was a knock on the door. Inman reluctantly broke his embrace with Mary and said, "**Entrez s'il vous plait**." (Please enter.) The door opened, and Ken Cracker said, "Sorry to disturb, Monsieur Carnes, but Monsieur Soleil asked me to tell you that lunch would be served in ten minutes." Inman graciously thanked his employee. After he left, Mary observed, "He's our age!" Inman instinctively felt what Mary was alluding to. "Yes, I know how truly lucky I am. I didn't work up to my position, it was handed to me. I have a lot to prove. I want our employees to respect me. It'll probably take a long time." Mary smiled, "I doubt that, look what you've accomplished in a couple of weeks! You're revolutionizing the shipping business." Inman was truly honored by his sweetheart's kind words. He strode, peacock confidently, with Mary proudly on his arm through the complex to the General Offices, then to the Board Room for a delightful luncheon with Millicent and Danton.

In September, Blackjack successfully scheduled his first two Saturday funerals. He was enormously proud of his business acumen, and did not shy away from boasting of his marketing genius. Blackjack had no idea that he'd been played. The extra funerals allowed date days for Mary and Inman at **Maison Soleil**, and for Millicent and Danton at Maison Blanche. September passed too quickly for all four.

The day that both Millicent and Blackjack couldn't wait for was Wednesday, the first of October, the Cadillac New Model Release Party. Millicent was going to receive her brand new, first edition, Cadillac Eldorado Convertible. Blackjack was going to receive kudos and votes from Garden District elites who would practically swoon over what a great provider he was to his wife. Blackjack enlisted Johnny Hardwick to drive them to Earl Kemper's Cadillac dealership and stand by the Fleetwood. He had earlier partnered with Harry Cawe to return the loaner that wouldn't be needed after the party. When Millicent and Blackjack arrived at the dealership, all of the windows were covered in kraft paper. In truth, they had been covered for a week. Earl had closed the dealership in order to load the new models in. They had been delivered swaddled in unbleached Baft cotton fabric. Earl's trusted employees rolled each model into it's appointed place in the showroom. Earl had the Eldorado moved, ever so carefully, onto a revolving platform at the center of the googie monstrosity.

As usual, Blackjack insisted on being early, even though the invitation clearly stated that the doors would open at precisely 6:00 p.m. He started grumbling, almost immediately, that they had to wait outside in the early autumn heat. Millicent and Mary did their best to ignore Blackjack. At last, 6:00 arrived, and the doors opened. The Day family went in. Mary hung back away form the action. Blackjack went into full campaign mode, and worked the room pressing hands. Millicent went into full defense mode, greeting her life-long friends and making up for her husband's deficiencies. Earl took a corded microphone to the center of the room in front of the slowly revolving, shrouded, Eldorado. He welcomed his guests to the New Model Release Party, warmly. "I hope you all have drinks and snacks!" After polite applause, Earl continued. "This is truly an amazing year. Cadillac is presenting some major technological innovations. ...but you all know that, now don't you?" After another round of applause, he continued, "I know what you all want to see, but that will have to wait. First, let me show you Cadillac's beautiful line of automobiles for 1953.

Earl started with the Series 62 lineup. There was a Sedan, a Coupe, a Coupe de Ville, and a Convertible Coupe. After that, Earl introduced the new

Fleetwood Limousine. "Ladies and Gentlemen, this is the finest limousine ever offered. It is six inches longer than any of their previous models. Please notice the Kelsey-Hayes wire wheels. ...and it is equipped with Cadillac's Autonoic-Eye." He added, almost as a postscript, "Of course we'll have the commercial chassis for funeral service, hearses and flower cars. At least one of you will be interested in those models." A round of laughter irritated Blackjack, and tried his patience. He was offended by it, but he managed to hold himself together. Millicent had been an able teacher. At long last, Earl got to the highlight of the evening. Only one car was still draped, the first edition Eldorado convertible. Earl went into full-blown sales mode. "Our last new Cadillac is the brand spanking new Eldorado. Many of you competed for this revolutionary automobile. ...but only one of you is going to be able to drive this amazing piece of engineering home. Earl waved his hand and the Baft cotton covering was removed. A wholehearted "Ahhhhh" emerged from the party-goers. The Eldorado was exquisitely beautiful. The chassis of the model 62 had been lowered by several inches and the doors had been cut down. It featured the first "Wrap-around" windshield of any automobile, wire wheels, and a "Parade Boot." Automotive lust was in the air and shared by all. Earl said that the Eldorado was truly the most beautiful "Sports Car" yet produced. In truth, it was a massive land yacht posing as a sports car.

Earl kept the crowd on tender hooks, making them wait for the name of the new owner of the Eldorado. He baited them, stalled them, and procrastinated. At last, Earl announced, "The new owner of Cadillac's best car ever, the Eldorado, is.... ...Mr. and Mrs. Andrew Jackson Day." The guests had no idea that Earl had sold and received payment for the car already. The sham had it's intended affect. But, while the gentlemen attendees were congratulating Blackjack, many of the wives were looking critically at Mary. Millicent carried on as if nothing in her life had changed. Time after time, she said, "I've known you for uncountable years, please vote for my husband. ...and please tell your husbands to vote for Jackson too!" Overall, the evening was a huge success for the Day campaign for Coroner, in spite of Blackjack's overall unlike-ability. ...but then it started. Millicent found herself with a group of mothers of girls in Mary's graduating class at Miss. McGraw's. Not all of them were

"Old New Orleans." Several of them were **nouvelle**. While they had married into old money, they had never assimilated the culture or the manners of the gentry. "Milly, is Mary gaining weight?" Millicent turned to look at Mary. She hadn't noticed. After a quick moment's thought, she said, "I suppose it's the Blanchard family curse. She probably has fibroids. We're going to have her seen, then have them taken care of. I hope you'll all pray for her on Sundays." Millicent's passive-aggressive lie had it's intended effect. The gaggle of women abandoned the subject of Mary's unexpected weight gain and returned to talking about various upcoming parties.

Millicent knew that it would be a good idea to get Mary out of the public spotlight so she could find out what was really going on. She found Blackjack and pulled him aside. He wasn't happy about being pulled way from his stump speech. "Jackson, something I've eaten hasn't agreed with me. I've been nauseated for almost an hour. ...and I think there is diarrhea coming. Can't we please go home. I don't want to embarrass you!" Millicent's series of convincing lies caught Blackjack off guard. His mind was reeling, and he bought into the fantasy of the effects of an "accident" on his campaign. Blackjack made his apologies to Earl, and told him that he'd be back in the morning to retrieve the Eldorado. "Milly's under the weather, I really need to get her home." When they pulled into the motor court, Millicent hopped out and ran to the house. She went up to her bathroom and locked the door. For thirty minutes, Millicent made odd noises, on the slight chance that Blackjack had followed her up. He hadn't. When she finally came out of the bathroom, Millicent went directly to Mary's bedroom.

Millicent knocked, then opened the door. "Are you still up?" Mary said, "Yes, of course. I'm just reading. Please come in and join me." Millicent walked over the the **bergère à oreilles**, and sat next to Mary. Mary closed her book and said, "Mama?" Millicent breathed in deeply, "There were several ladies at Earl Kemper Cadillac tonight asking about the weight you've gained." Mary looked confused. "Have I gained weight?" Millicent sighed. "Yes, a little, and that's unusual for someone your age." Mary said, "Hummm." After an awkward silence, Millicent found the strength to ask, "Is it at all possible that you are 'with child?'" Mary's jaw slacked. "What? With child? No! That's not possible! I don't have a husband!" Millicent's neck weakened, and her head tumbled forward. After a few forlorn moments, Millicent lifted her head. "A husband is not a requirement to have a child. All that is required is being intimate with a man. Do you know what that means?" Mary began sobbing uncontrollably. "We made out. …but we're in love. I can't imagine that we did anything that would cause me to be pregnant."

Millicent sighed, and asked, "What if you are, do you think that Inman would marry you?" Mary smiled broadly, "He told me that he could never love anyone else. Yes, I truly believe he would." Millicent said, "That's good. He has probably the best job in New Orleans for anyone his age, and there's lots more money in his family than he could even imagine. If you two really love each other, the way you say that you do, it would be a good match." Mary wiped her eyes on a tissue. "Mama, do you hate me?" Millicent said, "Well, we don't know for certain that you're pregnant. I should probably be angry with you for what you've done, but I can't lie to you. A part of me envies the relationship you have with Inman. I had that once with Danton, but your father destroyed it." Mary said, "Mama, with this seriousness about us, would you please tell me about how father stole you away from Danton Soleil."

Millicent nodded her head. "Yes, okay. …but I'll have to tell you the story of your father's family first. You never really knew any of them, and your father never speaks of them. Your father, Andrew Jackson Day, later nicknamed "Blackjack" by his card gang, was born on May 31st. 1903. His parents were James Edward "JED" Day and Madeline Clancy. After his mother died of Yellow Fever in 1905, Jackson was brought up by his father JED, who was a Streetcar Conductor. One of Jackson's father's friends, another Conductor, named Clarence J. Laughlin had a son by the same name, but went by John. John was two years younger than Jackson, but neither of them had any real friends, much less a mother, and bonded almost immediately. John's father died unexpectedly in 1918 when he was just 13 years old. Jackson was just 15, but made a reasoned argument, and talked his father into allowing John to move in with them. John was devastated by his father's death, and JED went out of his way to offer support and encouragement to him. Your grandfather was an exceptionally nice man, nothing like your father. A part of me feels that if your father had been like his father, we might have had a reasonably happy marriage."

"C. John Laughlin fought his demons, but eventually dropped out of school after his Freshman year in 1920. He was able to find odd jobs, and JED made sure he had a place to live, and meals on the table. In 1928, Jackson and John were walking through the **Vieux Carré** and stopped at the window of a pawn shop on Rue Chartres. John pointed to a small view camera in the window. He told Jackson that it had been there for some time. Your father asked him, "How much is it?" John had no idea. Jackson said, "We're going in to ask." John had been afraid to even ask in the past. He had learned from an early age not to hope for anything. So many wishes had been denied him in his short life. Even so, John fell victim to Jackson's enthusiasm, and followed him into the pawn shop."

"Jackson asked about the camera. The shop proprietor said, "That, gentlemen, is a Century Grand Dry Plate Camera. It was previously owned by a famous **Vieux Carré** studio photographer who died recently." John was impressed, but Jackson wasn't. Your father snarled, "How much is it?" The proprietor reacted to John's obvious interest, and said, "It's only ten dollars." John frowned, and dropped his face because there was no way he could afford $10.00. Your father saw John's reaction and squinted his eyes. He paused for a moment and said, "You know, as well as we do, that camera has been in your window for well over a year now, probably because most people are buying Kodak roll film cameras. We'll give you two dollars for it." The proprietor winced, "...but there's a tripod, plate holders, and a bag of equipment that goes with it. I think there are even unused plates in the bag too. How about Seven Dollars?" Jackson stayed cool. "Four Dollars." The proprietor sighed. He knew that Jackson was right. He had paid too much for the camera in the first place, and was resigned that it needed to go. "Five Dollars," was his response. Jackson wasted no time, "Four Fifty." The proprietor agreed. John immediately started to panic. He pulled your father aside and told him that he had only Three Dollars on him. Jackson pulled two Morgan silver dollars out of his pocket. "I believe in you." John assured Jackson that he'd pay him back, and made the purchase. Helping C. John Laughlin start his storied career in photography was the only unselfish or generous act your father ever performed."

"1928 just happened to be the year that Huey Long was elected Governor of the Great State of Louisiana. That same year C. John Laughlin and Jackson Day were selected to join the Choctaw Club, also known as the Old Regulars, or the Regular Democratic Organization. Other members included New Orleans Mayor, T. Semmes Walmsley, Inman Carnes, the Third, and Danton Soleil. Jackson Day was still trying to achieve social standing, so he was on his best behavior. John Laughlin wasn't trying to prove anything, and was just an extremely nice guy. Jackson and John fit in completely in the Choctaw Club. By the summer of 1928, Danton Soleil invited both of them to join his Card Gang."

"By 1929, Huey long had advocated for policies that got on the bad side of the Choctaw Club, and the members tried to have him impeached. They failed, and in 1930 Long was elected to the U.S. Senate. He promised Mayor Walmsley a bridge, an airport, and various infrastructure improvements in exchange for a truce. The Choctaw Club buried their hatchet, at least for a while. In 1930, your father was given the sobriquet "Blackjack" by the Card Gang because of his fearless card playing. It was supposed to be a compliment, but, as usual, Jackson took it as an insult. Later that year, Jackson was nominated to be a member of the Boston Club, the **Ne Plus Ultra** of New Orleans Gentlemen's Clubs. On the night of the election, your father was blackballed. He blamed Danton Soleil, Inman Carnes, the Third, and Mayor Walmsley. None of them had blackballed him, and, in fact, Danton Soleil had been the member who had nominated him for membership."

"All Jackson could think about was getting revenge for his horribly public insult. He asked three of his employees from the Esplanade Avenue Bank House to pose as unemployed dockworkers who wanted to join the Choctaw Club to improve their chances of getting a job. They agreed to meet Mayor Walmsley, Inman Carnes, the Third, and Danton Soleil at **Broussard's** for lunch. Your father arranged for the party to sit at a table in the courtyard, and for John to perch in a secluded niche overlooking the courtyard. Jackson instructed John to inscribe the date into each negative, and keep detailed records of the date and time of the meeting. Your father had another friend, attorney Adrien Emile LaRoque draw up affidavits for the three potential Choctaw Club members stating that during their meeting with Danton, Inman and the Mayor, they had each each been offered $1,000.00 ($15,000.00 in 2019) to assassinate Senator Huey Long as a means to settle the feud with the Choctaw Club, but that they had refused. Blackjack had the wherewithal to have them sign numerous copies of the affidavits in the presence of a Notary Public."

"John printed four 8"x10" prints of each negative he shot at **Broussard's** for Jack. One copy of the affidavit accompanied with a set of the 8"x10" prints went into LaRoque's safe. another went into a Safe Deposit Box at the Whitney Bank. John and Jackson held the other two sets. At the next Card Gang night, your father asked Inman, Danton, and the Mayor to stay for a while after the last game ended. They sat at one of the card tables, and Jackson dropped a manilla folder onto the center of the table and waited for them to open it and peruse its contents. All of their faces went completely white, and they all, of course denied the allegations. It was Inman Carnes who became indignant and asked Blackjack what he wanted.

Your father laid out his demands:

First: $10,000.00 from each ($500,000.00 in 2017)

Second: Their social status would continue unchanged. Card games, EtC. would go on as if nothing had happened.

Third, and of primary importance, Danton was to break off his engagement to Millicent Blanchard, me.

Mayor Walmsley politely asked Blackjack to step out of the room so that they could discuss his demands. While your father was just out of earshot, both Inman and Danton come to the realization, that they have no choice. Mayor Walmsley, too, found that there was no negotiating with Blackjack."

"Danton was impacted the worst. To him the money was nothing, but I had always been the only love of his life. Still, he was determined to fight to the end. He asked Blackjack to come back into the room. "Is this the only copy of this affidavit, Blackjack?" Jackson laughed, "No, three attorneys have identical sets of this dossier, and instructions to send them to the press, the police, and to the Cathedral, if anything were to happen to me." Danton asked, humbly, how long he had before he had to break up with me. Blackjack said, coldly, "You have until Valentines Day for that, but the money is due by the end of the month." Sadly, your father thought that if he could convince me to marry him, his acceptance in the Boston Club would be assured, and he would at long last be deemed worthy and accepted by the upper crust of New Orleans."

"Tom and Inman looked at Danton. They both knew that he, most certainly, had the most to loose. Danton hung his head in despair for what he described as an eternity, then nodded in agreement. It was, at the base level, a choice between the love of his life, and his life itself. Blackjack beamed, "Excellent, thank you gentlemen! I for one am looking forward to our continued friendship." Danton couldn't help himself, "You know that you can kiss your hopes of the Boston Club goodbye!" Blackjack was unfazed and didn't miss a beat 'We'll see. Time will tell. I know for a fact, that none of you will stand in my way now.'"

"Inman, Danton, and Tom waited until the very last day of the month to hand your father certified checks for their extortion payments. Blackjack wasted no time opening an account at the Whitney Bank. With the Great Depression settling in, he was suddenly an extraordinarily wealthy man. He negotiated with the family that owned the funeral home and was able to buy it lock, stock, and barrel for far less than its true value. He started immediately, after the Act of Sale, to make improvements to the building, and his livery."

"Valentines Day, February 14, 1931 was on a Saturday. That evening, The Old Regulars held a ball. Mayor Walmsley was the Grand Marshall. Inman, Jack, and John were already there when Danton arrived with me. Danton had been morose all day, and I had been asking him what was wrong for hours. We danced, but I noticed that Danton was distant, and seemed distracted. I stopped in the middle of a dance and asked Danton what was he so upset about. He closed his eyes and let his head sink. After a moment, Danton opened his eyes and took my hand. He led me off of the dance floor to a quiet space."

"Danton explained to me that "Politics" was swirling around him, "I have people who aim to hurt me, and I can't let anything happen to you." In a state of shock, I asked, "Are you breaking off our engagement?" Danton looked off into the distance. "I have never loved you more than I do today, and will never love you any less, or love anyone else, ever, but I could never live with myself if anything bad happened to you." I was thunderstruck. I could hardly breathe. I started crying and pleaded with Danton to stay engaged to me. Danton broke down in tears as well. I threw my arms around Danton and said, "I don't care about anything else, I love you, and you only!" Danton fought his tears and broke free of my embrace, "I've loved you from the moment we met. I love you now, and you alone. I will love you for the rest of my life. I beg you to always remember that! I have to go. I wish you, always, the best that life has to offer, but I can't allow you to be hurt. Danton kissed me on the forehead and sprinted out of the building. I collapsed onto a **canapé**. Danton's sister Caroline rushed over and sat with me. She offered me her handkerchief, monogramed with a scarlet 'S' in a golden sun. I dried my eyes and removed the engagement ring that Danton had given me. I wrapped the ring in the handkerchief and handed it to Caroline. "I can't talk about this right now, even with you, my oldest and most treasured friend. Please get this back to Danton for me." Caroline was heartbroken. She took the linen wrapped ring, hugged me, and returned to the party."

"Your father, who had been lurking in the shadows, like a spider, stepped out into the light and asked, "Are you alright, Millicent?" I said, "Oh, Jackson, I really don't know. Danton told me that we can't be together anymore. I, I, I just don't understand." Your father had been running this moment through his psychopathic mind for at least a month. He sat casually in a **bergère** next to my **canapé**. He listened to me "respectfully" and let me talk for as long as I wanted. In truth, your father's deception was a difficult one. He didn't love me. Love wasn't a disability that he could conceive of allowing himself.

Marrying me was merely a tick mark on his grand scheme to climb the New Orleans social ladder. ...and it was payback for his imagined betrayal by Danton of his joining the Boston Club."

"The next day, Caroline went to the Wharf and met with her brother, Danton. He refused to talk about the break-up. He assured his sister that he would always love me completely, but there were political forces in play, beyond his command, that he couldn't discuss. Carolyn sighed. She handed Danton the engagement ring wrapped in her handkerchief, and left to go back to **Maison Soleil**. Danton placed the ring in his trouser pocket. Unseen by anyone, Danton later told me that he cried for the better part of the next four hours in the seclusion of his **bureau**."

"Over the next couple of months, your father gave me all of the room I needed. He doted on my every word and anticipated my every need. None of Danton's real friends, friends with social standing, would have dared ask me out, because they all knew, instinctively, that Danton was still completely in love with me. By May of 1931, your father had found a way to have me believing that he was my knight in shining armor. Now, with time and understanding, I know that he'd been 'gaslighting' me. He had bought the Funeral Home, and renovations were nearing completion, when I accepted his proposal of marriage. We wed on Saturday, June 20, 1932."

Mary asked, "So you never loved my father?" Millicent grasped, "**Je ne peux pas vous dire combien j'ai essayé**! (I can't tell you how much I tried!) Mary reluctantly accepted the new reality of her life. Millicent said, "Try to get some sleep. We'll go out tomorrow, get our hair done, have lunch, shop, and figure some things out. We have the rest of the month to figure out what this is, and how to get past it. Your father will be in the final push of his campaign. You should probably try to avoid him for as long as possible." Mary nodded. Millicent left Mary's bedroom and retired for the night. Neither sleep well.

The next morning, they were both at the table very early. Hattie and Marie Cosette had to change the order of their morning routine to get the juices and Coffee out early. Millicent, who had done a lot of thinking overnight, said, "We need to agree to talk to **no one** about what 'might' be." Mary nodded,

"…not even Inman or uncle Danton." Millicent nodded. "I don't want to worry any of them with just a suspicion. We need to wait until we know, one way or the other." Mary agreed. At last Marie Cosette brought the juices and coffee out. Mary poured herself an orange juice, and Marie Cosette poured Millicent's **café au lait**. Blackjack heard Hattie and Marie Cosette placing the chafers, and practically sprinted out of his office and snatched his plate off the table. As he heaped food on his plate, Millicent asked, "Jackson, what time do you want to go to Earl's to get my new Cadillac?" Blackjack, who had just stuffed three rashers of bacon in his mouth, muttered, "I'll have Johnny drive you, big funeral today. I don't need to be there, that damn car is paid for. Don't keep Johnny, though, I need him here, ready to go." Millicent said, "Okay, Jackson," as her husband walked quickly back to his office with his plate. After a deep cleansing breath, Millicent's famous **La Gioconda** smile enveloped her face.

Millicent called for Marie Cosette. "Please go down and find Johnny Hardwick. Tell him that Mary and I will need for him to drive us to Kemper Cadillac at 9:30." Marie Cosette said, "Yessum," and rushed through the kitchen and out the back door to the motor court. Millicent and Mary finished their breakfast in peace, then went upstairs to adjust their hair and makeup. At 9:30, Johnny was standing in the motor court with the back door of a Fleetwood standing open. Millicent brushed past him without making any contact. Mary made eye contact, for one brief moment, then looked down. Johnny drove them to Earl's dealership. Even though Millicent said that she wouldn't require him any longer, Johnny lingered just long enough to make sure that the Eldorado was ready to cross the curb. Earl Kemper was surprised that Blackjack hadn't joined Millicent and Mary on such a "joyous" occasion. Millicent said, "Business always comes first, now doesn't it, Earl?" Earl had to agree, although he was taken aback by Millicent's familiarity. Earl finalized all of the paperwork while the Eldorado was being detailed in the back lot. When the drop top Tunis Blue Iridescent land yacht cruised around the corner of the dealership, it was an instant sensation. Salespeople and guests alike gathered around it, gasping. Earl escorted Millicent and Mary to Millicent"s new Cadillac. Earl opened the driver's side door for Millicent, and offered his hand to steady her entrance. Being a Blanchard, Millicent had no need for Earl's assistance. She blew him off, and slid onto the brilliant white leather upholstered seat. Earl pushed the massive door until it latched, and said, "I hope that you get many years, and many miles out of this fine Cadillac." Millicent smiled and said nothing. She was, however, wondering just how many times he had said that to customers in the past. Millicent pulled the Eldorado off the lot, and headed toward the Central Business District.

During the drive, Millicent reiterated, "We say nothing to your father, nothing to Inman, nothing to Danton, nothing to ANYONE, until after the election. Mary agreed. Millicent parked, and she and Mary walked to **Maison de Bringer**. After a two hour session of beauty, Millicent asked Mary where she wanted to go for lunch. Mary thought. She thought about the story her mother had told her the night before. "Would it be okay with you, if we went to Broussard's for lunch?" Millicent closed her eyes. "We've never dined there as a family, have we? …and I suppose you now know why." Mary nodded. Millicent sighed, "There's a lot that both you and I need to come to terms with. Perhaps, Broussard's would be a good place to start that painful process." Broussard's was only three blocks away from Canal Street so Millicent left the Eldorado in the lot, and she and Mary walked to the restaurant.

When they were seated, a wicked smile emerged on Millicent's face. Mary was intrigued. "What's going on?" Millicent chuckled, and said, "You'll see, in just a moment or two." Their waiter showed up and asked for drink orders. After Mary ordered a soft drink, Millicent asked for it to be "sweetened," then, very dramatically, ordered a Brandy Napoleon. The waiter was impressed. **"Très bien Madame! Donnez-moi juste une minute."** (Very good Madam! Just give me a minute.) As the waiter arrived with Millicent's and Mary's drinks, the other waiters gathered around a statue of Napoleon, the lights dimmed, a bell was rung, and the staff and many of the diners engaged in a lively rendition of "**La Marseillaise**." Mary enjoyed her mother's antics immensely. "Thank you so very much, mama! I needed a boost." Many of the other diners had forgotten about the old custom, but enjoyed the experience so much, several of them ordered Brandy Napoleons and contributed to the festivities. Millicent and Mary allowed themselves to forget about the potential serious problem that was hanging over them, and enjoyed a wonderful dining experience. They strung the luncheon on for as long as possible, but at last it was time to walk back to the Eldorado and return to the funeral home.

On the drive back to the Garden District, Millicent turned completely serious. "Mary, you need to know that I am completely on your side, what ever the truth is. I can handle a medical condition, or even a pregnancy. Your father won't be able to willingly accept a pregnancy, even if you and Inman get married. ...if that's what it is. It's the 1950's and it'll hurt his social climbing schemes. Right now, we can't let him blame an election loss on you. He'd take it out on both of us. ...and the thought of what he might do frightens me." Mary started to sob. "I'm sorry mama." Millicent was pragmatic. "Now isn't the time for tears. Now is the time for us to be strong. Like I said before, no one can know. Is that clear?" Mary nodded. She had only one question. "Will we be lying to Inman and Danton?" Millicent sighed. "Have you been told by a doctor that you're pregnant?" Mary shook her head. "No ma'am." Millicent continued, "Well, as far as I'm concerned, you aren't pregnant until we have a diagnosis. Not telling them anything that isn't proven, isn't lying." Mary was relieved.

Millicent and Mary treated October just like they had treated September. They had lunch with Danton and Inman during the week when there were funerals, and had "dates" with their beaux during Saturday and Sunday funerals. Fortunately for Mary, only the busy-bodies at the New Model Release Party noticed Mary's slight weight gain. Inman and Danton certainly didn't notice, and Caroline never looked critically at her friends. By Halloween, Blackjack was winding his campaign up. The final Rotary meeting had been the day before, and both he and Milly started making last minute phone calls over the weekend. They attended all of the services at Christ Church Cathedral on Sunday, November the second. Blackjack made his last round of calls, especially to gamblers who owed him money on Monday. On Tuesday, both Millicent and Blackjack were in line to vote when their polling precinct opened. After they voted, Blackjack had to let his campaign go. He had a big funeral. Blackjack was nervous all day, but encouraged by the mourners who told him that they had voted for him. Millicent spent the afternoon in Danton's arms at their "place" at Maison Blanche. Mary spent the afternoon at **Maison Soleil** dancing and "making out" with Inman. By the time Millicent and Mary returned home, Blackjack was pacing the home. It would be a long night for Blackjack. Millicent and Mary went up to bed, but Blackjack stayed in his office downing an unhealthy amount of **café noir**. He had sent several of his Bank House employees to sit as poll watchers. By two in the morning, positive final results started coming in.

Blackjack refused to leave his office on Wednesday morning. He had his radio tuned to WWL 870, and was listening to updates with baited breath. Around 8:00, Blackjack screamed for Marie Cosette. When she came into his office, he asked her to bring him breakfast. Marie Cosette almost worried about what to serve him, but Mary helped, and they giggled as they piled his plate high with scrambled eggs, grits, bacon, and buttered toast. By 10:00 Wednesday morning, the final results were in. Blackjack had won by just enough votes to avoid a recount. His competitor phoned shortly after the announcement, to concede. Millicent and Mary were sitting in the parlor chatting when they were accosted by raucous laughter and shouting emitting from Blackjack's office. They looked at each other and grinned. Millicent said, "Well, that's a relief! Now we have only one thing to worry about." Mary's elation dwindled. Her head dropped and she started weeping. Millicent said, "We need to know." Mary nodded her bent head. Millicent moved over to the **canapé** where Mary was sitting, and put her arm around her daughter. "No tears! We'll get through this, one way or another." Mary smiled and sat up. She leaned her head onto her mother's shoulder and sighed. Blackjack stormed into the parlor. "I won!" Before Millicent could react, Blackjack shouted for Hattie. When she made her way into the parlor, Blackjack said. "No lunch today for us. We're going to Brennan's! You and Marie Cosette make whatever you want to eat. Today is a day of celebration!" Blackjack looked at Millicent and Mary. He frowned. "Go upstairs, and put your best clothes on. This is a BIG day!" Millicent looked at Mary. Mary looked at her mother. Neither said a word. Blackjack heard the phone ring and turned to return to his office. As he left, Blackjack said, "We'll be leaving at 11:30!"

Blackjack hadn't asked Millicent about where she might like to celebrate and enjoy lunch. He instructed Johnny Hardwick to drive them to Brennan's. When they arrived, the staff and the patrons applauded the victor, the newly elected Coroner, Andrew Jackson "Blackjack" Day. None of them knew the extent of what they had voted to allow to happen in Orleans Parish. Millicent had no idea what her choice to aid in Blackjack's campaign would eventually cost her. ...or Mary! As they tried to enjoy their wonderful luncheon, supporters and sycophants of Blackjack pressed themselves into their peace. Blackjack was in heaven, but Millicent and Mary found themselves very much piqued. One of the sycophants who forced himself on the family was Dr. Scrope, of Commander's Palace infamy. He insisted upon greeting the entire family, and proffered congratulations to Blackjack. In her disdain, Millicent neglected to notice the look on Dr. Scrope's face as he o'r looked Mary. While he said nothing on the night following the election, Dr. Scrope had a strong suspicion that Mary was pregnant, and called Blackjack the next day. On Thursday the sixth of November, Blackjack got the call from Dr. Scrope that he never expected. Dr. Scrope told Blackjack his suspicions. Blackjack was more worried about his ambitions than if there was a baby or not. "Scrope, this has to be confidential. When can she be seen when no-one will be there?" The Doctor said, " We're closed on Armistice Day. Could you send her over then?" Blackjack said, "Yes, expect her next Tuesday."

CHAPTER SIXTEEN

THE ARMISTICE DAY WAR

Millicent and Mary were sitting at the dining table on the morning of Armistice Day enjoying their **café au lait** and waiting for Blackjack to join them for breakfast. Hattie and Marie Cosette had already brought the chafers out and placed them on the **buffet de chasse.** Unlike his usual custom, Blackjack was running late and their food was cooling. Jackson had been in an uncharacteristically good mood since winning the election for Coroner the previous Tuesday, and Millicent was cautiously optimistic that today might be yet another calm day. When he finally came in and poured himself a cup of **café noir** in his stained old mug, Millicent and Mary rose and took their plates to the **buffet de chasse** and selected their food.

They returned to their seats and waited for Blackjack to return from getting his breakfast. "Jackson, are you going to have a busy day, today?" Millicent asked. Blackjack scrawled, "I have a busy day, everyday!" he said with a mouth full of scrambled eggs. After Blackjack guzzled down his breakfast, he started to rise, but sat back down and stared at Millicent. "I don't think you two are being truthful." "Truthful?" Millicent asked, "Truthful about what?" Blackjack pointed to Mary. "About her. About what's wrong

187

with her." Millicent looked surprised. "I told you, she has fibroid tumors. I'm going to take her to a specialist after Thanksgiving." Blackjack stood up. "You're taking her to see Dr. Scrope today at 10:45." Millicent said, "...but Jackson, his office will be closed today, it's Armistice Day." "He's going to meet you both there at 10:45. It's all arranged. Johnny Hardwick knows to have the car out by 10:30." With that, Blackjack returned to his office and slammed the door.

Mary asked her mother if would be okay for her to go up to her room to read. "Of course, just be down by 10:30. I have a lot to figure out here." Mary hugged Millicent and walked slowly through the parlor and up the stairs. Millicent walked through the parlor to the front window and stared out at the Streetcar stop in the Neutral Ground of St. Charles Avenue. She sighed. She had an idea what was wrong with Mary, but couldn't process how it could have happened.

At 10:30, Mary walked down the stairs and into the parlor. Millicent was still staring out the window. Mary joined her for a moment. "Is it time?" Mary asked. "Yes." was all that Millicent said. Millicent spun around. "Okay, let's go." They walked through the dining room, and into the kitchen. Hattie was sitting at the table prepping vegetables for lunch. Millicent passed Hattie and said, "We're going now, Hattie. Luncheon at 12:00?" "Yes'um," was all Hattie said. She didn't look up from her cutting. She knew what was about to happen, and that it wouldn't be pleasant. Millicent and Mary got into the back seat of her Cadillac Eldorado. Johnny Hardwick got behind the wheel and cranked the car up. He pulled out on Louisiana Avenue and drove a couple of blocks, turned right onto Coliseum Street and pulled into the parking lot at 3424 Coliseum Street. Millicent and Mary got out of the car at the medical practice of Henry Scrope, M.D., Richard Cambridge, M.D., and Thomas Grey, M.D.

Millicent tried the door. It was open. The lights in the waiting room were off, and no one was at the receptionist's desk. They took a seat. After a few minutes, Dr. Scrope opened the door. Millicent, you can bring Mary back, now. Millicent looked at Mary with a quiet look of fear. They stood up and followed Dr. Scrope back to one of his examination rooms. Dr. Scrope handed Mary a hospital gown and asked her to go behind the screen and change out of her clothes and have a seat on the exam table. While Mary was changing, Dr. Scrope asked Millicent several questions. "When did you notice that Mary was gaining weight?" Millicent thought for a moment. "I wasn't the first to notice. I remember that we were at the new model release party at Earl Kemper's Cadillac dealership, and several of my friends noticed. That was the first of October. Dr. Scrope scribbled notes in Mary's chart. "Has she complained of any pain?" Millicent said, "No, not that I remember." "Has she said anything about constipation?" Millicent frowned, "No, I don't think so." Dr. Scrope continued to write notes on Mary's chart.

Mary walked around the screen in the hospital gown and sat on the examination table. Dr. Scrope spun around on his stool and continued her history by asking Mary questions directly. "Mary, have you had any changes in your urination, or any pain when urinating?" Mary seemed perplexed. "No, not really." Dr. Scrope then asked, "Have you been experiencing heavy or prolonged menstrual bleeding?" Mary sighed. "No, Dr. Scrope, it's been a while since I have had a period." Millicent lost all of the color in her face. Dr. Scrope raised the back of the examination table and asked Mary to lay back. He then asked Mary to put her feet into the stirrups. Dr. Scrope stood next to Mary and began palpating her abdomen. "Does this hurt?" Mary showed no distress and said, "No, not at all." Dr. Scrope wrote some more notes down and told her that he needed to do a digital examination. Mary looked at Millicent. She was quite nervous about the exam. Dr. Scrope put gloves on, applied lubricant to his right fingers and performed the digital examination. When he finished, he removed his gloves and helped Mary sit up.

Millicent could barely dare to ask, "Well Dr. Scrope, is it bad?" Dr. Scrope was still busily writing notes on Mary's chart. He didn't look up, but said, "Well, the good news is that Mary doesn't have Leiomyomas." He sighed, and bit his lower lip, causing the beard hairs below his lip to stand up like a warning flag. Had Millicent and Mary not been terrified, it would have been quite amusing. "Millicent, Mary doesn't have fibroids, she's with child." Millicent put her right hand over her chest, looked down at the floor, and said, "That's impossible. There is no way that could be true." Dr. Scrope replied, "I'm afraid that it's true, and sometime during the summer, it did happen." Millicent wasn't mad at Mary, she was worried about how Blackjack would react.

Dr. Scrope asked Mary to return to the screen and change back into her clothes. He looked at Millicent. "I don't suppose that she has gotten married recently?" Millicent lowered her head and moved it back and forth. "No, she's only seventeen years old." Dr. Scrope chuckled. "My dear, in some countries, even today, a woman of seventeen is considered an old maid! Don't worry, she has options." Millicent raised her head and stared at Dr. Scrope. "Options, what options?" Dr Scrope schooched his stool closer to Millicent. "Well, she could marry the boy. —or— She could leave New Orleans, have the baby, and give it up for adoption. —and— There's the other option." Millicent looked deep into Dr. Scrope's eyes. "What other option?"

Dr. Scrope averted her stare, "Well.... well, it's called a D & C." Millicent looked confused. "A what?" Dr. Scrope explained, "A D & C is a 'Dilation and Curettage.' The cervix is dilated, and the uterus is 'gently' scraped to remove it's 'contents.' It's a therapeutic gynecological procedure." Mary burst into hysterics. "No! You can't kill my baby! Mama, please, don't. We didn't know that this could happen. No one ever told either one of us! Millicent took Mary's had and squeezed it tightly and reassuringly. "**Mon cher agneau**, (My dear lamb) nothing is decided. Please don't get too worked up." Millicent turned to look at Dr. Scrope. "I don't suppose that I can persuade you not to tell Jackson about this 'situation.'"

Dr. Scrope looked Millicent straight in the eyes. "No Millicent, I'm afraid not. You may not know, but I owe your husband a lot of money, and I have to be completely honest with him." Millicent sighed, "I suppose that he'll know by the time we get home." Dr. Scrope hung his head. "I'm sorry, Millicent, but I promised to call him as soon as you leave." Millicent breathed in and out extraordinarily deeply. "I understand. Could you at least give us some time to talk about this before we go home, before you call Jackson?" Dr. Scrope didn't hesitate. "Of course. I have a consultation room that is far more comfortable than this examination room. If you don't mind, let me know when you leave. I won't call Jackson until then. There's a phone if you want to call any family members." Millicent thanked Dr. Scrope and she and Mary followed him to the consultation room.

Millicent and Mary sat down in the consolation room. Nothing was said for several minutes. Mary was weeping. Finally she said, "Mama, I'm so sorry. This wasn't supposed to happen." Millicent shushed Mary. "**Chérie**, I know. Of course, I'm extremely disappointed, not so much with you, but with the situation you've placed yourself in. I don't doubt the love that you and Inman share. To be truthful, I'm more than a little envious. Everything between you and Inman can be worked out. I couldn't pick a better person for you to fall in love with, but that's not the issue. Inman is not the problem; Your father is the problem." Mary slumped in her chair. "**Mon Dieu**, you are so right." Millicent knew that Mary didn't know the sordid truth about her father, and didn't know how to tell her. Telling her would burst all of Mary's life-long misconceptions about her father.

Millicent continued, "Mary... I find myself in one of the most troubling situations I've ever experienced. It's not so much that you're going to have a baby. Baby's are gifts from God. ...and I have no doubt that Inman will be happy and glad for you both to get married. The real problem is that, when we get home, you are going to begin to learn the dreadful truth about your father, at least part of it." Mary looked perplexed. "Dread.... What? ...Dreadful? What are you talking about?" Millicent's face sank to a low Mary had never witnessed. She planted her elbows on the table and rested her forehead in the base of her palms. She sighed deeply. Millicent was considering exactly what to tell Mary, and what to hold back for another day. She released another heavy sigh. "Mary, I have a question for you.... How many of your friends, growing up, ever invited you over for a sleepover?" Mary didn't even have to think. "No one ever invited me to a sleepover, or a birthday party. Do people really do that?" Millicent replied, "Your father and I led you to believe that those things never happened." She continued, "How many of your classmates came to your birthday parties?" Once again, Mary had no need to hesitate to think about the question. "My birthday parties were always with family. ...There were never any friends." Millicent paused for a moment.

"Every year, we invited every girl in your class, but none of their parents would let their 'precious' daughters come to a funeral home for a birthday party." Mary looked shocked. "I... don't know how to feel about this. They were… they were all so nice to me at school." Millicent was shaking her head in agreement. "Of course they were. They saw the real you; Their parents saw you as the daughter of Andrew Jackson Day, and a resident of a creepy funeral home. None of the parents wanted any of 'that' influencing their 'precious' daughters." Mary sank deeper into confusion. "Mama, I don't understand, those girls, who I thought were my friends, at least at school, voted me to be the May Queen." Millicent cocked her left eye up. "**Douce fille**, I can't say that your friends didn't vote for you, but your father made it clear that certain debts owed by certain fathers would be 'reconsidered' if you were elected May Queen." Mary scrunched her brow. "Debts? What debts? Funeral debts?"

Millicent shook her head. "Certain debts… That's a story for another day. The problem at hand is that we must go home and face your father. I'll be able to handle it, but you need to know the severity of the situation." Mary looked at her mother inquisitively…. Millicent looked down at the floor for a few moments. "The Boston Club." Mary looked at her mother with a look of complete bewilderment. "The Boston Club???" Millicent smiled one of her 'Mona Lisa' smiles. "Yes, dear, the Boston Club. Your father has been trying to get in since 1930. When he was blackballed, your father used three of his employees to apply for membership in the Choctaw Club, had the meeting photographed, and had them sign affidavits that Inman's father, uncle, and the Mayor had offered them money to assassinate Governor Huey Long. It wasn't true, of course, but your father extorted a fortune out of them. It was more than he needed to buy and renovate the funeral home. Ever since, your father has planned and schemed how to be invited to join the Boston Club and move up the social ladder."

Mary looked perplexed. "What is the big deal? He's a successful businessman. What's stopping him?" Millicent chuckled, "Mary, your father has two businesses. You don't need to know too much about it right now, but for years he's been working overtime to overcome his negative perceptions in Society. He was looking forward to your Debut at the Rex Ball to cement 'his' place in society." Mary was suddenly indignant. "What do I have to do with his place in society?" Millicent let out a slight, "Ha." "I have no answer for that, I sure couldn't do it for him!" She paused for a moment. "His place in society shouldn't rest on either of us."

Millicent noticed that there was a phone on the table. She opened her purse and took out a little address book. After thumbing through it, she picked up the receiver and dialed a number. When her call was answered, Millicent asked for Danton Soleil. Lucy Butler recognized her voice, and put her through. Danton answered, and Millicent said, "Danton, I have Mary here at Dr. Scrope's office." Danton asked if she was sick. "No, Mary's not sick, but she is in the family way." Danton was shocked and couldn't reply for what seemed like an eternity. "Are you sure?" Millicent assured him that Dr. Scrope was confident in his diagnosis. Danton said, "...but they were always chaperoned...." Millicent retorted, "None the less, she's going to have Inman's baby."

There was a long silence on the line. At last, Danton asked, "How are we going to deal with this." Millicent thought for a moment, "There is no doubt that they love each other. I suppose that we should talk to them with Caroline and figure out how to proceed." Danton agreed, but asked, "Does Blackjack know yet?" Millicent admitted, "No, not yet, but as soon as we leave, Dr. Scrope is going to call him." Danton asked, "Do you have a copy of our evidence?" Millicent had an Epiphany. "Yes, I do. It may be time to play our hand." Danton agreed. "It's time he quit bullying you. Let him know, in no uncertain terms, that you are in charge of this situation." Millicent thanked Danton and told him that she'd be back in contact. Danton wished Millicent "**Bonne chance**" and told her that he'd be at her complete disposal any time she needed him. Millicent thanked Danton and hung the receiver back on the telephone cradle.

Millicent looked at her daughter and smiled. "We're going to get through this, but I'm going to need you to follow my lead. It will most likely get extremely ugly, and I may need to send you out of the room, if necessary. You don't need to be there if I have to engage the 'nuclear option.'" Mary suddenly felt suddenly uncomfortable. "What's going to happen to me?" Millicent did her dead level best to reassure Mary. "Now's not the time to worry about that. We just need to band together to survive your father's shock and anger."

Millicent changed gears and asked, "Mary, have you noticed your father being unusually nice to Marie Cosette lately?" Mary didn't even have to think, "Yes, now that you mention it, he has. It's almost like he's flirting with her." Mary instantly felt the impact of her statement. "I... I'm... I'm not sure if that is what I meant to say, mama." Millicent bristled, "That's okay, dear. It's exactly what I thought. Has Marie Cosette received any 'gifts' that she couldn't afford to buy for herself?" Mary thought. "She gets all of her clothes from me. She gets so little pay, she couldn't afford much, but she has new handkerchiefs, a brush and comb set, and a new necklace. At first I thought she had borrowed mine. You remember the one you bought me at Adler's at the beginning of the summer, don't you?" Millicent smiled. Mary continued, "I thought it was mine, but mine was in my jewelry box." Millicent's head was now cocked to the left. "Is that so?" She tried her best not to reveal to Mary how angry and distraught she was. "Well, I need to figure out how to protect both of you, now. Your father is liable to hurt you both."

Mary began to weep. Through her tears, she said, "Hurt me, Mama?" Millicent softened her rhetoric, just a little, "Don't worry, dear. He's not going to hurt you, or Marie Cosette, or even me, for that matter, ever again. I promise." Millicent stood up. "Come on, let's go home and face your father. As they walked to the waiting area, Millicent told Dr. Scrope that they were leaving. They went out of the door to the sound of Dr. Scrope's dialing the phone. Johnny Hardwick opened the door for them, and drove them back to the funeral home. As they got out of the car, Millicent stared Johnny Hardwick down. You won't ever need to drive me again, unless I ask you to, especially in my own car. Got it?" Johnny was taken aback. "Yes ma'am." Millicent added, "I need for you to take my car back to the porters and have it detailed. Can you get that done?" Johnny shook his head, "Yes, ma'am." Millicent turned to Mary, "Come on, dear, let's go in. It's almost time for luncheon."

Blackjack had heard Millicent's mini tirade and came out of his office into the motor court to confront Millicent and Mary. He was followed out of the office, after a couple of moments, by Marie Cosette. Blackjack yelled, "You've got a lot of explaining to do Millie!" Millicent charged over and got right up in Blackjack's face. She slapped her hand over Blackjack's mouth, and in a forceful, but hushed tone, said, "We're not discussing any family business out here, Andrew Jackson Day." She leaned in and whispered, "I doubt seriously that you want any of our 'socially acceptable' neighbors to hear any of this 'basket of dirty laundry.'" Mary's eyes almost bugged out. She had never seen her mother act that aggressively, or call her father "Andrew Jackson Day" to his face. Blackjack grabbed Millicent's wrist and ripped her hand off of his mouth. "Okay, we'll go into the house."

Mary and Marie Cosette had already scurried into the kitchen. Millicent and Blackjack followed. The door had scarcely closed. "PREGNANT? How the hell did that happen?" He looked at Mary. "Didn't I FORBID you from leaving the house at night?" Mary was, for the first time in her life, afraid of her father. She had never seen him this mad. His hair was disheveled, his face was beet red, and the veins in his neck and face were bulging. "Yes sir, you did." Blackjack swung his arms in the air wildly and carelessly. "...and you deliberately disobeyed me!?" Mary took a couple of steps back. "Father, I haven't left the house after sunset since you told me not to." Blackjack bellowed, "Lies, and more lies, and now you're going to lie to me even more!" He closed his fists, maniacally, and took a step toward Mary. Millicent stepped in his way, and pushed him back by hitting his shoulders with her hands. "ENOUGH!" She turned to Mary and Marie Cosette. "Girls, would you two go upstairs, Jackson and I have a few things to discuss." Neither Mary nor Marie Cosette dared to utter a word. They slipped through the swinging door leading to the dining room, and scampered through the parlor and up the stairs. Both had been utterly terrorized by Blackjack's words and actions.

Millicent could tell that Blackjack was starting to wind back up. His eyes were closed and he was shaking his head, and balling and unbarring his fists. Millicent puffed herself up. "JACKSON!" Blackjack was startled. He opened his eyes. Millicent stared straight through him. "Jackson, you need to sit down, NOW." She slapped the table forcefully and waited until he sat down in a chair at the kitchen table. Perhaps it was the shock of Millicent's acting in a way that he'd never seen, but Blackjack breathed in and out deeply, and buried his face in his hands. Millicent went into the pantry, rummaged around and opened a hidden cereal box. She retrieved a manilla folder. As she walked over to the table, Millicent said, "Jackson, you might be the Coroner-elect, but there's a new Sheriff in town." Before Blackjack could slap his palms on the kitchen table, Millicent slapped the folder on the table and pushed it in front of Blackjack. Blackjack looked perplexed. "What's this?" Millicent sat down in the chair across the table from Blackjack. "Read it, look at the pictures, and understand that you're NOT going to hurt me anymore. You're not going to hurt Mary, and you're not going to hurt Marie Cosette. We all know what you're trying to do to her!"

Blackjack started to stand up. The red was, once again, rising in his face, and his veins were bulging. Millicent summoned all of the rage of her decades of "imprisonment" AKA marriage to Andrew Jackson Day. "Oh yes, you go ahead and do what you think you want to do to me, but you better read that file first!" Blackjack looked down at the folder, and sat back down. He opened the folder and was, at once, confronted with an 8"x10" picture of the blood soaked, bullet riddled I.O.U. pledging the funeral home to Inman Carnes, III. He looked up at Millicent. All of the color in his face had drained away. "Where? …How?" Millicent stared him down. "Flip the photograph and read the notarized statement." Blackjack flipped the photograph and started to read the sworn statement. He paused and looked up at Millicent. "This won't hold up. There's spousal immunity."

Millicent smirked, "Spousal immunity means that the court can't compel a spouse to testify against their wife or husband if they don't want to. …besides, none of this information was told to me by you. I - observed - it - happening. You let Inman Carnes die in the ambulance behind the funeral home in the motor court. I directly observed you rummaging through his pockets to find the I.O.U., and taking his pulse, over and over, until you were sure he was dead, before you drove him over to Touro Infirmary." Millicent allowed Blackjack to finish reading the sworn statement, and stew in his own juices for a while. "Jackson, it's time for you to consider what exactly what you want, because I'm going to tell you the ONLY way you're going to get what you want." Blackjack was massaging his brow. Neither he, nor Millicent were unaware of the irony of the " Dossier Situation." Sheepishly, Blackjack said, "I'm listening."

Millicent asked, "Are you still using your father's house on Esplanade Avenue as a Bank House?" Blackjack seemed perplexed. "Yes…." He paused for a moment and continued, "I have an accountant who works there, and a couple of 'Card Guys' who live there." Millicent said, "Fine. They can use the front of the first floor. I'm moving Mary and Marie Cosette over there until the baby is born." Blackjack bowed up. "My daughter can't bear the child of a Carnes! Scrope told me that he could take care of it." Millicent bowed right on up with Blackjack. "You won't let MY daughter have a child with a Carnes, but you're doing your dead level best to fuck Inman Carnes's daughter!" Blackjack's knees gave way. He collapsed back into the chair, white as a ghost. "I don't know what you're talking about." Millicent moved in really close to Blackjack's ear. "You know goddamn well what I'm talking about, you backwoods, social climbing, claiming horse. Even your daughter has seen how you are manipulating Marie Cosette! Once again, it's time for you to shut the fuck up, and listen to me."

Not seeing any other path, at least for the moment, Blackjack bowed his head. "I assume you have these dossiers spread out all over New Orleans." Millicent smiled. "More than you could ever imagine, or begin to find." Blackjack sighed, "The girls are moving to Esplanade Ridge. Anything else?" Millicent sat down, and got down to business. "First of all, you're going to renovate the upstairs the way I want it renovated, paint it the way I want it painted, and decorate it the way I want it decorated. You'll have no contact with either of them. I'll make sure that they have everything that they need. You'll instruct Dr. Scrope to make house calls and tend to Mary, and Marie Cosette, if she has a need, but you need to make sure that he knows that he's on MY short leash. As long as they are taken care of, and safe, this dossier stays buried, and I'll keep up the appearances of our 'storybook' marriage. I'll come up with a reason Mary is gone, and won't debut at the Rex Ball. Most of our friends already think that she has Fibroid Tumors."

Blackjack resigned himself that he was defeated, at least for the moment, "When are they moving to Esplanade Avenue?" Millicent thought about the time of year. "We'll wait until the weekend after Thanksgiving. Until then, you'll have to keep your distance from both of them. ...but that won't be too difficult for you. You'll probably stay in your lair, now won't you?" Blackjack grimaced, "Probably, if that's what you want me to do." Millicent couldn't resist a **coup de gras**. "Don't beat yourself up, Jackson. You have a funeral home, and an extensive gambling empire to run. Don't worry, I'll keep the home fires burning, clasp hands with anyone you want me to, and advocate your irritating social-climbing agenda. ...as long as you play by MY rules. Blackjack stood up. He was hunched over at first. Slowly, he stood up straight. He threw his head back and paused. Blackjack took a step toward the door. "My dear, I have a lot of phone calls make. Would you ask Hattie to leave me a plate in the oven?" Millicent stood, painfully erect, clothed in her seaming victory. "Yes, dear, I'll make sure your lunch is here when you're ready for it." Blackjack left the kitchen, completely unsure of how Millicent had summoned the force necessary to completely decimate him. He hadn't been in this position for many, many decades.

Millicent waited until she heard his office door close. She went outside and found Hattie. "It's safe to go in and finish luncheon." Millicent gave Hattie her dinner instructions, then went into the funeral home and went up to Mary's bedroom. Mary and Marie Cosette stood up when Millicent opened the bedroom door. Millicent closed the door behind her, and walked to the center of the room. Marie Cosette asked, "Is you wantin' me da go down an' hep Hattie with da lunch, Mz. Day?" Millicent smiled at Marie Cosette. "Shortly. I came up here to talk to both of you. They all sat down. Millicent sat in Mary's desk chair, and Mary and Marie Cosette sat in the matching polychrome silk **bergère à oreilles**.

Millicent started, "First of all, everything is going to be okay. I'm going to make sure that everything is going to be okay, but we have some challenges to deal with. Millicent looked at Marie Cosette with no sense of malice or judgement. "Has he gotten to you yet, Marie Cosette?" Marie Cosette froze in place and started to shiver. "Who dat? Whad zackly is you sayin'?" Millicent turned her chair, and slid closer to Marie Cosette. She took Marie Cosette's hand. "Mary and I both saw you run out out of Jackson's office after him.

Till The Stars Burn Out Above You

We've seen the change in how he has been interacting with you. ...and he's been giving you gifts. Isn't that true?" Marie Cosette nodded her head. "Yes'um." Millicent squeezed Marie Cosette's hand reassuringly, and said, "All I want to know is how far he has gone. I'm not angry with you. He's doing something incredibly wrong to you. How far has has he gone?"

Marie Cosette began to sob. "Whil's y'alls was gone, Mista Day say'd he want to show me somethin'. I went back'n his desk da looka did. He put his han' on my leg. He got afu'm close, but y'alls drove up. He herd da commotun, an' went out'n da office. I'z still frozed fo a moment, den came oud'n da office. Millicent smiled. "Good, he hasn't forced you into a bad situation." Millicent paused. "Marie Cosette, Jackson's been up to no good, but it's finished. He's to have no more contact with you. I'm in charge now, and I promise to keep you safe! ...and, of course, your job is safe." Marie Cosette relaxed and smiled. Millicent stood up, as did Marie Cosette. Marie Cosette knew instinctively what that meant. "I'z'l be headed down do da kitch'n do hep Hattie." Millicent smiled broadly at Marie Cosette as she left the room. As the door closed, Millicent moved her chair closer to Mary. She took Mary's hand and smiled tenderly at her daughter. "**Chère douce fille**, this really isn't about me, or your father. You heard the options this morning. What do you want to do?"

Mary wiped her tears. "Mama, I have nothing but love for this baby. There's no way I could ever allow anyone to harm her." Millicent looked confused. "Her? You think that the baby is a girl?" Mary smiled, "I can't explain it, mama. Madame Delphine came to me in my dreamscape, and told me that my baby was a girl, and would make our family proud. You know full well that Inman Carnes is the only man for me. I feel a strong connection to him. Is that crazy?" Millicent tightened her grasp on Mary's hands. "No, sweetheart, that's not crazy. I had that same connection once, but it was ripped away from me." Mary was confused. "Father?" Millicent looked down at her lap. "No. No. ...you keep wanting to believe that, but before your father... Mary waited and looked at her mother with an inquisitive look. Millicent smiled. "You know who it is, but it's just too painful to talk about right now. ...one day." Mary understood. "It would be easier to do what father

199

must want me to do, but I can't. Other girls might decide to, but that would be up to them." Millicent grinned, "I know how much you love him." Mary let go of Millicent's hands and walked to her bed. "Completely. …and I know he feels that way too."

Millicent let that sink in for a moment. "Does he know?" Mary stared off into the distance and blinked a couple of times. "I can't see how. You called his Uncle Danton earlier. He might have told him." Millicent leaned in closer to Mary. "You might find this unexpected, but I truly want you to have the happiness that was stolen from me. I'm so tired of being a prisoner in my own life, and I refuse to allow your father to continue to hold you prisoner and hold you up as a reason he should be allowed to join that damn Boston Club." Mary was confused. "What are you saying?"

Millicent sat back in her chair and took a deep cleansing breath. She rubbed her brow and eye lids. "I'm not going to go into details. It's best for you not to know everything just now. After you were born, it became clear that I was only a trophy to your father. He became completely distant. His only interaction with me was in making sure that you became an even better trophy. He insisted that we go to church regularly, so that the Episcopalians at the Cathedral could see you grow up. He made sure that you had the best of everything. He paid for Ballet lessons, Piano lessons, and even paid that horrible old crone who taught you manners. Mary laughed. "Oh, I forgot about her. It never seemed like I could do anything to please her! My curtsey was never up to her standards. …but I think that my manners are acceptable." Millicent smiled and nodded. "I tell you all of this to help you understand what is going through your father's mind right now. He's thinking that twenty years of scheming and social climbing is about to go down the drain because of your condition. Obviously, there is no way that you can make your Debut at the Rex Ball.

Mary was tearing up. Millicent handed her a tissue. It's also obvious that you can't be seen by any of your father's friends. We also have to keep Marie Cosette away from your father. That's another story, for another day. Now's not the time for that. I got your father to agree to fix up your grandfather's house in Esplanade Ridge. You and Marie Cosette will move over there, out of sight, until the baby arrives. I'll visit often and make sure you and Marie Cosette have everything you need. Millicent paused, then said, "I'm almost jealous of you. It would be so nice to get away from the smell of death, and that dreadful Muzak downstairs."

Mary sat up and slid over next to her loving mother. "What about father? Will he ever forgive me?" Millicent thought about it for a few moments. "Time will tell. I suppose it depends on how well I cover this up, and if he gets what he really wants. ...to get into the Boston Club. Millicent stood up. "I'll have Marie Cosette bring up a tray so the two of you can eat in peace and won't have to run the risk of getting in your father's way." Millicent kissed Mary on the forehead and squeezed her hands lovingly. She walked quickly to the door, opened it, turned to smile at Mary for a moment, then turned and softly closed Mary's bedroom door behind her.

The next morning, Millicent slipped out to "run an errand." She drove almost to Tulane and pulled over to a public phone booth. After dropping a nickel in the slot, she dialed Danton's office. "Millicent could tell that Danton was nervous when he answered the call. "Milly, is that you?" Millicent said, "Yes, of course it is! **Bonjour mon cher amour!**" (Good morning my dear love!) Millicent's loving French and relaxed demeanor put Danton at ease. "**Je ne savais pas si vous pourriez être en colère contre moi.**" (I wasn't sure if you might be cross with me.) Millicent laughed. "Why would I be cross with you? You haven't committed a social **faux pas!**" Danton sighed, "How did Blackjack take the news?" Millicent replied, "At first I thought that he'd be capable of violence, on Mary, and on me. ...but I launched the 'nuclear option' on him." Danton asked, "You showed him the dossier?" Millicent replied, "Um hum." Danton paused to take in the scope of the situation. "I suppose you told him how things were going to be handled?" Millicent sighed, "Yes, I did. ...and he accepted my terms, at least for now. He's probably in his office right now trying to come up with ways to get back at me. I don't care. I've only ever loved you, and we'll work together to fix this for our loved ones."

Danton hesitated for a moment, then asked, "What does Mary want to do?" Millicent's pregnant pause made Danton extremely uncomfortable. Finally, Millicent said, "Mary is head-over-heels in love with Inman. She want's desperately to have his baby and 'live happily ever after' with Inman." It was Danton's turn to offer an uncomfortable interval as he thought through the scenario. At last, he said, "Milly, my gut says that Inman feels the same way about Mary, and that he'll want to marry her and have a family with her." Millicent then asked, "How is Caroline going to feel about this?" Danton didn't have to hesitate, "Caroline? Caroline loves Mary, she'll probably be the easiest to convince. …but, what about Blackjack?" Millicent said, "Jackson knows that he's to have nothing to do with either Mary or Marie Cosette. I'm moving both of them to one of his Bank Houses on Esplanade Avenue to get them away from him, and anyone who might malign Jackson in public." Danton finally asked, "So, when do we tell Caroline?" Millicent replied, "There is a funeral tomorrow, and there aren't any planned so far for the week of Thanksgiving. Shouldn't we get it over with?" Danton thought for a moment and said, "Yes. Inman and I will plan on going to **Maison Soleil**, tomorrow, for luncheon with Caroline. Please join us around 11:30. We'll get the truth out, and hopefully be able to enjoy a nice luncheon." Millicent agreed. She then said, "You realize that 'we' are untouchable, at least for now. …We'll have to be discrete, though." Danton sighed. "**Je t'aime Millicent. Je n'ai jamais cessé de t'aimer. Je t'aimerai tant que je vivrai!**" (I love you Millicent. I've never stopped loving you. I'll love you as long as I live!) Millicent started to weep. "**Mon précieux Danton, je t'aime de tout mon cœur, et je le ferai toujours!**" (My precious Danton, I love you with my complete heart, and always will!) …until tomorrow morning." Danton said, "Until tomorrow morning. My dreams will be of you tonight!"

After Danton reluctantly returned the headset back to the phone cradle, he walked out of his office and to Inman's **atelier**. Inman and his team were putting the final touches on the Patent Application for his Banana Box. Danton was extremely proud of his nephew's brilliance, and his efforts in getting his product patented, and put into production. Inman was happy to see his uncle. "Do you have news from our attorneys?" Danton said, "No, but there is news. Could you step out for a moment?" Inman made his apologies and stepped out to hear Danton out.

Danton cut to the chase. "Mary and Millicent are going to have luncheon with us tomorrow." Inman was enthusiastic, "That's wonderful!" Danton hedged a bit, and asked, "Am I correct in assuming that you two are in love?" Inman closed his eyes and practically melted. "Uncle Danton, she is the most amazing young lady. I adore her. I love her. All of my thoughts are about how to make her happy." Danton smiled and sighed. "I can see that. She truly is an amazing young lady!" Inman added, "She truly is." Danton continued, "I don't want to keep you from your team for too long, but I wanted to let you know that we're having luncheon with your mother, Aunt Virginia, Millicent, and Mary tomorrow at **Maison Soleil**." Inman was overcome with joy, "That's so wonderful, what's the occasion?" Danton hedged, "Well, it wasn't my idea, your mama, Millicent, you know…" While he really didn't know, Inman nodded and said, "Luncheon tomorrow, **Maison Soleil**, our ladies, fantastic!"

The next morning, at breakfast, in the amazingly peaceful complete absence of Blackjack, Millicent told Mary that they would later be going to **Maison Soleil** to break the news to Caroline and Inman. Mary, completely contrary to Millicent's expectations, was fine with the news. "Good, let's get this out, and get it settled." Millicent suddenly found herself tense. "What if he doesn't agree with what you want to do?" Mary closed her eyes and shook her head. "I may have misjudged you a bit, and I know that I truly misjudged my father completely, but I am completely sure of Inman." Mary's sting hurt Millicent, although she knew that it was completely accurate. She also knew the Carnes/Soleil family, and knew that Mary was right. Had Blackjack not forced Danton's hand, she'd have been happily married to him to this day. Millicent responded, "I honestly believe that you are right. …and I truly hope so!"

When Millicent and Mary walked out the kitchen door and down the stairs to the motor court, Johnny Hardwick had already moved Millicent's Eldorado to a place of convenience. He had left the keys in the ignition, and gotten well out of sight. Millicent and Mary got in and drove to Howard Avenue. As Millicent pulled the Cadillac to the curb at the main gate of **Maison Soleil**, Danton and Inman were sitting in Caroline's **salon principal** regaling her with the progress on Inman's new invention, the Banana Shipping Box. Caroline was terribly intrigued at the financial implications of its implementation. "**Votre cher papa serait extrêmement fier de vous, cher fils!**" (Your dear papa would be so extremely proud of you dear son!) Inman beamed.

Mary reached through the gate and rang the bell. Caroline sat up straight and said, "**Nos invités sont arrivés.**" (Our guests have arrived.) Monique slipped out the kitchen door and opened the gate. "**Madame vous attend et ravie de vous voir tous les deux!!**" (Madam is expecting you, and excited to see you both!) Monique escorted Millicent and Mary to the **véranda** of the **manoir** and introduced them. "**Madame Day, et mademoiselle Day.**" Millicent stepped into Caroline's **salon principal** followed by Mary. Caroline and Virginia rushed over to great their oldest friend and her charming daughter. Danton hung back looking at the ladies, with great desire for Millicent, and at Caroline, marveling at how much pleasure she had been receiving from the recent visits of both Millicent and Mary, but mostly from the visits of Millicent.

After many hugs and kind words and salutations, Millicent, still holding Caroline's hands, said, "**Caroline, nous avons des nouvelles dont nous devons discuter.**" (Caroline, we have some news that we need to discuss.) Caroline said, "Millie that is wonderful, but we'll eat first. Monique has been preparing all morning, and it's just ready to serve." Millicent agreed. During luncheon, Danton went on and on about what an amazing job Inman was doing in the family business. "His Banana Transport Box is going to revolutionize the industry. We'll be able to move our employees to other more important endeavors, and cut the transportation costs of bananas more than in half." Caroline was curious, "What would old Sam, the Banana Man think about Inman's innovation?" Danton answered her, "I'm going to find out, but only after it is patented. Inman and I will be going out to Audubon Place, and present him with one of Inman's boxes of bananas and see what he says!" Caroline clapped her hands in delight. "Ohh, I'd almost risk leaving the property to see his reaction!" Everyone completely enjoyed Caroline's sentiment.

As they finished their dessert, Caroline looked across to Millicent. "Milly, you said something about some news earlier." Danton's, Millicent's, and Mary's faces lost complexion. Millicent cleared her throat. "Yes, I did. Ahem, please excuse me, this is awkward and difficult." Caroline scrunched her brow. "Awkward? Really? How so?" Millicent stared into Caroline's eyes with a pitiful expression. "Caroline, Mary is with child." Caroline froze completely to contemplate Millicent's simple five words. To Millicent's surprise, Caroline displayed no shock or displeasure. She was simply working the situation out in her mind. "I suppose that you're sure?" Millicent replied, "Yes, I'm sure. Dr. Scrope diagnosed her on Tuesday. Jackson forced him to see us when the office was closed for Armistice Day." Caroline then turned her attention to Inman. "**Est-ce possible, mon fils?**" (Is this possible, my son?) Inman stood and walked to Mary. He put his hands on her shoulders. He looked at his aunt, his uncle and his mother in turn. He then stared into Mary's loving eyes. Her lack of shame or fear gave him courage. "**Oui, mama, c'est possible. Je pensais que nous avions pris des précautions, mais c'est arrivé si soudainement** "(Yes, mama, it is possible. I thought that we had taken precautions, but it happened so suddenly....) Mary put her hand over Inman's hand and squeezed it lovingly.

All eyes turned to Caroline. She looked at Inman. "I understand that you aren't as big of a fan of tennis, as Danton, Millicent, myself, and your late father, but the ball is, indeed, in your court right now." Inman turned his gaze back to his beloved. There was no fear in either of them, only love. Inman dropped to one knee and took Mary's hands. "**Très chère Mary, je vous aime depuis la première fois que je vous ai rencontré. Nous avons passé l'été dernier à grandir dans l'amour et l'affection les uns pour les autres. Faites de moi l'homme le plus heureux du monde et épousez-moi!!**" (Dearest Mary, I've loved you from the first time that I met you. We have spent the past summer growing in love and affection for each other. Please make me the happiest man on Earth and marry me!) Mary started to cry tears of overwhelming joy. She threw her arms around Inman and said, "**Oui, mon seul amour!**" (Yes, my only love!) As they hugged, and Millicent, Caroline and Danton were reduced to tears, aunt Virginia blurted out, "...but, he doesn't have a ring to give her!" Caroline became indignant, "Oh, yes he does!" She removed her engagement ring and handed it to Inman. He looked at Caroline and mouthed, "Are you sure, mama?" Caroline smiled and nodded her head. Millicent said, "**Mon Dieu**, Caroline, Inman's father gave you that ring!" Caroline smiled, "Yes he did, and his father gave it to his mother before him. It goes back many generations. All who have worn it have been truly in love. Some have experienced great difficulties, but love was always evident." Danton excused himself. After a few moments he returned with two bottles of **Veuve Clicquot la Grande Dame 1949**. Monique brought in a tray of antique Baccarat cut-crystal champagne coupes. As Danton handed Caroline a glass, she frowned, "This isn't from my cellar. ...and it's chilled. Danton made up a white lie. "I remembered seeing them in the Frigidaire a week or so ago. I must have brought them over some time ago for some event, and they weren't used." Danton couldn't tell if Caroline believed his scenario, or simply accepted it. When everyone had a glass, Danton raised his glass, "To Mary and Inman! May the happy couple have countless years of joy together!"

Millicent was over the moon happy, and let the celebration go on for as long as she dared. She hated that she was looking at her Cartier wrist watch so often, but she was worried about enraging Blackjack. Caroline noticed, and understood. At last she said, "Goodness, look at the time, Jackson must be expecting you two for dinner shortly!" Millicent smiled a sad smile, and sent Caroline a look that communicated, "Thank you my dear old friend. I love you!" She stood up and said, "Yes, Caroline, Mary and I should be going. We want to thank you for your gracious hospitality!" Caroline stood and said, "Nonsense, we're finally going to be family. ...and it's about time!" Caroline linked arms with Millicent and walked her through the door out to the **véranda**. Millicent said, "Can we meet on the first to plan a secret wedding here?" Caroline immediately understood that Millicent didn't want to involve, or even tell Blackjack. "Yes, send dear Marie Cosette with the details." Millicent agreed, and she and Mary made their way back to the gate. Inman went along to let them out onto Howard Avenue. By the time that they got into the Eldorado, Millicent was lost in thought. It was interesting to her that Caroline referred to Marie Cosette as "dear Marie Cosette," and not "your girl." Millicent's thought process was interrupted by Mary, "Mama!" Millicent snapped back and asked, "What???" Mary laughed, "Mama, it's hot, and we need to get home." Millicent laughed. She cranked the huge Cadillac and pulled away from the curb.

After Millicent and Mary left **Maison Soleil**, Inman returned to the **garçonnière** to regroup. Caroline and Danton went into the **bibliothèque**. (library) Caroline shut the door and they sat on either side of a green leather topped **bureau plat**. (an 18th century flat desk) Danton asked, "What can I do to help you prepare for this wedding?" Caroline said, "I want you to go to Saint Patrick's and find that young priest who's been bringing us the Sacraments on Sunday." Danton asked, "What was his name, 'Julian' something?" Caroline thought for a moment. "Yes. ...something like 'lash a cot.'" Danton laughed, "Okay, so what do you want me to tell him, or, would it be, ask him?" Caroline responded, "I want you to tell him our 'situation.' Tell him that I want him to marry Mary and Inman. ...but he'll need to know that she's an Episcopalian. I'm not sure how much of a problem that'll be. Hopefully it won't be too much of a problem, because they mostly have the same beliefs and ceremonies. Ask him if it would be possible for him to stay a while after he brings the Eucharist this Sunday." Danton, of course, agreed. "I'll just run over there now. It's Thursday afternoon. I'm sure that he's preparing for some sort of service, Compline, perhaps."

As Millicent pulled away from the curb, Mary was thankful for the breeze. Millicent noticed Mary massaging her belly, and admiring her 'new' engagement ring. In truth, Millicent was completely envious of her daughter, because Mary was on the verge of marrying her true love. Mary was, however, confused when Millicent turned for town, and not to the funeral home at the next intersection. She turned a confused face to her mother. Millicent smiled. We're going to Adler's. Mary smiled, but was still confused. Millicent parked the Cadillac, and she and Mary walked to Adler's. Millicent led Mary to the Jewelry Department. The salesman asked, "How may I help Madame?" Millicent said, "To start with, we'd like to look at 18kt. gold chains." The salesman said, "Very good, Madame, if you'll follow me." He led them to a display case that was dripping with fine gold chains, Crucifixes, Stars of David, and other non religious medallions.

The salesman asked, "What length chain was Madame considering?" Millicent looked at Mary. "Please know that this is in your best interest." Mary pulled a face, but said nothing. Millicent looked back at the salesman. "It would need to come down to here on her." She pointed to a spot deep within Mary's breasts. Both Mary's and the salesman's eyebrows raised in surprise. After a moment, the salesperson told Millicent, "Our longest chains are Matinee length, 21 to 24 inches. They generally would fall just above mademoiselle's, umm, **décolletage**." Millicent looked at Mary. That wouldn't work. She asked, "What if a small gold ring were placed on the chain and a bracelet were strung through the ring?" The salesman thought for a moment. "Madame is quite the genius! You should be a jewelry designer!" Millicent asked, "May we please see some combinations? I'd like to start with your longest Matinee chain and matching bracelets." The salesman said, "But, of course," and brought out several square mahogany felt lined trays. Millicent asked, "Mary, do any of these designs appeal to you?" Mary looked at each with interest. She liked the Mariner chain very much. "His family is in shipping, but it's too heavy, I think." Millicent agreed. Mary said, "a Box Chain or a Cable Chain would work." Millicent was patient. At last, Mary found one that spoke to her. "What is this style called?" The salesman told her, "That is a Figaro chain."

Mary looked at her mother, "What do you think, mama?" Millicent said, "It's beautiful! Why do you like it?" Mary said, "I like the fact that all of the links are't uniform. Inman and I have had perfect dates, and dates that we had to get through because things didn't go as we had planned." Millicent clasped her hands and said, "What an extraordinarily beautiful sentiment!" She turned to the salesman, " Could we put this combination together to see if it works?" The salesman obliged, "Of course!" Millicent's only worry was how much flare the bracelet would have once suspended below the necklace. To her surprise, and delight, it produced very little flare. When the combination was assembled, the salesman asked Millicent if she wanted to see how it looked around Mary's neck. "**Oui! beaucoup!**" The salesman handed both ends of the necklace to Millicent who placed it around Mary's neck from behind and fastened the clasp. When Mary turned around, Millicent said, "**Mon Dieu, c'est la pure perfection!**" The salesman turned a massive oval mirror around so that Mary could see the necklace. To her, it was so beautiful, she let out a great sigh. Millicent was convinced, "We'll take it!" The salesman smiled, "Shall we write this sale up, or would Madame like to consider something special for herself?" Millicent, all puffed up, said, "Madame would! May Madame see your range of Cocktail Rings?"

The salesman picked up Mary's chain and asked Millicent to follow him to another display case. Before he could even ask what Millicent was interested in, she pointed to one ring. "That one. That one right there!" Not knowing exactly which ring Millicent was pointing to, the salesman pulled the tray out and let Millicent pull the ring out and try it on. It was an especially jazzy diamond and platinum dazzler. The primary design was diagonal in nature, and resembled a perfect bow on an elegant Christmas present. It was a size six and fit Millicent perfectly. As she slid it on, the platinum complimented her skin tone and the assortment of old European mine-cut and emerald-cut stones lit up the room. Millicent looked at Mary. Mary's face lit up, and she nodded her head enthusiastically. Millicent said, "I'll wear it out, if you don't mind." The salesman said, "…but of course, Madame!" The salesman wrote out the ticket, and Millicent presented him her charger plate. The salesman said, "**Pardonnez-moi madame, mais je dois autant obtenir l'approbation d'une charge.**" (Pardon me Madam, but I must get approval for a charge this much.) Millicent smiled politely. The salesman flagged down a floor walker who called the business office. Approval was swift. The floor walker sincerely apologized to Millicent for delaying her. Millicent was truly gracious. "You were just doing your duty to the store, and, I think, protecting my account from fraud. …so, I thank you!" The floor walker was sincerely humbled by Millicent's magnanimity, and bowed, "Thank you, Madame. We appreciate your patronage of Adler's, truly!"

Millicent took her receipt and bags of jewelry boxes, and she and Mary wore their new acquisitions out of the store. Mary was still unsure of why her necklace had a bracelet dangling below. As Millicent cranked the Eldorado, she explained, "Look at your left ring finger." Mary looked down and smiled. "Yes, I'm engaged to the finest young man in all of New Orleans!" Millicent had to agree. "…but, the one young man your father despises the absolute most."

Mary, not knowing the full story yet, frowned. "…but, mama, this engagement solves our problem." Millicent sighed, "Don't underestimate your father. He can't be trusted with this information. I'll have to work with Caroline to plan this wedding without your father's involvement." Mary started crying, "…but why?" Millicent, on the verge of tears herself said, "If Jackson even suspects what we're doing, he'll force Dr. Scrope to kill your baby. We'll have to keep you and your baby safe, and get you married, in private, away from your father."

Mary suddenly knew what the necklace was for. "I suppose that I can't wear my engagement ring on my finger, then." Millicent wiped her eyes. **"Mon cher chéri, je souhaite vraiment que tu puisses, mais non, tu ne peux pas."** (My dear darling, I truly wish that you could, but no, you can't.) Millicent paused, then added, "But your engagement ring will rest above your heart. …and the connecting ring will be replaced by your wedding ring until we settle this unhappy business."

Danton was able to speak to Father Lachicotte at Saint Patrick's that afternoon. The good Father listened to the family's dilemma with great interest. "Do you have a clue when Madame Carnes wants to hold the wedding?" Danton said, "No, only soon. …and it'll have to be at **Maison Soleil**, naturally. Her biggest worry is that the girl is an Episcopalian." Father Lachicotte let out an abbreviated chuckle, "Thank God the girl isn't a Baptist. That would be so much more difficult." Danton laughed. "If it helps, her mother is a Blanchard, and is a confirmed Catholic." Father Lachicotte reassured Danton. "We'll get through this. When does she want to meet?" Danton smiled and said, "She was hoping that you would be able to stay after bringing the Sacraments this coming Sunday." Father Lachicotte thought for a moment. "Yes, that will be the best time. We're closing in on Thanksgiving, and Advent will be here the following Sunday. Tell her that Sunday the 16th. works for me." Danton returned to the **manoir** at **Maison Soleil** after his meeting with Father Lachicotte. To Caroline, he said, "He'll want to meet with Mary and confirm her Baptismal Vow." Caroline said, "Well, that's fair. Is that all?" Danton sighed, "No, Mary will have to sign a pledge that her children will be brought up Catholic." Caroline grinned, and thought to herself, "Mary can promise that, but what control does the Catholic Church have to enforce it?" To Danton, she asked, "Do you think that she'll sign that pledge?" Danton shrugged his shoulders. There was absolutely no way that he could answer that question.

After pulling into the motor court, Millicent and Mary wiped away their tears. Mary had already suspended her engagement ring and secured it safely in her bosom. Millicent left the Eldorado to the porters and went into the kitchen. Hattie and Marie Cosette were finishing up dinner preparations. As Millicent and Mary walked into the kitchen, Millicent could tell that Marie Cosette was on tends hooks. "Hattie, I'd like to borrow Marie Cosette for a few minutes if that won't hurt your efforts." Hattie expressed none of the emotions she was feeling and said simply, "Yess'um." The three went upstairs and into Mary's bedroom and closed the door securely. Marie Cosette could hardly contain her anticipation. She asked, "Well, how'd id go?" Mary looked at Millicent who only smiled. Mary pulled the chain slowly out of the gap between her breasts and revealed the ring. Marie Cosette squealed. "You'z engaged!" Millicent said, "Yes, but it's secret. Mr. Day can't know, the staff, all of them, even Hattie, can't know. No one can know. Do you understand. Marie Cosette said, "De bodh ob ju has been drully good to'un me. Jaw secred be safe wid me!" Millicent hugged Marie Cosette. "Thank you, dear one. I wish my husband could see what a dear, wonderful person you are!" Marie Cosette blushed, "I'z bedder go on down an' hep finish de dinna'" Millicent smiled broadly and said, "Yes, my dear, please do."

After Church on Sunday the 16th., Blackjack begged to not have to go to a long luncheon. "There is so much I need to familiarize myself with before I assume this position in January. I'll eat whatever is leftover in the refrigerator. Will you two be able to go to lunch on your own?" Millicent was impressed with Blackjack's feigned humility but pretended to be unhappy. "I suppose that we can manage, Jackson." When they pulled into the motor court behind the funeral home, Blackjack jumped out of the Eldorado, and bolted for his office. Millicent gracefully exited the passenger door and made her way around the massive bonnet of the car and to the Driver's seat. As her mother strolled around the Cadillac, Mary pushed the passenger side seat forward, exited the car, let it fall back into place, and slid into the front passenger seat. Millicent fired the massive motor up. "Antoine's?" Mary nodded approvingly, and they were off to a date with culinary perfection in the **Vieux Carré**.

One of the best perks of being a regular at Antoine's was that their waiters were quite simply the best. Regular customers quickly achieved their own waiters. By the second or third visit, their waiter knew the pallet of their entire family, or group. Millicent and Mary's order was almost placed before they were seated. As usual the cuisine was better than perfection. They both wished that they had room and time for dessert. Millicent settled the bill, and she and Mary drove to **Maison Soleil**. Father Lachicotte was already there. He had just finished administering the Sacraments to Caroline, and Inman. Danton had actually gone to Mass earlier. Mary reached through the gate and rang the bell. Monique came out and let them in. She led them cautiously to the **véranda**. "I'z not shu' if'n de be finnish wid de Mass." Monique quietly opened the French door just enough to see in. When she saw that the occupants of the room were standing and chatting, Millicent felt comfortable enough to swing the door open and introduce herself, and Mary.

The first thing that both Millicent and Mary noticed was the kind look at them from Father Julien Lachicotte's eyes. They were both comforted by the fact that he seemed to get it, and wasn't judgmental. Caroline made the introductions. "Father Lachicotte, this is my oldest and dearest friend, Millicent Blanchard Day, and her daughter, Mary Day." Father Lachicotte smiled and took both of their hands in turn. "Delighted." Caroline said, "We should have some **rafraîchissements**! Father Lachicotte smiled. "Madame Carnes, please assemble them, but I feel that I should have a meeting with the intendeds first." Caroline said, "Yes, of course, Father. Please use the **bibliothèque** for your meeting, if you please. Father Lachicotte thanked Caroline, and invited Mary and Inman to accompany him into the **bibliothèque**.

Caroline and Millicent suddenly found themselves alone in Caroline's **salon principal**. Caroline apologized to Millicent, "Virginia has a 'caller.'" Millicent, with an extreme display of class, showed none of what she was thinking. She said, "I'm so glad to be spending this afternoon with you, my dearest friend." Millicent's magnanimity touched Caroline deeply. She had to catch herself before she broke down and cried. After a deep sigh, Caroline said, "I noticed a new extraordinarily beautiful chain around Mary's neck. May I assume that her engagement ring is tucked away from Jackson's view?" Millicent confessed, "Yes it is, but I wanted it to be near her heart." Caroline sighed, "…and I suppose that her wedding ring will have to replace that plain gold ring suspending the chain holding her engagement ring?" Millicent started to tear up. "Yes, at least for a while. I doubt you know what Jackson is capable of." Caroline thought for a moment. "I truly wish that I hadn't read all of those books over the years, but I have a pretty good idea of what he's capable of."

She continued, "Look at what he did to you and Danton, all of those yeas ago, when he was just a rank amateur." Before Millicent could respond, the door to the **bibliothèque** opened and Father Lachicotte and Mary and Inman strode into the room. Both Caroline and Millicent were breathless in their anticipation. At last, a smiling Father Lachicotte said, "These two young people are quite extraordinary! Not only are they in love for all of the right reasons, their expressions of love and all of its ramifications, propelled me to a greater hope for mankind!" Millicent and Caroline looked at each other questioningly. However, they both remembered, almost concurrently, that he was quite young, and unaffected by the grotesque that society had to offer.

Caroline took the lead. "So, are they ready to be married?" Millicent held her breath. Father Lachicotte beamed, "Yes, they are. Mary recited her Episcopal Catechism perfectly, which falls in line with ours. …and she signed the pledge." Millicent had been away from the Church for so long she had forgotten, and looked at Caroline and asked, "What pledge?" Caroline said, "It's nothing. I'll explain later." Father Lachicotte asked, "Does the family have a preferred date for the sacrament? Caroline took a cleansing breath and looked at Millicent. "It's not going to be a big wedding. …but we are entering Advent. What if we have the ceremony on Rose Sunday, the 14th. of December?" Millicent thought for a moment, then said, "What a beautiful day on the Christian calendar for a wedding! Yes, of course, if that suits our children." Caroline asked for input from Mary and Inman. They were both enthusiastic. In truth, they would both have been delighted to have been married right there on the spot. They were that much in love.

After Father Lachicotte left, Caroline looked over at Mary and Inman. "Why don't you two go down to the **Garçonnière** and spend some quality time together while Milly and I do some planning. After Inman grabbed Mary's arm and pulled her toward the **véranda**, Millicent looked at Caroline with a horrified look. Caroline sank back in her chair, "Milly, they're in love, they're engaged, and Mary is pregnant. What else can they do?" Millicent roared with laughter, "Not much, I suppose!" ...and the two lifelong friends then got down to business. Their first obstacle was their suggestions for Best Man and Maid of Honor. Millicent suggested, "I think that Danton should be Inman's Best Man. He's really the only choice." Caroline agreed. "...okay, but what about Mary's Maid of Honor?" Millicent laid her forehead in the palm of her hand. "Caroline, I don't know. She doesn't have close friends, at least friends close enough not to rat her out to her father."

Caroline confidently said, "She has one person who is truly her Maid of Honor." Millicent closed her eyes and thought. At last, Caroline said, "Marie Cosette!" Millicent opened her eyes. She was somewhat confused. Caroline said, "You know as well as I do, that girl isn't a servant. You don't treat her like one, now do you?" Millicent said, "No I don't. ...and you know, don't you?" Caroline said, "Yes, I figured the whole thing out recently. I'm going to make it all right, when it's time. ...but that's my timeline, all right?" Millicent said, "Yes, of course!" Carolyn asked, "We have our Best man and our Maid of Honor, do we need anyone else? Millicent couldn't think of another necessary participant, other than the father of the Bride, but he wouldn't even be told about the joyous proceedings.

When it was time to get back to the Garden District, Danton and Inman escorted Millicent and Mary to the main gate. As they walked, Danton showed Millicent a picture. She looked at it and asked, "This looks so familiar.

What is this building?" Danton said, "It's called 'Morro Castle.'" Millicent nodded her head, "Yes, of course, the old, haunted Spanish garrison building. Why are you showing me this picture?" Danton said proudly, "I bought it. …or rather, Inman and I bought it." Millicent stopped dead in her tracks. "Why ever did you buy an apartment building?" Danton rocked back and forth on his heels. "Well, we're renovating it at the moment. …but around Christmas we'll be running ads in the **Times Picayune** for our home for single pregnant women and single mothers. They'll be supervised by matrons, and have excellent security." Millicent was intrigued. "…but you're leaving out something, I sense." Mary was now interested. Inman said, "We wanted to make sure that everything was in place before telling you. We didn't want to get anyone's hopes up only to be disappointed." Mary was chomping at the bit to know the rest of the story. Millicent looked at Danton with a pleading look. Danton, all puffed out and proud said, "There is a second building on Burgundy that is attached, and Inman and I found a secret passageway from the upstairs of Morro Castle to a stairway down to the other building. We're building Inman a bolt-hole there."

The gears were turning in Millicent's mind. "You know full well that I can't tell Jackson we're moving the girls over there." Danton pursed his lips, "No, of course you can't. It'll have to be old Blackjack's idea. I suppose that he still reads the **Times Picayune** every morning." Millicent nodded, "Yes, he does… Make sure you have ads in the Sports section. He studies that section like seminarians study the Bible." Millicent's joke amused everyone. They all burst out laughing. Danton agreed, "I suppose we'll have to push things so he can't trust his goons, and looks for an alternative." Danton opened Millicent's door, and Inman opened Mary's. Millicent cranked the Eldorado. Danton and Inman were propped on the door frames, not wanting to say goodbye. Finally, Millicent looked over at Mary. "Why are you being so coy. Go ahead and kiss him!" Mary looked over at her mother, "I will. Why don't you kiss him too? I know you both want to, and Inman and I both know what you've been up to. …and we're both extremely happy for you both!" Millicent and Danton exchanged shocked looks that didn't last long, and melted into looks of great love and affection. They kissed, and Inman leaned in and kissed

Mary. When Millicent pulled away from the curb, both she and Mary were practically breathless. Nothing was said. Nothing needed to be said, but both were happy that their loving relationships were out in the light of day, and approved by everyone, at least everyone who mattered.

Thanksgiving came, and it was difficult, at the very least, for almost anyone to be thankful. Millicent and Danton were angry that they couldn't be together, officially. Caroline missed her dear husband Inman, and had for over 20 years. Mary and Inman were engaged to be married, but only in complete secrecy. There was nothing that could ever make Blackjack thankful. Well, perhaps, membership in the Boston Club, but what chance of that was there? Virginia was the lone exception, and she had several 'callers' that gave her a long list of things to be thankful for.

Monique prepared Thanksgiving dinner at **Maison Soleil** for Caroline, Virginia, Danton, and Inman. Inman was truly thankful for his new job, and that he was to be married to the love of his life. He couldn't understand why he couldn't be with his **fiancée**. Caroline and Virginia were happy that their family and the Blanchard family were soon to be united, but worried about what Blackjack was capable of. Monique ate her Thanksgiving Dinner quietly in the kitchen, perhaps the most thankful of all. She felt the love of a family that appreciated her work and treated her like more than just a servant.

Hattie and Marie Cosette prepared a sumptuous Thanksgiving dinner at Andrew Jackson Day's funeral home on Saint Charles Avenue. ...but a malaise infected the house. Blackjack did everyone a favor by eating his feast in his intake garage with his cronies. Millicent and Mary ate in silence together in the dining room. They both knew full well that they lived in a prison, and that it would be an endeavor for them to both escape their confinements. Hattie and Marie Cosette ate their Thanksgiving dinner, after serving Millicent and Marie, like Monique, in the kitchen, but, unlike Monique, they were worried about the ramifications on their livelihood, of recent developments.

For dessert, Hattie had gone all out and made a **Gâteau de Sirop aux Figues**. (Syrup Cake with Figs) Marie Cosette had spent the better part of the morning cranking the ice-cream churn to turn Hattie's boiled vanilla custard into a velvety-smooth decadent frozen treat to be paired with the **Gâteau**.

Millicent, however, found it quite impossible to finish her dessert. She had the girl's impending move to Esplanade Ridge locked into focus. She went to the kitchen door. "Hattie, Marie Cosette, you both really out did yourselves this year. Everything was delicious!" Hattie nodded and went back to her dishes. Marie Cosette smiled so deeply that Millicent sighed and cracked a smile.

Millicent then walked down the hallway that led to Blackjack's office. He had finished his meal, and was going over the books of one of his Bank Houses with his accountant. Millicent pushed the door open and walked into Blackjack's office. He jumped up, protesting, "Excuse me!" Millicent lunged behind Blackjack's desk and slammed her fist on the ledger. She shouted, "Sit down, Jackson!" Millicent then turned her gaze to the accountant, "You, …you get the hell out of here! You two can do this later." The accountant looked at Blackjack. He nodded, and the accountant hurried out of the office. Blackjack, hiding his wrath, in the knowledge that there wasn't a damn thing he could do about Millicent, asked, "What can I do for you Millie?"

Millicent stood up straight and looked down at Blackjack over her bony, but elegant Blanchard nose with a dead stare that almost burned two holes in Blackjack's forehead. "We're going to the Bank House on Esplanade Avenue. I'm damn well determined to make sure that the upstairs is going to be ready on Saturday, when Mary and Marie Cosette are moving." Blackjack said, "Millie, I've got so much work to get done; I assure you that it'll be ready." Millicent's hands tightened into fists. "I don't care if you have to work all damn night for the two next weeks, you're going to get your ass out of that damn chair, and we're going over there to check on progress. Got it?"

Blackjack sighed stiffly, and nodded. He got up to have the Eldorado pulled out while Millicent went back to the kitchen to tell Hattie and Marie Cosette that she'd be out for a while. "Marie Cosette, would you please run up and tell Mary that I'll be back as quickly as possible?" Marie Cosette agreed, and ran through the door to the dining room, through the parlor and foyer, and up the stairs. Millicent thanked Hattie again for a truly delightful Thanksgiving dinner, then slipped out the kitchen door, and down the steps to the motor court. Blackjack was sitting behind the wheel. Millicent walked calmly to the driver's side, looked at Blackjack, and said, "Shift it on over, this is MY car, remember? You've told everyone in New Orleans." Blackjack slid across to the passenger side and Millicent assumed her position behind the wheel.

Millicent turned the Cadillac onto Louisiana Avenue, then South Claiborne Avenue. South Claiborne became North Claiborne. She turned right onto Esplanade Avenue, then left onto Marais Street and pulled into the back yard of the Bank House. They got out of the Eldorado and went in the back door of the Bank House. Blackjack's goons were startled when they heard the door open and close. They jumped up and rushed back to the kitchen to an even greater shock. "Boss, we din't 'spect you today!" Millicent looked at the pair of goons garbed only in boxer shorts and stained singlets. "Obviously!" Blackjack asked them to put some clothes on. "Madame Day wants to inspect the renovations upstairs." While they waited for the goons to get dressed, Millicent looked around the kitchen. The sink was piled with dirty dishes. The garbage can was overflowing, and there were piles of dirty laundry in the corner. She winced from a pervasive funk of decaying food, sweat, and God-only-knows what else. "Jackson, this can't be like this on Saturday!" Blackjack hadn't expected their living conditions to be so rough, but to be fair, he'd only ever passed quickly through the kitchen on his way to the business room on his visits. "I'll make sure that this is cleaned up, and that it won't ever be like this again."

Millicent was getting impatient and said, "We're going on up now. Hewie and Dewie can catch up when they're presentable." She walked into the central hallway and made her way up the stairs. Millicent and Blackjack looked first at the bathroom in the central hallway. It was finished and cleaned up to Millicent's satisfaction. Next, they went into the rear bedroom, Marie Cosette's. The floors were done, but the painting hadn't been finished. Millicent tilted her head and breathed deeply. Blackjack started taking some notes and said, "I promise you, this will be done by tomorrow afternoon." That left Mary's bedroom and sitting room. Millicent wasn't optimistic. They went into the sitting room first. To Blackjack's relief, it was completed and met Millicent's approval. They then stepped into Mary's bedroom. Blackjack held his breath as they stepped through the door. Millicent was relieved, "This is wonderful, it's exactly what I asked for." She stepped to the French doors that led to the gallery. "Jackson, the gallery needs to be painted, and they'll need some furniture out there. Can you make that happen?" Blackjack agreed.

When the goons caught up, Blackjack gave them a punch list. "These things have to be done by tomorrow afternoon. Do you understand?" The goons looked at each other. "Yes, Boss." Millicent looked at Blackjack and pointed through the floor. "Oh, yes. ...and that kitchen is a pig sty. I don't care if you both have to work through the night, but it had better be so clean that my 'loving' wife could eat off the floor by the time my daughter gets here!" Both of the goons were afraid to show any emotion. They hung their heads and nodded. Blackjack added, "...and that funky smell has to be gone too." "Yes, Boss." Blackjack looked at Millicent, "Did I leave anything out?" Millicent looked at the goons, "Don't let me hear that either one of you has said anything to either of my girls that I'd take offense to. Understand?" "Yes ma'am!" "...and don't even think about going up those stairs unless it's a damn emergency!" "Yes ma'am!" Satisfied, Millicent walked back through the sitting room toward the stairs. "Good." She started down the stairs, "Jackson, I'll be waiting for you in the car. Don't be too long, or you'll have to take the streetcar home." Blackjack said nothing but noticed that his goons had smiles they couldn't contain on their faces. "Wipe those smirks off your faces, or I'll have to do something that I don't want to do." They both straightened out. "Sorry boss, we didn't have no idea..." Blackjack started down the stairs. "Don't make my wife unhappy. That'll make me more unhappy. Got it?" The goons responded, "Oh, yes boss. We'll make sure everyone here is happy!" Blackjack walked swiftly down the stairs and out to the Eldorado. It was a quiet drive back to the Garden District.

After a mostly silent Thanksgiving dinner, Inman stood up and exclaimed, in desperation, "I don't understand why I can't see my **fiancée** when I want to!" Danton said, "That's a question I'll never be able to answer!" Caroline shot the 'Soleil Glare' at Danton, and he quieted down. She gave her twin sister, Virginia a similar look, and Virginia blew a breath out of puckered lips and decided not to say a thing. After an appropriate pause, Caroline looked at her son and said, "**Votre situation est compliquée. Le père de** ilом

Mary est aligné avec des criminels odieux. Sa mère et moi travaillons pour résoudre ce problème." (Your situation is complicated. Mary's father is aligned with heinous criminals. Her mother and I are working to solve this.) Inman, still disgruntled, accepted his mother's explanation and spent the rest of the day with his family, quietly dreaming of Mary.

On Friday, Danton and Inman went into work. Inman wanted to finish his final presentation versions of his Banana Transport Box, so the attorneys could present the Patent requests the following week. Lucy Butler agreed to come in, but the rest of the office employees had been given the day off. Cargo was being unloaded and loaded when they got to the Wharf, as it was almost every other day of the year. That day however, bananas were being offloaded and loaded into trucks and rail cars. Danton and Inman walked out onto the Wharf to watch. Danton mentioned, "We won't be seeing this much longer." Inman said, "No, I suppose not. Does that make you sad?" Danton laughed, "Oh hell no! You're going to greatly improve our bottom line." The two stayed, and watched for at least a half an hour. While they watched, Danton said, "Millicent is moving Mary and Marie Cosette to one of Blackjack's Bank Houses on Saturday for protection." Inman asked, "Protection? …from whom?" Danton shook his head, "From Blackjack, actually. Millicent want's to keep their Garden District friends from knowing that Mary is pregnant, so Blackjack won't force Dr. Scrope to abort your child. …and then there's the inappropriate attention Blackjack has been paying to Marie Cosette." Inman frowned, "How could he?" Danton sighed, "You'd be surprised to know what that damn bastard is capable of." Inman shook his head, "That's so completely horrible." They agreed to go in and finish the preparations so they and Lucy could go home early.

Mary and Marie Cosette spent Friday packing their clothes and personal items to be ready to move to the Bank House on Saturday. Millicent slipped into Mary's room. She could see that Mary was depressed about having to leave the only home she'd ever known. "**Chéri, cette décision n'est que temporaire. J'ai juste besoin de montrer à ton père que ce n'est pas la fin du monde pour lui**." (Darling, this move is only temporary. I just need to show your father that it's not the end of the world for him.) Mary forced a smile that didn't convince Millicent one bit. "Anyway, I thought you would like to have a touch of home, so I'm having the porters bring over these **bergères à oreilles,** these floor lamps, and a few other pieces of your furniture. I wish that I could move the bed, but the room over there is just too small for it." Mary hugged her mother. "**Oh, mama, je sais que tu as mon meilleur intérêt à l'esprit, merci beaucoup!**" (Oh, mama, I know that you have my best interest in mind, thank you so very much!) Millicent reiterated, "I'll only be a phone call away. We'll go shopping, I'll take you to see Inman when possible. …and then, there's the wedding!" Mary finally smiled convincingly. "I wish you knew how much I love him!" Millicent grinned. "I have a pretty good idea. …and I suspect he feels the same for you!" Mary's eyes welled up and she hugged her mother again, tightly. "I know that he does, here, in my heart!"

CHAPTER SEVENTEEN

ADVENT AND A NEW PARADIGM

Johnny Hardwick pulled one of the Cadillac hearses out into the motor court early on Saturday morning and started to pack Mary's and Marie Cosette's luggage and furniture. Blackjack watched from his office window with his horribly stained diner mug of **café noir**. Hattie was trying to give Marie Cosette a crash course in all she'd have to do for Mary until the baby was born. "You'z'll be jus fin. …an you'z wan hav him tryin' do git add ju, needer." Marie Cosette sighed, "I'm'a gonna miss ju sumthin' awful!" Hattie was unexpectedly moved. She hugged Marie Cosette, and said, "I wish you only de bes' sweet chil'. I'z hard on ju, bud ju were de bes'. I'll miss ju, mo dan ju can no!" Upstairs, Mary took a shower, dressed and packed her nightgown and toiletries into the Louis Vuitton valise her aunt Irene had sent for her graduation, "…just in case you can come to visit me. …anytime you want to."

Mary walked down the stairs and through the foyer and parlor. She placed her valise by the kitchen door and filled her juice glass. Mary set the glass on the table and walked over to the **buffet de chasse to** fix her plate. Millicent smiled as Mary returned to the table and sat down. Millicent could see that Mary was depressed, so she started talking enthusiastically about their "shopping trip" Sunday afternoon. Mary enjoyed coming up with shopping euphemisms for their afternoons with their **beaux**. Marie Cosette stepped in to see if Millicent or Mary needed anything. Millicent smiled, "We're just fine dear. ...but you could take Mary's valise out to Johnny." Marie Cosette reached down and picked Mary's valise up, and walked through the kitchen and down to the motor court. Johnny was parking Millicent's Eldorado. He got out and took the valise from Marie Cosette. Johnny put the valise into the hearse and went over to an old bent-oak cane-bottom chair and sat in the shade while he waited for the ladies to finish their breakfast.

As Marie Cosette got back to the kitchen, Hattie was packing a large wicker hamper with cooked and uncooked food. "I'z ain't gonna cook da rice now. Ju gots da do dat donight." Marie Cosette protested. "I'z ain't neva cook'd no rice afore!" Hattie shook her head. "Chil, you'z smart. You'z goddz book smartz. Idz jus rice. One do doo. ...one cup'o rice, doo cups wader. A dash'o sald, maybe some budda, das all. Brin id do a boil, den turn de fire down real low. ...leabe id be twenny'o mo minids afo you dake de lid off'n de pod." Marie Cosette was relieved. "I 'speck I'z'n do dat!" Marie Cosette helped Hattie by fetching provisions for the hamper. She had just asked Hattie what she was to prepare for lunch when the door swung open and Millicent and Mary stepped into the kitchen. Millicent grinned. "You won't be preparing lunch, we're going out to luncheon." Marie Cosette seemed puzzled. "...but, wad'aboud me?" Millicent laughed, "Dear child, you're going out with Mary and me. ...you can change into something nicer when we get to Esplanade Avenue."

Marie Cosette's face erupted into an infectious look of complete joy. When the hamper was packed, Marie Cosette hugged Hattie, and hefted the heavy basket and struggled with it down the back stairs. Johnny jumped up, overturning the chair, and ran to take the hamper. As he placed it in the back of the hearse, Mary stepped to the Eldorado and pulled her seat back so Marie Cosette could get into the back seat. "Lordy! I'z ain't nevva been in a car dis nize!" As Millicent pulled the Eldorado onto Louisiana Avenue, she looked at Marie Cosette in the rear view mirror. "Marie Cosette, please do me a favor and take that horrible **tignon** off. You're not Jackson's servant anymore, you're

Mary's companion." Mary turned around and grinned as Marie Cosette unwrapped her beautiful chestnut hair. It was the first time Millicent or Mary had ever seen Marie Cosette with her hair uncovered. Millicent had to fight to stop from tearing up. She couldn't believe how beautiful Marie Cosette was. Her hair had graceful waves and flowed like water in the breeze. She thought to herself that it had been a sin for Blackjack to hide Marie Cosette's beauty, and condemn her socially by insisting that she wear the **tignon**.

Millicent took the Claiborne Avenue route to **Tremé** then Esplanade Ridge. She pulled the Eldorado behind the Bank House. Neither Mary nor Marie Cosette thought much of the house from the outside. Millicent said, "I think you'll both like the inside much better. Millicent pushed open the kitchen door and called for Blackjack's goons. "Ya'll go on out and help Johnny unload the hearse." "Yes ma'am!" Millicent led the way and guided the girls upstairs. Their first stop was the sitting room. "It'll be even nicer when the rest of the furniture arrives." From there, Millicent showed them Mary's bedroom. Mary walked over to the French doors and looked out onto the gallery. She noticed a bird nest in the shade tree and smiled. She nodded her head, "This isn't so bad." Millicent beamed, "Come on, let me show you the bathroom and Marie Cosette's bedroom." Marie Cosette sighed. "Id'z nizer den my room back ad de fun'ral home!" Millicent placed her hand over her **décolletage** and said, "I wanted you to have a room you'd feel comfortable in." As Millicent and the girls strolled back to the sitting room, Johnny Hardwick and the goons started bringing luggage and furniture upstairs. Millicent asked Marie Cosette, "Do they have your suitcase?" Marie Cosette looked at the load and said, "No'm." Millicent said, "Why don't you run down and get it so you can change for luncheon?" Marie Cosset hopped up and ran downstairs and to the back yard. She retrieved her second hand suitcase, and ran back upstairs. Marie Cosette popped her head into the sitting room and said, "I'z foun id. I'z be ready in'a minud."

While Marie Cosette changed, Millicent sat across from Mary. She opened her purse and removed an envelope. Millicent handed the envelope to Mary, who asked, "What is this?" With a glint in her eye, Millicent said, "Why, it's some of your precious father's money. You're going to need it for day-to-days." Mary opened the envelope. She gasped audibly as she counted the bills. "There's $200.00 in here!" ($1,941.00 in 2019) Millicent cocked her head and sighed, "You'll need to make groceries. …buy cleaning supplies. …and clothes! You're about to be a different size every week, it'll seem!" Millicent stood up and peeked into the hallway where the luggage and boxes were being placed. She found one marked "Ceramics" and brought it into the sitting room. Millicent cut the paper tape on the box and opened it. She rummaged around the *Times Picayune* protected objects, and pulled out a rather large one and a somewhat smaller companion. Millicent pealed the newsprint, away, to reveal a chamber pot and lid. Millicent noticed Mary's confused look. "Oh, I know that you don't need one of these. You have a thoroughly modern bathroom just out in the hallway. …but for generations, pregnant women have kept one under the bed for 'middle of the night' emergencies." It took a half of a minute but Mary got it. She laughed and took the chamber pot from her mother, put the envelope of cash in it, and went into her bedroom and slid it under her bed, discretely behind the dust ruffle.

When Marie Cosette had changed, the three ladies went downstairs. After last minute instructions to Johnny Hardwick and the goons, Millicent and her girls piled into the Eldorado and made their way down Esplanade Avenue. As they turned onto Royal Street, Millicent sighed, then said, "Marie Cosette, this afternoon I want you to be treated like the lady that you don't know that you are. No one will judge you by your appearance. …but would you be okay with my ordering for all of us? …I know what you like, and the menu will be **en Français**. I never got to teach you any written French." Marie Cosette was happy to allow Millicent to order for her. She'd never been to a restaurant before, and was terrified that she'd embarrass Millicent. "Das fine wid me!" Mary looked lovingly at her mother and nodded enthusiastically. Millicent found a place to park near The Court of the Two Sisters, and walked with her daughter, and her "almost" daughter to one of her favorite **Vieux Carré** restaurants.

As they entered the restaurant, the **Maître d'hôtel** greeted Millicent personally. "**Madame Day, c'est un honneur et un plaisir de vous voir aujourd'hui!**" (Madam Day, it is an honor and a pleasure to see you today!)

Millicent said, "It's nice to see you too, may we sit in the courtyard, please." The **Maître d'hôtel** looked down at his book and said, "But, of course, Madame. Please follow me." The **Maître d'hôtel** escorted Millicent and her girls to the patio. Millicent was aware of the approving looks being sent their way as they walked through the restaurant. Marie Cosette was not only being accepted, she was being approved, even desired. Millicent also noticed that Marie Cosette was instinctively returning the approving looks with warm smiles and glistening eyes. Millicent no longer had any doubts. Marie Cosette was undoubtably a Carnes. After they were seated, Millicent was informed, "Madam, your regular waiter isn't here today, his **grand-père** has passed. Would it be alright if Jean-Luc served you?" Millicent said, "**Ce serait merveilleux!**" (That would be marvelous!)

Jean-Luc was dispatched to Millicent's table. Millicent greeted him and said, "Might we order off of the dinner menu?" Jean-Luc replied, "**Certainement, chère madame! Veuillez m'excuser un instant afin que je puisse vous fournir les menus du dîner!**" (Certainly, dear Madam! Please pardon me for a moment so I can provide you with the dinner menus.) Jean-Luc returned with the over-sized menus and handed one to Millicent, Mary, and Marie Cosette. He paused as he handed Marie Cosette her menu. Their eyes met and it was almost too much for Jean-Luc to bear. He sighed, and summoned his composure with all of his might. It might not have been love at first sight, but it was surely lust at first sight. Jean-Luc had never before been instantly aroused by a mere glance from a beautiful woman. Millicent noticed. Millicent noticed the look in his eyes, and the impressive bulge in his trousers. Jean-Luc found it necessary to ignore his other tables for a few minutes to drink some ice water and settle himself in multiple ways.

While Jean-Luc was away, Millicent pointed out the interesting parts of the Courtyard. "Take that well over there. It's called the 'Devil's Well.' Anyone who tosses a coin in it and makes a wish runs the risk that the Devil will answer the wish." Marie Cosette's eyes opened wide. Mary's eyes just rolled, and she sighed. Millicent continued, "Do you see that ancient Willow tree over there?" Marie Cosette nodded her head. "Well, the story passed down for generations says that the pirate, Jean Lafitte, was part of three duels in one evening under that tree. He won them all, killing all three men!" Marie Cosette was overwhelmed, and had to look away. Millicent noticed that Marie Cosette's face mellowed into a smile, and that she started waving to the upper windows. "Who are you waving to, Marie Cosette?" Marie Cosette said, "Dose doo ladies up dere!" She pointed up to the windows, but neither Millicent nor Mary could see another soul." After a moment, Millicent chuckled, "It's probably Emma and Bertha." Mary laughed too. Marie Cosette didn't understand. Millicent explained, "Bertha and Emma are the two sisters. They're long gone. They both died late in 1944, but their spirits live here, or so they say." Marie Cosette let the encounter go. Mary had no idea, but Millicent knew that the spirits of the deceased at the funeral home regularly reached out to Marie Cosette seeking comfort that they weren't abandoning their families.

When Jean-Luc had his act together, and returned to Millicent's table to take orders, Millicent said, "Let's make this easy. I'll order for all of us." Jean-Luc nodded, but couldn't help watching Marie Cosette from the corner of his eye. Millicent said, "For Aperitifs, I'll have the Carriageway Martini, Mary and Marie Cosette will both have Champagne. For Appetizers, I'll have the Fresh Bayou Cook Oyster Cocktail, Mary will have the Shrimp Cocktail, and Marie Cosette will have the Shrimp Remoulade. We'll all have the Dinner Salad with French Dressing." Jean-Luc said, "**Très bien, madame**, and for **Entrées**?" Millicent said, "Yes, I'll have the Fresh Tropical Lobster Thermadore, Mary will have the Combination DeLuxe Seafood Platter, a la Court, and Marie Cosette will have the Jumbo Louisiana Shrimp a la Creole and steamed rice. We'll all have the **Haricots Verts à la Française** (Frenched Green Beans), and Mary and I will have the Brabant Potatoes." Jean-Luc asked, "... **et votre sélection de vins**?" Millicent looked at the selection. "Two bottles, chilled, of course, of **Bâtard-Montrachet** if you please." Jean-Luc was suitably impressed. Deep down, where no one could see it, he was silently calculating Millicent's growing tab, and the tip that he might very well receive. All he said was, "...and for dessert, Madame?" Millicent answered, " Crepes Suzette for me. Bananas Gregoire for Mary, and **Pêches flambées** for Marie Cosette." Jean-Luc asked finally, "Would Madame like to gild the Lilly?" Millicent chuckled. That peculiar of The Court of Two Sisters always amused her. "Sure, why not! I'll have a Hennessy, Mary will have Kahlua, and Marie Cosette will have Creme de Cacao.

Jean-Luc thanked Millicent for her orders, then rushed them to the kitchen. While they waited for their food, Marie Cosette pondered her luck to be sitting there in that fine establishment surrounded with fine and wealthy people. She didn't dare say anything or ask any questions. Millicent recognized Marie Cosette's rigidity and tried to get her to relax by offering her wonderful truthful compliments. Marie Cosette smiled and relaxed somewhat, but was still reluctant to speak. Millicent was almost ashamed of herself for suggesting that Marie Cosette not speak that afternoon. After all, people's judgements really only affect themselves, if the intended victims refuse to be affected by them. While Millicent and Mary truly enjoyed the fine cuisine that they were used to, Marie Cosette found herself in a place she never expected. It was one thing to be eating food that she hadn't had to prepare, but still another to be eating food so sublime and impossibly delicious.

As much of a surprise that the potential ecstasy that food could provide was, Marie Cosette was truly unprepared, and shocked when the bill arrived. Millicent looked over the tab and confirmed that it was correct. The total was $32.00, which included two $8.00 bottles of wine. She opened her wallet and placed two twenty dollar bills on the tray. ($40.00 in 1952 = $385.00 in 2019) She handed it to Jean-Luc and thanked him. "We'll look forward to your service in the future. Marie Cosette's eyes opened wide. She'd never seen that much money in one place, much-less shelled out for one meal for three people.

As they left the restaurant, Millicent paused. "Marie Cosette, these gates are called the 'Charm Gates.' They were forged in Spain, and legend says that they were personally blessed by Queen Isabella herself before they made the sea voyage here. It's said that if a person touches these gates, he or she will be granted a charmed life. ...or was it that he or she would return to New Orleans?" Marie Cosette said, "Eider way, can'd hurd." She laid her hands on the ancient wrought iron. She was joined by Mary. "I forgot about this! I can't remember how many times I've touched these gates hoping for a charmed life!" Millicent sighed, and joined in. They were all three embracing the Charm Gates, hoping for a charmed life.

Millicent drove Mary and Marie Cosette back to the Bank House on Esplanade Avenue. She got out and went upstairs with the girls to help them get everything in order. Before she left, Millicent picked up the phone receiver. There was a gambling call in progress. She put the receiver back on the hook. Under her breath, Millicent said, "I told him a private line, not a damn party line!" Millicent made her goodbyes and told Mary to be ready to go to **Maison Soleil** the next afternoon after church. Mary agreed. After Millicent left, Mary asked Marie Cosette if she could help prepare dinner. Together they started their new adventure as a team.

Sunday morning was difficult for Millicent. She kept expecting Mary to come down for breakfast, even though she knew full well that Mary and Marie Cosette were safely ensconced at the Bank House. Then there was having to go to Church with just Jackson. Almost immediately, fellow communicants began asking where Mary was. Millicent lied, "She's traveling." As much as Millicent hated the lies she was telling, it was perhaps the first time Blackjack had appreciated anything she'd done for him. Millicent, for the first time, wanted the service to go on longer, so she wouldn't have to deal with Blackjack. After the service, Coffee Hour seemed to last for an eternity. Evidently, winning that first election had hooked Blackjack. Something clicked, and he showed signs that he was in permanent campaign mode. Blackjack was finally ready to leave when there weren't any wealthy and influential people left at Coffee Hour. As he pulled into the motor court behind the funeral home, Blackjack said, "I'm assuming that you're going to see Mary, and that you won't want me to come." Millicent said, "Yes, I'm going to see Mary...." Blackjack cut her off. "...lot's of work. I'll eat leftovers." He jumped out of the Eldorado and sprinted to the funeral home.

Millicent refused to allow Blackjack to live in her head. She took a cleansing breath, then started her drive to Esplanade Ridge. After she parked behind the Bank House, Millicent went into the kitchen. The two goons were still not used to the goings on with the two girls and Millicent. They charged the kitchen, only to be confronted by Millicent. They immediately noticed the look of extreme displeasure on her face. Millicent balled her fists, and her eyelids closed to slits. "This is the last time I'm going to have to see you two dressed only in soiled underwear. NOT ONE GOD-DAMNED MORE TIME! ...and don't even think about trying to fuck with me you worthless troglodytes. I'll hang your shriveled balls on my Christmas tree. ...got it?" The two big bad goons were left trembling in fear. "Yes ma'am. So sorry. ...won't happen ever again." As Millicent started up the stairs, an awful stench assaulted her. Evidently, one or both of the goons had soiled themselves. She took that as a good omen and grinned.

When Millicent got upstairs, Mary and Marie Cosette were together in the sitting room enjoying the music evanescing from Mary's new Philco radio, record player combo. Mary hugged her mother, "Isn't the tone dulcet? Uncle Danton had it delivered." Millicent silently enjoyed the irony of her daughter referring to her lover as "uncle Danton." She admired the mahogany mid-century moderne cabinet and declared the sound, "sonorous." Jo Stafford's hit *You Belong to Me* was playing. Millicent was taken in by her voice. "She's got real talent! I wish that we could just listen to the radio at the funeral home!" Mary said, "Yes, I know! Muzak is the worst!" After the top hit faded into a commercial for Earl Kemper's Cadillac Dealership, Millicent asked, "Should I go on over to **Maison Soleil** by myself?" Mary guffawed, "No, I'm perfectly ready. Just let me get a sweater."

As Millicent turned onto Esplanade Avenue, she asked Mary, "So how was your first night at the Bank House." Mary thought for a moment. "It was much better than I expected. The goons downstairs could be a little quieter, but it was nice to have Marie Cosette for company. She asked me to help her with her diction. She really enjoyed being treated like a real person yesterday." Millicent was overcome with happiness, "Good, be a true friend, and teach her to speak standard English so she can have all in life that she deserves!" Mary said, "I don't think this is going to be the easiest challenge I've ever faced." Millicent nodded. "Yes, I can see that. Start with those damn 'd's. Get rid of 'dat, dose, dem, dhey, doday, dere, dheir, ...ad nasaum...'" Mary laughed. "That'll be a big bulk of it, but there's more." As Mary agreed, Millicent pulled to the curb on Howard Avenue at the main gate of **Maison Soleil**. Mary ran to the gate and rang the bell.

Inman popped out onto the **véranda**, and ran to the gate. He opened the gate and held it for Millicent and Mary. Without any fear or embarrassment, Mary threw her arms around Inman and they kissed passionately. Millicent, secretly jealous, smiled and walked ahead, albeit slowly. Mary and Inman caught up to Millicent and walked the rest of the way to the front **véranda** of **Maison Soleil** together. Inman opened the French doors and Millicent and Mary stepped in. Caroline stood to receive her guests. Mary rushed over and embraced her future mother-in-law, then returned to Inman's side. As Millicent greeted her dearest friend, Inman said, "Mama,…." Caroline cut him off. "Why don't you two go down to the **garçonnière** and enjoy the time you have together for today. In her excitement, Mary almost yanked Inman's arm out of its socket. They ran down to the **garçonnière**. When they reached the dance pavilion, Mary grabbed Inman's neck and bent him into her realm. She kissed him so passionately, that Inman almost fainted. Mary knew that they had only a couple of hours while their mothers made the final preparations for their upcoming wedding. She found an appropriate time to pull back from their embrace, then grabbed Inman by the crook of his elbow and pulled him toward the stairs up to the bedrooms.

As they got to the staircase, Inman pulled Mary to a stop and started to say… Mary cut him off, "Your mama said to "Enjoy our time together! …and that's exactly what we're going to do!" Inman couldn't argue with that. He and Mary ran upstairs holding hands and lovingly undressed each other. Mary pushed Inman onto his ancient four poster bed and jumped on top of him. Inman lay back and let Mary conduct the symphony of love. He was confident that he'd have a happy ending, and wanted Mary to have as many as possible. They concentrated on the experience, not the destination, and soon found themselves becoming experimental. They made passionate love for almost two hours, before deciding that it might be a good idea to check in on their mothers. After all, Caroline had probably had Monique put out a sumptuous spread of **rafraîchissements**. They strolled back to the **manoir** holding each other tightly at the waist.

As Mary and Inman walked up the stairs to the front **véranda**, the sexual musk of their carnal activities preceded them into Caroline's **salon principal**.

231

As they stepped into the room, Caroline and Millicent looked up from their writing tablets. The smell of love wafted over them, and they both noticed the warm relaxed nature of their children. Oh, they knew, but they said nothing. Caroline suggested that they have some **rafraîchissements**. "I think you'll find that Monique has stepped up her game!" As Mary and Inman made their way to Caroline's **salle à manger**, Millicent pulled a face and mouthed, "I'm jealous!" to Caroline. Caroline who had pulled the same face mouthed "Me too!" to Millicent. Caroline fanned her face with her hands, then she and Millicent got back down to the final details.

Mary and Inman returned with dessert plates, punch cups, and linen napkins. They sat together on a late 1920's caned sofa with overstuffed pillows. Mary took a moment to look at the furniture. Aside from Caroline's antique **bergères confessionnelles**, all of the furniture seemed to date from the late 1920's. Mary was intrigued, and couldn't resist asking, "Madame Carnes, your **bergères** are antique, but the rest of your beautiful furniture seems newer, and not French." Millicent almost fainted, but Caroline was gracious. "**Ma chère fille, le père d'Inman et moi avons reçu sa maison comme cadeau de mariage avec une somme d'argent pour la décorer à notre style.** (My dear girl, Inman's father and I were given his home as a wedding gift with a sum of money to decorate it in our style.) We kept the family heirlooms. They're in the **garçonnière** and the **atelier**." Millicent sat up straight and sent Mary a "I can't believe you asked that" stare. Mary smiled and said, "I hope that I haven't offended you Madame Soleil, it's just that your furniture is just so beautiful!" Caroline smiled warmly, "There was no offense, and your question reminded me of a beautiful memory. **Merci beaucoup mon cher!**" Millicent relaxed back into the comfort of her **bergère**.

Caroline asked, "Milly, are there any funerals scheduled this week?" Millicent thought, "Yes, I know that there is one on Wednesday. Why do you ask?" Caroline replied, "Because of their age, we'll need to take Mary and Inman to get their marriage license." Mary and Inman beamed with joy. Millicent was puzzled. "...so, you're willing to leave the property?" Caroline sighed, "Yes, but, just this one time. ...at least for now. It's that important." Millicent assured Caroline that both she and Mary would be there in time to go to lunch, then get the license. "I'm treating you to lunch at Antoine's, and don't even argue with me!" Caroline's eyes teared up. "My dearest friend, Milly, I won't argue with you. I may cry. …I may cry a lot. I haven't been to Antoine's in so many years, and it was Inman's and my favorite restaurant." Millicent had to catch herself to keep from crying. "Good! Mary and I will be here before noon. …but it's getting late. Mary and I should be going." Caroline stood and hugged her oldest and truest friend. "Until Wednesday…." "Yes, until Wednesday…."

During the drive back to the Bank House, Millicent wanted desperately to be Mary's friend and have her tell her all about her afternoon with Inman, but she knew that she couldn't. She was Mary's mother, after all. All she allowed herself to say was, "It was so wonderful that you and Inman got to spend time together today." Mary, still experiencing the waves of erotic sensation from her epic love-making session with her beloved, confessed, "I can't wait to be married. I can't imagine loving anyone as much as I love Inman!" Millicent said, "Yes, I understand, but there will be at least one more." Mary thought for a moment, then was embarrassed. "Oh, yes, the baby!" Millicent smiled, "Yes, but it's not a competition." Mary agreed. Millicent asked, "Have you asked Marie Cosette to be your Maid of Honor?" Mary said, "I haven't told her anything other than we're engaged. Is it time to ask her?" Millicent said, "Yes, but with the caution that no one can know." Mary agreed as her mother pulled the Eldorado behind the Bank House. Millicent didn't get out, and Mary ran through the kitchen to the stairs up to her sitting room. Marie Cosette was there waiting for her, listening to the radio. Mary caught Marie Cosette up with the goings on of the day and asked her to be her Maid of Honor.

Marie Cosette was completely stunned by Mary's request that she be her Maid of Honor. "Iz you suah?" Mary pulled Marie Cosette close, looked her directly in the eyes, and said, "Yes, I'm completely sure! As far as I'm concerned, you're my sister." Marie Cosette began to cry. "No one'z eve benn dat kind do me!" Mary couldn't contain her tears, "It's a new day for us. You and I are on this journey together. I don't know where it will go, but we'll do everything together. …and by the way, my name is Mary, not Miz Mary! Okay?" Marie Cosette threw her arms around Mary and said, "**Je t'aime ma sœur!**" (I love you, my sister!)

They went downstairs and cast the troglodytes out of the kitchen so that they could prepare their dinner. After dinner, they went back up to the sitting room, listened to the radio, and engaged in girl talk. Marie Cosette wanted desperately to know what it was like to be in love. Mary waxed lyrical about all of Inman's amazing characteristics. "From the first minute that I met him, Inman wasn't at all like most boys. The boys I met at Church were all puffed up and self-centered. They paraded around and talked incessantly about how great they were. It was like they'd be doing me a favor by asking to date me!" Marie Cosette giggled. "Do's ju dink dat I'll eva fin a boy do date?" Mary considered Marie Cosette's question. "I believe that you will. Didn't you see how that waiter at The Court of Two Sisters, Jean-Luc, fell all over himself when he looked in your eyes? ...just don't go looking for it and don't try to force a relationship." Mary and Marie Cosette talked until it was very late. They went to their rooms and slept peacefully.

The next morning, Marie Cosette came into Mary's bedroom and woke her up. "Iz you gonna hep me wid de brefus'?" Mary jumped out of bed and threw on her chenille robe. She and Marie Cosette scampered down the stairs and started their breakfast. Mary had to rely on Marie Cosette to teach her what needed to be done. She'd never actually cooked anything on her own. Thankfully for Mary, Marie Cosette had been trained, meticulously, by Hattie. They got the breakfast prepared, they ate, and Marie Cosette insisted that they get the washing up done. When they were done, there wasn't a single dirty dish in the kitchen. Marie Cosette went to the front of the house and requested that one of the goons take the garbage out. When he protested, Marie Cosette said, "Ju no dat Madame Day'll be hea in'a lill bid. Do I needs tell her whad a lazy bones you iz?" That was all it took. From then on, both of the goons were at the girl's beck and call.

Millicent arrived shortly after 11:00 to pick Mary up. As Mary slid into the Cadillac, Millicent asked,"**As-tu bien dormi, ma chérie**?" (Did you sleep well, darling?) Mary smiled, "**Oh, oui mama, et Marie Cosette et moi nous entendons bien**!" (Oh, yes mama, and Marie Cosette and I are getting on famously!) Millicent was relieved. "Did you ask her?" Mary beamed, "Yes ma'am. She was so happy that she started crying." Millicent said, "Goodness, what did you say then?" Mary looked off into the distance, "Well, I told her that I considered her my sister, and that we were going to go on this adventure together, …and to drop the Miz. I'm just plain Mary." Millicent sighed, **"C'est tellement merveilleux! Je suis content que tu vois plus en elle que ton père ne l'a jamais fait!"** (That is so marvelous! I'm glad that you see more in her than your father ever did!) While they waited at a traffic signal, Millicent reached under her seat and pulled out a distinctive orange paper bag with chocolate cloth loop handles. It had a distinctive logo of the letter "H" in a circle, topped with a **Duc** carriage with horse and jockey. "I have a small gift for you." Mary instantly recognized the bag as being from **Hermès**. She opened the bag and retrieved a beautiful silk scarf. **"Merci mama! Quelle est l'occasion?"** (Thank you, mama! What's the occasion?) Millicent giggled, "You'll need it when we pick Caroline and Inman up. You'll be riding in the back with Inman, and you'll want it to keep your hair in control." Mary laughed. "Mama, you think of everything. I could never love you enough!" Millicent sighed, "I know that you love me, and you know that I love you. Just know that I love Inman too, and will be over the moon in love with your baby. …but then there's your father. I'll find a way to deal with that, though."

Millicent pulled the Eldorado to the curb outside the main gate of **Maison Soleil** and Mary rang the old cast iron farm bell. Inman dashed past Monique and opened the gate for Millicent and Mary. Millicent looked at Inman. "Is Caroline really ready to venture out of her secured cocoon?" Inman sighed. "Yes, and no. She is awfully excited about having lunch at Antoine's, but her old anxieties are trying their best to get in the way." Millicent grinned at Inman. "You just leave that to me! I'll give her the best day she's had in years!" Inman was extraordinarily thankful. Millicent strode confidently across the threshold of Caroline's **salon principal**. "Dearest Caroline, your chariot has arrived!" Caroline was taken aback, and charmed. **"Comme c'est excellent! Nous devons absolument partir.**" (How excellent! We must, by all means, go.)

Millicent smiled broadly and linked arms with Caroline. Together they strode out onto the **véranda**, down the stairs and to the gate. Inman took Mary's hand and tenderly placed it in the crook of his arm. Mary smiled lovingly at Inman and they followed their mothers to the gate. Caroline seemed to grow apprehensive at the gate, but Inman pulled it open and buoyed by excitement, Caroline stepped out onto the Howard Avenue sidewalk for the first time in decades. Inman secured the gate and ran to open the door of the Cadillac for his mother. Caroline slid onto the plush leather seat and Inman closed the door. He ran around to the driver's side. Millicent had opened the door and leaned the seat forward. Inman allowed Mary to get in first, then followed her. Millicent returned the seat and got in. She cranked the Eldorado, and they were off to the **Vieux Carré** and Antoine's for lunch.

After Millicent parked the car, and she and her party started walking toward the restaurant, Caroline was truly amazed how little the French Quarter had changed. As they stepped into Antoine's, the **Maître d'hôtel** greeted Millicent. After a moment, he noticed Caroline. He studied her for a few uncomfortable moments, then he gushed, "**Mon Dieu dans le ciel, est-ce possible? Madame Carnes? Oh, tu m'as manqué toutes ces années. Je suis ravi de vous revoir!**" (My God in heaven, can it be? Madame Carnes? Oh, I have missed you all of these years. It's so wonderful to see you again!) Caroline was completely taken aback. She raised her left hand to her **décolletage** and her right hand to cover her mouth. She'd have started sobbing if she hadn't been a strong Soleil lady. "Well, Jules, I'm delighted to see you today too! As much as Jules wanted to hug Caroline, he knew his place, and escorted the group to one of the best tables in the establishment. Lunch exceeded anything that Caroline remembered. For most of the meal, her bottom eye lids were full of tears of joy.

After Millicent settled the tab, they walked back to the parking lot and got back into the Eldorado. Mary folded her scarf into a triangle and tied her hair up in it. As they drove, Millicent engaged Caroline in conversations about their time at Miss. McGraw's. Caroline was so hungry to talk about her memories that she failed to notice that Millicent was headed away from the Orleans Parish Courthouse. Mary and Inman couldn't have cared less. Mary buried her head into the curve of Inman's neck and shoulder. Inman massaged Mary's thigh knowing that neither of their mothers could see them. Mary was in heaven. She and Inman engaged in "love talk." It took a while, but

Caroline finally asked, "Millicent, where are we going? We should have been at the Courthouse a while ago." Millicent replied, "Yes, if we were going to the Orleans Parish Courthouse." Caroline thought a moment. "Ohhhhhhh, I see, Blackjack!" She got it, but Mary and Inman didn't. They simply let it go. One day they would both understand Blackjack's political network in both Orleans and Jefferson Parishes, and why Millicent decided to drive to Carrolton for the Marriage License.

Millicent smiled and said, "We're going to the Saint Tammany Parish courthouse in Carrolton. Caroline grinned. "Well then, we're going on a road trip. This IS a red letter day!" Millicent laughed, "Yes, I suppose it is. ...just like old times!" The two friends told tales, and enjoyed their company all of the way to Carrolton. Mary and Inman enjoyed the sun on their heads and the wind on their faces. They snuggled, they kissed, and they made small talk. After just over an hour, Millicent pulled the Cadillac to the curb outside the old Saint Tammany Parish Courthouse. They all went in and signed the register at the Clerk of the Court's office. When they were seen, the Clerk went through the application with them. There was a waiting period, and she asked, "When do you intend to be married?" Inman said, "We'd planned on Sunday, December 14th. Will that work?" The clerk smiled, "Yes, that will be just fine." With all of the paperwork completed, and the mothers' written consent, the clerk typed the license and handed Inman the original. She kept a carbon copy.

As they left the Courthouse, Inman asked his mother to safeguard his and Mary's Marriage License. Caroline slid into the front seat of the Cadillac and folded the paper, first into thirds, then in half. She placed it in her hand bag and snapped it closed. They set off back to Orleans Parish and **Maison Soleil**. Mary and Inman were thankful to have time to snuggle. However, in truth, they'd rather have had that much time to make love in the **garçonnière**. It didn't take long for Inman to notice that their mothers were completely engaged in their reminiscences, and basically ignoring them. Inman slid his hand under Mary's skirt, and up her thigh. She froze for a minute. Inman mouthed, "They aren't paying any attention to us." Mary looked at both of their mothers to confirm Inman's observation. She relaxed once she had shifted completely out of her mother's view in the rear view mirror. Once they were settled, Mary allowed Inman to run his hand up her thigh and dive his fingers into her Labia. She allowed Inman to pleasure her until she was on the verge of climaxing, then grasped his wrist. She couldn't risk any exclamations. Mary keep Inman's fingers inside her for most of the ride back to **Maison Soleil**. It was comforting to her.

Millicent parked on Howard Avenue. She got out and walked with Caroline to the gate. They hugged, and Caroline told her, "My dear friend, this has been the best day I've enjoyed in over 20 years!" Millicent went out on a limb, "Perhaps you'll consider going out with me in the future?" Caroline smiled, "That's a distinct possibility." Inman walked with his mother to the **véranda**, then excused himself and walked to the **garçonnière**. When he was sure he was out of sight, Inman balled his right hand up and raised it to his nose so he could smell his beloved on his fingers. The intoxicating odor almost caused him to faint over into the Jasmine border.

While their wedding wasn't scheduled until the 14th., Millicent and Mary came to the Wharf every day that Blackjack had scheduled a funeral. Sunday the 7th. was a special day. Millicent and Caroline greeted one another warmly. Caroline announced, "**Rafraîchissements** are in the **salle à manger**, if you please." She and Millicent piled into the **bergères à** oreilles, and started their reminisces. Mary and Inman held themselves closely and intimately, and hurried to the **garçonnière**. They were undoing buttons and zippers all the way up the stairs. When they finally arrived in Inman's bedroom, they had to force themselves to not rip the clothes off of one another. At last they were naked, and looking at each other lovingly. Mary pushed Inman onto the bed and jumped on top of him. Inman barely managed to pull another pillow behind him so that he'd be semi-reclined before Mary grabbed his penis and guided it into her engorged vagina.

Once Inman was inside of Mary, she collapsed onto Inman's massive chest. She started breathing extra deeply. As Inman lifted Mary up and down with his legs, Mary writhed, and dragged her breasts over Inman's muscular chest. Inman's respiration intensified. They kissed. They kissed passionately. …wildly passionately. As Mary experienced her first orgasm, she ran her fingers through Inman's luxuriant hair. She started to moan and pant. She grabbed Inman's hair and tugged as she climaxed. Inman made no protest. They waited a few minutes with passionate kisses, then Inman started Mary on her next journey to orgasm. In all, Inman was able to send Mary to Elysium five times before he couldn't control his climax any longer. Mary and Inman climaxed together, without caring how loud they were, or who heard them. When it was accomplished, Mary collapsed onto Inman, and they lay there together for over a half an hour. While they didn't want to get out of bed, they both knew that it would soon be time for Mary to be driven back to the Bank House, and Millicent to return to her own personal hell at the funeral home.

When Millicent dropped Mary off at the Esplanade Avenue Bank House, Marie Cosette was already prepping their dinner. Mary sauntered into the kitchen, and collapsed on a chair. Marie Cosette instantly knew. "Sweed sistuh, you dun did de deed!" Mary laughed, mostly because she actually understood Marie Cosette. "Yes, Marie Cosette, Inman and I did indeed do the deed. ...many times!" All Marie Cosette could think to say was, "Lordie!" Mary asked, "Can I tell you a secret? No one can know, no one!" Marie Cosette said, "You'ze my sisduh, you'ze secrets safe wid me!" Mary leaned in close to Marie Cosette and said, "I'm addicted. I'm addicted to my **fiancée**. My overwhelming desire is to be naked with him in bed, making passionate love." Marie Cosette had no idea how to respond. She hedged, "Iz you su'a?" Mary was sure, completely sure. "Yes, Marie Cosette, Inman completes me. ..and I complete him, too."

Marie Cosette found herself in a dilemma. As much as she relished hearing Mary's sagas of her exceptional love, she found herself finding it painful to hear of Mary's exploits because she found herself wanting to experience love too. ...with zero prospects. Mary reminded Marie Cosette, "Next Sunday, we'll both be going to **Maison Soleil** for the wedding. That will be a wonderful occasion. Who knows, you might meet a fine young man there. Uncle Danton has invited the entire management staff to the wedding. Marie Cosette perked up with the thought of eligible bachelors competing for her attention. Suddenly, Marie Cosette frowned. "What's wrong," Mary asked. "Iz remembrin' dat cude waita ad dey Doo Sistuh's. Jean-Luc. He'us so cude, dhe way he god all 'cited afder I smil'd ad him. Whad ju dink he'd say if'n I'd open'd my moudth?"

Mary nodded, "I see your point. …but I have an idea. She picked up the receiver of the telephone. One of the goons was accepting a bet. "Hello, this is 707648, I'd like to put two bucks on…" Mary put the handset back on the hook and waited for a minute. She picked it back up and this time, got a dial tone. She dialed the funeral home. Blackjack answered the phone. "This is Mary, I'd like to speak to my mama." Blackjack yelled for Millicent. She stepped into the hallway from the kitchen to the office, "Yes, Jackson, what is wrong." Blackjack said only, "Pick up the phone in the kitchen, it's for you." When Millicent picked up the receiver, both she and Mary were assaulted by the noise of Blackjack slamming his receiver down into the hook.

Millicent said, "Hello, this is Millicent Day." Mary giggled, "Oh mama, it's just me!" Millicent cooed. "**Oh, ma douce, comment allez-vous et Marie Cosette?**" (Oh, my sweet, how are you and Marie Cosette?) "**Nous allons bien, et vous?**" (We're doing well, and you?) Millicent said, "I'm just fine, thank you." Mary then asked, "Mama did you get rid of those flash cards from when I learning sound combinations? What were they called? Sight Words?" Millicent thought for a moment, "I think I put them in one of the boxes that I was going to send over the the Cathedral Bargain Shoppe. Why?" Mary said, "Well, Marie Cosette now really wants to learn better diction." Millicent exclaimed, "I've been trying for years to do that, what changed?" Mary confessed, "She said that she was jealous of my loving relationship with Inman. I told her that Uncle Danton had invited the entire management team to the wedding, and there were several handsome, available bachelors in the group." Millicent was over the moon. "That is fantastic! I'll have Johnny Hardwick find those boxes. If he can't find them, I'll go to the book store and buy you some new ones. I'll drop by tomorrow, and I'll take you girls to lunch to celebrate!"

The next morning, Millicent pulled quietly into the back yard of the Bank House, and quietly entered the building. She surveyed the kitchen. She could smell that breakfast had been prepared, but was happy to see an empty sink, and an empty trash can. She then slipped into the business room. She scared the living day lights out of Blackjack's goons. Fortunately for them, they were appropriately dressed. "…just checking." Millicent shot them a glare, and turned. She walked to the stairway and climbed graciously to the second floor. Millicent knocked softly on the sitting room door and opened the door a crack, "It's only me." She entered the sitting room, and Mary ran over and hugged her mother. "**C'est si bon de te voir, mama!**" (It is so good to see you, mama!) Millicent held Mary's hands. She thought to herself how much Mary didn't look any different from the young lady that had graduated from Miss. McGraw's School for Girls only months before. Millicent smiled and stared at Mary a little too long. At last Mary said, "Mama!" Millicent snapped back into reality. "Mary, look what I found." She reached into her purse and produced the old set of sight words. Mary exclaimed, "Oh, this is wonderful. We'll get started immediately!" Millicent chuckled, "Could you at least wait until we've had luncheon?" Mary looked at Marie Cosette, and they both burst into girlish laughter. Mary nodded her head, and the trio made their way down to Millicent's Eldorado.

As Millicent turned onto Esplanade Avenue, Mary asked, "Would it be possible for us to go to The Court of the Two Sisters?" Millicent tried her best to contain her grin, "Yes, I think that's a wonderful idea." After Millicent parked the Cadillac, they walked the short distance to The Court of The Two Sisters and passed through the Charm Gates. Marie Cosette paused and planted her hands on the gates. As the **Maître de Hotel** greeted them warmly, Millicent asked, "Would it be possible to be seated in the courtyard? The **Maître de Hotel** looked at his book of reservations, and said, "**Oui, madame Day**." As he picked up three menus and started to lead the way to the courtyard, Millicent asked, "Is it possible that Jean-Luc is serving today?" "**Oui, Madame**." Millicent then asked, "We'd like very much for him to serve us today, if it possible." Mary and Marie Cosette looked at each other and their eyes grew wide. They both let out a "Haw" in excitement.

Even though they knew that Millicent would be ordering, Mary and Marie Cosette held their menus high, obscuring their faces as if they were considering their options. Jean-Luc greeted Millicent and offered to take their orders. As before, Millicent ordered for herself and the girls. When she was done she asked if there was anything else the girls wanted to add. Mary dropped her menu, and said, "**Non, ma commande est magnifique.**" Millicent said, "Marie Cosette?" Jean-Luc turned to Marie Cosette. She slowly lowered her menu and stared deeply into Jean-Luc's eyes. She breathed deeply and smiled slightly. When Marie Cosette could tell that Jean-Luc was almost breathless, she said, slowly and sultrily, "**Ma commande est la perfection!**" (My order is perfection!) Jean-Luc found himself paralyzed in lust. He was finding it difficult to breath, and nearly passed out on the spot. He made a feeble excuse, and retreated to the service hallway. Jean-Luc asked another waiter to put his order in and drank a large glass of ice water. ...then another. When Millicent's order was up, Jean-Luc asked two other waiters to help him serve his table. He personally served Marie Cosette and did his best to remain professional. "**Votre commande, mademoiselle.**" Marie Cosette looked him in the eyes and batted her eyelashes. "**Avez-vous échantillonné pour voir à quel point c'est bon?**" (Have you sampled, to see how good it is?) Mary and Millicent were on the edge of their seats, amazed at Marie Cosette's torture of the poor waiter. Jean-Luc marshaled some modicum of control and said, "**Mademoiselle, je n'ai aucun doute sur sa qualité!**" (Miss, I have no doubt as to how good it is!) After Jean-Luc finished his initial service, he left, and all three ladies enjoyed their luncheon immensely. To say that Jean-Luc was attentive to Millicent's table would be a gross understatement. They wanted for nothing.

As Millicent and her girls walked back to the Cadillac, Millicent said, "Thankfully there is a funeral today, because we need to make one more stop." Mary and Marie Cosette looked at each other with confused looks. Mary asked, "Where are we going?" Millicent tossed her head up and back and said, "Maison Blanche. ...We need dresses for next Sunday!" Marie Cosette didn't realize at first that Millicent was including her in the "We." They piled into the Eldorado and Millicent drove them around to a lot just off of Canal Street, close to the department store. As they went into Maison Blanche, Marie Cosette's face positively bloomed. She had never been into a department store, much less one as large or grand as Maison Blanche. The experience, at first, was extraordinary overwhelming. Millicent led the way to the Ladies Department, and then deeper, into the Bridal Department. A rakishly thin **vendeuse** (saleswoman) stepped from behind a curtain. She was wearing a black Christian Dior Faille dress with a white portrait collar, nip waist, and dolman sleeves. "**Bonjour, Madame, comment puis-je vous aider?** (Good afternoon Ma'am, how may I assist you?) Millicent replied, "**Nous aimerions voir vos robes de mariée et robes pour la demoiselle d'honneur et la mère de la mariée.**" (We would like to see your wedding dresses, and dresses for the maid of honor and the mother of the bride.)

The **vendeuse** suggested that they start with the wedding gowns. Millicent agreed, but asked if she might use the department's telephone. The sales lady agreed, picked up the receiver and requested an outside line. She handed the phone to Millicent and escorted Mary and Marie Cosette to an oversized rack of wedding dresses. Mary was requested to turn around slowly, and the **vendeuse** studied her form. "Size 3, I'd say. We may need a size larger and take the waist in." Mary was impressed, "**Oui**, I normally wear a size 3 or 4." The sales lady flipped through the dresses and pulled several out for Mary to review. Both Mary and Marie Cosette liked them all, but Mary's favorite was a ankle length Crêpe de Chine gown designed to be worn over multiple crinolines. The gown had an embroidered deluxe Organza over-skirt with a lace edged sheer illusion neckline. "It's Chanel." Mary went into the changing room to try it on.

Millicent had called the Wharf and requested to speak to Danton. He picked up and greeted Millicent warmly, "**Quel plaisir d'avoir de vos nouvelles, mon amour.**" (What a pleasure to hear from you, my love.) Millicent sighed, "**Tu me manques tellement mon amour!**" (I miss you so much, my love!") Danton asked if everything was okay. "Oh, yes, of course. The girls and I went to lunch, and we're dress shopping. I thought that while I was here, at Maison Blanche, I would get Caroline and Virginia dresses, EtC. for the wedding too." Danton sighed, "You are so kind and considerate! Please do, but have the **vendeuse** call me so I can put them on my account." Millicent said, "I don't mind spending Jackson's money on them!" "Even so, please let me pay for them. Spend his money on the girls." Millicent said,

"Yes, alright, I'll have her call you for your account information. Do they both still wear a size six?" Danton said, "Yes, that was the size they last requested I get for them. You'll probably pick better styles that I would!" Millicent laughed. "I'll let you get back to work, my darling." Danton said goodbye, and Millicent walked over to the rack of gowns as Mary came out of the fitting room. When Millicent saw the dress she gasped. It was absolutely beautiful, and suited Mary's physique.

"Would mademoiselle care to try one of the others?" Mary looked at here reflection in the triple mirror and shook her head. "No, this is the dress." Millicent reminded Mary that she was lucky that her wedding wasn't going to be in the church. "You'd have to have your shoulders covered there." Both Millicent and Marie Cosette overwhelmingly approved of Mary's choice. Mary went back into the fitting room to change. Millicent said, "Let's find this young lady her dress next. When we get the dresses figured out, we'll go on to gloves, hats and shoes. "First we need to decide on a color." Mary emerged from the fitting room and Millicent looked at her, "Given the date of the wedding, I'd say that rose would be the perfect color for Marie Cosette's dress." Mary grinned broadly. "Oh, yes, and my favorite color too!" Millicent looked at the **vendeuse** and requested, "I'll leave this to you and the girls. I'll step away and look for matronly dresses. "**Mais bien sûr, madame** ..." (But of course, Madam...)

While Millicent was shopping on her own, for herself and Caroline and Virginia, the **vendeuse** showed Marie Cosette her range of rose colored bridesmaid dresses. After trying on several, she tried on one that was an ankle length Empire gown in rose Charmeuse topped with matching lace, and a blouse with matching rose open lace half sleeves. The **vendeuse** was hanging the two dresses at the sales counter and draping them in paper dress bags when Millicent arrived with three distinctive Chanel Wrap Dresses. Purple for her, Gold for Caroline, and Green for Virginia. "**Trois robes, madame**?" (Three dresses, Madam?) Millicent smiled slyly, "Yes, one for me and the other two for the mother and aunt of the groom." Mary explained, "**Mon Dieu! Sérieusement?**" (My God! Seriously?) Millicent laughed, "No worries, Danton has insisted that he be called to put his sisters wardrobes on his account." Mary was relieved, not wanting her father to explode in anger over her mother's extravagance.

With the dresses sorted, Millicent turned her attention to gloves, hats, and shoes. The **vendeuse** retrieved a pair of elbow length kid gloves for Mary. "Mademoiselle will notice that the ring finger of the left glove is slit on the inside. Your husband-to-be will be able to slide your rings onto your finger without your having to remove your glove." Mary threw her hands to her mouth and let out a polite yawp. "That's ingenious!" The **vendeuse** replied, "That's Maison Blanche!" Pink kid gloves were chosen for Marie Cosette, and plain white kid gloves were selected for the other ladies. Once suitable shoes, stockings, and hats were chosen, Millicent helped the **vendeuse** sort the items into two piles. She produced her Charger Plate and settled her bill. When she requested that the **vendeuse** call Danton, that charge was elevated to a Floor Walker. He called accounting and had them use their account information to contact Danton Soleil at his office.

After describing what Millicent intended to purchase, the accountant, shocked at Danton's indifference to the purchase, said, "Monsieur, are you sure, it's quite a large purchase?" Danton assured the accountant, "This is my sister's only son's wedding. I couldn't care less if it was ten times that much!" Please allow Madame Day to complete this purchase for me." The accountant rang the Bridal department and approved Danton's charge. It was $325.00. (Just over $3,100.00 in 2019) Millicent's tab was closer to $475.00 ($4,500.00 in 2019). She knew that Blackjack would blow a stack when he received the bill, but couldn't find it in herself to care any less. Part of her sincerely wanted to go ahead and turn Blackjack over to the authorities and get rid of him once and for all. ...but, then, there was the fact that he was, after all, "financially useful."

Millicent's purchases were loaded onto a garment trolly, and a porter took them to the main floor on a goods lift. Millicent asked Mary and Marie Cosette to wait with the porter until she could return with the Eldorado. Once the bags and boxes were loaded into the boot of the Cadillac, Millicent drove to Howard Avenue. Mary got out and rang the bell. Monique came out of the kitchen and opened the gate. Millicent said, "We have wedding clothes, that we'd like to store here." Monique was extremely moved. "**Oui, madame**. Please come in and visit with Madame Carnes. I'll have some of the staff help me move these upstairs." She called to one of the gardeners, young Tom Foster. "Please wait here until I get back with help. Guard these packages, if you please." Tom was happy to oblige. Monique led the ladies to the **véranda** and introduced them. Caroline was delighted to see them. "**A quoi ai-je l'honneur de cette visite?**" (To what do I have the honor of this visit?) Millicent said, "I apologize for dropping in without notice, but I thought it best to bring our wedding dresses here so that you and Virginia can try yours on, and the rest of us can change confidently into ours on Sunday."

Caroline was taken aback. "You bought my sister and me dresses?" Millicent said, "Well, we picked them out, but Danton paid for them." Caroline thought for a moment, "...so, Danton enlisted you to find these dresses?" Millicent half-lied and said simply, "**Oui**." Caroline smiled, "Thank you dear friend! God only knows what I'd be wearing if Danton had picked it out!" Millicent said, "You both have complete outfits with hats, gloves and shoes. There's time to exchange if necessary." On the verge of tears, Caroline said, "Every day I spend time with you, I regret all of the time I missed out with you over the years. Yes, I've enjoyed my countless books, but oh, what I'd give to have back all of the happy memories of time I could have spent with you!" Millicent said, "I feel the same way. I allowed myself to be kept cooped up in a dreary funeral home, thinking that you hated me." Caroline said, "Dearest Milly, you didn't step on Danton's heart, he stepped on yours!" Millicent sighed deeply. "We know the whole story now. One day, all of this will be fixed." Caroline cooed, "I can't wait!"

Worrying that she had been gone too long, Millicent made her excuses and drove the girls back to Esplanade Ridge. She made a point of sneaking in and scaring the goons. She stared them down until she could see that they were noticeably shaking in their boots. "I'll be back. ...and you won't know when!" Mary and Marie Cosette waited for Millicent in the kitchen and started prepping dinner. Millicent strode triumphantly into the kitchen. Mary and Marie Cosette burst out laughing. Mary said, "You're getting far too much enjoyment out of terrorizing those goons!" Millicent puffed up and shook her head, "Never!….." Mary and Marie Cosette convulsed in laughter. They laughed so vehemently, they almost peed their pants. Millicent said, "We had so much fun today, and got so much accomplished! You two have a good dinner, and get some well-deserved sleep. Rose Sunday will be here before you know it. I'll call you, Mary, and let you know if we'll be able to have lunch at the Wharf this week." Mary threw her arms around Millicent. **"Merci Mama! Je vous aime tellemen**t!" (Thank you mama! I love you so very much!) Millicent replied, **"Ma douce fille, je t'aime tellement!"** (Sweet daughter, I love you so completely!) Millicent took her leave, and traveled back to the funeral home on Saint Charles Avenue. After a quiet dinner prepared by Hattie, Millicent was happy that she could pour herself a tall Blanchard strength Gin and Tonic and decompress quietly in the darkened parlor. She wouldn't be bothered by Blackjack that evening.

For the rest of the week, Mary was as unhappy not to have her mother's visits and their joys, as the goons were elated not to have to deal with the dreaded Millicent, and her impossibly strict standards. On Sunday, December 14, 1952, Rose Sunday, Blackjack found himself burdened with a horrible cough and severe nasal congestion. He ached all over and was sweating profusely. Dr. Scrope would eventually diagnose a relatively severe case of the flu. He recommended that Blackjack stay in bed and avoid contact with anyone who wasn't wearing a mask for the next several weeks. Blackjack informed Millicent that he wouldn't be going to Church that day. Millicent reminded Blackjack that he had an entire staff to meet even his most selfish need. She said, "Hattie is preparing you some tonic to get you over this flu." Blackjack rolled his eyes. "I guess I won't see much of you today." Millicent said, "You heard what the doctor said. Besides, if you take Hattie's tonic, it's unlikely you'll see much of anyone today or for the next couple of weeks, but you just might get better. …and, besides, I told you that my sister and brother are arriving today. With you sick and probably contagious, I'll stay with them at the Hotel Monteleone." Blackjack huffed. "How much is that going to cost?" Millicent rolled her eyes. "You have more money stashed away than almost everyone I know. You just drink Hattie's tonic, and I'll see you at the first of the year." Blackjack raised himself up to protest such a long hotel stay, but fell back, completely exhausted, and sighed. Millicent took that as her queue to leave.

Instead of driving to the Cathedral, Millicent drove to the Bank House on Esplanade Avenue and rounded up her girls. She took them to Brennan's for breakfast. "Breakfast" lasted until after 1:00. It could have easily lasted all afternoon, but they all had a wedding on Howard Avenue to get to. While Millicent and the girls were enjoying their "Breakfast at Brennan's," Danton had dispatched a car and driver to the airport to meet Irene and Phillippe. By the time their flight landed, they were exhausted. The DC-3 had flown through too many storms to keep track of. They had been bounced around in turbulence so much that Irene commented, "World War Two was such a more enjoyable experience." They were driven to the Hotel Monteleone to check in, rest, and dress for the wedding. Their driver promised to wait for them in the parking garage.

Millicent and her girls showed up much earlier than expected at **Maison Soleil**, much to the delight to both Caroline and her twin sister Virginia. They were both proudly wearing the Channel dresses Millicent had chosen for them. Millicent put both of her hands over her mouth when she saw her lifelong friends. "**Mon Dieu, comme c'est beau!**" (My God, how beautiful!) Caroline embraced Millicent, "**Ce sont les plus belles robes que j'ai jamais vues!**" (These are the most beautiful dresses I have ever seen!) The two teared up, but were careful not to allow their tears to stain Caroline's dress.

Millicent sighed and asked where she, Mary, and Marie Cosette should change for the wedding. Caroline rang a small crystal bell. Monique walked into Caroline's **salon principal**. "**Oui madame?**" Caroline said, "Monique, please take these ladies up to change for the wedding." Monique was happy to oblige. She led the ladies up the stairs from the lower loggia at the rear of the **manoir** to the upper loggia. Monique took Millicent to one bedroom, and Mary and Marie Cosette to another bedroom. She asked if she could bring them anything, but all were far too excited to think of anything that they could possibly need. As she left, Monique reminded Millicent that the front center room was a **salon**, and would be a comfortable place to wait until the wedding. Millicent changed quickly into her outfit, as did Marie Cosette.

Together, Millicent and Marie Cosette helped Mary into her dress, masked the neckline with washcloths and touched up Mary's makeup. As they both brushed Mary's luxuriant hair, Millicent said, "It's a shame we couldn't go by **Maison de Bringier** today!" Mary said, "Inman won't mind. He's more interested with what's inside of me." Millicent smiled inwardly at Mary's unintentional "**à double entente**."

When they had finished perfecting Mary, Millicent and the girls went to **Maison Soleil's salon au deuxième étage** to wait for the **fête** to begin. The "Orchestra" had begun playing Jules Massenet's ***Méditation*** from the opera ***Thaïs***. Caroline escorted Father Lachicotte up to the salon to visit with Mary and make sure that she knew the Order of Service. By then, guests had begun to arrive. Shortly, the small orchestra/jazz band ensemble that Lucy Butler had assembled continued playing the prelude music. Millicent peeked through the shutter and marveled at the number of Danton's employees who had accepted his invitation to the impromptu wedding. It was a blue-clear cloudless December day. The humidity was low and the temperature moderate. Millicent thought to herself that she couldn't have ordered a better day for Mary and Inman's wedding. The orchestra started their prelude with Johan Pachelbel's ***Canon in D***.

Marie Cosette looked at Mary. "Dat's... That's such beautiful music!" Millicent was so happy a rogue tear burst from her left eye. "Yes, it is, Marie Cosette. Yes, it is!" Millicent dabbed her cheek and hugged Mary. "It's really happening. Are you truly happy?" To the strains of ***Gesegnet Soll Sie Schreiten*** from the Wagner's opera ***Lohengrin***, Mary confided to her mother, "I'm happier than I've ever been in my entire life!" Caroline was truly amazed. "**Ma chère, tu es si calme, si détendue, j'étais une épave complète avant mon mariage!**" (My dear, you are so calm, so relaxed, I was a complete wreck before my wedding!) Mary embraced Caroline tenderly and tightly. She whispered in her ear, "**J'ai peut-être un avantage sur les plus jeunes. Je n'ai aucune crainte sur ce qui vient ensuite. Je sais, dans mon cœur, ce qu'est l'amour complet. Cela me rassure et me calme.**" (I may have an advantage over the younger you. I have no fears about what comes next. I know, in my heart, what complete love is. That reassures me, and calms me.) Caroline hugged Marry even tighter and began to cry uncontrollably. She was jealous. What Mary possessed was completely unusual, almost impossible. Millicent and Marie Cosette took sides and blotted her tears away from Mary's splendid lace neckline. Millicent asked, "Caroline, what ever is wrong?" Caroline said that she needed to sit. Marie Cosette poured her a glass of water, for which Caroline expressed her thanks, warmly.

The orchestra transitioned into Johann Sebastian Bach's **Arioso**, as Caroline began her story. "Well, you see, it's complicated." Millicent smiled broadly at Caroline. "Please go on…" Caroline sighed, "Well, it was September of 1933, a few days before Inman was born. Danton had persuaded Inman to go with him to the World's Fair in Chicago. They had been gone for a week, and were due back on Saturday. For me, the week had been horrible. It was the first time Inman and I had been separated for more than simply a long work day. I picked up the phone and asked the operator to connect me with the Factorage. I asked them if a car was going to be dispatched to Union Terminal to pick up Inman and Danton. They said that an employee had, indeed, been requested. I requested that the driver stop by and pick me up, so that I could meet them at the station." Caroline paused for a moment to dab her eyes. Mary leaned in and asked, "Well… did you meet them at the station?" Caroline smiled, "Yes, but after a rather long wait at the station. The train had been late leaving Memphis. There had evidently been a car crash on a crossing south of the city that had to be investigated and cleared before the train could leave the station." Marie Cosette asked, "What did ju… you do den… then?" Caroline said, "I had no choice; I had to wait for the train to arrive."

Caroline continued, "I was restless, and started walking through the station. I was near the colored section when this large colored woman with scary hair started laughing." Mary grasped, "Delphine!" Caroline said, "Yes, Madame Delphine Voyante, but I didn't know her name back then. She caught my attention and said, 'Ju gon be deliver'd ob ju boy on Wids-day, in dee dark moon.' I was both frightened and fascinated. I was paralyzed with fear, but something told me to hear her out. I asked her how she knew. She said, 'Papa Legba, himself dold me dis.'" Marie Cosette had a sudden realization. "Papa

Legba! Yes, I remember hearing dis, …this name!" Mary was confused. "Who was this Papa Legba? Was he a doctor?" All of the other women had to work hard to contain their laughter. Caroline added, "Papa Legba is the Voodoo Loa, or **mystère**, associated with crossroads. He intercedes between Human Beings and the **Bondye**, the Voodoo 'Good God.'" With Mary's questions answered, she pressed further. "What else did Madame Delphine say to you?"

Caroline sank back into the luxury of the **canapé** in which she was seated and said, "Madame Delphine told me that my son would make me extremely proud, but that he and I would both go through periods of challenge. She told me that Inman would be the one to see the end of all of our family's troubles. That part was a tad confusing. I didn't know, at the time, for sure if she meant my family, or my family and other families, Milly." Millicent sighed deeply. "It seems that she meant both of our families, but we have a few more miles to walk on that path." Caroline agreed. "Yes, Jackson hasn't been convinced, has he?" Millicent shook her head.

From the open window, Caroline heard the orchestra beginning to play Bach's *Jesu, Joy of Man's Desiring*. Caroline jumped up. "It's time! Virginia and I need to get down to the kitchen door now. Our carriage will be waiting for us! Danton has an entrance for us! Oh my! …let's go Virginia!" Virginia agreed, but said, "We'll be seated in that carriage for a while!" Caroline and Virginia hurried out of the salon and down the stairs to the kitchen door. They were helped into the carriage, and sat there for four minutes in the heat. There was a pause as the orchestra and choir finished the Bach selection, before they launched into Georg Friedrich Handel's *The Arrival of The Queen of Sheba* from *Solomon*. All three ladies were curious about the "arrival," and each went to a window to peep through shutters to the lawn and drive below. After the first few bars of the piece, thanks to their height advantage, Millicent and her girls could see a pair of white stallions both with ostrich plumes pulling a freshly lacquered antique black **Vis-à-vis Barouche**. Its doors were emblazoned with gleaming golden suns and the Soleil coat of arms. As the coach came into view, Millicent and the girls could hear audible gasps form the attendees. Caroline and Virginia were helped out by attendants, and the

251

Vis-à-vis Barouche left the compound to travel down Howard Avenue to the Carriage gate just below the **garçonnière**, to retrieve Danton and Inman.

Caroline and Virginia greeted many of their guests, until the orchestra started playing ***La Primavera*** (Spring) the allegro movement from Vivaldi's ***Concerto Number 1 in E major***. Aside from the fact that they were wearing Morning Suits and not military uniforms, Danton and Inman looked, for all the world, like nobility. In this company, and in New Orleans, they were nobility. Mary gasped when she saw Inman in all of his splendor arrive. She watched him, like a hawk, until he and his uncle Danton alighted from the carriage and evanesced to the **belle étage véranda** below her view. Millicent looked at Mary. "It's almost time. Are you ready?" Mary threw back her head, and said, "There has never been any doubt!"

When the orchestra began playing Charles-Camille Saint-Saëns' ***The Swan*** from ***The Carnival of the Animals***, Millicent paused for a few bars, then opened the French door and led Mary and Marie Cosette slowly out onto the upper **véranda**. They paused at the center of the balcony just long enough for the attendees to notice Mary, her Maid of Honor, and her mama. There were gasps as everyone stood. Millicent then guided Mary to the grand circular stairs. Mary locked arms with her mama and her Maid of Honor, Marie Cosette, and the trio slowly and graciously made their way down to the **belle étage.** Inman was about to pass out from desire. When he finally saw his **fiancée**, he gasped. She was a vision of loveliness. As the song ended, Millicent placed Mary's hand into Inman's hand, and kissed Mary, and then Inman. Father Lachicotte beamed.

The service went perfectly. The banns were pronounced. The Eucharist was shared, and the ***Ave*** was sung. When Father Lachicotte said, "I now pronounce you Man and Wife, the congregation erupted in celebration. It being just a tad premature, Father Lachicotte finished the service, recessed to the rear of the congregation and gave all the Great Benediction. Wild applause broke out once again. Several members of the orchestra, really members of Jazz bands, stepped out of rank and began playing ***Just A Closer Walk with Thee***. Millicent and Danton presented Mary and Inman with stylishly emblazoned parasols.

Mary and Inman began to lead their Second Line in the approved manner. They started, ironically, funeral like, by extending their right feet out at a 45 degree angle, then bringing their left feet even with their right feet. After that, they extended their left feet out at a 45 degree angle and pulled their right feet even. Time after time, Mary and Inman repeated these steps. After a few verses of ***Just A Closer Walk With Thee***, the Jazz Band changed to an upbeat tempo, and the dirge steps were abandoned. After the end of ***Just A Closer Walk With Thee***, the Second line Band played numerous songs on the parade to the **garçonnière**. They played ***When the Saints Go Marching In***, ***Yes Sir, That's My Baby***, ***Tiger Rag***, ***Mazie***, ***West End Blues***, ***Sugarfoot Stomp***, ***Shake It and Break It***, ***Bill Bailey***, and ***Dippermouth Blues***.

The family and friends attending the service started waving the white handkerchiefs, embroidered with an "M" for Mary and an "I" for Inman that had been gifted them when they arrived. The I was in the Middle of the M and a little bit larger. It was an incredible monogram for the couple! The friends and family lined up, and formed the Second Line behind the jazz musicians. When they made it through the maze of serpentine driveways and foot paths, they all found themselves at the **garçonnière**, and more specifically the Dance Pavilion and Terrace.

Millicent was over the moon when she realized that Lucy Butler had convinced Professor Longhair to take turns with the Jazz Band. She walked over to the piano and said, "Thank you for agreeing to play for us tonight, Roy. You're the best, and it means an awful lot to me that you are here." Fess stood up from his piano bench and shook Millicent's hand with his silk gloved hand. "Madame, the pleasure is all mine!" Millicent added, "Roy, I'll make sure that the waiters and circulating bartenders take good care of you this afternoon. ...and we'll get you to your night gig at the Caldonia Club too!" Fess smiled, and as the band finished their first set, said, "...afternoon ladies and gentlemen, I'm so happy to be here today, on this happy occasion. As a special treat for the Bride and Groom, I'd like to play my new song. I hope to be recording it in the new year. It's called ***Tipitina***." Henry "Roy" Byrd, had a unique rolling syncopated style of piano playing. He belted the song out to an enthusiastic audience. The words were, on that occasion, mostly unintelligible, but the rhythm and syncopation of the piano music was compelling. As he finished the song, Fess received an enthusiastic ovation.

Millicent made the rounds engaging with the guests, and thanking them for coming. It was impossible for her not to hear the idle chit chat of the guests about Caroline and **Maison Soleil**. "I had heard that Caroline had gone crazy." "I'd heard that too, but she hasn't changed. She's still the charming and sophisticated lady she always was." "I heard that the property had been left to ruin." "Well, look at it! It looks as good, or even better than it did twenty years ago." "I know! Isn't this a fantastic wedding party!" "Yes!" Millicent finally made it to General and Mrs. Long. "Alice, Alexander, I am truly happy that you both could be here today." General Long said, "I wish that whoever planned this wedding had been with me while we were marching through Europe. We'd have been better rationed!" Alice took Millicent's arm. She snickered, "That's high praise coming from such a gruff old soldier!" The General harrumphed. Alice confided to Millicent that she had heard rumors. Millicent pulled Alice Long aside, away from prying ears. "Alice, I know that I can confide in you, and that my revelations will be kept close to your heart." Alice replied, "Yes, of course. I won't even tell the old bulldog if you don't want me to." Millicent sighed. "I think that I could trust him too." Alice asked, "What is it that you are so worried about confiding in me?" Millicent said, "The rumors are true. Mary is expecting. That's not the problem. Mary and Inman are hopelessly in love. He has means, and a lifelong career. I love him, and Caroline loves Mary. The problem is Jackson." Alice's complexion soured. "Why you married that vile human being still baffles me!" Millicent looked down and scratched the back of her neck. Alice added, "Everyone knows that you still love Danton Soleil." Millicent started to cry uncontrollably. Alice embraced her. "I'm so sorry, my dear! Decades of marriage to the good General have driven me to bluntness." Millicent breathed in forcefully and regained control of her emotions. "No, you're right. I do love Danton Soleil, to this day, and he loves me every bit as much. We're working on our situation, but at this point, the children are more important."

Alice Long understood Millicent's dilemma completely. "Milly, how can Alex and I help you through this?" Millicent confided in her dear friend,

"Jackson was pinning his hopes on finally being invited to join the Boston Club after Mary's debut at the Rex Ball. I've had to move her and Marie Cosette out of our home for their safety." Alice frowned, "The servant girl too?" Millicent sighed, "Marie Cosette is so much more than she appears to be. She is anything but a servant girl. Jackson has been 'grooming' her." Alice's eyes grew wide. Her hatred for Blackjack intensified. "I had no idea, my dear." Millicent confided, "I have no expectations that anything can be done to win Jackson an invitation to join the Boston Club. My only desire is for my friends to accept Mary and Inman's marriage and not judge them. They were both, after all, very sheltered before meeting each other. ...and they are madly in love with each other!" Alice Long pledged to Millicent, "My dear friend, you can count on me. None of our friends will have any negative impressions of Mary and Inman. Their union will be celebrated when it's announced officially! I'm just glad you don't have any expectations of Jackson's desire to be welcomed into the Boston Club. I'm afraid that will never happen!" Millicent thanked Alice. "I'm hoping to spend more time with you in the New Year." Alice said, "I'm looking forward to it!"

All of the guests were delighted to get to know Inman, Mary, the illusive twins Caroline and Virginia, and the insanely beautiful and **mystérieuse** Marie Cosette. The wedding reception lasted longer than anyone could have predicted, but no one minded. Marie Cosette flirted with a host of eligible managers from the Soleil and Carnes Factorage. As the last of the guests made their way out onto Howard Avenue, Mary and Inman collapsed onto a bent bamboo sofa. They were joined by Caroline and Virginia, Millicent and Danton, Irene and Phillippe and Marie Cosette. Uncle Phillippe asked Inman, "Do you feel changed?" Inman looked at his bride, then at uncle Phillippe, "No! Mary's and my relationship hasn't changed even one bit. ...but I do feel sanctioned. ...and I feel that our relationship is accepted." Aunt Irene said, "Inman, your confidence in your relationship is quite refreshing! I applaud you and Mary. I wish you both a lifetime of happiness!" Inman and Mary beamed. Mary looked over at Marie Cosette. "Well, did you meet anyone?" Marie Cosette's cheeks blushed only a bit. She grinned, "Perhaps.... There's two or three that have promised to call. We'll see." Millicent clasped her hands and brought them lovingly to her chest. "Marie Cosette, **Mon Dieu**! Your diction! Did you work 24 hours a day on it?" Marie Cosette beamed, "I let Mary have at least one hour of sleep a night." Everyone let out hearty laughs. "Well, I hope at least one of them is good enough for you!"

Millicent looked at Danton, "Should we tell them now?" Danton pretended to think for a moment. "Well….. I suppose we could…" Millicent used her pause to put Mary and Inman on tender hooks. At last, she said, "Danton and I have reserved suites at the Hotel Monteleone so that we all can spend Christmas with Irene and Phillippe. You two will have as proper of a honeymoon as we can give you. Jackson is horribly ill, and won't interfere with our happiness. Marie Cosette was sad. All she could think was that she'd have to go back to the Bank House and endure the goons her own. Millicent could see her despair. She asked, "Marie Cosette, why are you so sad? We have a room for you too." Marie Cosette could hardly believe what she was hearing and began to cry. Mary jumped up and ran to her "sister." She threw her arms around Marie Cosette and said, "**S'il vous plaît, pas de larmes. Nous vous aimons et nous voulons que vous profitiez de ce temps avec nous!**" (Please, no tears. We love you, and we want you to enjoy this time with us!) Marie Cosette smiled and told Millicent how happy she was. "**C'est le meilleur Noël que j'aie jamais eu.**" (This is the best Christmas I've ever had.)

Millicent looked at Mary. "Monique has moved your clothes to Inman's room upstairs. Why don't you two go up and change clothes. Marie Cosette and I will go back to the **manoir** and change before we return to the hotel. Inman and Mary didn't have to be asked a second time. They sprinted upstairs and stripped out of their clothes in record time. By the time they were done, they realized that they had removed their underwear as well. Unable to contain themselves, they jumped into the bed and made mad, passionate love. They knew that they had to keep it brief, much to their consternation. Wanting so much more, they resigned themselves to get out of bed, and dress. They went down to meet up with the family. No one said a word. Millicent asked Danton and Marie Cosette to ride with her and Mary and Inman. She had asked Danton earlier to provide a car for Irene and Phillippe, and Virginia and Caroline to the hotel. Virginia and Caroline had been spending some time recounting the day, and were happily amazed that they were going to be treated to dinner at the Hotel Monteleone with the rest of the family. When it was time to leave, Millicent and crew made their way to her Eldorado on Howard Avenue. Millicent said, "We have one stop to make first. Mary and Marie Cosette were terrified as Millicent made her way to Esplanade Avenue.

Millicent pulled behind the Bank House and parked. "I'll handle this by myself," was all she said. She got out of the Cadillac and stomped to the kitchen door. She disappeared inside the Bank House and was gone for only a few minutes. She emerged from the Bank House with a broad smile on her face. As she turned back onto Esplanade Avenue, everyone wanted to know what had transpired in the Bank House. After a few tortuous miles, Mary couldn't take it any longer. "What happened in there?" Millicent grinned. "I went in, and the goons were once again in their underwear. They weren't expecting me, evidently. I told them that you two would be with me until the first of the year, and that Blackjack was terribly ill. I also reminded them that they should always be prepared for a visit from me. I'm thinking that as much as I don't want to, I may need to gift them with a couple of surprise visits between now and the first of the year."

Millicent then drove her family to the Hotel Monteleone on Royal Street. As they got out and prepared to go into the lobby, Mary, Inman, and Marie Cosette suddenly realized that they didn't have any luggage. Millicent started to laugh. "Well, it's about time. …but Danton and I didn't want you to have to spend time planning. We had Monique and Lucy Butler pack for you. Your bags have been delivered here to the Hotel, and have probably already been unpacked and placed into bureaus. That's the kind of service this hotel insists upon."

Inman asked, "Is there anything that we have to do?" Millicent chortled, "Why yes, as a matter of fact, there is one thing. You must enjoy yourselves!" Everyone laughed and they left the Cadillac in the garage. Millicent and Danton ushered their family to the lobby. Millicent and Danton registered, and received their keys. Danton gave his keys to Mary and Inman. "This is your suite. It has a salon, an ensuite, and a second ensuite for Marie Cosette."

As Inman thanked his uncle and took the key, Millicent said, "Dinner will be in the **de Bienville Suite**.

When they go off of the elevator, and walked to their suite, Mary and Inman felt a sudden and unexpected feeling of freedom. They were married, on their honeymoon, and no one could say anything. They conveniently forgot that Blackjack was sick, and unable to interfere with their happiness. Inman unlocked the door to the suite, and, in one sweep, lifted Mary to his chest and carried her across the threshold. Although Inman was a tad perplexed when he entered the salon, he quickly recovered his bearings and carried Mary to the master suite. Although they both knew that dinner was planned in forty five minutes, they couldn't resist. They shucked out of their clothes and dived under the covers. They couldn't help it. They made love, and regrettably had to stop early, once again. They got dressed, and went down to meet their family.

When they got down to the **de Bienville Suite**, Mary and Inman embraced intimately before pushing through the door. They entered the room, and the rest of their family was already seated. They made their apologies, which were accepted without exception. As they walked to their seats, they passed Virginia. As they passed, Virginia sighed and said, "Oh the sweet musk of true love! I wish you two happiness for a lifetime." Mary, Inman, and the rest of the family chose to ignore Virginia's somewhat inappropriate, if not accurate, comment. The meal was delicious and the expert hotel service was spot-on. During the meal, uncle Phillippe asked Inman if Danton had mentioned that they had both attended the same boarding school in Memphis. "Why, no, he didn't. I knew that he and my papa were roommates at Fordwright Academy, and later at Tulane.... You were there too?" Phillippe puffed up. "Yes, and Adrien LaRoque." Millicent interjected, "Adrien goes by 'Emile' these days." Inman perked up, "Emile is my middle name!" Caroline sighed and put her fork down on the gold band dinner plate. "...and your father's, and his father's, and his father's father's before that. Adrien started using that name to mock your father." Inman was dumbfounded. "W...what?" Caroline continued, "Yes, believe it or not, Adrien and I dated for a short while. He was always so cocksure and aggressive. He was actually convinced that I was going to marry him. …but he wasn't 'noble,' if you will, more Creole, and it did't take me long to realize that he was completely wrong for me, and that your father was the only man for me." Mary was fascinated at the convoluted web that spun around the families of the Boarding School buddies. "…so, that's how Emile ended up marring my aunt Alice-Varina? Millicent added, "Yes, and ever since, he's been mobbed up with Jackson, and can't be trusted."

Phillippe thought for a moment and asked, "Didn't Jackson take my place in the card gang?" Danton took that question. "Yes, Chief Guillotte nominated him enthusiastically. I suppose that Jean had been 'asked' by Blackjack's uncle 'King' Clancey to get him into our inner circle. I imagine that Blackjack thought that being in the card gang would automatically get him into the Boston Club." Phillippe jumped in, "Did he get in?" Danton said, "Phillippe, if you had ever visited your oldest and dearest friends, you'd know that he is still trying to get in. Once Blackjack joined the card gang, he introduced Adrien to Alice-Varina. Danton looked across the table at Millicent and Caroline. "…and like her brother, Alice was a second place trophy."

Millicent and Caroline both howled with laughter. Phillippe and Irene joined in on the laughter. Phillippe said, "Now, that's the damn truth! Danton, you haven't changed a bit. You always hit the nail on the head!" Danton grinned wickedly. "Thanks Phillippe, and to think, I've only had two Bourbons!" Phillippe jumped up and enthusiastically said, "**Serveur, un autre tour de boissons, s'il vous plaît!**" (Waiter, another round of drinks, if you please!) Irene gasped, "Phillippe Blanchard, I haven't heard you speak French in twenty years!" Phillippe flashed his sister a grin, "When in Rome…"

Mary and Inman were happy to see that dessert was being prepared to be served. Sommeliers were uncorking bottles of Veuve Clicquot, and Pastry Chefs were carefully slicing Doberge Cakes that looked suspiciously like they had been ordered directly from Beulah Ledner herself. Both Mary and Inman were enjoying their dessert, and the amiable company of their family, but were intensely eager to go back up to their suite. Their restlessness showed in their faces. Millicent looked at Caroline, and Caroline nodded. Millicent said, "**Mary, chérie, tu as l'air fatiguée. La journée a été longue, Inman**

et toi aimeriez-vous l'appeler une nuit?" (Mary, darling, you look tired. It's been a long day, would you and Inman like to call it a night?) Mary smiled, "**Oui, mama, merci beaucoup!**" Mary and Inman stood and made their way around the table hugging and shaking hands with their family. As they started to leave, Millicent reminded them. "Breakfast will be here in the morning at 8:00." Mary and Inman thanked Millicent and made their way to the elevator. Not long after Mary and Inman went up, Marie Cosette called it a night. Caroline and Virginia were driven back to **Maison Soleil**, and the rest retired to the Carousel Bar for drinks and stories.

For the absolute first time, Mary and Inman were safe, alone, and completely free to explore their deep passion for each other without any worries. Mary switched the radio on and they danced. After each song, they each discarded an item of clothing. Before they knew it, they were both completely naked. They danced a couple of more dances. Inman said, "This feels so wonderful!" Mary agreed, and foxtrotted Inman over to the bed. She collapsed onto him and they started kissing and making out. After a moment, Mary said, "...**juste un instant, s'il vous plaît.**" (...just one moment, please.) Mary got out of the bed and walked over the the radio. Inman rolled over and propped on his elbow. He grinned as Mary switched the radio off, then ran back to the bed. Mary launched herself, and Inman caught her in his arms. It proved to be a long passionate night.

The phone rang at 7:30 for their wake up call. Mary and Inman had only managed to get a couple of hours of sleep. Inman rolled over to wake up his bride. As she woke up Inman said, "**Je t'aime complètement, ma chérie. Je ne sais pas comment j'ai dormi sans toi à côté de moi!**" (I love you completely, my darling. I have no idea how I ever slept without you next to me!) Mary smiled and kissed her husband passionately. Deep inside, however, she knew that this paradise was only temporary. Come the first of the year, she'd have to go back to the Bank House until her mother could figure out how to talk her father down from his high horse of intransigence.

Mary and Inman bathed and dressed. They linked arms and rode the elevator down to the **de Bienville Suite**. They were only a minute or two late. The waiters had just started serving the **café au lait**. Inman pulled

Mary's chair out and helped her get situated. He took his seat and the waiter poured his and Mary's **café au lait**. The waiter asked if they wanted any juice. Mary asked for a glass of Orange Juice. Inman asked if he might have Pink Grapefruit Juice. "**Oui, monsieur.**" Danton had requested that breakfast be served Family Style. Platters of Scrambled, fried, and poached eggs were delivered with Dishes of Grits, Oatmeal, and Brabant Potatoes. There were also platters of Bacon, Country Sausage and Andouille Sausage, along with Toast, English Muffins and Biscuits.

After all of the dishes had been passed, and everyone was enjoying their breakfast, Millicent said, "I'll be taking Irene and Marie Cosette out today. Danton is going to the Factorage, and Phillippe is going to his warehouse at Maison Blanche. It wouldn't be good for you two to be spotted in public. Your father could still snap if you two get ratted out." Danton added, "You have a telephone in your suite. Room Service is just a call away. …order anything your hearts desire! While we're all here, we'll have breakfast and dinner together in this room. Luncheon will be up to you, in your suite." Mary and Inman were about to burst with excitement. Millicent added, "On the 24th, we're having a wonderful **Réveillon de Noël**. …**puis nous célébrerons le réveillon du Nouvel An**." (…and then we will celebrate New Year's Eve.)

Millicent tried to watch Mary and Inman enjoy their breakfast without being too obvious. Her heart was warmed because she could see and sense a love almost identical to that she shared with Danton. Danton pulled out his Patek Phillippe pocket watch and said, "Well, I need to get going." Inman had one request, "Uncle Danton, would you call the attorneys and check on the the Patent application?" Danton smiled, "Oh yes, dear nephew. I had Lucy put that on my planner on Friday. If all goes well, today is the day!" Inman walked over to Danton, shook his hand and bear-hugged him. "This is so exciting. Now I can focus completely on the shipping containers." Danton said, "God willing, you can get this project completed in a year or two!" Millicent was curious. "What project?" Inman said, "I found some drawings and models that my papa had worked on before he died. They were for a shipping container. …but it wasn't just the shipping container. It's a steel box, that a special crane can load onto a special ship, then unload and put on a rail car or a truck trailer." Phillippe chortled. "So, you're saying that I could have one of these boxes in Cherbourg, load it with fine French antiques, and ship it to New York, where it could be put on a truck trailer and delivered to my store?" Inman said, "That's right. Or, a container could be packed here in New Orleans at your warehouse, trucked to the rail depot, and carried by train to New York, and trucked to your New York warehouse." Phillippe got up and walked over to Inman. "Wouldn't that drastically cut the cost of transportation?" Danton said, "Yes by almost half!" Phillippe put his hands over his mouth and let out a pronounced "Hawwww." "How soon can I be your first customer?"

Danton said, "Well Inman, you've finished your Banana Transport Box. How long do you think this project will take?" Inman thought. "I was hoping that the proceeds from the Banana Boxes would pay for this. The prototypes will be expensive." Phillippe gave Danton an excited stare. Danton said, "Inman, you're on your honeymoon. Please don't worry about this too much until you come back to the Wharf, but when you do, please don't worry about funding. Spend everything you need. The money you're making from sugar and other commodities at **Beau Cadeau** will cover everything you need." Inman was buoyed by his uncle's words.

Mary and Inman made their way back up to their suite. Mary had all kinds of questions about the shipping containers. They got into the suite, and Inman tried to redirect their conversation to topics about Mary. Mary wasn't having it. "Damn it, Inman, you never talk about yourself. For once, I want to know about what you're working on! Inman walked over to the desk in their bedroom and retrieved a pad and pen. "I'll show you everything, but you'll have to get into bed with me naked." Mary huffed, "Those are easy terms!" They stripped off and climbed under the covers.

Inman started to sketch the scheme. He first drew a shipping container. "It's the same size as a Tractor Trailer. I have provisions for containers that are even longer, too." Mary asked, "What about the wheels when they're on the ship?" Inman smiled. "There are no wheels. The wheels are on carriages pulled by the semi-cabs. My cranes will lift them off of the ships, and place them on to my truck trailers, or on to my train beds for transport." Inman thought for a moment, then added, "...and once they reach their destination, the containers can sit on their own as storage units." Mary was flabbergasted. "You've thought of everything!" Inman replied, "Some things have taken time. Some things have required changes. My father had designed containers with flat steel walls. I figured out quickly that flat walls would allow a container to warp far too easily. I redesigned it with corrugated walls for strength. I also had to re-engineer and strengthen the load points, and the latching mechanisms." Mary gave Inman a coy look. "It sounds like you are further along than uncle Danton knows."

Inman blushed, just a little. "Perhaps." Mary asked, "Are you holding out on him?" Inman sighed deeply, "Maybe? **Oh mon Dieu**! Yes, I am. Are you happy? I can't keep anything from you!" Mary snuggled in closer to Inman. "Why would you think that you'd ever need to keep anything from me?" Inman calmed down. "I wouldn't. ...and I don't. It's just all so new. One of my problems is that I can't conceive of disappointing anyone. You can't comprehend how much it means to me that I can talk to you. I know that you won't tear me down, but I hope that you will always offer constructive criticism. Mary said, "Um hum." They lay there, side by side, staring into each other's eyes, until Mary asked, "should we order some lunch?" Inman snapped out of his state of Elysian. "**Oui, madam**!" The use of "Madame" caught Mary off guard at first. She quickly grew to love the sentiment. Inman jumped out of the bed and fetched the Room Service menu.

Even though it was difficult for both of them to decide what to order while they were still entangled in their passionate nakedness, Mary and Inman finally came to a room service order. Mary excused herself to go to the restroom while Inman placed the order. When Mary returned from the restroom, she and Inman put on the plush white pima cotton bathrooms provided by the hotel to wait for the room service order.

After a delightful luncheon, Mary and Inman spent the afternoon dancing and playing cards. Marie Cosette got back about 4:30. As she passed through the salon on her way to her ensuite, she noticed that the card-playing love birds were in bathrobes. She smiled and said, "Dinner is at 6:30." Mary and Inman thanked her, and decided that it might just be time to bathe and get dressed. Once back in their bedroom, Mary began reminiscing about all of the orgasms that Inman had gifted her in the pool at **Maison Soleil**. She dropped her robe. Inman gasped at her beauty, and closed his eyes. While Inman's eyes were closed, Mary yanked the belt of his robe open and pushed the robe over Inman's broad shoulders. As it fell to the rug in a heap, Mary grasped Inman by his hand and led him to the bathroom. She placed a towel on the white Carrera marble sink counter, and lifted herself up onto it. Inman pulled in close to Mary and placed his arms around her. As Inman kissed her face and eyes passionately, Mary maneuvered him into her. Inman began to make long strokes in and out of his wife. Mary was in heaven. As their session grew in intensity, Mary wrapped her arms around Inman and dug her nails into his back. Inman picked Mary up off of the counter and supported her by her thighs and continued to thrust. Inman was able to control his passion until Mary had come twice, but then, there in the center of the white marble bathroom, Mary and Inman climaxed together intensely. ...so intensely, they were both reduced to tears of joy and thanksgiving. They then got into the shower together and lovingly washed each other. After toweling off, they went back into the bedroom and dressed.

Dinner in the **de Bienville Suite** was, once again, a sumptuous affair. Danton had arranged for it to be based on native game and common vegetables grown in the local Parishes. Inman thought that the **Jarret de Chevreuil** (haunch of Venison) was perhaps the best he'd ever tasted. Mary leaned in close to Inman, "What part of the cow is this from?" Inman put his hand over his mouth to keep from laughing and breathed deeply. "It's not cow, my dearest, it's deer." Mary let her **faux pas** sink in for a moment, then recovered, "It truly is divine!" Inman agreed. By the time dinner was accomplished, the routine for the next couple of weeks was assured. Inman's only request was for Danton to bring him an Engineering notebook. "I may have an inspiration and want to jot it down." Danton agreed to bring him one by the following dinner.

Millicent and Danton spared no expense for the **Réveillon de Noël**. They ordered the finest seafood dishes and the fattest, most succulent Gulf Oysters. Expensive wines flowed, and the desserts were flamboyant and extravagant.

After the dinner, gifts were exchanged. Mary and Inman were somewhat confused, but overjoyed, that they had gifts from each other, and gifts for the rest of the family. Millicent, Irene, and Marie Cosette had handled that for them. Mary's gift from Inman was a sterling charm bracelet. The charms already on the bracelet included a book, a horse, a streetcar, several hearts, a horseshoe, and a lock. Inman's gift from Mary was a bespoke set of gold cufflinks featuring Chibcha Indians and Colombian emeralds. Inman took one look and then cast a glance over to Danton. They smiled at one another knowing that the cufflinks were a celebration of Inman's Banana Transport Box, that was now patented and in production. As the **Réveillon de Noël** wound down, Millicent told Mary and Inman that Christmas luncheon would be in the **de Bienville Suite** immediately following a Mass celebrated by Father Lachicotte at 10:30.

The week between Christmas and New Year's Eve passed far too quickly for the newlyweds. They made every last moment count, and their love for each other intensified geometrically. On the afternoon of the 30th. of December, Millicent called the funeral home. She was told that Blackjack was still confined to bed, and extremely ill. Dr. Scrope, who was making a house visit got on the line. He told Millicent, "It's probably for the best that you were able to be away. Several of your employees have come down with it." Millicent asked if Jackson was out of the woods. "Yes, his fever has broken. He's come a long way, but he's still weak and sleeping most of the day. I nearly lost him on Christmas Eve. If his fever hadn't broken, I'd have had to transport him to Touro Infirmary and place him in the Intensive Care Unit." Through her severe disappointment, Millicent said, "Thank you for your valiant efforts, Doctor Scrope."

Millicent hung the phone up. She'd heard what she needed to hear. Knowing that Blackjack was still incapacitated, she reasoned that it would be worth the risk to allow Mary and Inman to celebrate New Year's in the Carousel Bar and Swan Room with the rest of the family. Millicent would hold on to that tid-bit until lunch time on New Year's Eve, fearing that something might occur that would make having Mary and Inman make a public appearance impossible. She did, however, call Lucy Butler at the

Factorage and arrange for Inman's White Tie and Tails, and Mary's fanciest party dress to be collected and brought to the Hotel Monteleone. They were dropped off with the Concierge who had them cleaned and pressed. The Concierge, following instructions, dropped the fresh garments off at the Suite Millicent and Danton were enjoying.

As the family was enjoying breakfast on the morning of New Year's Eve, Millicent announced, "We'll be having luncheon in this room today. We're running out of family time together." Everyone was excited about a special family luncheon. "...and, we have the room reserved all day. We can visit, ...play cards, ...or board games, what ever!" As much as Mary and Inman wanted only to go back up to their room, get naked, and spend the day in bed together, they knew spending time with the family was the right choice. They were both overjoyed when a driver from Soleil et Carnes delivered Caroline and Virginia. As Millicent greeted Caroline, Caroline whispered in her ear, "I hope you don't think it too tacky that we wore our dresses from the wedding, but they are so extraordinarily beautiful!" Millicent pulled back for a view, still holding Caroline's hands. "How could I ever judge you, my dearest friend? The dress becomes you, and you both are positively radiant!"

Caroline greeted Mary and Inman. "**Comment allez-vous, monsieur et madame Carnes?**" (How are you, Mr. and Mrs. Carnes?) As Inman hugged his mother, Mary said, "**Nous sommes heureux. ... heureux de la lune!**" ("We're happy. ...over the moon happy!") Caroline and Virginia beamed with delight. Almost in unison they replied, "**Très bien!**" Danton hugged his sisters. "Twice!" Caroline pursed her lips and asked, "What do you mean, twice?" Danton laughed. "In less than a week you've left the estate twice!" Caroline looked at Millicent and winked. She turned back to Danton. "If you go back another week, it's three times. I accompanied Millicent, Mary and Inman to Covington to get the marriage license." Danton was impressed. "... all the way to Saint Tammany Parish!" Caroline laughed, "Yes, and back!" Millicent put her arm in the crook of Danton's elbow. "...and she's going with me to register the license next week." Danton was quite impressed. He guided his sisters to seats at the table and had a waiter bring them both **café au lait**. As Caroline and Virginia made their breakfast selections, Danton said, "I hope you gave Monique the day off." Caroline laughed. "I'd already given her the day off before Milly called and invited us to spend the day with the family. You might not believe it, Danton, but Virginia and I aren't completely helpless!"

Breakfast was dragged out as if it had been enjoyed at Brennen's. The family enjoyed small portions, many courses, and multiple drink options. Breakfast transitioned into Brunch, then Luncheon. As the food orgy came to an end, Millicent stood up. "It's New Year's Eve tonight, and our family time is coming to a close. Irene and Phillippe will be leaving for New York shortly, and we'll all have to go back to our routines. Tonight needs to be a big celebration." She looked directly at Mary and Inman, and said, "We, as a cohesive family, are going to celebrate what 1953 has to offer us tonight in the Swan Room and at the Carousel Bar."

In her excitement, Mary dug her fingernails into Inman's inner thigh under the table cloth. Inman's eyes bulged, and he exclaimed, "That's so amazing." Mary thought for a moment and remarked, "…but we don't have the proper clothes?" Danton replied, "Yes you do. Your mother and I asked Lucy Butler to get them and bring them to the hotel. The Concierge had them cleaned and pressed. They are in our Suite waiting for you." Inman's eyes grew wide wth excitement, but Mary was suspicious. "What if someone sees us and rats us out to father?" Millicent closed her eyes and tilted her head back. "I thought of that. I worried about that. …but I called the funeral home and spoke to Dr. Scrope directly. Your father is still delirious, and even if someone calls, he won't be able to comprehend, at least for several days. I think a grand evening out is worth the risk! We'll meet at the grandfather clock in the lobby at 6:00."

As the luncheon came to an end, Mary asked if she and Inman could spend a little time together before they had to dress for New Year's. Millicent said, "**Bien sur ma chérie**!" (Of course, my darling!) After Mary and Inman left, Marie Cosette asked if it would be okay for her to spend the afternoon exploring the **Vieux Carré**. Danton stood and walked over to her. "Yes, I think if that's what you want to do, you should. Although it shouldn't be, the quarter is foreign to you!" While everyone exchanged approving looks and words, Danton slipped Marie Cosette a twenty. She looked at him is shock. Danton whispered in her ear, "Eat, drink, be merry, or buy yourself something special. Just enjoy your afternoon. You'll have to go back to that damn Bank House hell hole, the day after tomorrow." Marie Cosette teared up and hugged Danton. "No one's ever been dis, ...this, nice to me. Thank you Monsieur Soleil." Danton smiled, "You're welcome, Marie Cosette, but I insist that you call me Uncle Danton!" Marie Cosette was even more confused, but said, "If dat, ...that will make you happy, Uncle Danton." Danton hugged Marie Cosette and said, "It will make me extremely happy, my dear Marie Cosette."

After Marie Cosette set off on her journey of exploration, and Mary and Inman returned to their suite to "dress," Millicent, Irene, Caroline, Virginia, Danton and Phillippe were left in the **de Bienville Suite** together. Danton suggested they play a card game called "Scrounge." When everyone agreed, Danton sent a waiter to request two decks of cards. They enjoyed their spirited gams of "Scrounge" all afternoon, until it was time to change for dinner and New Year's Eve.

The entire family met in the lobby of the Hotel Monteleone just before six, all dressed in their finest clothes. The ladies wore gowns, and extravagant jewelry. The gents wore White Tie and Tails. Millicent and Caroline were chatting when Mary and Inman stepped out of the elevator. They both gasped in unison, and were so happy and proud of their children, they hugged each other tightly. Mary and Inman embraced their mothers, then their aunts, Irene and Virginia, their uncles, Danton and Phillippe and finally Marie Cosette. Millicent and Danton then led their assault on the Swan Room. The **Maître d'hôtel** looked up from his book and smiled. "**Monsieur Soleil, c'est si agréable de vous voir ce soir! Neuf, je crois**." (Mister Soleil, it is so nice to see you tonight! Nine, I believe.) Danton nodded, "**Oui certainement. Pouvons-nous nous asseoir près de la scène?**" (Yes, certainly. May we sit near the stage?) The **Maître d'hôtel** smiled at Danton, "**... pour vous, monsieur, c'est tout à fait possible**." (...for you, sir, that is quite possible.)

Millicent and Danton's family was guided to the stage. Waiters moved three white linen draped tables together and held the chairs for the ladies. Menus were distributed, and drink orders written down. Midway through a leisurely New Year's Eve dinner, the **Maître des cérémonies** stepped out onto the stage. "**Mesdames et messieurs, j'ai le plaisir de souhaiter la bienvenue à Liberace sur notre scène** "(Ladies and Gentlemen, I have the distinct pleasure to welcome Liberace to our stage....) After an enthusiastic round of applause, Liberace stepped to the microphone, and said, "I'm so delighted to be in New Orleans for New Year's Eve. Tonight, I'd like to dedicate my show to all of the wonderful mothers in this exciting city. It's no secret how I feel about my mother. She's the most wonderful person in all of the world, and I've always felt that one day a year is hardly enough time to pay tribute to her, so I like to think of every day as Mother's Day. ... so to start out our program, here's a little bit of advice my mom gave me some years ago. I'd like to pass it on to you."

Liberace launched into the old standard, *I Want a Girl*. He sang, "When I was a boy my mother often said to me: 'Get married boy and see how happy you can be...'" Inman squeezed Mary's hand and looked at his mother lovingly. He started to tear up at the chorus, "I want a girl, just like the girl that married dear old dad. She was a pearl, and the only girl daddy ever had." The entire family looked lovingly at Mary and Inman. Their mothers thrust out their hands in unison, as if to say, "Well, there you go." The song was heartwarming and deeply meaningful for Mary and Inman. When the song was over, Liberace stood to address his audience of adoring fans. "Thank you all. Thank you so much. One of the dances we very seldom see anymore is the authentic Viennese Waltz. ...and I bet, if I play *The Blue Danube* by Johan Strauss, we might bring back that wonderful waltz. Shall we try?"

As Liberace played the prelude to the waltz, Inman stood up and offered his hand to his beautiful bride. Inman knew in his heart that the waltz was Mary's absolute favorite dance. They danced flawlessly, as if no one else was in the room. Their mothers were balling their eyes out, both in happiness, and in fear of what the next few days might hold for their children. Other couples found their waltz charmingly beautiful as well. When the song ended, there was a standing ovation. Mary and Inman returned to their seats. Liberace came to the microphone and said, " Thank you, thank you, all. I feel compelled to share that round of applause with the young couple who waltzed so elegantly and beautifully." He paused, opened his palm, and directed it at Mary and Inman. For a second time, the audience went wild with applause.

As it died down, Liberace had a sudden realization. "Well, this is a surprise. Our young couple is seated with people I recognize. He took the microphone and stepped off the stage. Liberace stepped to the family's table, and said to Irene, "Haven't we met before?" Irene replied, "Oh, Lee, you know we've seen each other many times at Paul Getty's home!" Liberace grinned, "Yes, it's true, but I didn't know you knew this fellow." He pointed at Phillippe. "Know him? Why, he's my brother! Do you know him too?" Liberace tossed his head back. "Why yes, I met Phillippe several times at parties that Paul Lynde gave in New York City." He paused for just a moment then asked if Irene had a request. "As a matter of fact, I've always been partial to your version of *I'll Be Seeing You*, could you play that?" Liberace kissed Irene on the forehead returned to his piano and played her request. For the rest of his show, Liberace was completely charming, engaged with his audience, and played their requests. He was truly "Mr. Showmanship!"

When the show ended, Liberace blew a kiss to the audience and asked Irene to save a place for him at the Carousel Bar. She nodded, and the family transitioned from the Swan Room to the Carousel Bar. Marie Cosette had developed a headache, and excused herself to go up to bed. The rest of the family somehow made it to the Carousel Bar before the rush of autograph seekers who mobbed Lee's dressing room door. Danton asked the bartender how they might reserve a seat for Liberace. "Well sir, you could lay your jacket over the stool." Danton's posture stiffened and grew quite formal. "Take off my jacket?" Phillippe began to laugh. "Oh dear god, Danton, it's almost 1953. Here, use my jacket. I'm not ashamed." Danton nodded his head and smiled at his old friend. "That's the thing about you Phillippe, you've never been ashamed of anything!" Phillippe laid his jacket across the stool, made a cat roar, and clawed the air at Danton. Everyone, including Danton, began to laugh uncontrollably.

Mary and Inman chose to sit at a table for two at one of the front windows looking out onto Royal Street. The table was set with its corner pointing to the window. Mary and Inman sat, side by side against the window. The crisp white linen tablecloth concealed their amorous activities below the table. While they weren't the first, or even nearly the last to engage in that kind of behavior, they both knew that they had to keep their heads about them and not go too far. They enjoyed themselves until about 11:00. They reasoned that after midnight, they could excuse themselves to go up to their suite, and didn't want it to be obvious what they'd been up to. At 11:00, the bartender dialed the radio to WWL 870 for the CBS broadcast of New Year's Eve with Guy Lombardo from the Roosevelt Grill in New York City. Mary and Inman got up and began to dance to the hits being performed by the Royal Canadiens. Very quickly, the bar's floor space became extremely crowded, but Mary and Inman didn't mind dancing extra close to each other.

As midnight neared, waiters scurried around ensuring that all of the patrons had flutes of Champagne. From the radio, the Carousel Bar patrons heard, "Ten, Nine, Eight, Seven, Six, Five, Four, Three, Two, One... Happy New Year! Happy 1953!" Mary and Inman kissed a long and deeply romantic kiss before raising their glasses. They then went over to their family and Liberace at the bar and wished everyone a happy and prosperous 1953. Once their glasses were empty, Mary and Inman made their excuses, and made their way through the tight crowd to the elevator and up to their suite.

After breakfast on New Year's Day, the family spent the day together in the **de Bienville Suite**. They told stories and played cards, all of them grateful for the time to be together. Knowing that this was their last night together for a while, Mary and Inman retired early, just after the completion of dinner. Mary and Inman made love for hours until they were both exhausted. As they reveled in the afterglow of their love-making, Inman confessed. "I don't know how I'll be able to live apart from you." Mary said, "Mama thinks that our marriage is a good first step to convincing my father to accept us." Inman replied, "I truly hope so." Mary and Inman engaged in pillow talk until they both fell asleep wrapped in each other's arms.

The next morning, after a luxuriant breakfast, Danton had Irene and Phillippe driven to Moisant Field for their flight back to New York. He drove himself and Inman to their Factorage at the Wharf. After a passionate goodbye with copious tears, Millicent drove Mary and Marie Cosette back to the

Bank House on Esplanade Avenue. Mary cried mournfully the entire journey back to her father's prison. As the girls got out of the Eldorado, Millicent hugged Mary and pledged to make things better. Mary was inconsolable. She was weeping uncontrollably. "I can't understand this. I'm married. I have a husband who has plenty of money, and a secure job. I'm happy, and I'm expecting." Millicent shook Mary. "I know that you can't understand this situation. It defies the laws of logic. ...but that's your father. He defies the laws of logic. ...but I promise you that I'll find a way to end this." Mary hugged her mother then resigned herself to her life in goon hell. She went into the Bank House with Marie Cosette and they made her way upstairs. Millicent followed them in and brought her wrath down on Blackjack's goons for any reason she could find. After Millicent caused Blackjack's goons to soil themselves for a third time, she left in triumph.

Millicent had no idea what difficulties would be coming in the months ahead.

CHAPTER EIGHTEEN

BLACKJACK'S EPIPHANY

Inman was restless at work. He sent Lucy Butler on an errand that would keep her out of the office for a long time. Once she was gone, Inman scoured through the papers on her desk, looking for the address of the Bank House on Esplanade Avenue. It took him almost thirty minutes to find it. Inman was completely disappointed in his performance. He decided to wait until the next day, Saturday, the 3rd. of January, to visit Mary. He had to put a plan into place. That Friday night he reconnoitered the property in Esplanade Ridge, on the verge of **Tremé**. The second floor had a gallery porch fronting Esplanade Avenue. To the left of the house was an Episcopal Church, Saint Anna's. The Marias Street side had a semi-octangular balcony surrounding the bedroom over the kitchen area. Much to Inman's surprise, there was an exterior staircase leading from the back yard up to the second floor. He was tempted to rush up the stairs, but thought it better to watch the goings on of the Bank House for the evening.

From a secluded vantage point, Inman observed the stream of gamblers that went to the front door and were serviced through openings in the door. The face level opening opened first. Only account numbers were used to establish legitimacy. After that, a counter level opening was reveled for the monetary transaction. Money flowed in, and money trickled out. Inman also watched the lights in the second floor rooms. As the evening dragged on, he noticed that the lights in the room that he supposed to be the sitting room went out, and the lights in the rear room came on for a few minutes, then went out. The lights in the front room burned steadily. After a few minutes, Inman saw Mary come out onto the gallery, lean on the rail, and look off into the distance. Inman perceived Mary to be looking toward **Maison Soleil**, and had to fight to keep from running to his loving wife. After a couple of minutes, Mary sighed heavily, turned, and returned to the front bedroom. It wasn't long before the lights in her room went out. Inman continued to observe the comings and goings for the next couple of hours before meandering his way back to **Maison Soleil**.

Inman had just gotten on the Saint Charles Line Streetcar when he saw Delphine seated on the back row of seats. He walked back, bowed and said, "**Bonsoir madame Delphine, comment ça va ce soir?**" (Good evening Madam Delphine, how are you this evening?) Delphine, unused to this level of polite greeting said, "**Vous êtes exactement le gentleman qu'était votre papa!!**" (You're exactly the gentleman that your papa was!) Delphine was so honored by their exchange that she started her well-known laugh, "Hee, hee, hee, hee…" Inman blushed, and took a minute, but summoned his courage. "Madame Delphine, it is an honor to see you tonight. May I assume that you have a message for me?" Delphine settled back on her Streetcar bench and said, "Papa Legba likes ju, boy. …but dey's compeding spirids oud dere who are fighding Papa Legba." Inman looked a tad confused. "Fighting with Papa Legba?" Delphine smiled. "Sounds wrong, don' id?" Inman nodded. Delphine continued, "Dey don' won ju do win. Dey are dark forces. Ju needs no, Papa Legba iz on ju side, boy. Ju'z shown him dat ju love dat girl. Ju need do keep da faidh."

Inman thought for a moment. "Dear Madame Delphine, is Mary's father going to make things worse?" Delphine looked off to the right. "Mo dan ju can know! Bud… Ju godda know dat ju hab peoples on ju side. Ju godda fight de gud fighd. It ain' gon be easy, bud, ju'll win if'n ju jus keep de faidh." Inman had so much more that he wanted to ask Delphine, but Howard Avenue was fast approaching. As the Streetcar pulled to a stop and opened the doors, Inman bowed and said, "**Merci, Madame Delphine**!" After Inman alighted from the Streetcar and started walking down Howard Avenue to **Maison Soleil**, he was surprised not to hear Delphine's accustomed laughter. There was no need for theatrics because of Inman's genuine respect for Madame Delphine Voyante.

Inman made his way down Howard Avenue and unlocked the gate to the **garçonnière**. He went in, locked the gate, and made his way to the dance terrace. There was a chill in the air and Inman snagged a throw blanket and went over to a **chaise longue**. He wrapped up and settled in for the night, knowing that he couldn't sleep, and needed to settle on a plan. His true and rightful wife was his objective, and her father was his adversary. After settling in, it wasn't long before Inman decided to make the obvious choice: climb the stairs and knock on the door. All of the activity he'd noticed had happened on the front **véranda** of the Bank House. Relieved, Inman unexpectedly fell asleep. His sleep wasn't exactly peaceful. His dreams were of difficult times, isolation, and a foreign city. Inman woke up scared and confused.

Inman showered and dressed. He ate breakfast and luncheon with Caroline and Virginia. After luncheon, after Virginia returned to her suite to do "whatever" with "whomever." (it was never questioned.) Inman sat with his mother in her **salon principal**, and asked, "Why can't Mary and I be together? I have means. I have class. I have everything her father says he wants for her!" Caroline closed her eyes and sighed deeply. She opened her eyes and looked straight into Inman's eyes. "Did you know that your uncle Danton and Millicent Blanchard were, at one time, very much in love?" Inman said, "I know that they have feelings for each other." Caroline continued, "Did you know that Millicent and Danton had been engaged?" Inman was completely shocked. "No, I didn't." Caroline said, "There's a whole lot more, but suffice it to say, there's a lot of bad blood between the Soleils and Carnes, with Jackson Day. ...not the Blanchards, of course!" Inman was stunned. "Can't he see we're madly in love?" Caroline responded, "Well, I can, and Milly can. We both love you both and want only the best for you, but Jackson has political power, and his 'bought and paid for' army of goons. Jackson would rather see Mary married to Lucifer than you."

Inman's head swam for a few minutes coming to terms with Caroline's last statement. "You can't be serious. That's hyperbole, isn't it?" Caroline looked down and placed her left hand over her forehead. "I'm sorry, but that's the truth. You needed to hear it. You also need to know that Millicent and I will do everything in our power to fix this situation." Inman thanked her. "I'll be going now. I'm going to try to see my wife tonight. I hope you understand." Caroline smiled at her son, "**Bonne chance**!" Before he left to make his way to Esplanade Ridge, Inman grabbed some leftovers and wrapped them in waxed paper. He placed them in a brown paper sack that he put into his World War II surplus backpack. He walked up Howard Avenue and rode the Streetcar to Canal Street. He transferred and rode the Canal Street Streetcar to Rampart Street, where he got off and walked to and through "Back of Town." Inman enjoyed looking at the historical residences and businesses on his walk through "Back of Town," **Tremé**. He paused when he got to the corner of Esplanade Avenue and Marais Street. Inman needed a moment to settle in and ascertain if everything was as before. It was. He proceeded cautiously to the back yard of the Bank House and made his way to the back stairs leading to the second floor. So far, so good. Inman stepped quietly up the stairs to the door. He knocked quietly. There was no response. ...probably because Mary and Marie Cosette were in the sitting room and didn't hear his knocks. Inman walked around the house and threw pebbles at the windows until one opened. He motioned to the back of the house and Marie Cosette acknowledged Inman's signal. She ran back and had the door open before Inman could return to the back of the house. He ran up the exterior stairs and into the door. Mary launched herself into Inman's arms. Marie Cosette cautioned quietness. Mary and Inman settled themselves down and walked together to the sitting room.

Mary said, "We can't do anything that will alert the goons. They're on high alert." Inman smirked. "They're idiots. ...but we'll be discrete." Mary looked at Marie Cosette pleadingly. Marie Cosette said, "Y'all go on in dere... there! I'll be just fine in here listening do da...to the radio." Mary hugged

Marie Cosette then grabbed Inman's hand and guided him to her bedroom. Once the door was closed she jumped into Inman's arms and began kissing him passionately. "**Emmenez-moi au lit, cher mari!**" (Take me to the bed, dear husband!) Against all odds, Inman successfully avoided all obstacles and sat on Mary's bed with her legs entwined around his waist. His mouth was quite busy, so he thanked Papa Legba mentally. ...or was it Saint Peter? It didn't take long before Mary began to unbutton Inman's shirt and run her hand across his broad chest. Inman, in the throes of love, unbuttoned Mary's shirt and reached around and unhooked her brassiere. He lifted the front of the brassiere up and Mary's breasts tumbled out. As Inman began to tenderly massage Mary's nipples, she couldn't take it anymore, and pushed Inman down onto the bed. She stood up and yanked Inman up too. They undressed each other and crawled into the bed. The bed was nondescript, nothing like the luxurious bed at the Hotel Monteleone, but neither noticed. They were in love, and in a rampant case of lust, and the only thing that registered was their overwhelming happiness to be together.

Try as they did, both Mary and Inman couldn't help make some exclamations. Marie Cosette had their backs and turned the radio up to keep the goons from hearing them. Well mostly. In truth, she didn't want to hear it either. It was partly because she didn't want to be eavesdropping, and partly because she was intensely jealous of their relationship. Mary and Inman made wild, eyes rolling back, passionate love for over four hours. At 1:00, Inman convinced Mary that he needed to go back to the **garçonnière** and regain his strength for later on that day, Sunday. Mary kissed Inman tearfully all the way to the back door. He slipped down the stairs and disappeared into the night. As Mary passed through the sitting room to go to bed, Marie Cosette, without meaning any negativity said, "You know dat...that he's gon' get caught." Mary took the high road. "Yes, that's a possibility, but Inman is smart, and the goons aren't." Marie Cosette added, "You's right, he is smart, an' they be dumb, but luck can favor the lowest of the low. Look at me, I spent a week at da...the best hotel in New Orleans!" Millicent saw Marie Cosette's golden heart and smiled. "Marie Cosette, you are so far from being the lowest of the low! ...and thank you for raising the volume on the radio!" Marie Cosette smiled, the two dear friends hugged, and both went to bed.

Sunday was a repeat of Saturday, except for the fact that Inman realized that he'd need to go to work on Monday, and forced himself to leave his dear wife at midnight. Two nights of bliss, fooling the goons made Inman just a bit cocky. Inman worked late on Monday, and snagged a couple of Po-boys from the Commissary to eat on the way to the Esplanade Avenue Bank House. It took only part of the journey for Inman to regret his dinner choice. True, the taste of the Po-boys were divine in every sense, but when the meal repeated on him, Inman was terrified about his breath. As soon as Inman entered the Bank House he asked Marie Cosette for some mouth wash and held a ravenous Mary at bay until he could rinse his mouth. Mary held onto Inman as he rinsed, kissing his cheeks. "This is so unnecessary, my love!" Once he spit, Inman launched into Mary, kissing her like he hadn't seen her in twenty years. They made their way to Mary's bedroom, and Marie Cosette turned up the radio. The evening of marital bliss fogged Inman's normally sharp senses. As he stepped out of the door to the back stairs, he failed to notice one of the goons at the back fence urinating and cursing the girls for taking the other bathroom in the Bank House. He heard Inman descending the stairs and turned. "Hey, you, what are you doing here?" Inman took off and ran toward the **Vieux Carré**. He had a head start because the goon hadn't finished relieving himself, and had to get it all tucked in and zipped up. The goon ran for a couple of blocks, but Inman had vanished into the night.

The next morning, the sixth of January, the goons placed a call to Blackjack to tell him that Inman was spotted leaving the second floor at midnight the previous night. Blackjack blew into a psychotic rage. "How the hell did that happen? Weren't you two paying attention!" The sacrificial goon tried to explain, "Boss, we was taking bets at the door. We don' know how he found the house, but he walked up the back stairs. We'll make sure thad don' never happen again." Blackjack didn't have any replacements and didn't really have a choice. He puffed up, "That better not ever happen again, you hear! I doubt you know what I'm capable of!" He slammed the phone down on the hook and stormed into the parlor. Millicent turned elegantly, only to see a raging bull approaching from the dining room. As much as Millicent should have been terrified, she wasn't. She bowed up in preparation for Blackjack's assault.

Blackjack stopped only a few feet from Millicent and, red faced and hyperventilating, said, "That Carnes vermin was at the Bank House last night. I don't suppose you know how that happened?" Millicent took a sip of her Gin and Tonic and stared Blackjack down. "Jackson, they're in love, and he is, after all, Inman Carnes' son, and quite brilliant. You and your goons aren't brilliant. If you weren't so petty and vindictive, you'd realize that Inman is perfect for Mary." Blackjack's face grew beet red and the veins in his face popped out alarmingly. "Those families repeatedly put me down in society!" Millicent flung her drink into Blackjack's face, to "cool him down." Blackjack froze in complete shock. Millicent said, "Jackson, none of them ever did any such thing! Neither Danton nor Inman blackballed your application to the Boston Club. They were your friends, and they sponsored your application. ...but you blamed them and and you turned on them. You extorted them so you could buy this damn funeral home and take me away from Danton!"

Blackjack calmed down, enough to say, "Milly, Emile just reminded me that, as Coroner, I have the power to have anyone committed to East Louisiana State Hospital." Millicent stared Blackjack down. "Is that a threat, Jackson?" Blackjack paused. "Take it as you will." Millicent moved in close to Blackjack's beady eyes and said, "Go on, pull the trigger. ...as long as you know that the holders of the 'packages' have instructions, that in the instance that Danton or I go missing, are killed in mysterious circumstances, or are 'committed,' that they are to turn the dossiers over to the State Patrol, and the news outlets. Do you want your various and sundry crimes reported in the *Times Picayune*? Blackjack froze. Millicent poked him in the chest and said, "Jackson, I asked you a question!" Blackjack said "No." and started walking toward the stairs. Millicent stopped him. "Don't you dare come up to the Master bedroom tonight! You sleep on that decrepit sofa in your office, do you hear?!?!" Blackjack said nothing and slithered back to his office.

279

On Wednesday, Inman tried to visit. Mary and Marie Cosette were at the open door when Inman came around into the back yard. They saw the goon calling out to Inman and telling him that he needed to get out of there or there would be consequences. Inman looked up at his beloved and blew her a kiss before leaving the back yard. Mary ran to her room and cried for the rest of the night. The next evening, Inman once again returned to visit Mary. For the second evening, there is a goon on guard duty. For the second time, Mary spent the night crying. As Inman left, he wandered around the property.

He spent a few moments contemplating Saint Anna's Episcopal Church next door. While it wasn't Catholic, in the strictest terms, Inman decided to try the door. It was open. It was dark inside, but the light of the Presence Candle drew him in. Inman genuflected and kneeled in prayer. Inman didn't pray for his needs or his desires. He prayed, instead, for his wife's happiness, for his unborn child's health, and for his mother, aunt, and uncle. In his tears, Inman plucked a Book of Common Prayer from the pew and found the General Confession.

He read, " ALMIGHTY God, Father of our Lord Jesus Christ, Maker of all things, Judge of all men: I acknowledge and bewail my manifold sins and wickedness, Which I, from time to time, most grievously have committed, By thought, word, and deed, Against thy Divine Majesty…. Okay, Inman personalized the confession. When he finished, Inman said the "Our Father" then slowly walked to the Narthex and out toward Esplanade Avenue. Inman was surprised that there was an extension ladder leaning against the church that he hadn't remembered seeing as he entered the Church. He looked up and said, "Thank you." Inman made his way back to **Maison Soleil** and spent a mostly sleepless night desiring his beloved wife.

On Friday, Inman threw himself into his containerized shipping project. The clock at times seemed to be stopped, and at other times seemed to spin wildly. Inman trusted that his next gambit would work. At 5:00, Danton and Inman drove to **Maison Soleil** for dinner. Danton and Caroline were quiet and pensive. They both knew that Inman was going to attempt to visit Mary. They both knew that they couldn't talk him out of it, but feared what Blackjack was capable of. Virginia looked at her brother and sister, morose in their fear. "**Connerie!**" (Bull shit!) Caroline gasped, Danton guffawed, and Inman began to laugh. He looked lovingly at his dear Aunt Virginia. "**Chère tante, qu'est-ce que la «connerie» exactement**?" (Dear aunt, what exactly is 'bull shit'?)

Aunt Virginia placed her fork on her plate and rested her knife on the edge of the plate. She finished chewing and dabbed her lips. "I think that it's bullshit that you can't be with Mary. God damn that ungodly Blackjack! He doesn't own Mary. You two are married. ... and you are half Carnes and half Soleil, and she is half Blanchard. You two are Louisiana royalty. I think that you should go down to the Wharf and take some of the stevedores over to Esplanade Ridge, and break Mary out of that prison and bring her here. That's all I have to say about that!" ...and suddenly, everyone knew that **dîner** was **complété**.

Danton took Inman into the **bibliothèque** to mitigate Virginia's outburst. They sat down and looked at one another. Danton breathed in and out deeply behind pursed lips. Inman remained attentive, but deathly silent. Danton had almost wanted Inman to be impulsive and speak out, but he did't. Danton saw that it was all on him. "Virginia isn't wrong. ...and we could go down to the Wharf and gather a posse, and break Mary out." Danton paused and looked off into the distance. "...but what Virginia doesn't know, and even you probably don't know, is that as Coroner, Blackjack can have any citizen of Orleans Parish committed to East Louisiana State Hospital. If we did the right thing and rescued Mary, he'd probably commit Millicent, and even your mother and Aunt Virginia. He wouldn't come after me. He wouldn't come after you. The price would be too high. Your Aunt Virginia would be low hanging fruit, even though there's nothing wrong with her. ...your mother too. They both have lived behind these stone walls for almost 20 years. People talk, and people judge, right, wrong, or indifferent."

Inman cradled his forehead in his left hand. "So, I can't be with Mary?" Danton shook his head. "No, you can't. Millicent, and I will need to find a way." Inman stood up. "I'm going to see Mary tonight. God has gifted me with a way." Danton stood up and wished Inman "**Bonne chance, cher neveu!**" (Good luck, dear nephew!) Danton parted ways with Inman and returned to the **salle à manger** (dining room). Inman left the property and decided to walk through the **Vieux Carré** to Esplanade Ridge to get a handle on his thoughts and plans. During his walk, Inman decided that he would need to carry the ladder to the Marias Street side of the front gallery, away from the front door.

When Inman made it to the Bank house on Esplanade Avenue, he passed the house and ducked into Saint Anna's property. He was delighted to see the large extension ladder laying against the fence. He picked it up and carried it past the Bank House and extended it up to the upper gallery. Inman scampered up the ladder and knocked gently on the french doors. Mary came to the doors and almost fainted when she saw her precious husband. She opened the door and embraced her husband tightly. After a few moments, Mary put their love on hold to tell Marie Cosette that Inman was there so she could distract the goons with loud radio music. They were astoundingly dumb, and never figured out that loud music equated to connubial bliss. Inman stayed until 2:00, removed and stowed the ladder, and wasn't caught.

For the next month, Inman was able to visit Mary by utilizing God's ladder. They didn't get to spend all of the time together that they both desired, but all of their time was quality time. During the month, Mary and Inman grew to understand that they were completely in love, and that the amount of time was less important than the quality of the time spent together. They both thanked God for any time that they got to spend together.

Monday, February 9th. would prove to be problematic. After a month of success, Inman was painfully cocky. Inman showed up way too early. The sun hadn't set and the ladder was a huge obvious eyesore. Inman hadn't been at the Bank House for two hours before a bettor asked about the renovations. The servicing goon was confused. "What renovations?" The bettor pointed to his right and said, "Well, that ladder, there." Even though it was against Blackjack's rules, the goon opened the door and looked to the left. He closed the door, and finished the transaction. After the transaction, the bettor left, and the goon alerted his comrade. The pair charged the stairs and burst into the sitting room and then Mary's bedroom.

The goons burst in on Mary and Inman making out. Mary and Inman hadn't had time to remove any clothing. One goon lunged at Inman. Inman moved away and allowed the goon to land hard against the wall. Several more times, the goons, separately, and in unison attacked Inman, to no avail. When he saw an advantage, Inman rushed out onto the gallery and launched himself onto the ladder. He locked the leather heals of his shoes against the uprights of the ladder and used them to guide his slide down the ladder. Once down the ladder, Inman made his way back to the **Vieux Carré**, and then back to **Maison Soleil**. The goon's ignorance of the basic tenants of warfare had condemned themselves to failure.

The next morning, as painful as they knew it would be, the goons had to call Blackjack and report the previous night's exploits. Blackjack lost his mind. He told the goon, "From now on, rough him up, badly. Do you understand?" The goon answered in the affirmative. He wasn't exactly happy about the violence, but his partner saw a chance to move up in the food chain and was excited about the prospect of pummeling Inman.

Blackjack then turned his wrath on Millicent. "You're encouraging this treason in MY family!" Millicent crunched an ice cube, clenched a fist, and said, "YOUR family? You have some gaul! You have ignored me in every sense of a marital relationship since I got pregnant with Mary. ...and don't think that I don't know that you enjoy the sexual company of Marie Catherine Jardin. We ceased to be a family, completely, when you forced MY daughter to that damn Bank House! Blackjack threatened his commitment powers, and Millicent reminded Blackjack of the consequences of using those powers on her or Danton. Blackjack threw up his hands and retreated to his office yelling for Hattie to bring him **café noir**.

The next morning, Inman sketched out a design for a lightweight rope ladder. He knew that many of his fabrication team were WWII veterans, and could build out his design quickly. Inman's team looked at his ladder design. It was supported by sisal ropes, knotted beneath each rung. Instead of wood, Inman opted for lightweight aluminum rungs. He designed aluminum hooks and a lightweight throwing rope with a monkey's fist to make getting the advance line up to the receiver easier. Not a single person on Inman's team questioned his motivation for getting this project done. They worked together and finished the project by 3:00.

After dinner, Inman packed the rope ladder in his backpack and made his way through the **Vieux Carré** to **Tremé** and Esplanade Ridge. Inman spent a long time reconnoitering the Bank house. He hid in shadows and watched the front door for a while, and the back door for a while. He noticed the balcony around the second floor bay. Inman was amazed that there weren't goons posted in the front or the back. He had no way of knowing that at least one of them was wanting to catch him, so he could beat him. Inman went to the side of the Bank House and threw pebbles at the sitting room window. Mary finally heard the taps at the window glass, and opened one of the windows. Inman pointed to the balcony and mouthed, " Send Marie Cosette out!"

Marie Cosette went to her bedroom and opened the window. She stepped out onto the balcony and waved to Inman. Inman waved back and retrieved the rope ladder. He showed Marie Cosette the monkey's fist and throwing rope. Marie Cosette smiled and indicated that she understood what was coming. Inman tossed the monkey's fist up to the balcony. Marie Cosette missed catching the monkey's fist the first two tries. On the third toss, Marie Cosette caught the monkey's fist. She grasped the throwing rope and pulled the ladder up to the rail. She hooked the ladder to the balcony rail and stepped back to allow Inman unrestricted space as he climbed onto the balcony. Inman sprinted up the ladder. He pulled the rope ladder up behind him, and ducked into Marie Cosette's bedroom. Inman hugged Marie Cosette and followed her to the sitting room. Before Mary and Inman retreated to Mary's bedroom, Inman described how the ladder would remain on the balcony, and deployed on his arrival. "Marie Cosette, maybe you can find an oilcloth to conceal the ladder?" Marie Cosette happily agreed to find concealment for Inman's ladder.

Mary and Inman enjoyed a leisurely night of marital bliss. Marie Cosette kept the radio turned up when necessary. As much as Inman didn't want to leave, he knew that he had to, and left just after 2:00. He had a similar visit the next evening on Thursday the 12th. Friday the thirteenth, however, would prove to be Inman's unlucky day. Inman arrived in darkness, after dinner, as usual. He had only to toss one pebble up to the window to attract the attention of Mary. She threw open the window. Thankfully, Marie Cosette had turned the volume up on the radio to cover the unusual sounds. Mary stared adoringly from the window as Marie Cosette went to her room and lowered the rope ladder for Inman. He scaled the ladder, watched the whole way by his adoring wife. Mary was waiting for Inman as Marie Cosette escorted him into the sitting room. Mary jumped into Inman's arms and kissed him passionately. Marie Cosette sighed and remarked, I don know if dat… if that radio has enough volume fo' you two tonight!" Mary laughed, "Let's hope so, and I hope it's something that you want to listen to!"

As Inman carried Mary into her bedroom, Marie Cosette said, ostensively to herself, "I'll be okay. I don' have a man now, but I will!" Inman used Mary's foot to swing the door closed, then walked over to her bed and sat her down gently. Mary stood up and began unbuttoning Inman's shirt. She pulled the tails out of his trousers and thrust her hands up over Inman's massive shoulders and pushed both his shirt and jacket over his shoulders. They cascaded down to the rug. Mary then guided Inman's hands to the buttons on her dress. He started at the top, and insisted on kissing Mary each time he achieved a button. Following Mary's lead, Inman caressed Mary's shoulders and caused her dress to float down to the floor. Mary pulled Inman's singlet from his waistline and pushed it up and over his shoulders as far as she could. Inman had to reach down and pull it up and over his head. After tossing it aside, Inman reached around Mary and unfastened her brassiere. He slid the straps just to the edge of Mary's shoulders and paused. He looked lovingly into Mary's eyes as she bent slightly forward and allowed the brassiere to slid down her arms onto the pile of clothes below.

Mary and Inman embraced lovingly, nude from the waist up for a few moments. Mary began to pant, and realized that she needed more from Inman. She unbuckled Inman's belt and unbuttoned his trousers. They fell to the floor. Mary then pushed her slip down to the mass of clothing and kneeled down to remove Inman's boxers. She slid them down slowly, kissing her husband passionately most of the way down until Inman's penis popped out from the waistband. Inman closed his eyes and tilted his head back as

Mary lavished her attentions on his manhood. Inman waited for a while, but pulled Mary back up into his arms. He kissed her passionately for a few moments before sinking to his knees and starting to slip her panties down. Inman kissed her entire body from Mary's waist to her mons Venus. As Mary's panties crossed her buttocks and fell to the floor, Inman began pleasuring Mary orally. As worked up as she was, it didn't take long for Mary to climax. After she did, Mary grasped Inman by his luxuriant hair and tugged him to a standing posture. They kissed passionately, as if it were for the first time.

It wasn't long before Mary couldn't take it anymore. As in the past, she backed Inman to the bed, pushed him down, and jumped on top of him. Inman was happy to let Mary be in charge of their lovemaking. He was completely in love with her, and would have been content to simply be with her. Inman hadn't been brought up to be needy, so the wild sex was at once unexpected, and at the same time deeply appreciated. Mary and Inman truly had a blessed relationship. They both were beginning to see the external challenges before them, but internally, they functioned like a well oiled machine. They were both in tune with their own needs as well as the needs of their partners. Understandably, their biggest shared desire was to make their intimacy last as long as possible. Inman became acutely aware of just how far he could go before it was necessary for him to retreat and find other paths to Mary's gratification.

When it became apparent that they were both completely exhausted, Mary refused to allow Inman to pull out. She dug her nails into his butt and held him just close enough for him to maneuver. They both exploded in orgasm together. Mary slid off of Inman and lay next to him, looking adoringly into his eyes with her arm and leg draped across his muscular body. They lay there together and planned an impossible future for quite a long time. Inman wanted to linger longer than normal because it was Friday night, and he wouldn't have to go to work the next morning. Around 10:00, there was a lot of activity from the goons below. They seemed agitated, and that worried both Mary and Inman. Inman regrettably decided that if he wanted to continue making these visits, he'd probably better leave. Both Mary and Inman got dressed without breaking their loving eye contact.

Inman put his arm around Mary's waist, and they walked out of Mary's bedroom. Marie Cosette looked at them and blushed. "I thought dat... that you two would stay together longer tonight." Inman smirked, and Mary replied, "Too much damn goon activity." Marie Cosette nodded and looked at Mary. "Well, go on, you know where the balcony is." Mary grinned and walked with Inman to Marie Cosette's bedroom and out onto the balcony. Inman lowered the ladder, stepped over the railing and kissed his bride. for some unexplainable reason, Inman got cocky, and decided to do some tricks going down the ladder. Two thirds of the way down, Inman lost his footing and in catching himself, caused the ladder to swing in and crash against the kitchen wall.

Mary ducked back into Marie Cosette's bedroom as Inman dropped the rest of the way to the ground and began to run. One of the goons, who had been getting a Dixie beer out of the refrigerator, heard the crash and ran out to see what was going on. He saw Inman and began yelling and chasing him down Esplanade Avenue. Fortunately, the goon hadn't seen the ladder, and Marie Cosette was able to go out and pull it up. Mary and Marie Cosette sat in the sitting room listening to the radio. They were both terrified about what might happen to Inman.

Inman turned down Rampart Street. Thankfully he was in much better physical shape than the cigar smoking, beer guzzling goon, and maintained a respectable distance. The goon, eager to keep his job, and his life, pushed himself. He saw Inman turn on Saint Peter Street and made his way there. By the time the goon made it down Saint Peter Street to Bourbon Street, Inman had vanished into the crowd enjoying the Krew of Hermès parade. Inman was dazzled by the spectacle that he encountered.

There were decorated floats illuminated by incandescent lights and multi-color neon tubes. As fantastic as the floats were, the detail that caught Inman's imagination were the Flambeaux. Groups of costumed Krew members were holding aloft long poles topped with kerosene reservoirs that fed fuel down to burners in front of reflective panels. Many of the poles were decorated with designs like music clefs. Utilizing leather Guidon Flag carrying harnesses, the Krew members could spin their Flambeaux in dazzling displays. They marched, slowly, in unison, with choreographed Flambeaux movements, to the drunken crowd's wild approval.

Distracted, Inman didn't notice the Krew's Captain, dressed in white and gold, masked, and wearing a splendid helmet surmounted by white ostrich feathers. He was riding a white steed, majestically. The Captain certainly noticed Inman. It was Danton, a charter member of The Krew of Hermes, from 1937. Instinctively, Danton looked over the crowd and saw the goon looking for Inman. Fortunately, Inman had crossed Bourbon Street and was making his way toward Canal Street. Danton watched the goon until he gave up and started making his way back to the Bank House. Danton breathed a sigh of relief, and returned his attention to the parade. He knew that tomorrow would bring yet another blow-up by Blackjack.

Inman made it to the streetcar. It appeared to be empty when he got on, but as he sat down a familiar voice called to him. "Dat was so cloze. …is a gud ding dat ju are in such gud shape." Inman stood up and turned around. Delphine was seated on the rear bench. Inman removed his hat. "**Madame Delphine, quel grand plaisir! S'il vous plaît excusez-moi de vous manquer la dernière fois!**" (Madam Delphine, what a great pleasure! …Please excuse me for running out on you the last time!) Delphine smiled and cocked her head. "Ju no dat de girl's fader hades ju, don ju?" Inman looked down at his feet. "Yes. …but I don't know why. No one will tell me." Delphine said, "Blackjack has whad he has, a'cause o ju papa and ju oncle, and dey frien, de Mayor." Inman was confused. "Are you saying that they helped Blackjack?" Delphine grumbled. "No, I'z sayin' dat Blackjack conned de money out'n dem. He had phodos, and sworn stademen's from his goons dat pud dem all in a bad way. Day gave Blackjack money. …and de girl's mama doo.

Inman was heartbroken. "Madame Delphine, I sincerely want to thank you for telling me this, but why are you telling me all of this?" Delphine sank back onto the bench and smiled. "Ju got's'a no wat ju's up agin'. Dat man is pure evil, I dell ju! He's dun dol' dem goons do beat ju badly when' dey catch ju." Inman's face communicated his shock and lack of understanding. "Ju ain' gonna dake dat box'o Laura's candy do dat girl domorro' neider! Dey's gonna call de boss domorro' an it ain' gonna sid well wid him. De girl's gonna hav' do visit ju fo a whil'.

As the streetcar started around Lee Circle, Inman found himself overwhelmed at all the Delphine had shared with him. His head was spinning. As the streetcar puled to a stop, Inman said, "**Bénédictions chères madame! ... jusqu'à ce que nous nous revoyions**." (Blessings to you dear lady! ...until we meet again.) Inman bowed, then sprinted off the Streetcar and down Howard Avenue to the **garçonnière** gate at **Maison Soleil**. He let himself in and paused on the dance terrace. He usually spent his troubled nights on the dance terrace, but it was a bit airish, and smelled of rain. Inman went upstairs to his bedroom and undressed for bed. He lay there, propped up for hours, trying to connect all of the puzzle pieces to understand why Blackjack hated him so vehemently. It was after 4:00 before Inman sank into Elysium, still propped up.

The next morning was Valentines Day. Inman slept in. The goons waited until 9:00 before calling Blackjack. They were taken aback when Blackjack didn't start yelling and screaming. They were mistaken to think that things would be okay. Blackjack was over the tipping point, and considering his options. After telling the goons to beat Inman unmercifully if they could catch him, Blackjack hung the phone up and considered his options. After a few minutes, Blackjack stood up and walked calmly into the front parlor where Millicent was standing, looking out across Saint Charles Avenue.

In an uncharacteristically calm and measured voice, Blackjack said, "That Carnes bastard was at the Bank House last night, again. I though you should know that I told my loyal employees that when they catch him, they should beat him unmercifully. ...if they value their jobs, and their lives." Millicent said nothing, and continued to stare out the window. Blackjack turned and slithered back to his office.

After telling Hattie that she was going to Maison Blanche, Millicent went out to the motor court and asked for her Eldorado. It was driven out of the garage for her, and Millicent got in and drove to the Central Business District. True to her word, Millicent went to Maison Blanche, but not the store, the rental spaces behind. She went up to her brother Phillippe's antique warehouse and called Danton. "Can you come over here? Now?" Danton agreed and made his way over from his flat. When he entered the warehouse, Millicent threw her arms around Danton. "It's bad! He showed no emotion this morning." Danton sighed, "So the goons called him and told him that Inman was there last night?" Millicent responded, "Yes, but how did you know?" Danton replied, I saw Inman on Bourbon Street running from one of Blackjack's goons." Millicent looked puzzled. "You were on Bourbon Street last night?" Danton grinned, "Yes, no one knows, but I was the Captain of Hermès last night, atop a giant white steed, leading the parade!" Millicent put her left hand over her **décélotage**, and said, "My, I wish that I could have seen that!" Danton reminded her that all of the members of the Krew were sworn to secrecy. "One day when you are my wife, I'll be able to tell you these sorts of things."

Danton asked Millicent if it'd be okay for him to use the phone. Millicent nodded her head. Danton picked up the phone and dialed **Maison Soleil**. Monique answered the phone, "**Bonjour, Maison Soleil**." Danton said, "Good morning, Monique! This is Danton Soleil. Would you please tell my dear sisters that there will be three guests joining us for lunch, and that we'll need to push it back to 1:30?" Monique said, "I think that will make Madam Carnes very happy, Monsieur! Is the delay for your guests or for Monsieur Inman?" Danton chortled. "Take your pick, Monique. They are both plausible reasons!" Monique assured Danton that a particularly wonderful luncheon would be prepared and ready to serve at 1:30. After hanging up the phone, Danton turned to Millicent. "The delay is for us. I'm sure there is a bed, or something upholstered somewhere in this vast furniture boneyard." Millicent almost burst with joy. "Yes, of course, but I need to make one call first." Danton had no choice but agree.

Millicent dialed the phone. After a couple of rings, one of the goons at the Esplanade Ridge Bank house picked up. He near soiled himself when he heard that it was Millicent. "I need you to politely go upstairs and tell the girls that I'm going to pick them up at 1:30. … do you think that you are competent enough to do that?" Shaking with fear, the goon said, "Yes ma'am, I can do that for you!" Millicent dropped the phone back into the cradle. Danton said,

"1:30? We're supposed to be… Oh!" Millicent let out a maniacal chuckle and grasped Danton's hand. She led him deep into the warehouse, and to a made bed. It wasn't made for very long.

At 12:30, Millicent and Danton decided to forgo their enjoyment of each other so that Millicent could go to the Bank House and torment the goons and retrieve the girls a little sooner. Danton got into his Packard and drove to **Maison Soleil**. After greeting his sisters, Danton made his way to the **garçonnière** to check in with Inman. He called upstairs for Inman. Danton's calls shocked Inman awake, and he answered Danton. Danton said, "Get dressed and come on down. I have news." Inman agreed. When Inman came down, Danton was sitting on one of the bent bamboo sofas. Inman sat on one of the matching chairs and asked Danton what was going on.

Danton started with the events in the **Vieux Carré** the previous night. Inman asked how Danton knew about his foray into the Hermès Parade, and that there was a goon chasing him. Danton grinned and said, "I saw a lot last night because I was sitting atop a huge white horse, behind a big ole white mask." Inman was astounded. "That was you?" Danton said, "It was!" He continued, "The goons called Blackjack this morning. He told them to 'beat you badly.'" Inman said, "Yes, I know." Danton asked, "How do you know that?" Inman said, matter-of-factly, "Delphine told me on the Streetcar last night."

Danton lowered his head. "Delphine doesn't always tell you what you want to hear." Inman closed his eyes and calmly said, "No, she doesn't." Inman slowly raised his head and looked his uncle in the eyes. "…did she warn you that Blackjack would take Millicent away from you?" Danton placed both of his hands behind his neck and sighed. "Yes, but I didn't believe it at the time. She also said that our relationship wouldn't be over, but when it happened, I didn't believe that either. I feel bad, that across the years, I forgot that Delphine said that Millicent's and my relationship wouldn't be over."

Inman asked, "Are you a believer now?" Danton smirked. "…to a point. Millicent and I are, and at the same time, aren't a 'couple.' We're exceptionally happy, when we're together, and we both see some hope for the future." Danton looked down at the sampler box of candy from Laura's on the coffee table. "I suspect that you were planning to take that box of candy to Mary tonight at the Bank House." Inman nodded. "I suspect that Delphine warned you that doing that would be a big mistake?" Again, Inman nodded. Danton continued, "From what I've heard, that would be a painful mistake." He paused for effect, then continued. "You won't have to take your chocolate to Esplanade Ridge tonight. Mary will be visiting you here."

Inman perked up. "Really? When?" Danton puffed up, just a bit. "Luncheon is scheduled for 1:30, but I suspect that they'll be a little early." Inman started fretting. Danton asked what was the matter. Inman said, "I won't have time to go out and buy Mary some flowers." Danton laughed. "Don't have any worries over that! I had Lucy Butler place a flower order for all of our lady friends. Inman sighed and sank back into the plush chintz upholstery of his chair. "Thank you so much, uncle Danton!" Danton laughed. "Don't thank me, thank Lucy Butler, Monday morning!" Inman laughed. "I sure will!" Danton suggested that they make their way to the **manoir** to wait for the ladies. Offering no objections, Inman jumped up and the two made their way up to **Maison Soleil's manoir** to wait for Millicent, Mary, and Marie Cosette.

Inman and Danton had just gotten comfortable in Caroline's **salon principal** when the main gate bell rang. Both Inman and Danton jumped up as if a bolt of lightning had struck them. Knowing that Monique would go and let the ladies in, Inman and Danton went out onto the **véranda** to form a welcoming party. At almost the last minute, Inman asked, "Where are the flowers?" Danton started to hyperventilate. "Kitchen, I suspect." Inman made a mad dash through the home to the kitchen, and found the bundles in a pail of water in the sink. He grabbed three of the five and ran back to the **véranda**. Danton said, "You hold them, and present them. I'll make the presentations." Inman agreed. As they turned and started up the front steps, Monique said, "**Puis-je présenter, Madame Day, Madame Carnes, et Mademoiselle Jardin**."

Danton and Inman were smiling from ear to ear. Danton said, "**Puis-je présenter à ces charmantes dames des bouquets de fleurs, presque aussi belles qu'elles son**t." (May I present these lovely ladies with bouquets of flowers, almost as beautiful as they are.) Inman presented each of the three blushing ladies with a monumental bouquet of flowers. Before they went into Caroline's **salon principal**, Danton sent Inman around the front of the **manoir** to the kitchen to retrieve the bouquets for Caroline and Virginia. When Inman returned, they all stepped in, and Danton honored his sisters, and Inman presented them with their extravagant bouquets.

Caroline was almost at the point of tears. It was the first time in decades that she'd received flowers on Valentine's Day. She summoned Monique, and asked for all of the lady's bouquets to be placed in water. Monique curtseyed and collected the bouquets from the ladies. She went back to the kitchen, trimmed the ends, put them in vases of water, and placed them all along the center line of the dining table in the **salle à manger**. At 1:30, Monique announced that luncheon was served. Her seafood menu was received wildly, especially her Crayfish Étouffée. When Monique presented her desert, most of the guests assumed that the Doberge Cake had come from Beulah Ledner, but Monique insisted that she herself had baked and constructed the intricate and delicious confection. As dessert was being served, Millicent announced that they would be booking suites at the Hotel Monteleone for Mardi Gras. Mary and Inman were overjoyed. They had both found it difficult to sleep without each other.

After their late luncheon, Caroline's guests retired to the **salon principal** for after luncheon drinks. It was then that Inman presented Mary with the sampler he had bought especially for her from Laura's Chocolates. Mary began to cry, almost uncontrollably. Inman was completely confused. Mary assured him that it was because she'd never received even a Hershey's Kiss from anyone ever before. Inman calmed down when Mary began to hug and kiss him passionately, even in front of the family. They all looked away and pretended not to see Mary's actions. After everyone left, Caroline would later tell Inman that Mary was entering her third trimester, and that she would be especially emotional until the birth, and quite possibly for a while afterwards.

As much as no one wanted the afternoon to end, it did. Millicent noticed the time and suggested that they call it an afternoon. She didn't, after all, want to raise Blackjack's suspicions. Monique ran to the kitchen and found a fruit crate. She placed Millicent's, Mary's and Marie Cosette's vases of flowers in the crate and insulated them with crushed newsprint from Virginia's extensive collection. Monique carried the flowers out to Millicent's Eldorado, and placed them in the boot. Monique returned to the kitchen, leaving Millicent and Danton, and Mary and Inman upset over the parting, and trying to prolong the encounter, with any means possible. Marie Cosette sat alone in the back seat of Millicent's Cadillac, upset that she didn't have a beau.

Ironically, it took less time than Marie Cosette imagined for Millicent to fire up the Eldorado. "Danton, you know that I don't want to go, but you also know why we must go." Danton hung his head. "Yes, regrettably." Millicent reached her hand out of the car and pulled Danton in for one final passionate kiss. Danton melted. Millicent said, "We'll be together Tuesday for Mardi Gras." Danton perked up and said, "**Laissez le bon temps rouler!**" (Let the good times roll!) Inman and Mary broke from their romantic embrace. Ironically, neither of them had ever heard the ubiquitous Mardi Gras greeting before. They both looked at one another with questioning looks. Millicent and Danton noticed their confused looks and began to laugh. Millicent said, "I hope you don't think that we're laughing at you two! You have to know that it's difficult for us to comprehend how we neglected to connect you both with Mardi Gras." Inman said, "I heard the parades growing up, but never experienced one until recently. I also never heard, '**Laissez le bon temps rouler!**'" Mary added, "I always saw the parades from my bedroom, week after week, every year, but never heard the phrase, '**Laissez le bon temps rouler!**'" Millicent was deeply saddened by these confessions that condemned both Mary's and Inman's isolated upbringing.

Before pulling away from the curb, Millicent said to Danton. "I have an idea, can we meet tomorrow, at say, 10:30" Danton pulled a face. "At church? What about Blackjack?" Millicent tried in vain to conceal a grin. "No, at our place. Jackson has no need to go to church right now. He doesn't have his perfect family to show off, and he won his election. ...but he has no reason to suspect my reasons for going." Danton began to smile, and said, "Well, I, for one, am looking forward to a religious experience tomorrow!" Millicent's eyes opened wide, at first, then she winked at Danton as she pulled away from the curb. Millicent drove the girls back to Esplanade Avenue, but instead of turning on Marais Street, she went to the next block and turned right on North Villere Street, then right again on Kerlerec Street, and finally onto Marais Street. Millicent slowly and quietly pulled in behind the Bank House. She switched off the massive motor of the Eldorado, stepped out of the car, and rushed the back door of the Bank House.

As soon as Millicent crossed the kitchen threshold, she immediately started yelling her disgust at one thing or another. The goons, who weren't properly dressed and were eating TV dinners on collapsible tables in front of a cheap (relatively) Philco black and white set, lost it. They jumped up, knocking their tables and "dinners" across the room. They ran into each other several times trying to get to the stair hall to greet Millicent. They were both shaking with fear. Millicent sized them up and said, "My husband is not exactly happy with your care of my daughter. You really don't want to know what he said after your phone call this morning!" Millicent left them hanging for a moment then said, For God's sake, one of you put on a shirt and go get the girl's Valentines flowers out of the boot of my car and take them upstairs!" The two goons looked at one another. One was too terrified, and the other wanted to impress Millicent. He put his shirt on, and tucked it in, before running to the back yard and removing the vases of flowers from the boot of the Eldorado. After making his delivery to the girl's sitting room, the goon returned to the stair hall and waited for what Millicent would dish out next.

She stared them down for almost two minutes, then said, "I doubt that either one of you is religious, but I assure you that God is watching your actions. I, for one, want to encourage you to consider your souls. I can tell you with certainty, that you are both skating on thin ice with my husband. Chasing an innocent young man through the **Vieux Carré**? What were you thinking? I'll tell you this. I'm surprised that Jackson has put up with you two this long! The only thing I can surmise is that you keep his books 'well managed.' None of that will matter if you you expose my husband to bad press. I can assure you that your families will never know what happened to you two. ...and that will be a blessing for them." Millicent knew that it was an appropriate time to leave when she smelt the now familiar smell of fear.

Millicent turned and started toward the kitchen. Suddenly, she stopped and turned around, "You boys watch yourselves!" Millicent then spun around and left the Bank House.

The next morning, Millicent got up, dressed for church, and went down for breakfast. Danton looked over the Sports Section of the ***Times Picayune*** and grunted. "We're not going to Church today." Millicent sat down, and as Hattie poured her **café au lait**, said, "We may not be going to Church, but, I am." Midway through her breakfast, Millicent brought up the Rex Ball. Blackjack became furious. "Damn it Milly, you know full well that I can't go to that damn ball. Your daughter destroyed everything with that Carnes dog!" Millicent sighed. "Okay, I get it, you're not going to the Ball. That's quite alright, but I AM. …and I'm going to spend time with my friends, my friends that got you elected as Coroner. I'm going to enjoy myself, in spite of you. …and I'm going to enjoy myself to the point that I won't be able to drive myself home. I'll be staying at the Hotel Monteleone, just so you know! …but don't worry, I'll be making your excuses, and lying to people by telling them how much you wanted to be there. They'll all be feeling sorry for you by the time I'm done. Blackjack grunted. "Whatever!" He then shouted for Hattie. When she stepped into the dining room, Blackjack slammed his horribly stained diner coffee mug onto the table, stood up, and demanded that Hattie bring him coffee in his office. He stormed off. Millicent looked embarrassed, and tried to apologize. Hattie cut her off, "Miz Day, you'z a righteous soul. Taint no need to apologize fo sins dat ain't you's." Millicent wanted to thank Hattie for her wisdom and understanding, but she found herself paralyzed in her seat and weeping uncontrollably. By the time Millicent recovered, it was time for her to motor over to Maison Blanche on Canal Street and spend time with the only man she had ever loved.

Danton arrived at the corner of Canal Street and Dauphine Street well before Millicent was due to arrive. He strategically took a seat in a diner on the corner across from Maison Blanche, so that he could watch for Millicent's arrival, and follow her up to Phillippe's warehouse after an appropriate interval. After an acceptable breakfast, but challenging coffee, Danton saw Millicent pass his vantage point. He settled his bill, and went into the back lobby of the

Maison Blanche building. He rode the elevator up and knocked on the door. Millicent opened the door, and yanked Danton into the warehouse space. She slammed the door shut, and pulled Danton by the wrist back to their accustomed place. They undressed and got into bed. As much as they didn't mean to, they took their love-making slow. It wasn't until they were holding each other in the after glow, that Danton remembered that Millicent had said that she had an idea the day before. He propped himself up on one elbow and asked, "What did you mean, yesterday, about having an idea?"

Millicent propped herself up too. "Well... I don't know about you, but I was shocked and disheartened by our children's lack of understanding of Mardi Gras." Danton looked down. "Yes, I was too. So... What do we do about it?" Millicent collapsed back onto her back and looked off into the distance. "I thought that they should be able to wander the **Vieux Carré** on Mardi Gras, at least until midnight when the **gendarme** shut the district down." Danton replied, "I like the idea immensely, but what about Blackjack's goons?" He lay back flat on the bed and snuggled his arm around Millicent. She said, "Well, actually, that brings me to my idea.

What if Mary and Inman were allowed to enjoy Mardi Gras with the protection of, say, four of your stevedores, each armed with slapjacks, brass knuckles, or even pistols?" Danton didn't even have to think. Millicent's idea was genius. "I don't think it will be difficult to recruit guards tomorrow. I love this idea!" After a suitable period of intimacy, Millicent and Danton dressed and went to lunch at Antoine's. By this time, Millicent had not a care in the world who saw her with Danton. If it was anyone she cared about, they'd understand. If it was one of her husband's goons, Millicent had developed the courage to both challenge them and then make them look weak in Blackjack's blighted sight. Reluctantly, Millicent had to call it a day after a truly memorable feast at Antoine's with Danton. As she left, Millicent told Danton, "Mary and I will be at the Wharf tomorrow, for Lundi Gras luncheon." Danton seemed a bit perplexed. "Lundi Gras?" Millicent said, "Why not Lundi Gras?" Danton had no objections, it just hadn't ever been vocalized before.

Millicent got up early on Monday the 16th. of February, 1953 to enjoy her breakfast and plan the next day, Mardi Gras. Blackjack, thankfully, ignored her at breakfast. Her only comment was, "Jackson, I'm going shopping today, do you need anything?" It was ignored. The sports section of the **Times Picayune** was far more interesting to Blackjack than anything Millicent had to say. When breakfast was concluded, Millicent called for her Eldorado and drove to the Central Business District, parked, and walked to Adler's. After a while, Millicent found suitable pieces of Mardi Gras jewelry for both Mary and Marie Cosette. After completing her purchase, Millicent transitioned to Maison Blanche and looked for suitable ensembles for Mary and Marie Cosette for Mardi Gras. ...and she bought them all suitable masks.

While Millicent was shopping, Danton and Inman were at work down on the Wharf. Danton sent for Dominic DeLaVigne, his Chief of Security. As Dom got over to Danton's desk, he extended his hand, "I haven't had a chance to thank you for inviting me to Mr. Inman's wedding. It was the most beautiful and heartwarming wedding I've ever been to!" Danton shook Dom's hand and motioned for him to take a seat. "Inman and I were both happy that you and Mrs. DeLaVigne could be there." Danton paused for a moment to gather his thoughts. "Dom, sometimes I feel like I don't show my appreciation for what you, Clement, and the rest of the Security Team do for this operation. How long have you worked here, 18 years or so?" Dom leaned forward, "It'll be 22 come June." Danton smiled, "That's right, I think that Big Inman hired you, didn't he?" Dom sat up proudly, "Yes sir, he did! ...and I can tell you, without shame, that I cried like a baby when he was murdered! It's amazing how much like him young Mr. Inman is." Danton replied, "Yes, I've noticed that for many years. I suppose that the gang are taking to him like they did to his father?" Dom grinned from ear to ear, "Oh, yes! Everyone on the Wharf loves him!"

Danton was pleased. "Dom, I sent for you because I have a special request for the security department. I think that you know that Inman's father-in-law, the Coroner, hates my family. It goes way back, well before Big Inman died in the back of his ambulance. Lately, he's made threats against his wife, his daughter Mary, and Inman. He even tried to get Dr. Scrope to abort their baby." Dom put his hands over his mouth in abject horror. "I had no idea that it was that bad!" Danton looked over toward the safe. "There is a package in there, and duplicates in the safes at several of the big attorney firms. They contain evidence that would send Blackjack to Angola for a date with 'Gruesome Gertie.'"

Dom's eyes grew wide. Danton continued. "Inman can't know this just yet, but Blackjack sent his goons to retrieve an IOU for the funeral home that Big Inman had won at our poker night. The goons, for whatever reason, shot Big Inman. We loaded Inman into Blackjack's ambulance, and I was told that he would transport him to Touro Infirmary. The god-dammed bastard pulled behind his funeral home, stole the blood stained and bullet riddled IOU, and let Inman bleed out." Dom's ire began to rise. "Why don't you turn the bastard in?" Danton looked across the room. "For starters, Blackjack has a deep web of criminals working for him, and is protected by King Clancy, and more importantly, he is the Coroner." Dom looked confused.

Danton added, "As Coroner, Blackjack can have anyone in Orleans Parish committed to East Louisiana State Hospital, for any reason. He only recently learned that he had that power. Before that, Millicent and I could keep him firmly leashed with our dossier." Dom thought for a moment, "So, there's an impasse?" Danton nodded his head. "Mary's mother and I are trying to find a path through this mess. It's just not right to keep newlyweds apart, but we don't have a choice." Dom, visibly upset at what he'd just learned, asked, "So what is this mission you want Security to handle?"

Danton said, "Millicent and I have arranged for suites at the Hotel Monteleone tomorrow. We want Mary and Inman to be able to fully experience Mardi Gras together in the **Vieux Carré**, but there is a chance Blackjack's goons will be there, and they have orders to beat Inman mercilessly." Dom knew instantly what Danton wanted. "You want a security detail." Danton smiled. "Yes. I want you to help me pick **quatre gardes**. We'll make sure they have brass knuckles, slapjacks, and pistols. I am also planning on giving them each a bonus of $10.00 so they won't have to come out of pocket for food and such." Dom gave his team some consideration. "Clement LaRoux isn't married. He should head the team. While everyone else would would love to take this detail on, I'm thinking that we should ask Kenneth Cracker, Chip Blunt, and Adam Nail to be on the detail. None of them is married."

Danton grinned, "That's a good team. I especially like sending Chip 'The Ripper!'" Dom and Danton had a hearty laugh together. Dom asked about what would happen if they had to engage the goons. Danton was prepared for that. "I've spoken to Mayor Morrison and he assured me that he would instruct the Police Command to leave our guys alone and arrest the goons." Dom stood up to go outfit the detail. He laughed, "If anything happens, it'll be a big slap to King Clancy's face!" Danton laughed. "It would, but let's hope that it doesn't come to that!"

Millicent pulled in behind the Bank House just before 11:45, and stormed in to retrieve her girls. She called up the stairs for Mary and Marie Cosette as the goons tripped over each other. Marie Cosette leaned over the banister and told Millicent that they would be down in a couple of minutes. Knowing that Mary and Inman would be in the Quarter that night, and that they would have discrete guards, Millicent played up Blackjack's anger at his goons. "Have you two been looking for other jobs? ...maybe in another state?" As the goons started babbling, Mary and Marie Cosette came down the stairs. Millicent looked over her shoulder and said, "We'll be back tomorrow. You two have the night off."

The ladies walked out and piled into Millicent's Eldorado. Millicent Drove them to the Hotel Monteleone and parked in the garage. As they walked into the lobby, Mary suddenly realized, "We didn't bring any clothes!" Millicent smiled. "That's okay. You have clothes up in the suite." Mary then asked, "Is Inman here?" Millicent replied, "No not yet, he and Danton are still at work. They'll join us by Captain's Hour, though." Marie Cosette looked at Mary first, confused, then at Millicent. Millicent explained, "Captain's Hour is when the bar in a Garden District home officials opens." Marie Cosette nodded her head.

Millicent and her girls went up to the deluxe suite that would house Mary, Inman, and Marie Cosette. Millicent asked the girls to go into their bedrooms. Marie Cosette went into her bedroom, and Millicent followed Mary into her room. Mary's trousseau was laid out on the bed, even the necklace and the mask. Millicent caught Mary staring in confusion at the mask. Millicent said, "The mask is for tonight in the Quarter. Go on and get changed, we'll have what you're wearing cleaned for tomorrow. Millicent left and allowed Mary to change and place her clothes into a laundry bag. She walked over to Marie Cosette's door and passed the same instructions.

When Mary and Marie Cosette came out, dressed to the nines, with their regular clothes in laundry bags, Millicent called down to the Concierge and requested laundry service. With that small task accomplished it was time for lunch. Millicent looked at her girls and asked, "Court of Two Sisters?" Mary and Marie Cosette looked at each other and broke into smiles of delight. They both gave Millicent an enthusiastic, "**Oui!**" As they exited the elevator, Millicent said, "We'll walk, it's only a few blocks. The doormen opened the two large bronze front doors, tipped their hats, and, almost in unison, said, "**Mesdames!**" Millicent and her girls walked down Royal Street, crossed at Toulouse Street, and made their way the last half block to The Court of Two Sisters. As they entered, Millicent and the girls made sure to touch the Charm Gates to be blessed with charm. The **Maître de hôtel** greeted Millicent personally. "**Bonjour madame Day! La cour, je présume?**" Millicent smiled and said, simply, "**Oui merci!**" He led Millicent and the girls out to the courtyard and seated them at one of the best tables.

Millicent and the girls lingered over an extraordinary luncheon of multiple courses. They were finally done around 2:30. Millicent suggested that they shop their way back to the Hotel Monteleone. They spent the rest of the afternoon visiting jewelry stores, fashion stores, and antique emporiums. Marie Cosette liked the antique stores the best. She enjoyed learning the names of the pieces of furniture and **objets d'art**. Both Marie Cosette and Mary loved seeing the new fashions in the couture clothing stores. All three ladies enjoyed dreaming about owning and wearing the expensive jewelry in the jewelry stores. Shop after shop, block after block, the ladies made their way back to the Hotel Monteleone. It was after 4:00 when they made it back. The doormen tipped their hats, and pulled the bronze doors open. Millicent led Mary and Marie Cosette inside, and turned and entered the Carousel Bar.

As they took seats at the revolving bar, Marie Cosette leaned in close to Mary and whispered, "I've never been to a bar before."

Mary snickered. She whispered back, "They're a little like restaurants, except the role of the food changes places with the role of alcohol." Marie Cosette snickered. "Okay!" It being early, Millicent asked if they could reserve two more seats for Danton and Inman. The bartender said, "Absolutely, for you Madame, …that is a small request." When he asked for their order, Marie Cosette confessed that she had no idea what to order. Millicent took into consideration Marie Cosette's lack of "alcohol conditioning" that was common with youth of the upper classes. "I suggest that you try a Daiquiri, my dear." Marie Cosette agreed to take Millicent's advice. When the bartender asked for their orders, Millicent said, "Mary and I will have **Vieux Carré** Cocktails, and Marie Cosette will have a Daiquiri, if you please." The bartender said, "Very good, Madame," and stepped aside to mix the drinks.

While they were waiting for their drinks, Mary asked her mother, "Are we to be confined to our rooms again tonight?" Millicent sighed. "No, Danton has arranged for a discrete security detail for you, Inman, and Marie Cosette." Mary asked, "Is that really necessary?" Millicent said, "We hope not, but your father has told the goons to beat Inman without mercy if they find him. You may remember that I told them that they had the night off. They, or their cohorts might be in the **Vieux Carré** tonight. None of you have a fundamental understanding of your birth city. Danton and I want you three to be able to experience Mardi Gras without any worries. The security detail will be out of the way, unless needed. If needed, they'll squash any of Blackjack's goons, with impunity."

The drinks arrived and all eyes were on Marie Cosette. She sipped her Daiquiri, and pronounced it "delicious." Mary enjoyed sipping her **Vieux Carré** Cocktail and dreamed of her night out on the town with her beloved. Before the gents got to the Carousel Bar, Millicent leaned into Marie Cosette and whispered in her ear, "You should ask to go to Pat O'Brien's tonight." Marie Cosette replied, "Why." Millicent said, "Well, your mother was a big star there, some time ago. No, she was the biggest star there in the 1930's and 1940's. She'd still be a big star, but…." Marie Cosette asked, "…but what?"

Millicent said, " That's a story for another day. Today, you, Mary, and Inman need to learn about your heritage, about Mardi Gras, and have a wonderful evening out."

As Millicent was encouraging Mary and Marie Cosette to enjoy their evening, Danton and Inman walked into the Carousel Bar and joined the ladies. As Danton came into the view of the bartender, he exclaimed, "**Bonjour, monsieur Soleil, comme d'habitude?**" (Good afternoon, Mr. Soleil, the usual?) Danton smiled and said, "**Oui, pour deux!**" Inman was slightly amused. "What did you just order for us?" Danton grinned, "Nothing too fancy, double Bourbon/rocks." Inman was happy. Danton and Inman took their seats next to their ladies. Marie Cosette slid over to the far stool to allow Danton to sit next to Millicent and Inman to sit next to Mary. Inman smiled at Marie Cosette, "**Merci chère mademoiselle!**" Marie Cosette nodded and blushed. She wasn't used to being thanked or complimented. Danton turned to Millicent. "Our reservation at Antoine's is at 5:00. Do we have time for another round?" Millicent looked at her diamond encrusted Cartier watch. "I suppose we do. …but isn't Antoine's closed on Mardi Gras?"

Danton hailed the bartender and ordered another round. He once again turned to Millicent, "Yes, to the public, but they take reservations for private parties. …for their best customers. You've been out of the loop too long my dear Milly!" Millicent blushed, "That's true, I have. It's nice to be back." Danton continued, "The crew will meet us out on Royal Street at 4:45 and walk us to Antoine's. They'll have a table near us, just in case, although I doubt Antoine's will admit any of Blackjack's goons tonight." Millicent said, "I trust that you're paying for their meal." Danton laughed, "Of course, and I gave them all $10.00 for other expenses tonight." Millicent expressed her hope that they wouldn't get too drunk. Danton wasn't the least bit worried about that possibility.

After their "Second Round," Millicent, Danton, and their party made their way, with the Security Detail the few blocks to Antoine's. The **Maître d'hôtel** at Antoine's was delighted to see Danton and his party. "**Bonsoir, monsieur Soleil! Laissez le bon temps rouler!**" (Good evening, Mr. Soleil! Let the good times roll!) Danton laughed heartily at the festive greeting. "**…**

au moins jusqu'à minuit!" (...at least until midnight!) The **Maître d'hôtel** summoned two waiters. One was assigned to Danton and his party, and the other was assigned to the protection detail. Their waiter was informed that Danton would be settling their bill. The protection detail was positioned where they could watch the front door and the room.

When the waiters asked for drink orders, the protection detail all ordered water and iced tea only. At Danton's table, Mary and Marie Cosette had been informed by Millicent that there would be a lot of Beef dishes, so red wine was the proper choice. Both Mary and Marie Cosette asked Millicent to order for them. Millicent asked the waiter, "**Auriez-vous Château laFleur Pomerol 1950?**" (Would you have Chateau laFleur Pomerol 1950?) The waiter smiled, "**Mais bien sûr, Madame!**" (But of course, Madame!) Millicent asked that the first bottle be opened and decanted, and that a second bottle be opened to breath, with a third bottle kept ready to open in reserve. Millicent continued, "In the mean time, you might bring us Gin and Tonics." The waiter turned to Danton, who said, We're easy, double Bourbon/rocks, and don't let our ice cubes dry out!" The waiter chuckled. "**Bien sûr que non!**" (Of course not!) He left to order the drinks from the bar, and decant the wine.

While the family waited for their drinks, Danton said, "After tonight, we won't be eating meat until Easter. I'd suggest that we save the seafood for Lent, and enjoy beef, pork, chicken, EtC. Marie Cosette and Inman weren't familiar with the menu selections, so Danton and Millicent described the various dishes. **Bouchées à la Reine** was veal and chicken cooked 'Vol au Vent' in puff pastry. **Steak Robespierre** was a butterflied, marinated flank steak served with a sauce prepared from bacon drippings, onions, mushrooms, chicken livers, and veal sweetbreads, garnished with artichoke hearts marinated in extra-virgin olive oil, splashed with wine vinegar and parsley. **Filet de Boeuf Périgueux** was beef tenderloin sautéed in grape seed oil and duck fat with Madeira, tomatoes, and dry white wine, and demiglace. It was served on a slice of ham, and coated with the pan sauce to which truffles had been added. **Bécassine sur Canapé**, or Snipe on a Sofa, was Snipe and sweetbreads in a rich sauce served on toast points. **Paulette Rochzmbeau** was a pair of poached chicken breasts over French bread rounds, ham, and Marchand de Vin Sauce, topped with Béarnaise Sauce and freshly chopped parsley.

Danton suggested that everyone order a **petit** bowl of **Soupe aux oignons gratinée**. (French Onion Soup). He also said that he was going to order two somewhat unusual and exotic dishes for the group to share. He ordered two servings, with an individual ramekin for each diner, of **Tripes à la mode de Caen**. Without going into too much detail, it was a stew of a cow's stomach and large intestine cooked for hours with bones and hoofs (which were removed) a bouquet garni, and apple cider. Danton also ordered three orders of **Escargots à la Bordelaise**, Snails in a Bordelaise sauce.

Once the orders were in, what followed was just short of a two hour feast of epic proportions. Inman was happy to dive in and try all of the unusual dishes. Marie Cosette remembered eating much worse before moving into the funeral home, and cautiously approached the unfamiliar menu items. Mary already knew that she didn't care for tripe, but gave the Escargot a chance. She adored it! As the diner's slowed down, the waiters presented the Baked Alaska. They even presented a Baked Alaska to the protection detail. Inman had asked that it display "Thank you for your service!" in piped icing. While Danton's generosity wasn't necessary, it went a long way with the stevedores.

When Mardi Gras dinner was done, Danton settled the bill, and everyone went out onto Saint Louis Street. Danton and Millicent said to Mary, Inman, and Marie Cosette, "**Laissez le bon temps rouler!**" They all snickered. Danton turned to the security detail, "I know you'll take good care of them." They nodded their heads. Millicent looked at the girls and Inman. "The police will shut everything down at midnight. We'll be in the Carousel Bar. Join us, or not. We'll sleep in tomorrow, and go to Ash Wednesday service at Saint Patrick's, as a family. Millicent looked at Marie Cosette and said, "Don't forget Pat O'Brien's." Marie Cosette smiled as Millicent and Danton turned to make their way back to the Hotel Monteleone.

Inman asked his employees, "Are we very far from Pat O'Brien's" They laughed, "No sir, it's two blocks down that a way." They said, " We'll turn left on Royal, go two blocks, and turn left on Saint Peter. It'll only take a couple of minutes." Inman looked at Mary and Marie Cosette and said, "Let's go!"

As they walked, Inman asked, "What's the big deal at Pat O'Brien's?" The detail said, almost in unison, "Hurricanes!" Inman looked perplexed. "What is a Hurricane?" Chip "The Ripper" said, "Mr. Carnes, a Hurricane is a tall rum-based fruit drink. It's a crowd pleaser. You should try one." Inman looked at Chip and said, "Chip, I think that's a good idea! Thank you. My uncle thinks we need to learn about our heritage. If you think of anything else, please let me know!" Chip affected a look of accomplishment, and raised his eyebrows at his companions.

After a few minutes walk, Inman and his ladies arrived at Pat O'Brien's on Saint Peter Street. They entered the salmon colored, ancient establishment, and were greeted by the **Maître de hôtel**. He was older than one would expect, and began to stare at Marie Cosette. Inman raised an eyebrow, and turned to look at Mary. She looked back at Inman, not knowing why the **Maître de hôtel** was staring at Marie Cosette. At last the **Maître de hôtel** apologized for staring. "It's just that you resemble our star singer in the thirties, and forties, Marie Catherine Jardin." Marie Cosette smiled and said, **"C'est parce qu'elle est ma mère."** (That is because she is my mother.) The **Maître de hôtel** sighed and said, " Your mother was quite beautiful. You might be even more so!" Marie Cosette sighed and blushed. Inman asked where the best seats were. The **Maître de hôtel** suggested the patio. Inman agreed and they were escorted to a pair of tables next to the fountain. Based upon Chip's recommendation, they all ordered Hurricanes. Inman added, "… and a round for our friends at the next table." When the drinks arrived, Inman lifted his mammoth glass to the security detail, and they returned the honor.

Mary, Marie Cosette, and Inman enjoyed their Hurricanes, and were enthralled by the small combo that was playing Jazz classics under an overhang next to the carriage-way entrance to the patio. As they were nearing the bottom of their gargantuan Hurricane glasses, Inman leaned in to Mary and asked, "Would you like to stay here a while, or explore more of the Quarter, like our family suggested?" Mary asked, "What do you want to do?" Inman drew in a deep breath behind a massive smile, and said, "I don't care. …just as long as you are with me!" Marie Cosette's face erupted into a grand smile of complete joy. "I feel the same way. …but maybe we should explore. …just to make everyone happy." Inman smiled and nodded, although deep inside, he could think of one person they wouldn't be making happy that night.

As Inman was settling the bill, he asked the waiter, "Where can we go to hear some more great music?" The waiter said, "You should go to Dixie's." Inman inquired further. "Where is Dixie's?" The waiter said, "When you leave, turn left and go to Bourbon Street. You can't miss it." Inman thanked him and left a generous tip. The entourage pulled up stakes and started their march to Bourbon Street. When the group had walked the half block, they were all shocked to see a throng of masked people, mostly in costumes, overwhelming Bourbon Street. Some of the costumes were outright scandalous. Inman commented, "I never knew that it was such a short walk between gentility and depravity." Mary and Marie Cosette both laughed. After a moment spent getting over the shock of seeing so much exposed flesh, Inman commented, "Well, the waiter was right. There's no way we could have missed it. There it is, just across the intersection."

Dixie's Bar of Music was in a large grey building at the corner of Bourbon and Saint Peter Streets across from the Saint Charles Hotel. The upper windows were concealed behind floor to ceiling shutters that opened onto a wrought iron wrap-around gallery. The doorway to the bar was at the intersection, in a notched corner. A large green canvas awning projected from under the gallery to the corner, with a neon sign announcing Dixie's BAR of MUSIC. Inman's gaze was drawn to the sad potted palms on the upper gallery. Their growth had been stunted by their tight confinement. Inman's mind raced with corollaries until he shut them down, and surmised that they most likely hadn't been given any proper nutritional support. That was the difference.... Inman and his entourage made their way through the mob of masked and costumed revelers and entered Dixie's.

Once they entered Dixie's, Inman knew something was different. They were escorted to a table near the band, and in eyesight of Dixie's famous mural. Neither Inman, nor Marie Cosette recognized any of the famous faces in the mural. It was up to Mary to identify the celebrities, and tell why many of them were famous. Both Marie Cosette and Inman were familiar with Nat King Cole and Louis Armstrong, and to a certain point, Frank Sinatra,

Lena Horn, Xavier Cugat and Benny Goodman. Neither were familiar with Salvador Dali, Jack Benny, Paul Whitman, Connie Boswell, Dorothy Lamour, or Kate Smith. There were plenty of others, but the band started a new set, and they wanted to enjoy the music and their cocktails. It was an all-girl jazz band, and highly competent.

Just before 8:00, the proprietress, Yvonne Fasnacht, Miss Dixie herself, joined Sloppy and the house band with her clarinet. It was only when the band started playing swing dance music that Inman had a sudden realization of what had seemed odd earlier. Only then did he notice girls dancing with girls, and men dancing with men. While it caught Inman off guard, it didn't enrage him like many so-called "Christian" people in the 1950s. He looked at Mary. She was fixated on a particularly handsome young man dancing with a somewhat older gentleman. Inman asked, "What's all of this going on?" Mary's jaw was hanging open.

She somehow managed to say, I, I…don't…..know…." During the song's bridge, Mary recovered, somewhat. She said, "I know that boy over there. His name is Bill, and he and his family go to my church. He's engaged to Judy Mangrum." Inman was still a trifle confused. "So, why… is he… dancing with a man?" Mary stared at the two men dancing and shook her head. "I have no idea." When the song ended and the band took a short pause to arrange their music, the young man walked over to Mary and her party. He immediately greeted Mary. "I never thought I'd see YOU here."

Mary smiled. "How is Judy?" "Oh, she's great. We're getting married in June!" It was then that Mary's friend Bill noticed her condition. As his eyes bulged out, Mary introduced Inman, "This is my husband, Inman Carnes, the Fourth." Inman stood, and he and Mary's church friend shook hands, "It's a pleasure!" Mary turned her gaze to the "boyfriend." "Does Judy know?" "No, and I really don't want her to know." Mary started breathing deeply, and thought for a few moments. She realized that she was in a trap. At last she said, "As much as I think that you should tell Judy the truth, I'll take your secret to the grave if you'll do the same for me." Bill agreed.

The encounter encouraged Mary and Inman to take their show on the road. …the road being Bourbon Street. They and their party were assaulted by revelers, costumed, or not, drunk, or not, the entire journey down Bourbon Street. They were astounded at the number of windows from which they could buy alcohol. They were astounded when they got to the 500 Club and could see a topless woman swinging on a swing and stretching her legs out over the top of an open window overlooking Bourbon Street. They decided not to stop there even though the music from Sam Buerra's Witnesses' was so excellent. When they got to Conti Street, they decided to step into Hyp Guinle's Famous Door. Santo Pecora's band was holding court, and swinging it with **Twelfth Street Rag**. Mary, Marie Cosette, and Inman ordered drinks and enjoyed the show until just before 9:00. They particularly enjoyed the selection, **The Land of Dreams**. They almost hated to leave The Famous Door in order to fulfill the admonishment of their family to explore the Quarter.

After they left the Famous Door, and continued back toward Canal Street on Bourbon Street, Mary, Marie Cosette, and Inman were overwhelmed by the the hundreds of multi-colored neon signs beaconing them. In the 300 block of Bourbon Street, they stopped to look at the cut sheets in the windows of Sid Davilla's Mardi Gras Lounge. The music emanating from with-in from Freddie Kohlman's Band was intoxicating, but the scandalous pictures of burlesque dancers with exposed breasts was off-putting for both Mary and Inman. Their security detail was very unhappy when they decided not to stop there.

Just after 9:00, they did decide to stop at Steve Valenti's Paddock Lounge. They were attracted to the band's name. "Papa" Crestine and The New Tuxedo Brass Band were playing that evening. Drinks were ordered, songs were appreciated, dancing was initiated. They stayed at the Paddock Lounge longer than any other establishment that night, and had a fantastic time. Inman told Mary, "Uncle Danton told me that my father loved racehorses, and was about to open a stable at **Beau Cadeau** shortly before he died." Mary asked, "Do you love racehorses, too?" Inman laughed. "How should I know? I've never seen a horse race." As ephemeral as the thought was, the idea of racing horses stuck with Inman. As it creeped closer to 10:00, Mary and Inman grew restless, and wanted to further their explorations. They led the gang out onto Bourbon Street. Once they were in the throng of revelers on Bourbon Street, heading toward Canal Street, there was a shout from the crowd. "Hey you, punk!" Inman initially paid it no attention to it.

Out of the Blue, one of Blackjack's goons lunged through the crowd and sucker punched Inman. Mary and Marie Cosette screamed. The Stevedores pounced into action. While Mary and Marie Cosette checked Inman for injuries, the Stevedores wasted no time and pulled out their slapjacks. They beat both of the goons into a pulp before the mounted police could arrive. When the police did arrive, Chip "The Ripper" produced a calling card from the Mayor, and explained that the two had attacked Inman for no reason. Inman and his party were not detained or even questioned. The two comatose goons were arrested, and transported to **Hôtel Dieu**. Mary and Marie Cosette were both amazed at how seamlessly the encounter happened.

Buoyed by the efficient protection of the detail, and the decreasing odds of goons who would recognize them in the Quarter, Mary and Inman decided to continue their tour. They spent a spell in the Old Absinthe House. Walter "Fats" Pichon was slaying the piano. Mary and Inman enjoyed "Fat's'" artistry until almost 10:45. They vowed to come back. They left and wandered down Bourbon Street. They passed up Ferrera's Sho-Bar and Prima's Shim Sham Club for reasons of morality. At last, at 11:00, they found El Morocco. Phil Zito's Band and George Lewis were headlining. They enjoyed cocktails and snacks, and even found themselves dancing to the infectious vibes of the Band. They were there, enjoying themselves, for almost an hour before midnight arrived and the **Gendarme** began their horseback rounds, shutting Mardi Gras down for 1953. They admonished everyone. "It's Ash Wednesday, and Lent. Go home and fast!"

The security detail accompanied Mary, Marie Cosette, and Inman back to the Hotel Monteleone before splitting up and going home. Mary, Marie Cosette, and Inman nodded to the doormen at the Hotel Monteleone as they entered and made their way to the Carousel Bar, where Millicent and Danton were holding court.

Danton stood to greet the kids. Millicent turned on her barstool. "**Eh bien, vous ne cherchez pas pire pour l'usure**! (Well, you all look no worse for for the wear!) She hadn't seen Inman's eye. "Come, join us, and tell us all about your adventures tonight." Mary sat on the stool next to Millicent. "To begin with, we all felt out of place because we weren't wearing costumes and our masks were bothersome." Inman added, "It seemed like if we'd had comfortable masks, we could have stripped down to our underwear and no one would have batted an eye lash." Danton was a trifle embarrassed, "We should have explained that to you." Millicent agreed. "We wanted you to see the beautiful architecture, and enjoy great New Orleans music." Mary smiled, "Yes, that's what we concentrated on." Inman backed his bride up and added, "There were several clubs that we wanted to go in for the music, but the other 'entertainment' wasn't to our liking." Marie Cosette added, "You should've seen de…the faces of dose…those guys protecting us. They wanted to go into those clubs!" Danton laughed, "If it weren't Ash Wednesday, they'd have made a bee-line back there once they got you safely back to the hotel."

Danton paused and looked at Inman. He had the beginnings of a black eye. Danton said, "I see it was a good idea for the lads to go out with you." Millicent turned and gasped when she saw Inman's war wound. She summoned a waiter, "Please go to the kitchen and bring us a raw steak. We'll pay for it, of course, and it's not likely that one will be ordered today, or for the next 40 days." The waiter left and returned with the raw steak. Millicent motioned to Inman who was completely confused. Danton said, "Hold it against your eye, it'll help with the swelling and help it to heal faster." Inman placed the Delmonico steak on a linen napkin and placed it against his left eye. The beef conformed to the shape of his eye socket and chilled the area down. "Danton said, "Well?" Inman said, "Aside from feeling foolish, this feels awfully good. Thank you both!"

After a couple of rounds of cocktails, everyone agreed that it was time to retire and get some sleep before they all went to Saint Patrick's for the Imposition of Ashes.

CHAPTER NINETEEN

UNHOLY WEEKS

At 9:30, the phone rang in Mary and Inman's suite. Inman rolled out of his embrace with Mary and picked the receiver up. "Hello?" It was Danton. "It's 9:30. Can you all meet Millicent and me in the lobby at 10:00?" Inman said, "That's pushing it, but we'll make it happen." As he returned the phone receiver to the base, Mary asked, "Make what happen?" Inman rolled back over and kissed Mary on the forehead. "We've been requested to join our family in the lobby in thirty minutes." Mary's face erupted in surprise and slight terror. **"Mon Dieu! Je vais devoir prendre une douche rapide!"** (My God! I'll have to take a quick shower!) Inman laughed, "You go first. I'd suggest that we share one, but that wouldn't be very quick." Mary laughed as she sprinted to the bathroom. Inman buried his face in Mary's pillowcase and luxuriated in her scent.

Mary and Inman shared a passionate embrace as they traded places in the shower. Inman decided not to wash his hair and finished his shower in only a few moments. He toweled off, and got dressed. It was 9:50, and Mary was still applying her makeup. Inman sat in a **bergère** and enjoyed watching Mary applying her layers of makeup as quickly as she could. He didn't dare try to engage her in conversation. 10:00 arrived just as Mary was putting on her finishing touches. Inman stood and offered Mary his hand. Together they ran down the corridor to the elevator. When it finally came, a couple got off and Mary and Inman got into an empty car. Inman pressed the button for the lobby and, as the large bronze doors slid closed, wrapped his muscular arms around Mary. She melted in her husband's loving embrace. They kissed almost all the way down to the lobby. The bell rang and the elevator car stopped on the third floor. Reluctantly, the newlywed couple relinquished their embrace and smiled at the elderly couple who joined them for the final descent to the lobby.

Millicent, Marie Cosette, and Danton were standing by the massive lobby clock. Inman began apologizing for their tardiness, but Millicent said, "It's only been a few minutes. We'd have called earlier, but thought you might have wanted a few more minutes of sleep." Mary and Inman grinned, and held back chuckles. As a family, they went into **Le Café** and had a quick breakfast and **café au lait**. After Danton settled the bill, the family walked to the garage and piled into Millicent's Eldorado. As they pulled out onto Royal Street, Inman had a sudden realization. "How are we going to check out in time?"

Danton turned around and smiled at Inman. "Lucy Butler is going to be arriving shortly, if she hasn't already, and pack up for everyone and check us all out." Inman shook his head. "I don't know what we'd do without her. She's a wonder!" Both Millicent and Danton nodded their heads in agreement. After Millicent parked the Cadillac, the family entered Saint Patrick's, blessed themselves with holy water, genuflected, and sat together on the Gospel side in the traditional Soleil pew. After a few minutes the tenor bell was rung announcing the upcoming service. Attendance was sparse.

As the organ blared the processional, everyone stood up. They bowed their heads as the Crucifer passed, and were happy to see that Father Lachicotte was the Celebrant for Ash Wednesday. After the reading of the Word, Father Lachicotte said, "Dear friends in Christ, let us ask our Father to bless these ashes which we will use as the mark of our repentance." A pause was allowed for silent prayers. He continued, "Lord, bless these ashes ✠ by which we show that we are dust. Pardon our sins and keep us faithful to the discipline of Lent, for you do not want sinners to die but to live with the risen Christ, who reigns with you for ever and ever." All replied, "Amen!" Father Lachicotte sprinkled holy water over the ashes in silence then continued, "Daniel turned to the LORD God, pleading in earnest prayer, with fasting, sackcloth, and ashes. O LORD, we are shamefaced, like our kings, our princes, and our fathers, for having sinned against you. But yours, O LORD, our God, are compassion and forgiveness!" Father Lachicotte beaconed all to come forward and receive their ashes. As he made the sign of the cross on each forehead, he said, "Remember, you are dust and to dust you will return."

After the Imposition of Ashes, Father Lachicotte returned to the Mass, and presided over it regally. After the Recessional, Father Lachicott stood in the opening of the Great Western Door and greeted his flock. His face bloomed in a radiant smile when he saw Mary and Inman. "Bless you, my children! You both look so happy." Mary said, "Yes, Father, we are, when we can be together." Father Lachicotte sighed. "So your father is still against your union?" Inman said, "I'm afraid so, but my uncle and mother-in-law find ways for us to be together, and are working on some kind of solution so we can 'come out from under the basket' you might say." Father Lachicotte was impressed with Inman's Biblical reference. "I'll pray daily for that to happen." Mary and Inman stepped out onto the porch with Marie Cosette to wait for Millicent and Danton to speak to Father Lachicotte. When they were done, the family walked back to the Eldorado. Danton said, "Who's ready for some lunch?" Everyone was. He then asked, "Shall we dine at Maylié's?" Everyone agreed, so Millicent guided the Cadillac to Poydras Street.

As they stepped across the threshold, Danton saw William Maylié speaking to the **Maître d'hôtel**. The commotion of five people entering the space caused Monsieur Maylié to look up. He instinctively looked back down, but something caused him to look up again. He smiled broadly and said, "**Oh, quel plaisir de vous voir monsieur Soleil!**" (Oh, what a pleasure to see you, Mister Soleil!) Danton replied, "**Et également!**" (And likewise!) The **Maître d'hôtel** was given strict instructions to take Danton and his party to the best table, and assign the best waiter to serve them. After they were seated, and menus had been distributed, the waiter took their drink orders. Bus Boys were dispatched to deliver goblets of ice water. While the waiter was away arranging the drink order, the family reviewed the Bill of Fare. They knew it would be seafood. Meat was completely out of the question. That simplified their order, yet, only marginally.

The waiter returned and distributed the family's drinks. Once done, he took out an order pad and started with the Ladies. Millicent ordered Spanish Courtbouillion for her Soup Course, Shrimp Remoulade Salad, Broiled Pompano with Drawn Butter Sauce, Puffed Potatoes and Stuffed Mirletons with Shrimp. The waiter turned to Mary. She started with Crayfish Bisque, followed by a Spring Salad of Curley Shrimp, Romaine, and Watercress. For her main course, Mary ordered Caspurgot with Tartar Sauce, Irish Potato Croquettes and Cress Salad. Marie Cosette's soup choice was Shellfish Gumbo. Her salad was a Creole Salad Bowl. For a main course, Marie Cosette choose Stuffed Crabs with Red Beans and Rice Albert. The dish was named for Albert Booth Campbell, an ultra-loyal black employee who worked for Maylié's from 1897 until just before his death. He served as both a waiter and as a cook. For her vegetable, Marie Cosette ordered Squash au Beurre. The waiter then turned to Danton. His soup of choice was Creole Bouillabaisse. Danton also requested the Shrimp Remoulade Salad, Madame Esparbé's Crab Pontchartrain with Creole Rice and Asparagus Tips. Last, but not least, Inman ordered. He chose the Crayfish Gumbo and a Spring Salad of Curley Shrimp, Romaine and Watercress. Inman's main dish was Baked **Filet de Truite** (Trout) with Green Beans Almandine.

As the excitement of ordering culinary masterpieces waned, the reality of their situation began to sink in, at least with Mary and Inman. Inman was the fearless one who brought up the subject. "So what's going to happen now?" Danton asked, "What are you taking about?" Inman said, "Those goons are going to eventually recover enough to call Blackjack and tell him that they spotted us together during Mardi Gras." Millicent dropped her gaze to the linen napkin draped over her lap. Danton pinched his mouth and chin with his left thumb and forefinger to think. He sighed, and turned to Millicent. "He's right. Unless they were beaten so badly that they have amnesia, they'll be calling Blackjack. I doubt that it'll be while they are in **Hôtel Dieu**, but once they're booked, they'll be calling him to bail them out."

All of the color drained out of Millicent's face. She could barely breath. He can't know that we planned this rendezvous. He just can't know." Inman said, "He knows that you and Mary and Marie Cosette spent Mardi Gras at the Hotel Monteleone. He doesn't know that Uncle Danton and I were there, and has no way of learning that. Telling him that you spent the evening at the Carousel Bar with friends isn't a lie. It's the truth. Telling him that you sent Mary and Marie Cosette out to enjoy Mardi Gras isn't a lie. What if I just happened to find them at Pat O'Brien's last night? Can he be told that much of a lie?" Mary put her hand on Inman's thigh under the table and squeezed it lovingly. Millicent looked at Danton and her complexion returned, "It's perfect. It's simple, mostly true, and Jackson will believe it." Everyone sighed, knowing the backstory, just in time for their luncheon to arrive. Several waiters brought large trays with the entrées and baskets of Madam Esparbé's Hot Biscuits and Tante Ophilia's Plantation Corn Bread. They were all overwhelmed by the culinary experience, and all conversation ceased for the duration of their luncheon.

When the family was almost done with their meal, the waiter asked Danton if they had thought about dessert. Danton looked around the table. "May I have the honor of ordering a special dessert?" No one objected. Danton said, "Strawberry Floating Islands for everyone, and two bottles of your best Champagne." As the waiter was writing that down, Danton added, "**Coupes, pas flûtes, s'il vous plaît!**" (Coupes, not flutes, if you please.) A sudden realization hit the family, and dessert was served, as the corks were popped. A lot had to be decided in the next month and a half. Mary would soon be delivered of her and Inman's child, Blackjack had to get over his objections of Mary's new husband. Mary and Inman would need to start a household. ...and they'd also have to figure out what to do with Marie Cosette to keep her safe.

After luncheon, Millicent drove back to the Hotel Monteleone to drop Danton and Inman off. They got into Danton's Packard and drove, reluctantly, to the Wharf, and to work. Lucy Butler told them that all of the bags had been packed and delivered. She also told Danton and Inman that Millicent's bag was left at the Bank House with the girl's bags. Danton asked, "No one came out while you were dropping off the bags?" Lucy assured Danton that there was no one home. After she left, Danton said to Inman, "Good, we have just a little bit of time before Blackjack finds out."

Millicent drove her girls back to the Bank House. Finding their luggage on the back porch, Millicent put her bag in the boot of the Eldorado, then carried Mary's bag up to her room. Millicent was helping Mary unpack when she and both of the girls heard a horrible noise downstairs. It was Blackjack shouting for the goons. Millicent told the girls to stay upstairs, and went downstairs to find out what Blackjack was so mad about. She confronted him in the stair hall. "Jackson, why are you shouting so?" Blackjack said, "They haven't called in the book, there's no one to answer the phone. What the hell is going on?" Millicent stared blankly at her husband. "I have no idea, I was just settling the girls back in. I had no idea that they weren't here." Blackjack let out an exasperated roar, then got on the phone and called his uncle, King Clancy, over in Jefferson Parish. His uncle Frank told him to go back to the funeral home, and he'd make inquiries, and get back to him.

Blackjack wasn't happy that bets weren't being accepted, or that the girls had no guards, but he did go back to the funeral home to wait for King Clancy's call. Millicent went upstairs to explain the situation to the girls. "Your great-uncle Frank is going to find out that the goons were beaten up, arrested, and are at **Hôtel Dieu**, recovering. You know the story. ...but you don't have any idea who came to Inman's defense, do you?" Both Mary and Marie Cosette were quick to agree. Millicent said, "Good, your father can't know that Danton's stevedores were your security detail." Millicent added, I need to get home, it won't take long for Frank to find those goons. Please keep Inman far away from this place. Danton and I will find you both time together."

Mary agreed, and Millicent left and drove back to Saint Charles Avenue. She left the Eldorado in the Motor Court behind the funeral home, and went into the kitchen. Hattie was there, prepping for dinner. She had a look of distress on her face. Millicent took a glass out of the cabinet, and filled it with ice cubes from the Frigidaire, and made herself a Blanchard strength Gin and Tonic. To Hattie, Millicent said, "What ever it is, it'll be okay." Hattie didn't look convinced, but, none the less, Millicent took her drink, and walked into the darkness of the parlor.

Millicent sipped her drink, and stared out onto Saint Charles Avenue, as she had for decades. She shuddered every time the phone rang. Around 6:00, just before dinner was to be served, the phone rang. Millicent shivered, then the shouting began. Millicent knew that King Clancy had found Blackjack's goons, and knew that they had been arrested for assaulting Inman. Millicent took a long draught of her drink to prepare for Blackjack. He came storming into the kitchen and confronted Hattie. "Has Mrs. Day gotten home yet?" Hattie nodded her head and looked toward the swinging door to the dining room. Blackjack clenched his fists and barged through the Butler's pantry, and the swinging door into the dining room. He then stomped into the parlor.

Millicent steeled herself. She stared out of the window until Blackjack recognized her. "Milly, did you know that Mary was parading herself down Bourbon Street last night with that cur Inman Carnes?" Millicent turned around and looked at Blackjack with confusion. "She didn't say anything about it to me." Blackjack asked, " Did you allow her to go out into the French Quarter alone?" Millicent laughed, "No, of course I didn't. She went out with Marie Cosette." Blackjack asked, "She didn't say that she met up with that Carnes bastard?" Millicent chomped an ice cube. "Inman isn't a 'bastard.' He's from a much better family than you are. ...but no, she didn't mention meeting him." Blackjack exclaimed, "She's a lying little slut!" It took everything Millicent possessed to keep from attacking Blackjack both physically and verbally. In true Blanchard **sang-froid,** Millicent chomped an ice cube, showed no emotion, and said nothing.

Blackjack yelled, "You stay right here, I have something to show you." He stormed back to his office and returned with the Sports Section of the *Times Picayune*. Blackjack grabbed Millicent's arm aggressively, and dragged her into the dining room. He slammed the paper on the dining table and punched his finger repeatedly on an advertisement, aggressively. Millicent looked at the advertisement. "Home for Single Mothers." She read the ad aloud, slowly, and completely. There was a Matron to control access to the mothers, and counselors and medical staff to make the single moms whole, and care for baby. When she finished reading the ad, Millicent looked at Blackjack. "... and?" Blackjack said, "We're going to go and check that place out. If it's everything it seems, Mary and Marie Cosette will be moving there by the first of March." Millicent plunged the knife in, "Well, it's certainly evident that your goons can't keep Mary "safe" from Inman, now can they?"

That remark put Blackjack over the top. He was so angry, that he didn't even question who stood up for Inman and beat his goons to a pulp. Luckily for Inman, Danton, and Millicent, King Clancy couldn't get that information either. Blackjack told Millicent, I'll be busy with funerals until next Wednesday, the 25th. We'll go tour Morro Castle then. Millicent agreed. She then asked her husband, "Will you be dining with me tonight? Blackjack scowled, "No, I have a lot of work to get done. ...more now that those two assholes are at **Hôtel Dieu**, and under arrest. Tell Hattie to fetch me a plate to my office."

Millicent was offended by her husband's boorish ways, but agreed. Blackjack retreated to his office, and Millicent went into the kitchen. She requested that Hattie prepare a plate for Danton, and said that she'd make herself a plate from the kitchen to save Hattie a lot of effort. Hattie was grateful, and made Blackjack's plate, and delivered it to the funeral home office. Blackjack kept his face buried in his papers. He didn't thank Hattie, or even acknowledge that she'd been kind enough to bring him a plate of dinner.

The next morning, after breakfast, Blackjack told Millicent that he'd be back by luncheon. He left to go interrogate his two goons who were recovering at **Hôtel Dieu**, and inquire when they would be released, booked, and when he could post their bail. Millicent called Danton and updated him on what Blackjack was doing. After that, Millicent called Mary at the Bank House. She told her daughter what her father was doing. Millicent begged her daughter, "Please don't diverge from our narrative." Mary said that she wouldn't. She then asked her mother how long the goons would be away. Millicent said, "I'll know more about that when your father gets back. Please don't take any chances for a while." Mary agreed.

Blackjack arrived back at the funeral home just before 1:00. Millicent was sitting in the parlor, and heard him come in the back door. Blackjack asked Hattie if there was any lunch left. She said, "Yas'sir, I kept ju a plate in de oben." Blackjack said, "Okay, put it on a tray and bring it back to my office. ...and some sweet tea, too." He spun around, walked briskly to his office. Blackjack didn't even give Hattie the respect to thank her for keeping his lunch warm. Millicent made her way to the kitchen. Hattie was placing a tall glass of ice and a pitcher of sweet tea on the tray. Millicent smiled at Hattie in a way that let Hattie know that Millicent was embarrassed by Blackjack's actions. "Hattie, please let me take this tray back for you." Hattie thanked Millicent, and went back to dinner prep. She even smiled, but didn't let Millicent see it.

Millicent carried the tray back to Blackjack's office. She was relieved that the door was open. She placed the tray on a credenza. Blackjack looked over to the tray and complained, "Where's the lemon for the sweet tea?" Millicent huffed, "You probably didn't ask for any." She stormed out, and returned to the kitchen. She opened the Frigidaire and pulled out a covered pyrex dish of lemon wedges. Millicent placed several wedges in a small bowl, returned the pyrex container to the fridge, and stomped back to the office. Millicent dropped the bowl of citrus on Blackjack's desk and said, "Well?" Blackjack didn't stop stuffing food in his mouth, "Well, what?" Millicent couldn't look at him. She walked over to the window and looked down on the Porters washing the funeral home livery.

"What about your "employees?" Blackjack said, "Well, no one knows who attacked them. They're going to be in **Hôtel Dieu** for several days, and when they are released, they'll be booked. After that, I'll be able to post bond for them." Millicent pressed further, "So what about the Bank House? Who's going to manage that?" Blackjack took a swig of tea to wash his food down. "No one until the first of next week. There's a note on the door giving an alternative telephone number." Millicent said, "I hope that their impetuousness won't damage the bottom line." Blackjack sneered. "It's a minor setback. That is one of my smaller Bank Houses. ...that's why they're there. They couldn't handle a busier House."

Satisfied, Millicent told Blackjack that she needed to go to the Pharmacy for Mary's vitamins. Blackjack grunted, and Millicent left the office and called for her Eldorado. Once her Cadillac was delivered from the garage, Millicent motored to the Bank House. Once there, she phoned the Wharf and spoke to Danton. She said, "Would it be possible for us to meet at **Maison Soleil** in an hour or two?" Danton was completely amenable. Millicent said, "Good, I'll take the girls over now and visit with Caroline and Virginia, if she's available, until you and Inman can break away."

Millicent, Mary, and Marie Cosette piled into the Eldorado and drove to Howard Avenue. Marie Cosette got out and rang the bell. Monique, alerted by Danton that the ladies were on the way, rushed out of the kitchen to open the gate. "**Bienvenue mesdames et mademoiselle!**" Monique led the ladies to the **véranda**, opened the French doors to Caroline's **salon principal**, and announced their arrival. Caroline put a bookmark in her book, placed it on the **étagère** next to her **bergère à oreilles**. She stood up, extended her hands, and said, "**Mon cher ami, Millicent, c'est si merveilleux de vous voir, vous et vos jeunes filles!!**" (My dear friend, Millicent, it is so wonderful to see you and your young ladies!) Millicent rushed over and took her dear friend's hands. They embraced.

Caroline rang a small crystal bell to summon Monique. Monique returned to the room. "**Oui madame?**" Caroline said, "Monique, we'll need some **rafraîchissements!**" Monique curtseyed, "**Oui, madame, j'ai déjà travaillé dessus.**" (Yes, ma'am, I have already been working on them.) Caroline smiled and said, "**Très bien, Monique!**" Monique excused herself and returned to the kitchen to finish preparing the **rafraîchissements**. After Monique left, Caroline looked at Mary and Marie Cosette. "Why don't you two young ladies stroll down to the **garçonnière** and listen to the radio, or play some old records." Mary stood and thanked Caroline for her hospitality. "Nonsense, my dear, you'll both be happier down there, than up here listening to your mother and me drone on about the not so familiar past!" Mary and Marie Cosette fought to keep from laughing, and nodded before leaving the **manoir**. Caroline returned her gaze to Millicent. "Am I to suppose that this conversation would be easier without Mary and Marie Cosette?" Millicent confessed, "Yes, thank you, …at least for now. She and Inman are married. We have to include them in everything, but perhaps we can sort some things out before Inman and Danton get here." Caroline concurred.

Caroline said, "You must know that I know there was an altercation Tuesday night on Bourbon Street. Inman assured me that you ordered the finest steak in all of the **Vieux Carré**, on Ash Wednesday, no less, to soothe his wound. …at least he didn't eat it, and I thank you humbly for your care! When I noticed the ecchymosis, Inman was deliberate in telling me that Danton had arranged a protection detail, and that they had taken out Blackjack's thugs." Millicent asked, "Ecchymosis?" Caroline laughed. "The library was running low on novels, and as a jest, Danton brought me a Medical Textbook. I didn't have anything else to read, so I read it. A lot sank in, I think!" After a joint laugh, Caroline continued, "Ecchymosis is a discoloration of the skin, generally caused by bruising." Millicent was truly impressed. "Caroline, you could have been a Physician!" Caroline smiled, "Millicent, you are truly a sister to me, but I made my choice. I chose Inman, and as much pain as I've been through, I will never be able to regret that choice. He was an amazing man, a talented Engineer, and a devoted family man. …there was that one slip, but he redeemed himself."

Millicent beamed and said, "…and the apple didn't fall too far from the tree. Young Inman seems to be everything his father was." Caroline agreed and added, "Yes, and like his father and uncle, he's the third 'victim' of Blackjack." After a pause, Caroline recoiled, and added, "I'm so sorry, that wasn't meant to hurt you!" Millicent cast a warm glance into Caroline's eyes, "That didn't hurt me, dear friend, because, you see, I'm a victim of Jackson too. Young Inman is actually the fourth victim." Caroline's eyes welled up in tears. "Yes, that's true. You are the third, and he is the fourth." The irony wasn't lost on either, but it wasn't verbalized. Millicent opened her purse, removed a handkerchief, and wiped her tears. With resolve, Millicent said, "We are all victims. We are all at war, and we need to understand that there is only one enemy." Caroline agreed. Millicent said, "The goons are going to be in **Hôtel Dieu** for a few days. With caution, Inman could visit Mary at the

Bank House through the weekend." Caroline said, "Yes, with caution. We'll need to make sure that there are escape plans in place."

She thought for a moment, then continued. "What about after the goons get back?" Millicent said, "Well, Danton has bought Morrow Castle and turned it into a 'home for single mothers.' I insisted that he place ads in the Sports Section of the **Times Picayune**." Caroline was confused, "The Sports Section? Why the Sports Section? What single mother would ever see it there?" Millicent said, "They wouldn't. It was only there for Jackson. He reads the Sports Section religiously, word for word. He wants to go see if it's a better option for Mary and Marie Cosette." Caroline had a hearty laugh. "Oh, you two! Individually, you are both so brilliant, but together, no-one has a chance!" Millicent positively beamed. "**Merci beaucoup, cher ami!**" (Thank you so much, dear friend!) "**Non pas du tout!**" (No, not at all!) Caroline asked, "When will they be moving?" Millicent said, "Jackson said the first of the month. ...so we have a week to find ways for them to be together, more or less." Caroline was a tad confused. "A week, what about after they move to Morrow Castle?" Millicent laughed. "That's the best part. I can't believe that Danton hasn't told you yet! He bought the building next door that has a secret staircase to the second floor of Morro Castle. He and Inman have built a bolt hole there so he and Mary can spend time together." Caroline was delighted. She said, "That is truly wonderful! As they were celebrating, Danton and Inman made their way into Caroline's **salon principal**. Danton enthusiastically asked, "What is wonderful?" Caroline cut her brother an impish grin and said, "You've been busy!"

Danton grinned, but asked, "What are you talking about?" Caroline looked at Inman and said, "Your wife and Marie Cosette are down at the **garçonnière**. Why don't you go down and enjoy their company." She added, "If Marie Cosette would rather, she could come up and join us. She'd be completely welcome." After Inman left, Caroline knew that her brother was playing with her and smirked, "You know, ...Morro Castle." Danton flashed Millicent a reassuring smile. "Yes, Morro Castle. Mary and Inman can be together after business hours. ...at least until the baby has been born, and Millicent can convince Blackjack that it's in his best interest to accept this relationship, and embrace it." Caroline asked, "Do you really think that this will ever happen?" Danton looked into Millicent's eyes for a protracted period before saying, "I'm working diligently to help Millicent make it so." They all heard a door close, and Virginia joined them. Caroline asked further, "What is the plan for after the baby arrives?" Danton said, "Hopefully, Millicent can calm Blackjack down and show him how this marriage and the baby will raise his social standing, and won't injure it." Caroline thought for a moment. "Yes, I see what you mean. Aside from Blackjack's blood, the baby will be Louisiana royalty. Think about it. Carnes, Soleil, and Blanchard. What a winning trifecta!" Danton proudly rocked back and forth on his shoes. "Yes, he'd have to be a fool not to see how that would help his ambitions!" Virginia let out a guffaw. "Blackjack's not a fool, he's a psychopath!" Everyone was taken aback and they turned their gaze to Virginia. She bowed up and said, "I read that medical textbook too." They all had a great chuckle.

Caroline gave her bell a jingle. Monique popped into the room.. **"Oui madame? Comment puis-je aider?**" (Yes Ma'am? How may I help?) Caroline leaned forward in her **bergère à oreilles** and said, "I believe that we've come to a consensus here. Would you be kind and go down to the **garçonnière**, and invite the younger generation to join us for **rafraîchissements**?" Monique curtseyed and said, "... **mais bien sûr madame!**" (...but, of course, ma'am!) Monique disappeared into the back of the Manoir and out a side door. She returned to the **véranda** door to Caroline's **salon principal** within a few minutes with the younger generation. As they stepped into the room, arm-in-arm, Caroline put her hands to her face and nearly cried at how beautiful Mary and Inman were as a couple. They positively radiated love. **"Oh, bonne journée! nos jeunes enfants mariés!**" (Oh, happy day! ...our young married children!) Caroline strode over and embraced Mary and Inman. "... **de meilleurs voeux pour vous deux!**" (...such best wishes for you both!) Inman looked his mother in her eyes and nodded toward Marie Cosette. Caroline looked at Marie Cosette for a moment, then embraced her. **"Jeune femme, vous vous êtes épanouie tellement récemment. Tu ornes ma maison de ta présence!**" (Young lady, you have blossomed so much recently. You grace my home with your presence!) Marie Cosette, not used to social acceptance, blushed, and replied, "**Merci madame, vous êtes trop gentille!**" (Thank you ma'am, you are too kind!)

Caroline said, "**Rafraîchissements** are served, in the **salle à manger!**" Monique had outdone herself, yet again, thanks to Danton's warning call. The family filled the Limoges salad plates with Creole seafood delights, and stood around and talked about the future. Millicent opened the conversation. "Jackson's goons are going to be in **Hôtel Dieu** at least until Sunday. …then they will be booked, and Jackson will post their bond." Inman perked up. "So, who's running the Bank House?" Millicent said, "Amazingly, no one. There is a note on the door with an alternative number. To be honest, with the amount of ringing at the funeral home lately, I think the calls are coming there." Mary asked cautiously, "So no goons, no guards?" Millicent breathed in deeply, and out. "Yes, for now. It seems safe for Inman to visit you there for a couple of days, but promise me that you will all be listening for any goon activity, and promise me that you'll have a plan for it."

Marie Cosette said, "We still have dat… that ship's ladder. …and I will always be on lookout." Millicent closed her eyes and couldn't contain her tears. She hugged Marie Cosette. "I hope that you know how much I love you, dear child!" Marie Cosette broke out in tears. "You've been so nice to me, all these years, ma'am!" Millicent hugged Marie Cosette tightly and said, "Dear Marie Cosette, you don't need to call me ma'am any more. You may call me what ever makes you comfortable, Mom (I know 'mama' is taken), or even Millicent or Milly." Marie Cosette began crying. "I don't even know how my mama is coping. That tears at my heart. You have been so good to me, and that lifts my heart!" Millicent sighed, "Your mama will be okay." We want you to concentrate on taking care of Mary and the baby. There'll be a couple of easy days, but then many difficult days until the birth. Can we count on you?" Marie Cosette was overwhelmed, and could only nod.

As everyone finished their **rafraîchissements**, Millicent thanked Caroline and Virginia for their kind hospitality, and scrumptious **Hors d' Oeuvres**. With no objection, Millicent bid Caroline and Virginia **adieu**, and walked out onto the **véranda** with Mary, Marie Cosette, Inman, and Danton. Millicent suggested that, with the turn of events, it would be safe for her to drive Mary,

Marie Cosette, and even Inman to the Bank House for the night. Danton agreed. They all walked to the gate. Danton watched as Inman joined Mary in the back seat and allowed Marie Cosette to sit up front with Millicent. Millicent blew Danton a kiss, and pulled away from the curb. She drove her family to the Bank House on Esplanade Avenue. Millicent cautioned all three to be on their guard, and listen for any sign's that Blackjack or his goons were there. She received assurances from all that there would be an escape plan for Inman. Marie Cosette assured her that Inman's rope ladder hadn't been discovered, and was in place if needed.

As thy turned on Marius Street, just in case, Millicent asked Inman to scrunch down and let her go into the Bank House with Mary and Marie Cosette to check for goons. He agreed. Everyone was heartened when the house was dark. Millicent led the way. She barged into the kitchen, turned on the light and called out, "Where are you two worthless bastards?" There was no answer. She went room to room on the first floor, then went up stairs, and searched everywhere. Confident that there were no goons, Millicent went back downstairs and told Mary that it was safe to go up. She also sent Marie Cosette to tell Inman that the coast was clear. While Marie Cosette went out to fetch Inman, Millicent went up to the sitting room and spent a few precious minutes with Mary. "Do you need anything?" Mary gushed, "Mama, you are always bringing food, and anything we could possibly want! In a few days, we'll need to make groceries, but for now, we're fine."

Millicent smiled. How are you feeling?" Mary sank down into the tapestry of her love seat. "Well, my back hurts, but my heart hurts much worse. I can't get comfortable on a sofa, or in a bed. …partly because of my physical condition, but mostly because of my emotional and psychological condition. …being separated from my husband, and being hated by my father. The baby is kicking, but that is a true pleasure compared to how father has kicked me to the gutter." Millicent found herself weeping uncontrollably. "I'm doing my best. …and I'll keep doing everything to thaw your father's frozen heart."

Mary flashed a weak smile as Marie Cosette and Inman came into the sitting room. Feeling a strong need, Millicent stood and walked to Inman.

She embraced Inman, and held him tightly, saying, "I'm honored that you are my son-in-law, and embarrassed that Jackson has so much power to keep you two newlyweds apart. I hope that you know that Danton and I will do everything in our power to make things right." Inman did his best to hold back tears, "Yes ma'am, I know."

Millicent made her "Goodbyes" and left Mary and Inman in the sitting room. She went downstairs and spent a few moments with Marie Cosette who was prepping dinner in the kitchen. "Please keep an ear out. The goons may be back on Sunday, Monday at the latest. Jackson will be with them, and will probably assume that Inman is here and send them on a search. God only knows what would happen to Inman if he were caught here again. Marie Cosette assured Millicent that she would keep a look out, and an ear out. "I'll get him out safely, if dat, …that is what I have to do." Millicent thanked Marie Cosette, and took her leave. She drove back to the funeral home and poured herself a Blanchard strength Gin and Tonic. She was happy that Blackjack stayed in his office and didn't bother her.

Millicent was overjoyed that there were two funerals scheduled the next day, Saturday, February 21ˢᵗ. Around 9:00, Millicent threw caution to the wind, and dialed the number for Danton's flat. When he picked up, Millicent said, "Maison Blanche, 10:00." In a disguised voice, Danton replied, "**Oui!**" and hung up. Millicent strode back to the office and tried to explain to Blackjack that the was going shopping. He didn't even look at her. "Yea, whatever. I really don't have time right now."

Millicent turned in her tracks and went back to the kitchen. "Hattie, I won't be here for lunch, and I may not be here for dinner. He's in a fowl mood, and I apologize for that, but could you keep some food warm for him. …even if it's leftovers? Please don't go to too much trouble to make him happy. He won't know the difference, and probably won't thank you for your efforts anyway." Hattie said, "We'z gots some good leftovers from last night's dinner. I'll warm dem in de oven." Millicent added, "That's good enough for him, but you cook whatever you want for yourself." An uncharacteristic tear welled up in Hattie's eye. "Miz Day, you'se always been so good to me. You maks it possible to live in dis house wid him." Millicent smiled. "Well Hattie, there's been some friction lately, and it's likely to get worse before it gets better, but I don't want you to worry. Even though he won't admit it, we need you. ...and I have a deep respect for everything that you do for us." Hattie couldn't suppress her smile. She and Millicent made eye contact, and just knew.

Millicent went out to the motor court to a scene of mayhem. Hearses, Limousines, and Flower Cars were being detailed as quickly as possible. In the midst of the chaos, Millicent politely asked for her Eldorado to be brought out of the garage. When her request was ignored, she went full psycho on the employees. "One of you god-dammed ass holes better get me my Cadillac, or all of your sorry asses will be out of work!" All of a sudden the motor court looked like an ant hill that had been stepped on. The goons and porters were tripping over each other to be the one that finally found the keys and brought Millicent's Eldorado to her. When the Cadillac was brought out and presented to her, Millicent noticed the entire lot staring bug-eyed at her. As she started to slide into the driver's seat, she couldn't resist. "What the hell are you morons looking at. Don't you have two funerals to prepare for. Get back to work." Once again, they all scrambled. Millicent watched their Keystone Cop antics from the rear view mirror until she turned onto Louisiana Avenue.

Millicent found a parking space and walked to the rear of Maison Blanch. She rode the elevator up and walked the hallway to her brother's rented warehouse. Danton was standing there with a bouquet of flowers. Millicent took the bouquet and kissed Danton passionately in the hallway without regard to who might have been watching. Danton held the flowers while Millicent dug in her clutch for the keys to the warehouse. Once the door was open, they made their way back to their "room" and slowly and deliberately undressed each other. They got into the bed and enjoyed each other in numerous ways for the rest of the day.

On Esplanade Avenue, Mary and Inman had enjoyed a delightful afternoon, a passionate evening, and a worry free night of sleep. Marie Cosette had only half slept, keeping her senses on guard for activity, knowing that she could cat nap on Saturday. Marie Cosette made sandwiches for lunch, and both Mary and Inman thanked her for them. Mid afternoon, Inman asked if he and Mary could help prepare dinner. Marie Cosette was shocked, but agreed. They went down to the kitchen and Marie Cosette gave some basic knife skills instruction. Inman took to it naturally, so Marie Cosette tasked Inman with cutting the onions, bell peppers, and carrots. Marie Cosette and Mary pealed and deveined the shrimp. While Inman prepared the tomatoes and okra, Marie Cosette and Mary started the rice and red beans. There was a pie with only two pieces missing in the refrigerator, so they didn't bother with dessert. Marie Cosette was delighted with their help, and how easy it was to pull off a healthy and delicious dinner.

After dinner, Marie Cosette told Inman and Mary that she'd do the cleaning up, and they could go up and listen to the radio, dance, whatever. There was no argument from either. While they both had enjoyed working in the kitchen, and would enjoy it again, they pounced on the chance to spend quality time together leading up to bedtime. They were naked and in bed by 9:00. Mary's pregnancy made things a little different, but both Mary and Inman were thoughtful and caring, and found ways to satisfy their carnal needs. They fell asleep in each other's arms just before 11:00, and slept in Elysium until 8:00. They were both happy and stunned that Marie Cosette had breakfast ready for them.

On Sunday, none of the young generation had any idea that the goons had been released from **Hôtel Dieu**, or that they had been booked into the Orleans Parish Jail. They had no way of knowing that Blackjack had been told that he cold post bond for his goons the next day, Monday, the 23rd. of February. They only knew to stay on alert, and enjoy the time that why had to spend together. While they were constantly on alert, Mary and Inman enjoyed their day together, and gladly helped Marie Cosette in the kitchen. They spent Sunday afternoon and evening dancing together, and spending time talking, both together, and with Marie Cosette about all topics. As it got closer to time for Mary and Inman to go to bed, Inman said, "As much as I don't want to, I'll have to go to work tomorrow." Millicent understood.

Monday Morning, Inman woke up to the alarm clock. He showered and dressed, and made his tearful farewells, and promised to come back after work. By bus, by streetcar, and by foot, Inman made his way to the Wharf. His day of rendering designs for containerized shipping was productive, and

Inman decided to call it a day at 4:00. He made his way back to Esplanade Avenue by bus, streetcar, and foot. As a precaution, he threw a succession of pebbles up at the sitting room window. Mary opened the window and assured him that the goons weren't back yet. Inman entered the kitchen door and climbed the steps. Mary met him at the landing and embraced him passionately. She pulled him into the sitting room. Marie Cosette excused herself and went down to prepare dinner. Mary and Inman settled into the worn sofa and made out to the easy listening music from the radio.

The Bond process had taken some time for the goons. Blackjack couldn't come early that day because of a funeral. When he finally arrived at the court at 4:00, it took time for the goons to be released. For whatever reason, they were released at 7:00. Mary, Marie Cosette, and Inman had already eaten by the time Blackjack delivered the goons back to the Bank House. When they went into the kitchen, Blackjack noticed that the plates, bowls, and cutlery were in units of three. While he had no way of knowing that Mary, Marie Cosette, and Inman had heard them come in, Blackjack called his goons into a huddle. While Blackjack instructed his goons in a search of the upstairs, Marie Cosette guided Inman to her room, and out onto the balcony, where he could shimmy down the rope ladder to the yard and make his escape.

Blackjack called upstairs. "My employees are coming up, and will be making inspections." Mary and Marie Cosette were seated on the well worn couch when one of the goons knocked and entered the sitting room. As he entered, Blackjack bellowed from below, "Check her bedroom, and under her bed." The goon showed no compassion, and looked everywhere for Inman. Blackjack called out to the second goon, "Check the servant girl's room, and under her bed too." The second goon went into Marie Cosette's room and looked under everything. There was nothing to find in either room.

Blackjack left, unwilling to admit defeat, knowing that Inman had been there. He was especially livid. Blackjack was driven back to the funeral home, stewing in his own juices. He would have self destructed had there not been a funeral on Tuesday the 24th. of February. Millicent was thankful that Blackjack was otherwise engaged that day. She was able to spend a blissful afternoon with Danton at her brother's antique warehouse at the Maison

Blanche building. As they comforted each other, they both wanted to vent their grand gripes. It didn't take long, however, to see that their grand gripes were shared. As much as Millicent and Danton wanted to talk about their impasse with Blackjack, they refrained, knowing that Blackjack's visit to Morro Castle would be only two days away.

Waiting for Wednesday, the 25th. of February was difficult for everyone. While Blackjack yearned to keep Mary and Inman apart, Inman and Mary yearned to be together, and what was coming might just be a way. After breakfast on the 25th. Blackjack emerged from his office and told Millicent that it was time to tour Morro Castle. Millicent said nothing, and walked out to the motor court with Blackjack. They entered the Fleetwood limousine lovelessly, and were motored to the French Quarter. Their limousine pulled to a stop in front of Morro Castle, and Millicent and Jackson got out. Blackjack was cheap, even with his time. His questions were predictable. His primary desire was to get his goons back to work making book, and not 'protecting' his daughter from Inman Carnes. After the tour, Blackjack told the Matron that Mary and Marie Cosette would be moving in on the first.

The first of March was the following Sunday. Blackjack enlisted his goons to move Mary's and Marie Cosette's furniture to Morro Castle. Since there wasn't much furniture to move, they were done early. Mary and to a lesser extent, Marie Cosette settled in, and waited for for a sign. Millicent had previously told Mary about Inman's sign, and the rest of the secret details. Just before 6:00, a light came on in the courtyard outside the connecting building. Mary was overjoyed. She made her way to a door on the second floor that concealed a stairway to the first floor and to an apartment that overlooked the courtyard from a separate building. Inman greeted his wife with wild abandon. They hugged, and, at the same time, tore off each other's clothing. They fell into bed together and made passionate, but careful love. Later, worried there might be bed checks, Inman said that Mary should, regrettably, go back to her room, and that he'd go back to **Maison Soleil** for the night, "I'll be back tomorrow. You'll know when the light comes on." Mary covered Inman in passionate kisses and agreed to be on lookout for the light.

The elaborate, and quite expensive plan had proven to work. ...and it worked well almost all the way through Lent. Inman spent his days at the Wharf perfecting his patent applications for Containerized Shipping, and his evenings at Morro Castle perfecting his love for his wife. Before anyone knew, Good Friday was upon them. After Mass, Inman made his way to Morro Castle. He switched on the light and waited. Mary made her way down to Inman's bolt hole. Inman was just a little shocked that Mary hadn't delivered her baby during the past week. ...but he didn't care. He loved Mary, unconditionally, and their baby would make his or her arrival according to God's plan. They spent the afternoon together in a loving embrace. They made only one mistake. The blinds weren't fully pulled. To be fair, they didn't think that they needed an excuse to pull the blinds. Unfortunately for Mary and Inman, they did. Dr. Scrope had been in the building to make a house call on one of his patients. She had firmly planted herself in the courtyard, and refused to be uprooted, even for Dr. Scrope. After Dr. Scrope examined her, and started to leave, the goings on in Inman's window caught his attention.

Dr. Scrope called Blackjack immediately. Blackjack expressed only anger, and not a shred of thankfulness for Dr. Scrope's complete loyalty. Blackjack's goons were dispatched to extricate Inman from the equation. They broke down the door and burst into Inman's bolt hole. Inman stood up and confronted them. "What the hell are you two goons doing here? This is my property, and this is my wife!" One of the goons punched Inman in the gut. He fell to his knees, grabbed his mid section and doubled over in pain. Mary began shrieking. Marie Cosette heard her screams and ran to see what was the matter. The goon said, "Dis girl be de property of our boss, and he sent us to fix dis problem. You can' be seeing her anymore, god id?" The baby began kicking vehemently and Mary began pleading with the goons to leave them alone. Inman did his best to recover from the gut punch. With fierce determination, he stood up and stared the goons down. "You tell your boss that no two worthless goons or even an army of goons will keep us apart."

The second goon spun Inman around and punched him so hard in the jaw that he collapsed on the floor as Marie Cosette entered the room. Both of the goons began kicking Inman. Marie Cosette jumped one of the goons and began biting him on the carotid artery. He flung Marie Cosette across the room, and against the wall. When the goons were satisfied that Inman was incapacitated, they grabbed him by the wrists, dragged him out of the bolt hole, and tossed him into the back of a Ford Panel Delivery truck. One of the goons got in and continued the beat down, while the other got into the drivers seat and screeched off. Mary sat on the bed crying hysterically. Marie Cosette got up from the floor and sat with her. The radio was on, and as Jo Stafford's **No Other Love** continued to play, they both began to shake and cry uncontrollably. It took a while before Mary was calm enough to call her mother and tell her what had happened.

Millicent was furious. She told Mary that she would be there shortly, "You both stay there, and try to calm down. I'm going to call Danton before I come over." Millicent hung the phone up. She had never been as angry as she found herself. She stomped back to the office and threw the door open. Blackjack's accountant stood up. Millicent passed him, saying only, "Get the hell out, if you know what's good for you!" The accountant wasted no time running for the door. Blackjack leaned back in his office chair, rather smugly, and said, "Why, Milly, what an honor for you to visit. What's wrong, are you out of Gin?" Millicent charged Blackjack and slapped him so hard that he fell out of his chair and landed in a heap on the floor. As Blackjack picked himself up, he said, "I guess you know that my men have taken care of the Carnes problem. Blackjack returned to his chair. If that bastard is as smart as everyone says he is, he won't be bothering Mary anymore." Millicent couldn't take it anymore, "You are the bastard. You are a psychopath, a narcissist, and a worthless ass!" Blackjack smiled, "Stop, …too many compliments. I may just get a big head." Millicent said, "If you ever do this again, you just might, compliments of Hattie's black iron skillet, meet your end." Blackjack feigned fear. "Oh, no, don't threaten me, I may have to have the sheriff remand you to East Louisiana State Hospital. Maybe you and Hattie could be roommates." Millicent stormed off and, once in the kitchen, called Danton.

Danton said, "You go and take care of the girls; I'll find Inman and get him medical help." Millicent hung up the phone and went out of the kitchen door, shrieking for her Eldorado. When it was brought out for her, Millicent cast a glance of derision to the porter, got in, and spun the tires as she raced to the **Vieux Carré** to comfort Mary. Danton got into his Packard and started to patrol the Warehouse District and adjacent environs. On a hunch, Danton circled Lee Circle, to turn down Howard Avenue. As Danton made his way around the circle, he saw the goons dumping Inman at the main gate of **Maison Soleil**. A streetcar kept him from speeding to the gate and intercepting the goons. That was probably for the best, because he had a loaded revolver, and would have probably killed the two goons. When he got to the gate, Danton jumped out and rang the bell furiously. Monique came running from the kitchen, and the hubbub caught Caroline's attention. When she stepped out on the **véranda** and saw Monique helping Danton load a limp, beaten Inman into the back seat of the Packard, she rushed down to the gate. "What's happened?' Danton said, "Blackjack found out about the bolt hole and sent his goons in." Caroline climbed into the passenger seat and said, "Well, don't just stand there. We need to get Inman to Touro Infirmary!" Danton got in, and sped Inman to the Emergency Department.

CHAPTER TWENTY

THE ASCENSION

Millicent got to Morro Castle, pushed past the matron, and rushed up to Mary's room. She was lying on her bed in the fetal position. Millicent sat down on the bed and stroked Mary's hair. "Danton is going to find Inman and get him patched up." Mary sighed. She was completely spent emotionally for the day. As the sun set, Blackjack called, expecting to hear his daughter's voice. He was treated to Millicent's voice. "Hello." Blackjack said, "Milly, is that you? I thought I'd be speaking with Mary." Blackjack paused for a moment before saying, "Well, Milly, you just tell her that Inman Carnes has died from his wounds, and his bastard will be given up for adoption as soon as practical. She'll make her **début** at the Rex Ball next year." Millicent didn't want to say anything that would hurt Mary, but she did say, "Jackson, I no longer believe a word that comes out of your low class trash mouth. ...and don't bother reaching out to Mary. She knows what a base and foul person you are, and wants nothing to do with you, ever again." Millicent slammed the phone down and growled. In a weak voice, Mary asked, "What did he want?" It suddenly came to Millicent that Mary was her daughter, and truly a Blanchard in every respect. "He called to gaslight you. He was going to tell you that Inman was dead, and that you'd be giving the baby up as soon as possible." Mary turned her face into her pillow and began to cry.

Marie Cosette asked if it were possible that Inman was, in fact, dead. "They beat him badly, kicked him when he was down, threw him in the truck, and continued to beat him when they left." Millicent thought about the situation, then said, "No, I don't think he's dead. I truly believe that Danton would have called if that was true." Through her sobs, Mary said, "...but you don't know for sure, do you?" Millicent hung her head, "**Le temps nous le dira**." (Time will tell.) Millicent stayed with Mary until she calmed down, and ate some soup and crackers. Before she left, Millicent promised, "I'll call you the minute that Danton checks in with me, and updates me on Inman's condition." Millicent drove herself back to the funeral home and poured herself a tall iced gin with a splash of tonic. She carried her drink into the parlor and sat in the darkness pondering what would come next.

No news came that night. Holy Saturday was equally quiet. There was a funeral, so Millicent had to spend her time upstairs. She nursed Gin and Tonic, after Gin and Tonic in Mary's bedroom, looking down upon the streetcar stop on Saint Charles Avenue, waiting for the phone to ring. The sun set, evening came, and no phone call. Millicent started to worry that Danton was stalling, trying to find a way to tell her that Inman was, in fact, dead. Millicent finally went to bed just after 12:30 a.m. At 5:30 a.m. Millicent was awakened by the phone ringing. She sat bolt upright in her bed, and picked up the phone. "Danton?" The voice on the other end of the line said, "No, this is Dr. Scrope." Millicent apologized. Dr. Scrope said, "Mrs. Day, I'm on my way to Morro Castle. Mary will be delivered of her baby today." Millicent regrouped her thoughts and said, "Thank you, Dr. Scrope, I'll get dressed and come right over." After a moment she added, "Did you say Morro Castle?" Dr. Scrope said, "That's right," and hung the phone up. Millicent threw on some clothes and brushed her teeth and hair before walking quickly downstairs, through the house and out into the motor court. Not finding anyone on duty, Millicent threw open the door to the garage, found the keys to her Eldorado, and screeched out of the garage and into the early morning. As she flew past Christ Church Cathedral, she noticed that the Dean and congregants were standing around a newly kindled Vigil fire and about to light the Pascal Candle for 1953.

Millicent parked near Morro Castle and sprinted up to Mary's room. Marie Cosette was holding Mary's hand and trying to keep her calm. Dr. Scrope was taking her vitals. "She's starting to dilate, and the contractions are coming faster. It won't be long." Millicent took Mary's other hand and remembered how different it was when she gave birth to Mary in the embalming room next to Lulu White's still luke warm corpse. It suddenly occurred to Millicent that she was far stronger than she had given herself credit for those long years ago. The sun rose at 5:45 a.m. in New Orleans, and Agnes Day Carnes was born at 6:15 a.m.

When Dr. Scrope told the ladies that the child was a girl, Millicent began to weep. Her tears were tears of thanksgiving. She had hoped for a granddaughter, so the child wouldn't have any chance to bond with Blackjack. Millicent desperately wanted Blackjack's character defects to die with him. While Dr. Scrope dealt with the after birth, Millicent cleaned Agnes up, diapered her, and dressed her in a treasured Blanchard family gown. When Millicent placed Agnes on Mary's chest, Mary started to weep. "She's so beautiful. She looks so much like her father." No one would dare disagree. After a minute, Mary came to a realization. "What about Inman?" Millicent had to admit that she hadn't heard from Danton. "I can only surmise that Inman is being treated and that Danton is at the hospital with him. He'd have called otherwise."

What Millicent didn't know, as she sat next to her daughter, Caroline Carnes was sitting next to her son's bed at Touro Infirmary. While Dr. Scrope pronounced Mary in excellent shape and destined to be back in full form in a couple of days, the Physicians at Touro Hospital couldn't say the same for Agnes' papa. He had been beaten badly. Had Danton not found him as quickly as he did, Inman might have died. Even so, he was still in serious condition. Around noon, Inman finally opened his eyes. He turned his head and saw his mother. "Mama, I have a daughter!" Caroline dropped her book on the floor and jumped up. "Inman!" She leaned over her son and carefully embraced him. Inman said, "Mama, did you hear me, I have a daughter!"

Caroline let out a short laugh. "How ever could you know that?" Inman said, "I was just there, mama. Dear Madame Delphine took me to see the birth." Caroline felt like the wind had been knocked out of her lungs. "Okay, what's her name?" Inman said, "She's named 'Agnes Day Carnes' and she is quite beautiful, if I do say so myself." Caroline was conflicted over the Delphine connection. "Did you say that Delphine took you to see the baby?" Inman reiterated. "Yes, Delphine took my hand and led me to Morro Castle. We went upstairs to find Mary and Marie Cosette in the room with Millicent and Dr. Scrope. Millicent and Marie Cosette were holding Mary's hands. Agnes was born, and Millicent cleaned her and dressed her in a beautiful gown, while Dr. Scrope delivered the rest."

Caroline decided that it would be best not to challenge Inman. He might be making delusional statements, but what possible good could come from arguing with a man with traumatic brain injuries. She decided instead to read aloud from her book. Inman had always loved being read to. Millicent turned back to page 1, and began to read. Inman smiled and sank back into the hospital bed. He remained in a child-like state until just before 5:00. As the sun started to set, Inman rallied. He interrupted Caroline's reading. Inman asked, "What have you heard about Agnes?" Caroline was confused as to how to answer. After a moment, she said, I haven't heard anything from Mary or Millicent. Inman asked his mother to look in his pants for a scrap of paper with Mary's telephone number on it. She did, and found it. Inman asked his mother to give him the phone and dial the number. Caroline dialed the number on the scrap of paper and Inman waited as line rang. After a few rings, Millicent picked up the phone at Morro Castle. "Hello?" Inman said, "Is that you, **belle-mère**?" Millicent shouted, "Inman, is that you?" Inman said, "Yes ma'am, ...is Mary available?" Mary bolted up in bed and shouted, "Inman?" Millicent passed the phone to Mary. She could hardly breath. After a pause, Mary said, "Inman, is it really you?" Inman said, "Yes, ...it's me, ...why?" Mary said, "My father said that you were dead!"

Inman replied, "Well, ...he wanted me to be dead, ...but his goons weren't all that." Mary said, "You can't know how happy I am to hear your voice!" Inman smiled. "...and you can't know how happy I am to have a daughter." Mary said, "Who told you?" Inman said, "Didn't you see me? Delphine brought me to your side as you gave birth." Mary played along. "So... If you were here, what's your daughter's name?" Inman said, with clarity, 'Agnes Day Carnes.'" Mary found herself unable to breathe. After a few moments she asked, "How did you know that?" Inman replied, "I told you that I was there. Delphine brought me." The thought that Delphine had managed to guide Inman's soul to the room was too overwhelming for Mary to contemplate. She dropped the subject.

"Are you in any pain?" Inman said, "No, the nurses have been most attentive and managed any pain with medicines. What about you, are you in any pain?" Mary said, "No, sweetie, Dr. Scrope said that I will be awash in hormones that will keep me mostly pain-free for a few weeks. ...or did he say for as long as I nurse Agnes?" Inman told Mary that he couldn't wait to hold Agnes. Mary asked, "How long will you be in the hospital?" Inman said, "They tell me that I was lucky that I was in such good physical shape. There are no broken bones. Both of my eyes are blackened. I have a lot of cuts and horrible bruises; but, the main reason they're keeping me is to make sure that my kidneys weren't damaged. They reckon that I'll be here for at least a week. Then, home rest for another few days."

Mary asked, "Are you lonely?" Inman said, "You know that I'd give anything to be with you, but mama has been here since I arrived. She's been reading to me." Mary replied, "How wonderful that she was brave enough to leave **Maison Soleil** to be with you!" Inman said, "Yes, that's certainly true. Oh, here comes the nurse. Kiss Agnes for me, and tell her how much I love you both!" Mary said, "**Oui, mon amour, tu vas bien et tu reviens vers nous. Au revoir.**" (Yes, my love, and you get well and come back to us. Good bye.) Inman replied, "... **jusqu'à ce que nous nous revoyions. Baisers!**" (...until we see each other again. Kisses!)

Inman handed the phone to his mama and allowed the nurse to check his vitals. It occurred to Inman that she was only the third woman ever to hold his wrist. She was a handsome woman, and quite stately in her crisp white uniform. Her hair was pulled up in a bun and secured by her white nurse's hat. When she had finished making her notes on Inman's chart, the nurse took Inman's urinal. "I'll just take this to the lab. Do you want me to send an orderly with another, or do you think that you can make it to the bathroom?" Inman adjusted himself in the bed. "I'd like to try. I think that the exercise would do me some good." The nurse agreed, "Yes, and you don't want to get dependent on bed pans and urinals. You could get constipated." Caroline stood and thanked the nurse. "I'll come to the Nurse's Station if he needs another." After the nurse left the room, Inman turned to his mother and said. "Mama, I'm a little tired. Maybe I'll take a little nap." Caroline said, "Rest as long as you want. I have my book, and Danton will be bringing me more when he visits."

Back at Morro Castle, Danton showed up with a photographer. The matron said, "This is highly irregular. We don't allow this. He's a man." Danton reminded her, "If you'll remember, I own the Corporation that owns this establishment. Technically, you work for me. I'm truly appreciative of your devotion to the rules and procedures that have been established, and your extremely competent care of our young ladies, but, just this one time, I'm taking this photographer upstairs to Mary's rooms." The Matron fanned herself, and nodded her head. After Danton and his photographer cleared the lobby and started climbing the stairs, The Matron shook her head. "I just hope none of the other girls want pictures!" Danton had the photographer take the customary picture of Agnes laid on a pad in her gown, then a series of pictures of Mary holding Agnes. After that, Danton had the photographer take several shots of Millicent with Mary and Agnes. As he finished the shoot, and packed his gear away, the photographer said, "I'll deliver the proofs to the Wharf tomorrow afternoon, Monsieur Soleil." Danton thanked him. "... and you'll be able to find your way out, then?" The photographer nodded. As the photographer left Mary's room, Danton said, "Beware of the Matron!" Everyone was amused, and they could hear the photographer laughing all the way down the stairs. Millicent then asked Danton, "Would you like for me to meet you at the Wharf tomorrow after 4:00? We could take some pictures to Inman, and visit with him and Caroline." Danton thought that was an excellent idea. "Yes, I'll be looking forward to it all day!"

On Monday, Danton found it terribly difficult to concentrate on business. He decided that a walk might clear his head and allow him to get back down to business. As he walked through the massive central warehouse, Danton stopped to look at Inman, the Third's prized boat, *Terpsichore*, a beautiful 39 foot mahogany 1929 Chris Craft Combination Commuter. He reminisced about all of the wonderful voyages up river to Inman's family plantation **Beau Cadeau de Dieu**, and the fabulous dance parties held there. Danton had, in fact fallen in love with Millicent Blanchard at **Beau Cadeau**, and proposed to her there. *Terpsichore* hadn't been lowered into the river since Big Inman's death. She had rested, mothballed, on her keel and bilge blocks, covered by sheets of canvas. Danton sighed, and said, "One day..." He continued walking from one warehouse to another. When he got to the coffee warehouse, Danton noticed that Cap and Henry Saurage were in the tasting kitchen cupping the new arrivals. Danton stepped in to greet them. They were both extremely happy to see Danton. "May we offer you a cup of coffee? It's fresh!" Danton laughed. "It sure is, it was only unloaded on Saturday. Is there anything exotic?" Cap asked Henry, "You've become quite a cupper, what do you think?" Henry grinned at his father and said, "The most exotic in this shipment is from Sulawesi in Indonesia, and is called Kopi Iuwak." Cap coughed and spewed coffee. He looked at his son with wide open eyes. Danton said, "Yes, that does sound exotic. I'll try it." Henry started a batch, and started warming the cream. He knew that the Soleil family were all **café au lait** aficionados.

When the coffee was ready, Henry poured Danton a cup with warmed milk. When the sugar bowl was uncovered, Cap was embarrassed that there were only three cubes available. He apologized to Danton. "We seem to be running short of sugar. Danton laughed heartily. "Cap, we have over 350 tons of sugar in the sugar warehouse. I'll send you some!" Danton enjoyed his coffee and thought about how he and Cap and Henry might be great friends, if they only lived in New Orleans, and not in Baton Rouge. They talked, mostly about family. Danton confessed to his problems with Blackjack, and the newlyweds. He told them about Inman's brush with death. They were both shocked. When Danton finished his **Café au lait**, he stood up and thanked them for their hospitality, and their business. Henry looked at his father with a mischievous grin. "Should we tell him?" Cap paused and Danton asked, "Tell me? ...tell me what?" Cap said, "Oh, go ahead." Henry told Danton that the coffee he had just enjoyed was the most expensive coffee in the world. Danton asked what made it so expensive. Henry continued, "Evidently, Asian Palm Civit Cats have excellent taste in coffee cherries. They find and eat only the best. The beans are chemically changed during digestion, and people are willing to pay a small fortune for the cleaned, and sanitized beans." Danton thought about it for a moment, then burst out into laughter. "So, you're telling me, I just drank cat shit coffee!" Cap and Henry exploded in laughter and nodded their heads. Danton thanked them for their hospitality and laughed all the way back to his office. Later that day, Danton did, in fact send the Saurages a 25 pound bag of raw sugar.

Danton smiled the entire day, and couldn't wait until Millicent arrived. Around 1:00, Lucy Butler took possession of the photographs and paid the photographer out of petty cash. Millicent pulled her Eldorado into the warehouse just after 4:00. Lucy smiled, and thanked Millicent for her invitation to Mary and Inman's wedding. "It was the most beautiful wedding I've ever been to!" Millicent returned the compliment. ""It was beautiful, to a great extent, because of all of your hard work!" Lucy blushed as she opened Danton's office door. She closed the door and returned to her desk. A few minutes later, a florist delivered a huge arrangement of flowers. Lucy settled the bill and kept the arrangement on her desk until Danton and Millicent came out to drive to Touro Infirmary to visit Inman. When they did, Lucy gave them the double set of proofs and the vase of flowers. Danton took the vase and followed Millicent to her Cadillac.

Millicent drove them to Touro Infirmary, and they went up to Inman's room. Caroline placed a bookmark in her book and stretched out her hand to greet her lifelong best friend. Danton put the extravagant arrangement on a side table. Inman apologized, "I'd stand, but..." Millicent leaned over, hugged Inman, and kissed his forehead. "**Il n'est pas nécessaire de s'excuser. Ta femme et moi t'aimons, fier papa!**" (There is no need to apologize. Your wife and I love you, proud papa!) Inman teared up, and said, "Agnes is so beautiful!" Millicent asked, "How did you know her name?" Caroline said, "Inman tells me that Delphine took him to the room and he witnessed the birth." Millicent was almost shocked. Almost. In an effort to change the subject, Danton handed Inman a tissue and said, "Dry your eyes so you can look at these." He then handed Inman a manilla envelope with the pictures.

Inman stared intently at each shot, for what seemed an eternity. When he had looked at the last shot, Inman laid them in his lap and said, "She's so beautiful. She looks just like her mother!" Danton snickered. Caroline shot him "the glance." Danton got himself under control and mouthed, "I'll tell you later." Toward the end of a wonderful visit, Millicent told Inman, "Earlier this afternoon, I called the Police Commissioner and reported the attack." Inman sat up straighter. "What are they going to do?" Millicent said, "He sent detectives to Morro Castle and they took statements form both Mary and Marie Cosette. Marie Cosette was able to give them the tag number on the panel van they abducted you in. I gave the detectives the address of the Esplanade Avenue Bank House and the names of the goons. If they haven't raided the place yet, it'll be soon." Inman asked, "Did the Commissioner say anything about charges?" Millicent replied, "There may be more, ultimately, but for starters, Assault and Battery, Breaking and Entering, Kidnapping, and Attempted Murder." Caroline's eyes welled up. She closed them and silently wept.

Millicent said, "I think that knowing how well Inman is recovering, I should go back to Morro Castle, and take care of Mary." Caroline agreed. "He's going to be as right as rain in no time. Millicent kissed Inman on the forehead and said, "**Je porterai votre amour à Marie et à Agnès, et je vous rendrai bientôt visite, cher fils.**" (I will take your love to Mary and Agnes, and visit you soon dear son.) Before Millicent could turn, Inman grasped her hand. "**Voudriez-vous apporter ces belles fleurs à Mary. J'ai peur qu'avec ces photos, je ne puisse plus regarder autre chose avec plaisir.**" (Would you please take these beautiful flowers to Mary. I'm afraid, that with these pictures, I won't be able to look at anything else with enjoyment.) Millicent gasped at Inman's sentiment. She leaned down and kissed his forehead again. "Of course I'll take these flowers to Mary!" Danton picked up the vase, and they left Inman's room and walked to the Cadillac. Danton said, "Could we go directly to Morro Castle to visit Mary?…then you can drive me back to the Wharf." Millicent smiled, "I think that's a capitol idea." When they got to Morro Castle, Mary was sitting up in a **bergère** and holding Agnes. Danton smiled as he placed the enormous bouquet on a side table, and said, "These are from Inman." He turned to Millicent and said, "Where's that photographer when you need him!" Everyone smiled warmly.

Millicent walked to the phone, opened her Chanel purse, and retrieved a number. She dialed it and was connected with the Police Commissioner. She asked about "the matter." "Yes. Yes, I see. Thank you. That's good news." She hung the phone up. All eyes were on her. Millicent said, "The goons have been arrested, the Bank House was raided, and your fathers gambling books and cash were confiscated." Mary asked, "Is it safe for you to go home tonight, mama?" Millicent hadn't considered that. She covered her mouth with her left fist, looked down, and thought. Danton stood up. "Blackjack is going to be busy dealing with this situation. He won't notice if you don't come home tonight. He'd notice if you were there, and there might be problems. I think that we should book a suite at the Monteleone and let him cool down. You can always say that Mary needed you here." Both Mary and Marie Cosette thought the plan was ingenious. Millicent agreed.

Inman remained in Touro Infirmary until Friday the Tenth of April. He and Mary spoke on the phone every day several times. When he was discharged on Friday, Inman was cautioned to take it easy, at least until the Fifteenth. Inman was his own man, and when he got home to the **garçonnière**, he started exercising, to get his strength back. On Saturday, the 11th., Danton surprised Inman with a gift. He arrived at **Maison Soleil** and asked Inman to step out onto the **véranda**. When the two men got to the steps, Inman was facing a salesman standing beside a motorcycle. …not just any motorcycle, but Inman's father's restored Indian Scout. Inman could hardly contain his joy.

The Scout's red livery and gold lettering positively gleamed in the afternoon sunshine. Danton said, "I know that you're determined to find a way. Maybe your papa's bike will give you a bigger advantage." Inman, at the point of tears, hugged his uncle. **"Je n'ai peut-être pas eu de père, mais tu**

as toujours été là pour moi, cher oncle! Merci beaucoup." (I may not have had a father, but you have always been here for me, dear uncle! Thank you so much.) Danton and Inman walked down the steps so Inman could inspect the machine. The salesman asked, "Can you ride a bicycle?" Inman nodded. The salesman added, "Well then, you can ride this Indian. Inman said, "It looks just a little more complicated than a bicycle." The salesman laughed. "Yes, but just a little." The salesman was, by necessity, a patient man, and a good instructor. Inman was truly an apt student, owing, in part, to his competence in engineering. It took him almost no time to grasp the controls, the throttle, the brakes, the clutch, and the transmission. The salesman then had Inman get on behind him, on a temporary seat, and watch his actions as he navigated the lanes at **Maison Soleil** on the Scout. When they got back to the **manoir**, Inman was convinced that he could ride. ...and ride he did. The salesman looked at Danton. "Monsieur Soleil, this is truly amazing. I've never seen anyone take to a motorcycle like your nephew has." Inman roared by, attracting the notice of his mama.

Caroline walked out onto the **véranda**, and gasped. She shouted, "Danton Guillaume Soleil, what have you done?!?!" Danton thanked the salesman and bid him, "**Adieu**." He then went up to the **véranda** and reassured his sister. "Inman is determined to be with his wife. He deserves to be with his wife. He needs a way to get away from Blackjack's thugs." Caroline thought for a moment, "Those machines are dangerous, aren't they?" Danton said, "Yes, but thugs with slapjacks and pistols are more dangerous. Blackjack is more dangerous." Caroline shook her head. "Why can't they just set up housekeeping here? I'd be willing to move down to the **garçonnière** with Virginia and give them the **manoir**, for God's sake." Danton sighed. "That had crossed my mind, but Millicent assures me that Blackjack would never allow it." Caroline dug her heals in. "How can he have this much control?" Danton explained that, as Coroner, Blackjack could send anyone, for any reason, to East Louisiana State Hospital. Caroline huffed. "That man will be the death of me, I tell you!" Danton did his best to calm his sister down. Inman roared by and waved. Caroline couldn't help but see that Inman was growing into an accomplished motorcycle rider.

Inman decided to visit his wife and daughter on Wednesday the fifteenth. He asked Tom Foster, the gardener's apprentice to open and secure the gate behind him. Once free of his confines, Inman found himself learning how to deal with other vehicles in New Orleans. It didn't take him very long to get used to the other roadway competitors. He motored through the Quarter, turned on Esplanade Avenue, then onto Burgundy Street, and pulled up on the sidewalk next to his bolt hole. He went in and turned on his courtyard light.

Marie Cosette had been reading in the courtyard when the light went on. She closed her book and scampered up to Mary's room. "He's here!" Mary's face erupted into wild abandon. "Inman?" "Yes, he's down there! The light's on!" Mary stood up, not knowing which way to turn. At last she asked, Will you watch Agnes. I've already fed her. She should sleep for a while." Marie Cosette said, "Yes! She'll be fine! You go down and be with your husband. I'll come down if'n I need anything'." Mary hugged her and ran to the secret door to the staircase down to Inman's bolt hole.

Mary burst through the door into Inman's bolt hole and ran into his arms. They kissed passionately and collapsed onto a contemporary sofa. After a while of making out, Inman asked, "Is it safe yet?" Mary shook her head. "I want it so damn badly, but the episiotomy hasn't healed yet. Inman said, "**Il suffit pour l'instant d'être dans tes bras. Je t'aime tellement terriblement.**" (Just being in your arms is enough for now. I love you so terribly.) Mary sighed. "**Mon père m'a dit que tu étais mort, mais je ne l'ai pas cru.**" (My father told me that you died, but I didn't believe him.) Inman, remembering Easter morning, when he was still in a coma, and having Delphine escort his spirit to the birth of his daughter, said, "We are destined to be together. I hope that you won't ever let anyone tell you a lie about us. We'll know if anything ever happens. We need to trust God, we need to trust the Saints, we need to trust Papa Legba, and the Loa. Mary replied, "I've thought about it for a long time now. I have no doubt that Delphine brought your spirit here for Agnes' birth. I can't understand it, but I believe. We are connected. I promise you that I'll never doubt my connection between us and to the Spirit World. ...just don't ever leave me. Inman promised Mary that whatever happened, she was his soulmate, and no one would ever take her place. Mary made the same pledge.

Mary and Inman were truly happy, enjoying each other's company. Neither had considered that Blackjack might replace the indicted goons with fresh goons. He had. A fresh pair of goons entered Castle Morro and demanded to know where Mary's room was. The matron protested, and was promptly slapped into next week. Fearing for her life, she told them what they wanted to know. They went up to Mary's room, and weren't happy finding Marie Cosette minding the baby. They asked Marie Cosette where Mary was. When she declined to respond, they roughed her up. Agnes started crying uncontrollably, and Marie Cosette agreed to tell the goons what they wanted, only to protect Agnes. The goons charged the secret staircase and burst in on Mary and Inman. Inman knew better than challenge them. He sprinted toward the door, and out onto Burgundy Avenue. He kicked his Indian Scout to life and sped down Burgundy. As he roared around the corner onto Barracks Street, shots rang out. Mary fainted. The noise got Marie Cosette's attention and she came down to check on Mary. She screamed when she saw Mary passed out on the floor. Marie Cosette rushed to the phone and called Millicent. Millicent said, "I'm calling Dr. Scrope, and coming right over." She slammed the phone down. Marie Cosette slammed her phone down too, and rushed upstairs and brought Agnes downstairs to wait for Millicent and Dr. Scrope to arrive.

By the time Millicent and Dr. Scrope arrived, Mary had come around. She exclaimed, "Inman!" Marie Cosette said, "I think he's okay. We'll know more when your mama and Dr. Scrope get here. Millicent arrived first. Once she checked on Mary, she immediately called Danton. Danton hadn't heard anything but offered to go to **Maison Soleil** and call Millicent back. Millicent calmed down for the moment and waited for the doctor. Doctor Scrope arrived, checked Mary out and pronounced her healthy. While he was there, Danton called and reported that Inman was safe and secure at **Maison Soleil**. Millicent was horrified to learn that the replacement goons had fired guns at Inman. She was further distressed that she didn't know anything about them and couldn't take them out by calling the police, like she had with the previous two. Millicent suddenly realized that there was a new paradigm. It scared her more than she let on. She realized that she'd have to take the game to a new level, as much as she didn't want to. She realized that the next level would make everyone she cared about extremely unhappy. After Dr. Scrope left, Mary was slowly transitioned back upstairs to her room, and Millicent left to go back to the funeral home.

The next morning, Millicent made the call that she didn't want to make. She called her sister in New York City. Irene was ecstatic to hear from her younger sister. "How are the newlyweds?" From Millicent's silence, Irene deduced trouble. Millicent said, "They love each other more than any other couple in history, even in literature." Irene waited a minute, and said, "…but?" There was silence on the line. Irene accepted it, and waited for her sister to find the courage to say what she needed to say. At last, Millicent said, "Irene, you know how much I love Inman Carnes and his family." Irene said, "Yes, I do." Millicent said, "Things here have spun out of control." Irene said, "What in particular is wrong?" Millicent said, "Jackson has his goons actively trying to kill Inman. He just got out of Touro Infirmary, and they fired revolvers at him yesterday when he visited Mary and Agnes."

Irene sighed heavily. "I suppose that you are calling to ask if Mary and Agnes can spend some time with me." Millicent said, "Yes, but there's Marie Cosette too." Irene was confused. "Marie Cosette too? Why?" Millicent started crying. "Jackson has been grooming her." Irene exclaimed, "For sex?" Millicent said, "Yes, he almost had his way with her just before I got the girls out to the Bank House. She can't come back here, and she can't go back to Marie Catherine. Irene thought for a moment, then said, "They are all most welcome to stay with me, as long as necessary. I always wanted children, and wasn't lucky enough to be blessed. I'll be happy to stand in for you while they're here. When do you think that they'll travel to New York City?" Millicent said, "Dr. Scrope told me that they could travel safely on the 14th. of May." Irene said, "Don't worry about a thing. I'll take a larger apartment to give us all some room, and notify the management that I'll be hosting family." Millicent found it difficult to express the depth of her gratitude. After fumbling around trying, she said only, "Thank you Irene, I'll let you know the specifics when we get closer to the 14th."

When Millicent got off of the call with Irene, she called Danton. When Danton answered, Millicent asked, "Can we meet at **Maison Blanche** this afternoon?" Danton answered, "Yes, of course, why? Millicent said, "We have a difficult choice to make." Danton said, "I was afraid of this." Millicent added, "Let's leave it at that until 5:00." Danton agreed, and they ended their call. When Danton arrived at Millicent's brother Phillippe's warehouse in the **Maison Blanche** building at 5:00, Millicent had been there for some time. She had needed some time to decompress and seek clarity. The quietness of the warehouse, and the rows of antiques helped with her pacing. When Danton arrived, Millicent assaulted him with affection. She pulled him in, and guided him to a beautiful gilt **canapé**. They sat. Danton knew that Millicent had things to say, and remained quiet and respectful.

After a long silence, Millicent said, "Jackson is intent on killing Inman." Danton agreed. Millicent continued, "You and Caroline both know full well how much I love Inman, and support his marriage to Mary." Danton agreed. Millicent paused and steeled herself for the solution that, to many would be a **Coup d'État**. At last, Millicent came to the point. "Mary and Inman must be separated until we can fix this problem with Jackson. As much as he did't want to, Danton agreed. Millicent continued, "My sister has graciously agreed to host Mary, Agnes, and Marie Cosette in New York as long as necessary, to get us through this horrible crisis." Danton found himself in an untenable position. He said, "Caroline has offered to move to the **garçonnière** with Virginia and let Mary and Inman live in the **manoir** at **Maison Soleil**." Millicent said, "You know full well that that wouldn't solve anything. It should, but it won't. Jackson is a raving psychopath."

Danton agreed. Millicent continued. "We both know that the love between Mary and Inman is legendary." Danton agreed with emphasis. Millicent added, "I can't stand by and allow Jackson to cause Inman's death. He allowed Big Inman to die, deliberately, and will never be held accountable for that heinous crime. I can't allow him to cause my daughter's husband's death as well. Danton resigned himself to the solution, not knowing how long it would take to solve the sticky situation. He only asked, "When will they leave for New York?" Millicent said, "Dr Scrope said that, if everything presents positive, Mary and Agnes can travel on the 14th. of May. Danton wrenched his neck.

"The Day of the Ascension. …how ironic!" Millicent scrunched her brow. She hadn't thought of that. She replied, "None-the-less, that's the date they are all booked on the ***Crescent*** to New York. Regardless of what I think, or you think, or Caroline thinks, Jackson is happy with the solution. To him, it's more about keeping Inman away from his family." Danton's eyes teared up. He sighed deeply, and said, "He's doing the same thing to Inman that he did to me. No matter how long it takes, we can't allow him to succeed." Millicent dropped her head. She nodded in agreement. "No matter how long…"

For the next several weeks, Millicent and Danton insisted that Mary and Inman meet at **Maison Soleil**. Danton arranged for extra security at the gates and around the perimeter. Mary brought Agnes on her visits, and Agnes became the beloved of both Caroline and Virginia. Danton arranged for his photographer to visit and take formal christening portraits on the Tenth of May. A gilt **canapé** was moved out into the garden. Inman and Mary sat on the **canapé** with Agnes, flanked by Millicent and Danton on one side, and Caroline and Virginia on the other side. Father Lachicotte brought Holy Water for Agnes' Baptism. He blessed his garments, then worked slowly though the Sacrament and emphasized Agnes' parent's responsibilities. After the service, Father Lachicotte bemoaned the fact that Mary's father didn't approve of the marriage. "I've never known of two more well matched spouses!" While Mary and Inman looked down at the floor, aunt Virginia said, "In my book, it's a sin." Father Lachicotte couldn't disagree.

Regardless of anyone's feelings, the Fourteenth of May arrived. It was a Thursday. It was Ascension Day. …and the day Mary, Agnes, and Marie Cosette were booked on on the ***Southern Crescent*** to New York City. With feelings of resignation, Mary and Marie Cosette allowed Millicent to drive them to Union Station. Their baggage was checked, and they made their way through the waiting room. When their train was announced, Mary, Marie Cosette, and Agnes made their way to the platform with Millicent. They were greeted by their Conductor and Porter. They boarded, and were escorted to their their Pullman Drawing Room. They were told that their berths were ready whenever they were needed. Mary sighed, and replied, "Thank you. We're fine for the moment, but we're thankful that there are options."

Millicent looked for her girls through the windows in the Pullman Car. She stood there in her usual elegance, with occasional tears escaping her eyelids and descending slowly across her cheeks. As the train started to slowly pull out of the Station, Millicent was startled when Inman flew past, exclaiming, "**Bon jour, belle-mère.**" Millicent gasped, and hung her head. She began to cry uncontrollably. In their Pullman Drawing Room, Mary and Marie Cosette could hear shouting outside. They rushed to the windows in the corridor, and saw Inman running alongside the train. Mary began to hyperventilate. As the train started to outpace Inman, Mary made her way slowly, car by car, back to the end of the train and found herself trapped in the bubble of the Observation Car. Mary pounded on the windows and watched Inman making his best effort to keep up with the train. She stretched out her arms and called out to him. Inman cried out, "Mary, I'll love you to the end of the Earth!" Mary began to weep. Inman couldn't possibly hear her say "I'll love you forever!" ...but he read her lips, and shouted, "I'll love you 'till the stars burn out above you.'"

Mary winced when Inman fell while running along the tracks. She felt helpless. The **Crescent** started picking up speed, and Inman's visage grew smaller and smaller. When she could no longer see her dear husband, Mary turned, and left the Observation Car. On her way back through the train to her Drawing Room, Mary noticed Madam Delphine sitting at a table in the Dining Car. Delphine motioned Mary over to her table. Mary sat, almost catatonic. Delphine said. "Ju dink dis marriage iz ober, don ju." Mary shook her head, and replied, "No, It will be quite impossible for me to love anyone else." Delphine said, "Good. De boy dinks de same. Papa Legba iz still workin' fo ju bod. Ju got do drust dat."

Mary asked, "When will this hell ever end?" Delphine said, "Dat depends on a lot o' dings. Id won' be a shor' dime. Iz gone be yea's, sweet chil'. Mary started to cry, "...but, I need him. I'm connected to him. I'm not me without him." Delphine replied, "Dogethe' or apard, ju an the boy iz connecded. He will be wid ju on de journey, in ju soul." Mary asked, "Can you tell me that we will be together again?" Delphine laughed her trademark laugh, "Hee, hee, hee, hee, hee, hee, hee. Jes, ju will be togeder agin. Ju fader done dole you dad de boy was dead once. He'll dry dat ole lie again' Ju don' pay no heed do dad, ju hea'?" Mary nodded her head. Delphine added, "Ju iz gonna be dogedha agin. Ju keep da faidh, no madda' how long id dakes. Now, I godda go, de boy need me doo."

Mary thanked Delphine for her encouragement and left to make her way back to her Drawing Room She took a seat with Marie Cosette and Agnes. Mary cried quietly all the way to Birmingham. Marie Cosette understood Mary's pain but did nothing to try to minimize it. She instinctively knew that there was nothing that she could do to assuage Mayr's sorrow, but she, as always, made herself completely available to Mary. Mary, in her complete sadness, knew in her heart, that Marie Cosette would do anything in the world for her. For the first part of her journey, Mary's sadness was completely debilitating. Slowly, during the journey, Mary came to a sudden realization that her life was changing. There was no reason to continue to hide her marriage, Mary asked Marie Cosette to help her reconfigure her jewelry. By the time they pulled into Birmingham's station, Mary was wearing her Wedding Ring, closest to her heart, next to her Engagement Ring. She wore the rest of her jewelry as a matching set: a ring, a bracelet, and a plain necklace. She wore them all with pride.

Inman picked himself up from the gravel encrusted turf alongside the railway. He was bloodied, and devastated in what he considered his utter defeat. Inman stood up, momentarily watched the ***Crescent*** disappear around a bend, sighed, and limped back to the station, slowly, and painfully. When Inman got back to the station's grand waiting room, his bloodied face was hanging, and he considered himself utterly defeated. He had no reason to hope for any success in the future. Inman was about to give up the ghost, and sink into the defeated ranks of the "also rans," when he passed thorough the station, and was blocked from exiting by Madame Delphine, standing in his path, and laughing her trademark laugh. "Hee, hee, hee. hee, hee, hee, hee.

Inman looked up at Delphine, removed his motorcycle helmet, and bowed. "It is so nice to see you Madam Voyante." Delphine said, "I was hopin' ju wood walk wid me." She waved to the doors to the garden in front of the station. Inman followed her. Delphine said, "Boy, ju ain't defeeded. ...not now, an not eva'. Do ju unerstan?"

Inman thought for a moment, then said, "I didn't believe that there was any hope for Mary and me, coming back into this station, but if you say it is true, dear Madame Delphine, I'll believe." Delphine sighed. "Dat girl gona love ju dil deadh!" That didn't surprise Inman. Delphine continued, "Wat ju don no, is dat bastard, her papa, has dricks. ...an he has power. He's gonna use his power again' ju. Ju gonna haf do led him. Papa Legba be on ju side, bud de Loa be habin' fun wid ju. Ju drust Papa Legba. He make everydin' righd in de end." Inman was sad, but buoyed. "So it will all work out in the end?" Delphine nodded her head. "Jes. Ju godda drus' Papa Legba. All will be perfec', but id'll dake a lot o'dime." Inman took a few moments to consider what Madame Delphine had said. After careful consideration of her predictions, Inman thanked Madam Delphine. **"Chère madame, vous m'avez toujours dit la vérité, pas toujours ce que je voulais entendre, mais la vérité. Sachez que je vous aime et vous respecte, et j'espère croiser à nouveau votre chemin."** Dear Madam, you have always told me the truth, not always what I wanted to hear, but the truth. Please know that I love and respect you, and hope to cross your path again. Delphine said, "Don' ju worry none, we'll be meedin' again...."

Inman hugged Delphine and walked slowly, with his head bowed, back to his Indian Scout. He cranked it and rode slowly back to **Maison Soleil**. Inman was surprised that the gate was open. As he turned into the carriage round, Inman saw his mama standing on the **véranda**. He pushed his kick stand down, switched off the ignition, and made his way to his mama. Caroline opened her arms and embraced Inman. After the embrace, Inman sank down to the **véranda** floor. Caroline sat down next to Inman, and he collapsed into his mother's lap. He started crying. Caroline stroked her son's back, and waited patiently for him to express how she could assist him.

Inman's crying came to a close. Stoically, he sat up, and said, "Mama, you know that I love you. You have always done everything in your power to protect me. I also know how much you love my Mary and even my **belle-mère** too. I have no clue why Mary's father can't see how much we love each other." Caroline replied, "It's complicated, but Millicent, your uncle Danton, and I are all working on the problem. Just be patient, and concentrate on your work and your love of your wife and daughter. We'll solve this problem."

Inman rose up, followed slowly by his mama, Caroline. He hugged his mama, and said, "I have no choice but to trust you and all of the others to figure out this Gordian Knot. I love you so perfectly, mama!" Caroline closed her eyes and wept. Inman left the **véranda**, and made his way back to the **garçonnière.** He pulled his favorite **chaise longue** out onto the dance terrace. Inman sank onto the **chaise longue**, and stared, mournfully, up to the northern sky. Inman spent the rest of the day on the **chaise longue**, and as darkness arrived, fell sleep quickly. Mary and Agnes, his entire life, were gone. They'd been ostracized to New York City. On both sides of the great divide there was work to be done, plans to be made, and decisions to be pondered....

The story continues in…..

Let No Other Love Know the Wonder of Your Spell

Volume Two in the series…..

We May Never Pass This Way Again

9 781665 564601